D0049346

PRAISE FOR *THE EZEKIEL OPTION*

★   ★   ★

New York Times best seller
USA Today best seller
Publishers Weekly best seller
Christian Booksellers Association best seller

★   ★   ★

"If you only read one novel this year, this is it! *The Ezekiel Option* is brilliantly conceived and flawlessly executed—one of the most exciting political thrillers I've ever read. I literally could not put it down. Like an episode of *24* with a supernatural twist. Rosenberg has become one of the most entertaining and thought-provoking novelists of our day. Regardless of your political views, you've got to read his stuff."

★ Rush Limbaugh, #1 *New York Times* best-selling author

"Joel Rosenberg is one of my favorite novelists of all time. . . . *The Ezekiel Option* is another outstanding book. . . . What's so eerie about all Rosenberg's novels is that he brings them to life with modern events."

★ Sean Hannity, #1 *New York Times* best-selling author of *Let Freedom Ring* and *Deliver Us From Evil*

"Joel C. Rosenberg is a masterful storyteller, a true friend of Israel and of the Jewish people. He understands the real problems and threats in the Middle East better than any American novelist I know and turns it into a chilling, prescient, and unforgettable read."

★ Natan Sharansky, former deputy prime minister of Israel and *New York Times* best-selling author of *The Case For Democracy*

"Ripped from the headlines—next year's headlines."

★ *Washington Times*

"Eerily prophetic . . . unsettling and scary . . . Rosenberg documents his plot with extensive research. . . . A fast-paced story packed with action from beginning to end."

★ *Dallas Morning News*

"Another page-turner."

★ *WORLD* magazine

"*The Ezekiel Option* is perfect in every way . . . exciting, fascinating, well-written, character-driven, and above all, it is plausible. It will keep you on the edge of your seat and never let you go. This is a very powerful book."

★ *Kingston (Mass) Observer*

"Get ready for one of the most riveting reading experiences of your life. This book is too good to put down! . . . This heart-pounding end-times thriller is so close to what's happening in the world even as you read that it will hold you captive until the very end."

★ Crossings Book Club

"Better written and more complex than *Left Behind*, to which it will inevitably be compared."

　★ *Publishers Weekly*

"Absolutely fantastic! A must read! . . . The events that take place in this book are all too plausible and fans of action thrillers will find themselves thoroughly immersed in the storyline so much so that they will not be able to put the book down until the last page is turned."

　★ Harriett Klausner, #1 Amazon.com reviewer

"*The Ezekiel Option* is provocative . . . compelling . . . a roller-coaster ride through Washington, Iran, Russia, and Israel."

　★ ONEJERUSALEM.org

"Another direct hit on the dangers of a troubled world. . . . Joel Rosenberg again displays an uncanny eye for global realities along with his powerful storytelling ability— and a sense of the pressing spiritual challenges of our time. *The Ezekiel Option* is bound for well-deserved best-seller status."

　★ Ralph Peters, author of *Beyond Iraq: Postmodern War and Peace* and *New Glory: Expanding America's Global Supremacy*

"I was hooked on this book from the first two sentences. . . . *The Ezekiel Option* stands alone for a tension-filled reading experience. The characters are well-drawn and the dialogue is crisp in this contemporary novel. . . . The tension for the reader grows with each page until you reach a point of no return—where you have to complete the book in that sitting, even if you stay up until the wee hours of the morning."

　★ FaithfulReader.com

"The extant knowledge of the author and his ability to unravel world events is uncanny. The characters are as real as they can be, no doubt inspired by true life on the inside of Washington. My ears now prick up with anticipation when disturbing news comes out of Russia or the Middle Eastern nations. . . . No matter your political or spiritual leanings, *The Ezekiel Option* has something to offer you and it's going to be an exciting ride."

　★ *Infuze* magazine

"*The Ezekiel Option* is an exciting, action-packed thriller based on one of the most important end-times prophecies in the Bible. . . . This often-neglected prediction needs much more attention as we race ever closer to the very alignment of nations the prophet described 2,500 years ago."

　★ Tim LaHaye, #1 *New York Times* best-selling author of the Left Behind series.

THE COPPER SCROLL

★ ★
★

THE COPPER SCROLL

 Tyndale House Publishers, Inc., Carol Stream, Illinois

JOEL C. ROSENBERG

To Caleb, Jacob, Jonah, and Noah,
whom I love with all my heart.
May you never forget there is a treasure
more precious than gold.

★   ★   ★

Visit Tyndale's exciting Web site at www.tyndale.com

TYNDALE and Tyndale's quill logo are registered trademarks of Tyndale House Publishers, Inc.

The Copper Scroll

Designed by Dean H. Renninger

Scripture quotations are taken from the *New American Standard Bible*, © 1960, 1962, 1963, 1968, 1971, 1972, 1973, 1975, 1977 by The Lockman Foundation. Used by permission.

Scripture quotations are taken from the *Holy Bible*, New International Version®. NIV®. Copyright © 1973, 1978, 1984 by International Bible Society. Used by permission of Zondervan. All rights reserved.

Library of Congress Cataloging-in-Publication Data

Rosenberg, Joel C., date.
  The copper scroll : a novel / by Joel C. Rosenberg.
    p. cm.
  Includes bibliographical references.
  ISBN-13: 978-1-4143-0346-8 (alk. paper)
  ISBN-10: 1-4143-0346-7 (alk. paper)
  ISBN-13: 978-1-4143-0347-5 (pbk. : alk. paper)
  ISBN-10: 1-4143-0347-5 (pbk. : alk. paper)
    1. Copper scroll—Fiction. 2. Middle East—Fiction. 3. International relations—Fiction.
4. Polictical fiction. I. Title.
  PS3618.O832C67 2006
  813'.54dc22
                                                      2006010228

Printed in the United States of America

11 10 09 08 07 06
7   6   5   4   3   2   1

CAST OF CHARACTERS

★　★　★

THE PRESIDENT OF THE UNITED STATES
- James "Mac" MacPherson

THE VICE PRESIDENT OF THE UNITED STATES
- William Harvard Oaks

THE PRINCIPALS
- Jon Bennett, Former Senior Advisor to the President
- Erin McCoy Bennett, Former CIA Operative
- Natasha Barak, Hebrew University Professor of Near East Archeology

SENIOR ADMINISTRATION OFFICIALS
- Marsha Kirkpatrick, National Security Advisor
- Jack Mitchell, Director of Central Intelligence
- Lee James, Secretary of Homeland Security
- Scott Harris, Director of the Federal Bureau of Investigation
- Bob Corsetti, White House Chief of Staff
- Ken Costello, Senior Advisor to the President
- Indira Rajiv, Director of the NAMESTAN Desk, CIA
- Chuck Murray, White House Press Secretary

ISRAELI LEADERS
- David Doron, Prime Minister of Israel
- Dr. Eliezer Mordechai, Former Head of Mossad
- Avi Zadok, Current Head of Mossad

IRAQI LEADERS
- Mustafa Al-Hassani, President of Iraq
- Khalid Tariq, Chief Political Aide to the President

OTHERS
- Ruth Bennett, Mother of Jon Bennett
- Salvador Lucente, European Union Foreign Minister
- Dr. Yossi Barak, Chief Archeologist of the Israel Museum
- Viggo Mariano, Sicilian Operative

The journey that follows is fiction.

The prophecies upon which it is based are true.

In 1947, two Bedouin shepherds tending their flocks in the Judean hills not far from Jerusalem stumbled upon the greatest archeological discovery of all time. Over the course of the next few years, hundreds of manuscripts and fragments—what became known to the world as the Dead Sea Scrolls—were found in the caves of Qumran.

Some of the scrolls contained whole books of the Bible, including the oldest known copy of the book of Isaiah, foretelling key details of the coming Messiah. Other scrolls contained descriptions of religious life in the ancient community of the Essenes, a monastic Jewish sect. Still others foretold a coming "War of Gog and Magog" and the building of a great new Jewish Temple in the earth's last days.

But in 1952 another scroll was found in those same caves, and this one was strangely unlike all the others. It was not, for example, made of sheepskins or parchments. Instead, the message of the scroll had been engraved on copper, a costly and rare procedure. But why? What mysteries did this scroll possess? What message could it possibly contain that was more valuable, more worthy of protection, than Isaiah's messianic prophecies or the detailed architectural plans of a future Temple?

Members of a small team of experts entrusted with the scroll's care were eager to know. But they had a problem. Nearly two thousand years of oxidation had caused the Copper Scroll to become brittle and in danger of disintegration. They could not simply unravel the scroll without risking the very real probability that its precious contents would be lost forever. It took archeologists nearly four years to conceive a method to open the Copper Scroll, and when they did, they were stunned by what they found.

The *New York Times* broke the story to the world on June 1, 1956: "Dead Sea Scrolls Tell of Treasure."[1]

1 "Dead Sea Scrolls Tell of Treasure: 'Key' to Vast Riches Written on Copper Is Deciphered," Stanley Rowland Jr., *New York Times*, June 1, 1956, A1.

In a front-page, top-of-the-fold story that captured the imagination of readers around the world, the *Times* reported that the messages hidden within the Copper Scroll "sound like something that might have been written in blood in the dark of the moon by a character in *Treasure Island*." Somewhere, hidden in the forbidding hills of the Judean wilderness on the West Bank of the Jordan River, lay a treasure of almost unimaginable proportions. "The documents tell of hoards of fabulous value," said the *Times*. "If the treasure exists, it includes 200 tons of gold and silver," just waiting to be found.

Was it legend, or was it real?

In his groundbreaking 1960 nonfiction book *The Treasure of the Copper Scroll*, archeologist John Marco Allegro—a member of the original team that opened the scroll—concluded that not only was the treasure real, but its importance extended far beyond the wealth it listed. "There is," he wrote, "hardly an aspect of Near Eastern archeology, history, and religion that it does not in some way illumine."[2]

And yet, half a century later, the treasure has never been found, and so many questions remain unanswered.

Johns Hopkins University professor P. Kyle McCarter Jr. once told a gathering of archeologists at the Smithsonian Institution in Washington:

> *The Copper Scroll does not fit into any of the categories customarily included when the Scrolls are discussed. . . . It is not in the Rockefeller Museum in Jerusalem nor in the Shrine of the Book. . . . [I]t is written in a language that is different from the language of any of the other Scrolls. It is written on a material that is different . . . and its content has no parallel. . . . It does not resemble any of the other Qumran Scrolls— or anything else, except pirates' treasure maps in Hollywood. It is an unusual phenomenon, an anomaly.[3]*

2 John Marco Allegro, *The Treasure of the Copper Scroll* (London: Routledge & Kegan Paul Ltd., 1960), 25. Also published in the U.S. by Doubleday.
3 P. Kyle McCarter Jr., "The Mystery of the Copper Scroll," *The Dead Sea Scrolls After Forty Years: Papers Presented at a Symposium at the Smithsonian Institution*, October 27, 1990 (Washington, DC: The Biblical Archeology Society, 1991, 1992), 1, 45; cited by Dr. Randall Price, *Secrets of the Dead Sea Scrolls* (Eugene, Oregon: Harvest House Publishers, 1996), 265.

In the summer of 2005, just before the publication of *The Ezekiel Option*, a colleague and I traveled halfway around the world to see this "anomaly" for ourselves at the Jordan Archaeological Museum in Amman. We had the chance to study it up close, to read its text, to compare it with other Dead Sea Scrolls, and to hear whispers of a story that has never been published. Until now.

There are some who believe that the dazzling treasures of the Copper Scroll will be uncovered in our lifetime, perhaps very soon. What's more, some believe this "anomaly" of history—this "unusual phenomenon"—will lead us to an even greater discovery, to the most important archeological find of all time, one that will shock the world and in the process trigger the end of days.

Are they correct? Should such whispers be listened to or dismissed as ancient legends and myths? It remains to be seen. But it is here that our story begins.

JOEL C. ROSENBERG
Amman, Jordan
June 2005

PREFACE

* * *

Ezekiel's War was over, but the world was still reeling.

In a single day, millions had perished. Entire cities had been laid waste. Even now, many lay smoldering, virtually uninhabitable. The entire geopolitical system had been upended, and an eerie hush seemed to have settled over the world.

Where would the hammer fall next? Could what had happened to Moscow and Tehran and Khartoum and Damascus still happen to Washington or Chicago or Los Angeles? Some said no. They believed the worst was now behind them, that a new age of peace and prosperity was about to dawn.

It was a tempting premise.

I
★ ★
★

Their eyes locked for only a moment, but in that moment FBI Agent Marcus Santini knew something was terribly wrong.

He had seen that face. He knew that face. But how?

Santini's cab swerved violently to avoid hitting the man who had suddenly stepped into the flow of Washington, D.C., traffic. The man's eyes flashed with fear, but not of dying. He seemed oblivious to the danger of standing in the middle of Massachusetts Avenue, busy even on a Saturday. Instead, for that brief instant, he seemed rattled only by the look of recognition in Santini's eyes.

And then he bolted.

The cab started moving again, but Santini couldn't take his eyes off the man as he raced toward Union Station, clad in a thick winter coat and clutching a large backpack.

Santini had been trained to trust his instincts, but he had been with the bureau's Counterterrorism Division for less than a year. And this was his day off. What were the chances this guy was actually on a watch list? Two blocks from the Capitol? Less than a mile from the White House?

Then again, what if he was? What if something happened, and he had done nothing to stop it? Santini knew he would never be able to live with himself.

"Stop here," he ordered the driver.

"But, sir, we're almost there," the man replied.

"*Now*," Santini insisted, tossing a twenty through the small opening in the Plexiglas divider and jumping out the back door, even as the taxi was still slowing to a stop.

He had less than a minute, if that. If the man made it onto one of the trains, Santini would never find him until it was too late.

Sprinting like he had in college—like he had during training at the FBI Academy in Quantico for eight lonely months away from his wife and two-year-old son—Santini raced for the Red Line. Down the escalator. Through the turnstiles. Onto the platform.

The chimes began ringing. The doors were closing. The train was about to leave. Santini boarded the last car just in time, scanning the crowd to his left and right. The man was not there.

Santini's heart was pounding, and his doubts were rising. Was he overreacting? Was he in danger of winding up as a gossip item in the *Post*—"Junior Agent Mistakes Area Student for Suicide Bomber"?

The train began moving, heading west.

Santini glanced at his watch. It was 12:42. He knew the station at Judiciary Square was closed on Saturdays. That meant their first stop was Gallery Place-Chinatown. From there, nearly the entire D.C. Metro system was accessible—the Green Line to the Navy Yard, the Yellow Line to the Pentagon and Reagan National Airport, and only one Red Line stop away from FBI headquarters and the White House itself.

And they would be there in exactly three minutes.

Santini pulled out his phone and called a friend in the Directorate of Intelligence.

"Bobby, it's Marcus. I need a favor, fast."

"Whoa, whoa, slow down, big guy. You sound terrible."

"I need every watch-list photo you have of priority-one targets—males, European or North African, eighteen to thirty. Can you e-mail those to my cell phone?"

"That's a lot of photos, but I . . ."

Santini's phone chirped. His battery was dying.

"*Can you do it?*" he pressed.

"I guess so, but why?"

"Just send them—*now*. I'll call you back."

Santini hung up and glanced at his watch again.

12:44.

He had less than a minute to the next stop.

☆ ☆ ☆

George Murray was late, and he was never late.

Overworked, absolutely. Underpaid, it went without saying. But though the chief archeologist for the Smithsonian Institution was not one who typically tolerated a lack of discipline in his staff, much less himself, today it simply couldn't be helped.

Uncharacteristically disheveled and out of breath, Murray burst through the revolving doors of the Willard InterContinental, arguably Washington's grandest five-star luxury hotel, beautifully situated around the corner from the Treasury Building and the White House.

"I'm so sorry—I should have taken a cab," Murray confessed, wiping the sweat off his brow with one hand and shaking the hand of a literary agent from New York a bit too vigorously with the other.

"No, no, please, Dr. Murray. It is an honor to finally meet you in person. I've heard so much about you. You were very kind to call me."

"Well, I just wish I had more time, Mr. Catrell," Murray apologized. "I'm leaving for Israel tomorrow. I haven't even started to pack. My youngest is in bed with a fever. We can't figure out what he has. I've got to get my oldest to a basketball game in Annandale by four. . . ."

"Then let's have a seat," the agent insisted, guiding Murray over to some couches in a quiet corner of the lobby, where they could talk in private. "And please, call me Gene. Believe me, I would've happily waited longer. It's not every day a proposal as intriguing as yours comes along."

☆ ☆ ☆

The train began to slow.

Marcus Santini stepped to the door. His right hand moved to the sidearm holstered under his overcoat. His left hand reached for his badge.

A voice came over the loudspeakers, announcing their location. The doors opened. Santini waited a moment, then looked out. Only a handful of passengers stepped off the train and onto the platform. The man with the backpack wasn't among them.

Santini drew his weapon and, keeping it low and at his side, moved quickly to the next car. He ducked his head in but saw no one he recognized. He did the same for the next car, but again, Backpack wasn't there.

His doubts were rising again. Was this guy even *on* the Metro? There was only one train he could have gotten on, and this was it. But what if he had headed *into* Union Station instead, toward the shops or the movie theaters or perhaps the Amtrak trains? Which was worse: chasing a ghost or losing one?

Santini was about to call the whole thing off when he suddenly spotted Backpack. He was standing in the next car, nearly hidden by a group of giggling teenage girls. Santini's heart began racing again. If he was going to move, it had to be now. But was he really going to pull his weapon on this guy on a crowded D.C. subway car?

He still had no idea who the man was. He had no proof he was actually a threat. The backpack could be filled with schoolbooks or gym clothes or a ham sandwich and a six-pack of Coke, for all he knew.

Santini remembered an incident in London, shortly after the bombings there, when police had mistakenly shot and killed an innocent, unarmed man, thinking he was another suicide bomber. And yet, for all his doubts, Santini knew he had to move now, even at the risk of embarrassing himself and the bureau.

The chimes sounded again. The train doors began to close. Angry with himself for hesitating too long, Santini stuffed his sidearm into his coat pocket and quickly slipped into the train car behind Backpack's—just in time. The train began to move again.

Santini took a seat behind a large African-American woman carrying an armful of shopping bags, then noticed that the phone in his pocket was vibrating. He pulled it out and found that the e-mail had arrived. Actually, eight had arrived, the master file having been too large to send all at once. He scrolled through the photos as quickly as he could.

"Come on, come on," he whispered under his breath.

There were too many faces, and none of them matched.

He glanced up at Backpack. But with so many people around him,

Santini couldn't get a better look at his face. He would have to go by memory. His phone chirped again. His battery was almost dead.

He scrolled through another set of photos, then glanced back at his watch. He had less than two minutes until they reached the next station. More e-mails. More photos. Santini's pulse was racing. Sweat was dripping down his back.

And then his heart stopped. *That* was him. *That* was Backpack.

Santini saved the image, then speed-dialed the FBI Operations Center.

"This is Special Agent Marcus Santini," he whispered, his voice quaking slightly as he gave his authorization code. "I'm on the Metro. Red Line. Heading west. I have a positive ID on one Alonzo Cabresi. High-priority target. Suicide profile. Bulletin says consider armed and extremely dangerous. Requesting backup at—"

But Santini's phone died before he could give his location.

* * *

"What did he just say?"

For a moment, the watch commander in the FBI Op Center couldn't believe what she'd just heard and made her colleague who had fielded the call repeat himself, just to be sure. A priority-one target in D.C.? On a Metro train, no less?

It wasn't possible. They'd had no warnings. No chatter. Nothing that would indicate an attack, imminent or otherwise. Just the opposite. After all that had happened in Russia, Iran, and the Middle East recently, the world had gone quiet. The last three months had been the quietest of her entire ten-year career.

"Trace the call," she ordered.

"I'm doing it now, ma'am."

"Let's go, let's go."

"I'm going as fast as I can, ma'am."

"How much longer?"

"At least another minute or two."

"We might not have that long."

She grabbed the red phone on the console in front of her and speed-dialed the Secret Service command post.

"Sir, this is Agent Andrews at the FBI Op Center. We are going to threat level delta. Secure POTUS and crash the White House."

☆   ☆   ☆

"Next stop Metro Center. Please watch your step."

Santini raced through his options. But there weren't any. He was out of time. He would have to do this alone, he realized, and his hands began to tremble. At least he still had the element of surprise.

Then Santini looked up and saw Cabresi staring back at him from the adjoining train car. The man had a look of both shock and horror on his face. He'd been made, and he knew it. His hand moved to the backpack.

Instinctively, Santini drew his weapon. Cabresi ducked behind the teenage girls and moved to the exit. The doors opened. Cabresi made a mad dash for the escalators.

Santini moved to the door, but the woman in front of him did as well. He almost knocked her over trying to get out and in the process lost his footing and precious seconds. By the time he got back on his feet and onto the platform, Cabresi was nearly to the top of the stairs. Santini raised his sidearm and shouted, *"Stop, FBI."*

But it was too late. Cabresi had disappeared.

☆   ☆   ☆

He answered on the first ring.

"Secretary James?"

"Speaking."

"Sir, this is the FBI Op Center. You have an urgent call from Director Harris."

"Put him through."

Homeland Security Secretary Lee James was headed to Baltimore to give a speech to a conference of mayors when the FBI director gave him the news. Now he ordered his protective detail to turn around and get him back to Washington as quickly as possible. His driver instantly slammed on the brakes and spun the heavily armored Chevy Suburban into a lane of oncoming traffic, followed by the rest of their security convoy.

"Where's your man now?" James asked.

"We lost contact," said Harris. "But his last signal put him near Metro Center."

James froze. That was just a block from the White House. It wasn't possible. Not with all the safeguards they'd put in place. And what if Cabresi wasn't alone? What if this was a coordinated attack? Worse, what if Cabresi wasn't simply carrying conventional explosives, but a dirty bomb or a suitcase nuke? Even a small nuclear device detonated in the heart of Washington could kill fifty thousand people almost instantly. It could leave another quarter of a million dead within the next few days and weeks.

"Scott, tell me the president has already left for Camp David."

"I'm afraid not," said Harris. "Not until three. He's giving a speech right now."

"Where?" James pressed.

"The JW Marriott."

James' stomach tightened. The terrorist was heading right for the president.

☆   ☆   ☆

"Get him out, now."

That was all U.S. Secret Service Agent Jackie Sanchez heard in her earpiece. She didn't hear why. She didn't take time to ask. She simply moved like she'd been trained, like she had practiced a thousand times before.

President James "Mac" MacPherson was addressing the National Association of Manufacturers when Sanchez and two fellow agents grabbed him by his arms and jacket and escorted him quickly offstage. They were immediately surrounded by another dozen agents who created a security cordon around the president, while still other agents blocked the auditorium's exits and calmly ordered the confused audience members to sit down and stay put.

☆   ☆   ☆

The next sound Santini heard was a gunshot—and then screams.

He bounded up the escalator steps two at a time, weaving his way through a small crowd of terrified Japanese tourists as he did. Breathless, he finally reached the top, only to find Cabresi in the street—gun drawn—forcing a mother and her two young children out of a green Dodge Caravan.

The mother was hysterical. She was trying to get her youngest out of a car seat, but the child's leg was stuck. Cabresi now shoved the gun in the woman's face and yelled at her to move faster.

Santini raced for the cover of a mail truck parked along the street and carefully moved himself into position. He raised his gun again and aimed for Cabresi's head. He wanted to take the shot but he couldn't. Not without the risk of hitting the mother or her kids.

The child's leg was now free, and Cabresi forced the woman and the kids to lie on the sidewalk, facedown. Santini feared he was about to kill them all, execution style.

He moved to the other side of the mail truck, inched his way forward, and calculated the distance to the minivan. It wasn't more than twenty-five or thirty yards. If he sprinted, he could be there in a matter of seconds. There was still the risk that Cabresi would kill the family. But he might kill them anyway, and many more.

★　★　★

"Let's go, let's go, let's go."

Agent Sanchez and her team raced the president down a labyrinth of hallways, through the kitchen, out the service entrance, and down the loading dock. There Sanchez shoved him into the back of his armor-plated limousine, slammed the doors shut, and ordered the motorcade back to the White House.

★　★　★

Santini heard sirens in the distance.

They were coming from every direction. Cabresi heard them too. Panicked, he climbed inside the open driver's-side door and started the engine.

It was now or never.

As Cabresi peeled away—heading west down Pennsylvania Avenue—Santini bolted from the safety of the mail truck. He aimed his weapon and fired. He fired every round he had. The back windows of the Caravan exploded. The vehicle almost veered out of control, smashing through a trash can and a fire hydrant before turning a corner and vanishing from Santini's sight.

★   ★   ★

"And if you actually find this scroll?" the book agent asked.

Murray could see Catrell's eyes dancing with anticipation and he leaned in closer, oblivious to all the sirens and commotion just down the street.

"It will be the greatest archeological discovery of the twenty-first century," he whispered. "Which is why I wanted to meet with you before I left. You're actually the only—"

But Murray never finished his sentence.

A green Dodge Caravan suddenly jumped the curb and smashed into the front of the Willard. An instant later, a massive explosion ripped through the lobby. A ball of fire engulfed the famed hotel. Thick black clouds of smoke billowed high into the afternoon sky. Twisted metal and shards of glass were flying everywhere. The ceiling began to collapse.

When it was over, authorities would find George Murray and Gene Catrell among the dead and have no idea why.

2

★ ★
★

Jon Bennett's heart raced.

He'd been dreaming and planning and praying for this day for six months. He had considered every detail, spared no expense. But now that it was finally here, he couldn't shake the butterflies in his stomach.

He wasn't scared—just jittery, unsettled. His friends had warned him this was no time to get married or have children. Perhaps they were right. But Bennett couldn't help himself. Even if this day was his last, he wanted to spend it married to the woman he loved. And who knew for sure? Maybe they had more time than they thought.

He shifted from foot to foot in the back hallway of the small church near Winchester that they had been attending for the past several months and checked his watch. The music would be starting any moment.

Peeling back the edge of a curtain, Bennett looked out the window over the rolling hills of Virginia horse country. They were freshly covered with a thin blanket of snow, and he watched the small flakes still falling. It was so calm and quiet. It was so far away from the high-speed political life he and Erin had been living for so long, and it felt good. It was time to settle down and catch his breath and think of family.

His thoughts drifted for a moment. He had never really pictured his father, Sol, giving a toast at his rehearsal dinner or proudly sitting in the front row at his wedding. He had never spent much time trying to imagine introducing his father to the girl he loved, much less asking his advice. They had never been close enough for that. But suddenly he wished his dad could be here for this.

It had been more than four years since Sol Bennett succumbed to the heart attack that took his life, and so much had happened since that his son rarely had time to think about him. But somehow in the quietness of the moment, it suddenly struck Jon Bennett how much it hurt not to have been at his dad's side when he passed away, or to have had the chance to see him and talk to him one last time, or even to have been able to attend the memorial service or funeral.

He had been in Israel when he first got the news of his father's death. He had been recovering from gunshot wounds at an American military hospital in Germany when his father's services were held. He had never had the chance to say good-bye, and so much remained unsaid between them. An award-winning *New York Times* foreign correspondent and Moscow bureau chief, Jon's father had simply been too busy for him growing up. He'd missed countless birthdays, his graduation from Georgetown, and even his graduation with an MBA from Harvard. That was not the kind of man Bennett wanted to be. But what if that was the kind of man he already was?

He could see a large farmhouse down the road and could smell the smoke from its old stone fireplace. He turned and looked in the antique mirror hanging a bit askew on the wall and smiled as he picked some lint off his lapels.

Now forty-four, Bennett was beginning to look a lot more like his old man than he'd ever realized, and the last few months had only accelerated the process. His new glasses were no longer just for reading. They were now full-time accessories. What were once hints of gray around his temples, meanwhile, were slowly but surely starting to spread through the rest of his short dark hair. And he'd put on a good six or eight pounds since getting home from Russia, forcing him to rent a tux rather than use the one he'd owned for years. It was time to get serious about his running again.

One of his fondest memories of the years his father served in Moscow was waking up every weekday morning at exactly 5:30 a.m.—rain or shine—jogging in Gorky Park together, and then eating breakfast before the bus came to get him for school. It was about the only time they ever spent together, and they rarely said much. But Bennett had been an avid runner since.

He fixed his collar and straightened his tie and thought back to the last time he had worn a tuxedo. It had been a muggy July night in Moscow. The night he had proposed. The night the world had changed forever.

Red Square, the Kremlin, and most of the government buildings in and around Moscow and throughout the Russian Federation now lay in ruins. All of Russia's nuclear forces and nearly all of Russia's conventional military bases were destroyed. A recent U.S. intelligence analysis had estimated that nearly 90 percent of Russia's armed forces had been wiped out, including all of the forces that had been deployed to surround Israel in the weeks leading up to the now-infamous "Day of Devastation."

Much the same was true in Iran, Turkey, and Libya, as well as in the other hotbeds of Arab-Islamic radicalism. Tunisia and Algeria in North Africa, Sudan, Ethiopia, and Eritrea along the Red Sea, the former Soviet republics of Central Asia, and the once Fertile Crescent stretching from Lebanon and Syria down to Saudi Arabia and the Gulf States. Where ornate and imposing palaces, capitols, government ministries, mosques, and military facilities once stood, little now remained but smoldering wreckage.

Remarkably, the government ministries of Egypt and Jordan—which had not taken up arms against the Jewish State—had emerged largely unscathed, but their mosques and Islamic colleges, universities, and religious training centers had been consumed by fire.

Hundreds of millions of men, women, and children throughout the region were without homes, without adequate food and water and medical services. They were grieving their dead, bereft of leadership, like sheep without a shepherd, not sure where to turn next. And they were not alone.

In Europe, Germany and Austria had been hit hard. Tens of thousands lay dead. More remained critically wounded, even months after the fact. The Reichstag was gone. Much of Berlin looked like it had after the Allies carpet bombed the city and left it in ruins. Parts of Vienna were gone. Most government and military buildings in both countries were gone. Every museum and cultural center in both countries was gone. Every library was gone. One BBC reporter had put it like this: "It's as if every trace of the German past—notably the Nazi past—was consumed by fire in the snap of a finger, in the blink of an eye, without warning, without mercy."

And yet Bennett knew that was not entirely true. Warning had been given. He had helped give it. It was he who had passed Dr. Eliezer Mordechai's memo known as "The Ezekiel Option" on to the president and National Security Council. It was he who had encouraged Mordechai to leak his analysis of Ezekiel 38 and 39 to the American media, beginning with the *New York Times*.

It had cost Bennett his White House post, but it had ensured a global audience for Mordechai's perspective on the prophetic significance of the Russian-Iranian coalition arrayed against Israel. And by the grace of God, Bennett and McCoy had survived the firestorm that followed, as had his mother, Ruth.

Now Bennett prayed for a quiet, peaceful life, off the political bullet train and far from harm's way. He was exhausted. So was McCoy. They had given nearly everything they had trying to protect their country and bring peace to a troubled world, and now they desperately wanted a honeymoon that would never end.

A quartet of violins began to play Mendelssohn's *Wedding March*. His pastor popped his head in the side door and whispered, "It's time."

Bennett nodded and closed his eyes for a moment. He took a deep breath, and told himself to relax. He had nothing to worry about. Not anymore. Erin loved him as he'd never imagined someone could. She was as eager to marry him as he was to marry her. This was the first day of the rest of their lives, and it was going to be better than they had ever hoped for, dreamed of, or imagined. What more could he ask for than this?

3
★ ★
★

The doors opened with a rush and everyone stood.

Erin McCoy felt every eye upon her, and for a moment she wished she and Jon had just eloped. She was so grateful for all the family and friends who had come out for the ceremony. She needed their support and she appreciated it. But for months she and Jon had been in the glare of the public eye, and it was beginning to wear thin.

Their escape from Russia had been big news. Upon their return, they had been invited to the White House to meet with the president and First Lady. Together they had held a press conference to announce massive U.S. humanitarian aid and logistical support to all affected countries. They had been interviewed on every major news show in the U.S. and Europe and had even appeared on Al-Jazeera. *Newsweek* had put them on its cover. So had *People* and *The Economist* and numerous Asian and Latin-American newsmagazines.

At times Bennett and McCoy wondered if they should have just said no right from the beginning. They didn't want the spotlight. They didn't want fame and publicity. They didn't need the perks those came with, and they certainly didn't need the headaches. But it was true they had a compelling story to tell. They had a unique perspective on the horrifying events through which the world was suffering, as well as a powerful message of hope to share with millions without hope. It would have been wrong to keep silent.

But now McCoy desperately craved some privacy. It was why she had asked the president and First Lady and their daughters not to attend today's wedding. Not because she didn't love them. She did. Not because of tensions over the president's refusal to come to Israel's aid prior to the firestorm, though that's what the tabloids were reporting. The reason was simply this: welcoming the First Family to their wedding meant welcoming the entire White House press corps, and at the moment Erin couldn't think of anything worse.

Still, it pained her not to have the MacPhersons there. After the death of her father in Afghanistan in the eighties and the loss of her mother to ovarian cancer in the early nineties, the MacPhersons had practically become her adopted family. They had helped her through school, given her a place to stay, and supported her when she joined the CIA as her father had so many years before. They had even been responsible for introducing her to Jon in the first place.

McCoy had imagined the president walking her down the aisle one day and the girls serving as bridesmaids. She had cried herself to sleep the night before calling Julie MacPherson and asking her not to come. It had been the most difficult phone call she had ever made, but as best as she could see it, she didn't have a choice.

Fortunately, though the First Lady had sounded hurt, she and the president had been very gracious. They would give Erin and Jon the space they needed, and they would ask the media to do the same. They just asked that the Bennetts join them for a weekend at Camp David sometime after the honeymoon so they could properly congratulate them and try to heal the fresh wounds. McCoy had eagerly accepted, without even asking Bennett. He knew how important this relationship was to her, and just as she had hoped, he had backed her fully when she told him, his own strained relationship with the president notwithstanding.

And now here she was, walking down the aisle. With a single red rose in her hand and Dr. Mordechai at her side, McCoy tried hard to keep step with the music and keep from crying before the man she so loved and admired. She didn't want Bennett to think of her as weak or sentimental. She wanted to be a rock for him, like her mother had been for her dad. But then her eyes locked onto his. She saw them filling with tears. She saw his lip beginning to quiver. She could see him straining to hold it all back, and every fear she'd had that maybe this was all a little girl's fairy tale melted away.

Jon Bennett *really* did love her. This *really* was happening.

But why? How was it possible that God was being so good to her? Almost everyone she had ever loved had died terrible, premature deaths, and she couldn't help but fear Jon would be next. How could she love someone she barely expected to last in her life? And yet, how could she not? God in His graciousness had given her the gift she had always wanted. She'd done nothing to deserve it. She could do nothing to hold on to it. She would just have to trust—to "HALO jump," as Bennett liked to put it—and enjoy every day the Lord in His infinite love and mercy chose to give her.

It wouldn't be easy, but what in her life ever had been?

★   ★   ★

Erin was suddenly at his side.

She took his hand, and the pastor began to speak.

"Welcome, all of you, in the name of our Savior and Lord Jesus Christ, who loved us and gave Himself for us. I cannot tell you how much I've looked forward to this moment, though I suspect that my anticipation pales to that of the two lovesick children who stand before us."

A chuckle rippled through the room.

"Let us, therefore, not put off the purpose for which we have gathered: to witness and to celebrate the sacred union of these two dear friends in the bonds of holy matrimony. Two friends whose love and faith have literally been tested by fire. Two friends who have come to exemplify the words of our precious Savior, when He said, 'Greater love has no one than this, that one lay down his life for his friends.'"

Bennett had no doubt that whatever the pastor said next was what Mordechai called "VOSA," the voice of sound advice. But he heard none of it. Not the admonition to love Erin as Christ loved His church. Not the humorous anecdotes of the pastor's first married mistakes. Not the gentle but clear call to faith. It was all a dreamy fog, until these words snapped him back into reality.

"Jonathan Meyers Bennett, in the sight of God and man, do you take this woman to be your lawfully wedded wife—to have and to hold, for richer or for poorer, in good times and bad, in sickness and in health, from this day forward, for as long as you both shall live?"

Bennett felt the lump form in his throat and a tingling sensation in his fingers. As he watched the tears streaming down Erin's face, he managed a firm, "I do."

And then it was her turn.

"Erin Christina McCoy, in the sight of God and man, do you take this man to be your lawfully wedded husband—to have and to hold, for richer or for poorer, in good times and bad, in sickness and in health, from this day forward, for as long as you both shall live?"

Bennett's heart skipped a beat until he heard those precious, wonderful words—"I do"—emerge in that ever-so-slight North Carolinian accent. And then he could breathe again.

"Do you each bring a token of your love and affection for one another?"

"We do," they said together.

"Then, Jonathan, please repeat after me," said the pastor. "With this ring . . ."

"With this ring . . ."

". . . I thee wed."

". . . I thee wed."

Bennett slipped a simple gold band beside the diamond engagement ring he'd given her on the tenth-floor outdoor restaurant of the Ararat Park Hyatt Hotel, overlooking Red Square and the Kremlin, almost six months before.

"Now, Erin, please repeat after me. With this ring . . ."

"With this ring . . ."

". . . I thee wed."

". . . I thee wed."

With that she slipped a thick, 14-carat-gold wedding ring on Jon's left ring finger, squeezed his hands gently, and stared into his watering eyes.

"Very well," said the pastor, with an air of finality. "Then by the authority vested in me by the state of Virginia—and far more importantly, in the name of the Father, the Son, and the Holy Spirit—I now pronounce you husband and wife."

The room erupted with applause.

"Jonathan, you may kiss your bride."

It had been a long time coming, and he took his time. He kissed Erin for what seemed an eternity. Someone's pager began to go off, then another, and a third.

In that fraction of a second Bennett knew instinctively that another nightmare was beginning to unfold.

4

★ ★
★

Bob Corsetti was the first to bolt.

The White House chief of staff and his Secret Service detail quickly slipped out of the last pew, jumped in a waiting sedan, and sped off, presumably back to the Situation Room.

Ken Costello was right behind him. No longer undersecretary of state for political affairs, Costello, an old friend, now had Bennett's old job— and his old office—serving as senior advisor to the president and coordinating all U.S. emergency assistance and humanitarian aid to the countries affected by the devastation.

When Indira Rajiv left too, Bennett knew this one was bad. Rajiv was Erin's closet friend at the CIA. Erin had recruited her, trained her, and recommended her numerous promotions. Now, as director of the NAMESTAN desk, Rajiv was responsible for tracking all terrorist groups operating in and out of North Africa, the Middle East, and the "stans" of Central Asia. The only reason she'd be leaving Erin's wedding so abruptly would be if terrorists had struck again.

As the receiving line began, Dr. Mordechai pulled Jon and Erin aside.

"There's been an attack near the White House," he explained.

Erin gasped. "Where?"

"The Willard," said Mordechai. "It seems to have been a truck bomb or a suicide bomber. There are conflicting reports. But casualties are mounting, and my sources say the Secret Service is concerned about additional attacks. The police are sealing off the city. The airports are shut down."

"What about the president?" asked Bennett.

"He's safe," Mordechai assured them. "But it was a close call. He was at the JW Marriott at the time, giving a speech. But they've got him back at the White House now. The VP is safe as well. They've airlifted him to Camp David. Lee James is going to hold a press conference soon. That's all I've got for now."

Bennett asked him to make an announcement to let everyone know what was happening. In the meantime, he pulled Erin into the coatroom for a moment to gather their thoughts. All that remained was a private, secluded, candlelit meal with family members and close friends before they would finally have some time for themselves. But he could see the tension in Erin's eyes.

"You okay?" Bennett asked when they were alone.

"We need to do something," she replied. "*I* need to do something."

"I know," said Bennett as he took her hands in his and looked her in the eye. His new bride wasn't wired to sit back and watch events happen. She'd been trained to take action, and Bennett was certain every instinct in her body told her to race back to Langley and see if there was anything she could do to help. And he had no doubt they'd take her back in a heartbeat, even if it was her wedding day. "But it's not up to us anymore. We did our jobs. Now we need to let everyone else do theirs."

He could see the struggle in her soul as she tried to figure out their next move.

"We should at least call off the dinner," she said at last. "It's not a time to celebrate."

"Well, no," he said gently, "but we can't just send people home. Half of them are from out of town, some from out of the country. D.C. is shut down. They won't be able to get back to their hotels for a while."

"So what are you saying?" asked Erin, her eyes searching his for guidance.

"I'm saying we go forward. We have the dinner. We make it low-key, but we let people just be together, until it becomes clear what's going to happen next."

THE COPPER SCROLL 23

Twenty minutes later they pulled into The Inn at Little Washington, where Erin wiped the tears from her eyes, fixed her mascara, and tried to pull herself together. They had been listening to special coverage of the unfolding crisis during the drive over from the church. The more they learned, the more clear it became to them both that a new threat had just been unleashed. But for now they had guests waiting for them, and neither of them wanted to look gloomy on a day like today.

★　★　★

The newlyweds entered to an ovation they did not expect.

It was heartfelt and emotional, and Erin suddenly realized how much this small group of friends and family *wanted* to be together—and especially with them—at this moment of crisis.

Greeting them first with an enormous bear hug was Dmitri Galishnikov, founder and CEO of the Medexco oil empire and now number three on the Forbes list of the world's richest people. His beautiful wife, Katya, showered them with kisses. At their side was the widow of Ibrahim Sa'id, the assassinated prime minister of the Palestinian Authority, along with her sons, embracing the newlyweds with a warmth and a tenderness that came from deep in their hearts.

"You both have done so much for us all," Dmitri said in his thick, raspy Russian accent. "And we love you for it."

Erin felt herself choke up as she thanked them for coming so far to be with them. They had been through so much joy and sorrow together, and it felt good to have them there. She turned and winked at Jon, proud of his instincts and grateful to be his wife.

Nadia Mehrvash came up and gave Erin a hug and a kiss on both cheeks. Erin couldn't believe it was really her. She had asked Mordechai to track Nadia down and invite her to come. She and Jon had even offered to pay her way. But she had never heard if Nadia was really going to make it. And yet here she was, all the way from Iran, and Erin held her close.

Nadia was still in mourning, of course, for her husband, Hamid, who had died helping Jon sneak into Russia to rescue Erin. She was in mourning too for the baby she had miscarried in an Iranian prison camp just before the firestorm had set her free. But she was a woman of remarkable faith and resilience, and Erin was so happy to see her.

"I'm so sorry," Erin whispered, "for all you've been through."

"It is an honor to suffer for His name," Nadia whispered back. "I'm just sorry Hamid didn't get the chance to meet you."

"We will see him soon enough," Erin replied, and the two hugged again.

☆   ☆   ☆

Just after dinner, Eli Mordechai cleared his throat.

The graying, bespectacled, eighty-four-year-old former Mossad chief—who vaguely resembled Anthony Hopkins but sounded more like Sean Connery playing Marko Ramius in *The Hunt for Red October*—had news, and it was not good.

"Please forgive me for being the bearer of bad tidings amid this beautiful gathering," Mordechai began, "but I thought you might want an update."

Everyone nodded, including Jon and Erin, so Mordechai continued.

"Secretary James just finished his press conference. He confirmed that the explosion at the Willard was the result of a suicide bomber using conventional explosives. There are no traces of any nuclear or radioactive device. But the casualties are severe."

"How many?" asked Erin.

Mordechai paused, as if delaying the news would make it easier to bear. "Twenty-three people are dead. Forty-seven more are wounded."

A gasp swept through the room.

"Eleven are listed in critical condition at area hospitals. Several of them are not expected to make it through the night."

"Any suspects yet?" Erin asked.

Bennett noticed she was already scribbling a short list of her own on the back of a wedding program. He didn't recognize any of the names. But none of them were of Middle Eastern or Russian origins. True, Al-Qaeda was dead and buried, as were Hamas, Hezbollah, and Islamic Jihad. And Yuri Gogolov and Mohammed Jibril and their Al-Nakbah terror network were now history too. But who did that leave?

"The secretary said it was too early for hard leads," said Mordechai.

"You're saying they've got nothing?" asked Erin.

"I'm saying what they have isn't public yet."

Bennett looked around the room. It was obvious no one wanted to talk about anything else. Their city—their nation's capital—had been attacked. Again. It made no sense for Mordechai to hold back what little he knew at this early stage of the investigation unless it was actually classified.

Mordechai apparently drew the same conclusion.

"I can only say a little," said the old man. "Again, none of it is public yet, but I can tell you the FBI has already identified the bomber. They know who he is. They know where he's from. And they are hunting down every lead to find out who else he might have been working with. The odd thing is that he wasn't from the Middle East."

"Where was he from?" asked Bennett.

"Italy."

Italy? Bennett looked at his new bride, not quite sure what to say. He had never heard of an Italian suicide bomber. Neither, apparently, had she. The room quickly filled with cross talk as people developed theories and tried to make sense of it all.

"What do *you* make of it all at this point, Dr. Mordechai?" Ruth Bennett suddenly asked over the cacophony. "I thought 'The Ezekiel Option' was the end of all this."

"I wish it were," he said. "But I'm afraid Ezekiel never prophesied the end of evil, only the end of radical Islam as we've known it."

A hush came over the room.

"I don't understand," said Mrs. Bennett. "What exactly are you saying?"

Mordechai paused for a moment, then said, "I'm saying the War of Gog and Magog wasn't the end. It was just the beginning."

5

★ ★
★

It was not the wedding night they had planned.

But there was nothing they could do to change the events of the past few hours, and like all Americans, they were hungry to know more. FOX and CNN soon confirmed the outlines of the story Mordechai had revealed at dinner and began providing details. They broadcast a black-and-white passport photo of the suicide bomber that had been released by the FBI.

The terrorist was Alonzo Cabresi, a twenty-seven-year-old Italian national with ties to an obscure left-wing underground faction based near Rome known as the Legion. The group's Web site called for the overthrow of the Italian government and the disbanding of NATO. It also claimed responsibility for several assassinations of CEOs and diplomats in Europe over the years but had no history of operating in the U.S. and no obvious motive for today's attack.

Meanwhile, against the strenuous opposition of the Secret Service, President MacPherson and the First Lady visited the crime scene and comforted survivors at a local hospital before returning to the White House to hold a press conference with Homeland Security Secretary Lee James. James announced a $10 million reward for any information leading to the arrest and conviction of Cabresi's coconspirators. He also announced that Reagan National Airport would remain closed for several days but that Washington Dulles would reopen in the morning. The president announced that European Union foreign minister Salvador Lucente was en route from Brussels, ready to "offer the full support of the European police and intelligence services in hunting down the perpetrators of this crime and bringing them to justice."

But shortly before midnight, Jon and Erin had had all they could take. Emotionally spent, they finally turned off the television and their BlackBerrys and tried their best to set the world's troubles behind them. And then they lost themselves in each other's arms for the first time in their lives and found it had been well worth the wait.

☆ ☆ ☆

Seven hours later, the sun began to peek through the curtains.

Bennett rubbed his eyes and found himself staring up at the fan on the hotel ceiling. He couldn't remember the last time he'd woken up without an alarm clock or a hotel wake-up call—not since childhood, he was sure—and it felt good. Better yet, he was curled up beside Erin's warm, comforting body, and for a moment he forgot all the horror unfolding around them. She was even more beautiful asleep—so peaceful, so relaxed, as if she hadn't a care in the world—and for a while he just lay there staring at her.

Finally he slipped out of the soft cotton sheets as quietly as he could and went into the bathroom to splash some water on his face. Then he clicked on the news, careful to keep the volume low so as not to wake his adorable bride.

It was too early for the Sunday interview shows, but all the broadcast and cable news networks were still wall-to-wall with continuing coverage of the latest terrorist strike. The death toll had climbed from twenty-three to thirty-one, and at least a dozen Washingtonians had multiple serious injuries and were fighting desperately for their lives. Two had been in surgery for most of the night, and doctors were not holding out much hope.

Then the news anchor said something that struck Bennett as curious, though he wasn't quite sure why. The anchor said that among those who had perished in the bombing was Dr. George Murray, the chief archeologist for the Smithsonian Institution, who had been "expected to travel to Israel later today to meet with Prime Minister David Doron."

Bennett was pretty sure he had met Murray at a state dinner at the White House a few years back, and he certainly knew of the man's reputation as one of the world's leading experts on the ancient Near East. But why would he have been traveling to Israel right now—to meet personally with Doron, no less—with everything else that was going on in the world?

And there was something else. Bennett had a vague recollection of reading about another prominent archeologist—Mansfield or Manchester, some name like that—who had recently died somewhat mysteriously in London. Was he remembering that right? If so, was there a connection, or was it just an odd coincidence?

He made a mental note to track down the story, but then a report came on profiling the strange, sordid history of the Legion, and Bennett turned up the sound. In all his time at the White House and crisscrossing the globe for the president, he had never even heard of this group. So why were they crawling out of their hole now?

☆　☆　☆

Erin began to stir.

She kissed her new husband on the neck and whispered, "Come back to bed."

"I thought you'd want to know what was happening," Bennett said as he jotted down notes about the Legion: "founded in '71, funded by drug money . . ."

"I don't," she said in a seductive whisper.

"You don't?" he asked, turning to look at her now.

"Nope."

Jon hit the Mute button. "You are the same woman I married yesterday, right?"

"I say we go through political detox," Erin said softly. "No talking about the news. No watching the news. No papers. No magazines. No BlackBerrys. No checking our voice mail or e-mail for the entire honeymoon. Let's go cold turkey."

"Cold turkey?" he asked, bewildered.

"It's better than cold showers, right?" She smiled.

Now he was completely confused. "But yesterday, you practically wanted to . . ."

Erin leaned forward and put her finger to his lips. "That was yester-day," she whispered. "Now I know what I've been missing all these years." She caressed his face. "This is the only honeymoon we're ever going to get. Who knows how much time we've got left? Let's enjoy it."

Bennett didn't need to be asked twice. The world would have to wait.

★   ★   ★

They ate a long, lingering breakfast in bed.

Then they showered, dressed casually, and took a car service to Washington Dulles Airport. For their honeymoon, Bennett had promised to surprise Erin. And sure enough, she was surprised.

With their bags packed, they were standing in front of the Departures board when Bennett asked, "So, where would you like to go?"

"I'm sorry?" asked Erin.

"Where would you like to go?" he repeated.

"What are you talking about?"

"Name a place—anyplace in the world—and that's where I'll take you."

"I don't understand. I thought you were going to surprise me."

"I am. You can go anywhere in the world!"

Erin just looked at him for a moment, not sure whether to laugh or to punch him in the nose. *No plane tickets? No destination? No hotel reservations? Nothing? What kind of honeymoon was that? What kind of . . .*

"I know what you're thinking," Jon said.

"No, you don't."

"Yes, I do."

"No, you really don't."

"Yes, I *really* do."

"All right, Mr. Know-It-All, what am I thinking?"

"You're thinking, *What kind of moron surprises his new bride with no tickets, no reservations, zip, zilch, nada, nothing?*"

All right, maybe he *did* know what she was thinking. But that still didn't excuse . . .

Bennett suddenly pulled out his BlackBerry.

"Hey, I thought we weren't going to use those on our honeymoon," Erin said.

"I've got my travel agency on standby. They're ready to make all the arrangements. Just name the destination, and they'll have first-class tickets within minutes, the ritziest accommodations, the finest service, all the amenities, and no one will even know where we are."

Erin thought about that for a moment. She had never had the time, or the money, or the freedom to just look at a Departures board and pick any place in the world to go. Nor had she ever had someone to share it, even if it had been possible.

But now, for the first time in her life, time wasn't an issue. They didn't have jobs. They didn't have kids or a care in the world. No one was counting on them for anything but a postcard. Cost wasn't an object either. They had money in the bank from Jon's years on Wall Street—$22 million and change, to be precise. Why not go a little crazy? They could be gone for a week or a month or a year or more, if they wanted. Let Corsetti and Rajiv and Costello handle the nightmares. The Bennetts had served their time, and they were done.

"Anywhere?" Erin asked again, just to be sure.

"Anywhere," Bennett said.

She kissed him on the cheek and said, "Ronda."

★　★　★

The little resort town held a special place in her heart.

Nestled in the hills of southern Spain, Ronda was the birthplace of Spanish bullfighting, an occasional home for Ernest Hemingway at the peak of his writing career, and more importantly, the last place Erin had vacationed with her parents as a little girl before her father was killed in the mountains east of Kabul. It was quiet and serene and filled with bittersweet memories of the perfect life that once was hers. She had never mentioned it to Jon.

A few minutes later, Jon was off the phone. He took her by the hand and led her to the British Airways desk. There he handed over his credit card, purchased two first-class tickets, and explained the journey ahead.

"If it pleases you, my lady," Bennett began, "we will board Flight 918 aboard a Boeing 747, leaving Washington at 6:10 p.m. and landing at London Heathrow at 6:20 tomorrow morning. There, we will transfer to British Airways Flight 6982—an Airbus A320—leaving at 7:55 a.m. local time for Málaga on the southern coast of Spain, better known as the Costa del Sol. When we touch down in Málaga at 11:35 a.m. local time, we will be picked up by a limousine and driven to the lovely mountain resort town of Ronda, which, I might add, is the birthplace of Spanish bullfighting. I've reserved the honeymoon suite at the city's most beautiful hotel, the Husa Reina Victoria de Ronda. Our room overlooks the mountains of Andalusia and will be filled with roses and the best champagne in the country. How does all that sound?"

"Magical," said Erin, her eyes sparkling.

6

★ ★
★

MONDAY, JANUARY 12 – 4:24 A.M. – LOS ANGELES, CALIFORNIA

Barry Jaspers was a desperate man.

He glanced at his watch again and kicked a stray shoe across the bedroom floor. He had already finished packing his suitcase and had stuffed his briefcase with research papers that still needed grading. But no keys meant no car. No car meant no flight. He certainly didn't have the time to call for a cab if he was going to get to LAX in time for the 8:35 nonstop to Washington Dulles. So Jaspers bit his lip and kept hunting.

His wife, Leigh Ann, turned over and pulled the covers over her head. The last thing he wanted was to wake her. At forty-three, she was six months pregnant with "The Surprise" and needed all the sleep she could get.

Jaspers, known to most of his friends simply as Professor, was just shy of his fifty-eighth birthday. A widower before he met Leigh Ann, he had two grown sons and had been sure he was done with bottles and diapers. Now he was back at the starting line. His colleagues on campus were giving him a hard time. The truth was it had been a long time since there had been a baby in his arms, and the idea of going through it one more time with Leigh Ann, the woman who had rescued his heart and soul from the depths of despair, actually excited him, though he was loath to admit it to anyone else. He had not exactly been the best father to his boys. But maybe this time he could do it right. He certainly wanted to try.

For now, though, all he wanted was to find his keys. He had already checked the bedroom and the master bath. He raced back downstairs to the kitchen, checking drawers and counters and Leigh Ann's purse in an increasingly frantic hunt.

Jaspers cursed himself for booking a morning flight. Ever since his days as an undergraduate, he had hated getting up early. Back then, of course, it was because he was too hungover to get out of bed before noon. Now he was just getting old and lazy. He hated rush-hour traffic. He hated long security lines at the airport. The only thing he hated more was funerals. But what choice did he have? If he was going to make the viewing this evening and the memorial service tomorrow, he had to catch this flight.

George Murray had been his best friend for almost forty years. They had met as roommates at Johns Hopkins University. They had been Fulbright scholars at Hebrew University on Mount Scopus in Jerusalem. Together they had traveled the world, hunting down rare artifacts, speaking at archeology conferences, begging foundations for grant money, and helping each other write just enough journal articles and books to keep out of trouble. It was impossible to believe he was gone.

Even more impossible to believe was the way he had died. Violently. Horribly. In a suicide bombing less than a block from the White House. How could something like that happen? Murray had no enemies. He was incapable of creating them. Everybody liked the guy, right down to the doorman in his building and the janitors who kept his section of the Smithsonian shipshape. It made absolutely no sense.

What would happen to the project? to the book? They'd been working on both in secret for months. Not even their wives knew what they were doing, how far they had come, or how close they were to the most spectacular archeological find of all time. Could he carry it off without George? He would have to, of course. But how?

Exasperated and out of time, Jaspers finally grabbed his wife's key chain, removed the spare key to the Volvo, scooped up his bags, and raced out the front door. If he was lucky, he could make it to LAX in less than an hour. God forbid there be any accidents or road repairs. He had no margin for error.

Covered with perspiration, Jaspers threw his things in the trunk, hopped into the front seat, and pulled his door shut, hoping not to wake Leigh Ann or the neighbors with his racket. Then he flipped on the headlights and jammed the key in the ignition. The Volvo sputtered for a moment, as if its engine was flooded.

That was strange, thought Jaspers. He tried it again.

The force of the explosion could be heard for miles.

7

⭐ ⭐
⭐

The sleek black-and-gold helicopter gently banked to the east.

It descended to three thousand feet, and the pilots began their direct approach into Babylon. Stretched before them was a skyline of construction cranes and high-rise apartments and office buildings in various stages of completion.

To the east, on the shores of the Euphrates River, was the dazzling new Hilton, alongside the Marriott Grand, the Four Seasons, and the sprawling new regional headquarters for ExxonMobil, just weeks away from its grand opening. To the west were the Central Palace, the famed Ishtar Gate, and the newly expanded Royal Museum of Archeology, side by side with the nearly completed corporate headquarters for at least a dozen major American and European banks and oil companies. And dead ahead was their destination, the Great Tower of the People, the gleaming glass-and-steel parliament and executive administration building, rising seventy stories above the new Iraqi capital.

At a cruising speed of over 140 kilometers an hour, the pilots had no doubt they would reach the rooftop landing pad a good sixteen minutes ahead of schedule. But their hearts were still pounding. For this was no usual test drive, and theirs was no typical passenger. Seated in one of the plush leather seats in the back of the cabin was Mustafa Al-Hassani.

The seventy-five-year-old Iraqi president had said nothing to the pilots on the six-hour round-trip to Samarra and Karbala and back. Most of the flight he had spent talking on a satellite phone or with his chief political aide, Khalid Tariq. The men flying the helicopter were somewhat in awe, being in the presence of one of the few Arab leaders who had actually survived the firestorm, and they were dying to ask how had he done it. What did Al-Hassani know that the others didn't? Was he a god, as the buzz on the Arab street now claimed?

He certainly looked like a holy man, with intense dark eyes, a long and weathered face, a salt-and-pepper beard, and white flowing robes, and few seemed to doubt he had a spark of the divine.

Widely considered the intellectual grandfather of Iraq's profreedom movement, he had once been a beloved professor of Arabic literature and poetry by day and one of the country's shrewdest political strategists and revolutionary organizers by night. He had conceived a vision of what Iraq could be without Saddam back when few thought it was possible, and he had vowed not to rest until he helped bring it to pass. It had gotten him arrested and imprisoned by the Ba'ath Party, and he had been tortured without mercy. But now here he was, sitting behind them, a man who seemingly could not die.

The Iraqi-born but American-trained chopper pilots desperately wanted to talk with this rising icon. They wanted to hear his stories and ask him questions—not just about how he was enjoying his ride, but about his plans for the future. But they knew it was a line they could not cross. Their job was to fly, not to speak, and they could not afford to be fired. So they simply chose to be content with being in Al-Hassani's presence.

What was particularly intriguing to them was the fact that political, business, and tribal leaders from all over the region were suddenly converging upon Babylon for a series of apparently top-secret meetings.

The pilots themselves had been required to sign nondisclosure forms covering all of their time with the Iraqi president. Moreover, they had heard no specific names mentioned over their radios, but it was clear from the chatter of the air-traffic controllers that these leaders were coming from as far away as Algeria to the west and Kyrgyzstan to the east. They had even overheard a flight originating from Isfahan, Iran, being cleared into Iraqi airspace less than an hour ago. But why? What could possibly bring them all to Babylon amid all the horror going on in their own countries?

★   ★   ★

Viggo Mariano took the call on the balcony.

"Is it finished?" he asked.

"Almost."

"What's taking so long?"

"There are . . . complications."

"What kind of complications?"

"None, I'm afraid, we can talk about by phone."

Mariano seriously doubted that. Both he and the man on the other end of the connection were on secure satellite phones, unlisted, untraceable, and swept for bugs—as were their homes and offices—twice a week. But at this point, there was no reason to take more chances than absolutely necessary.

"How many are done?"

"Three."

"That's it?" Mariano sniffed, pacing obsessively and all but oblivious to the stunning views his 2,200-square-foot penthouse suite at the Rome Cavalieri Hilton afforded him.

"Like I said, there have been complications."

"What about the old man?"

"My team is in place. I just talked to them."

"Is he back in the country yet?"

"He lands in a few hours."

"He'll go through VIP service, right?"

"Every time."

"So when will you have a clear shot?"

"Highway 1—a few miles before his driver gets to the city limits."

"What about his security detail?" Mariano asked.

"He dropped it."

"When?

"Last week."

"Why?"

"How should I know? All I know is that this is his first trip without guards, without his bulletproof SUV, without a tail car. It's just an old Volvo and a kid driver who can't be more than twenty-five. Look, I've got another call coming in. It's them."

"When will I hear from you next?"

"When you hear the news break, wire the money to my account. I'll call you when it clears."

"Fine, but listen to me, Rossetti . . ."

"I understand, sir."

"This thing's coming from the top, and I—"

"Don't worry. I got it."

You'd better, thought Mariano, but he said no more. He clicked off the phone, tossed it onto the lounge chair, and poured himself another glass of wine.

He looked out over the sprawling ancient city at the dome of St. Peter's Basilica, practically glowing in the distance, and calculated his next moves. Time was running out. If he was to be paid in full, all of the targets had to be dead by sundown on the twentieth. That was just eight days away, and they were only halfway through the list.

8

★ ★
★

It didn't take long to fall in love with Ronda.

One of the last Moorish cities to fall to the Crusaders and one of the oldest towns in Spain, it was a hidden paradise of rolling hills, dazzling sunsets, fields, and mountains as far as the eye could see, and a two-hundred-year-old stone bridge spanning a breathtaking plunging river gorge in the center of town. No wonder this sleepy little town, tucked away so far from civilization, had captured Erin's imagination as a little girl. No wonder it had drawn her back more than two decades later.

It was off-season and a bit chilly, but the Bennetts had spent a lazy morning strolling Ronda's streets, visiting the ancient Arab baths, and touring the bullfighting arena known as the *Plaza de Toros*, which was built in 1784 and still held crowds of thousands in the crowded summer season. By afternoon, they were poking through various shops, looking for nothing in particular, and letting their imaginations run free.

"What are you thinking about, Mr. Bennett?" Erin asked as they ducked into a café and ordered cappuccinos.

"Nothing," he laughed.

"Come on, what is it?"

"No, no, let's talk about you," he said. "Where would you like to go to dinner?"

"Nice try. But you have to tell me. Those are the rules, remember?"
She sweetened the deal with a kiss.

"It's nothing, really," he said finally. "I was just thinking about what I'd like to do if time and money were no objects."

"And?"

Bennett wasn't used to daydreaming about any life other than the one he'd had on Wall Street for almost a decade and a half. Moreover, this idea seemed downright ludicrous, particularly in light of recent events. But it seemed fun and somehow comforting to have a "blue sky" session with his best friend.

"It's crazy, I know, but if Mordechai were wrong about all that's ahead, and if we could really do whatever we wanted, I would love to pull together some investors, buy a huge tract of land in northern Virginia, and build an exact replica of the White House and Old Executive Office Building, to scale."

"I beg your pardon?" asked Erin.

"Think about it," he said, his eyes wide with childlike delight. "What's the number-one place visitors from all over the country and all over the world say they want to see when they come to Washington?"

"The White House."

"Exactly. But with all the security restrictions, hardly anyone gets in anymore. And even if they do, they never get to see the West Wing, or the Oval Office, or the really fun stuff. But what if they could? What if there was a White House people could really explore? a White House where they could actually be invited to a state dinner?"

Erin was smiling, but it was clear she wasn't completely following.

"Imagine if there was a White House where families could take real insider tours every weekday. But every Friday and Saturday night, there'd be a state dinner—black tie, formal gowns, big celebrities, the whole nine yards. You'd call an 800 number and make a reservation and be told to arrive at the Visitors' Center at 7 p.m. sharp."

"Visitors' Center?" asked Erin.

"Exactly," said Bennett. "You'd park there, two or three miles away from our White House Resort and Conference Center, and you'd be assigned a position on a covered platform, sort of like at a train station, heated in the winters and cooled in the summers. You'd have to be there no later than seven, because at precisely seven-fifteen the real adventure begins.

"A presidential motorcade suddenly comes up over a ridge. Lights flashing. Sirens wailing. There are motorcycles, police cars, a fleet of black limousines with little American flags waving on the hoods, all followed by black Suburbans and more motorcycles. The limos pull up and you're assisted inside by ushers and security people dressed up as Secret Service agents. Then the doors close and the motorcade begins the two-to-three-mile drive through the Virginia countryside, until you come up over a hill and there it is—bigger than life, awash in big floodlights."

Erin looked more interested now.

"And as you arrive, the big black gates open and you're brought around to the driveway on the South Lawn. If you're in the first set of limousines, you're immediately escorted to a tour of the West Wing. If you're in the middle set, you get a guided insider tour of the East Wing and the secret underground facilities like the Sit Room and the Secret Service command center—that kind of thing. If you're in the last set, you get to tour the main floors of the White House, the Lincoln Bedroom, the private residence, the solarium—all the private stuff the public usually never gets to see.

"Then, at precisely 8:15 p.m., you're seated for an elegant dinner of filet mignon and lobster and the finest champagne, followed by a famous speaker or comedian. On some nights we'd have charitable concerts hosted by the First Lady or by former First Ladies. On other nights we'd bring in Dana Carvey or Will Ferrell to do a night of presidential comedy. Some nights could simply be ballroom dancing. The possibilities are endless. We could even host a weekend Global Issues Summit with former presidents or secretaries of state.

"Think about it: Easter-egg rolls where no kid is turned away, White House Christmas parties—every night of December—that everyone can attend, inaugural balls, helicopter rides over Washington in our own versions of *Marine One*. We could even rent out the Lincoln Bedroom and it wouldn't be illegal!"

Erin couldn't help but laugh. For all the years she had known Jon Bennett on Wall Street and in the White House, he had always been so serious, so focused, so consumed with cutting deals and bringing peace and democracy to the Middle East. She had never seen him with the time or the desire to dream such crazy dreams. She loved him for it all the more, but she still had to rib a little, at least.

"And this is what you think about in your spare time?" she asked.

"You have no idea."

★   ★   ★

"Dr. Mordechai?" said a stranger's voice. "Is that really you?"

Mordechai pulled his head out of the stack of e-mails he was reading, looked up at the passport-control officer, and handed over his passport. "I'm afraid so," he said at last. "I'm sorry; do I know you?"

"No, no, but I thought it was you," the young woman replied. "What an honor."

He waited for the punch line, but there was none. The officer seemed genuinely glad to meet him, and he couldn't help but be surprised. Most Israelis now considered Mordechai, the world's most famous messianic Jew, a heretic if not an outright traitor. The country's chief rabbis were pressuring Prime Minister Doron to strip Mordechai of his citizenship, claiming he had converted to Christianity and thus had renounced his Jewishness. Death threats against him were mounting. He had been cursed and spat upon. He had even been physically attacked on the streets of Jerusalem as well as in the airport. So to be greeted so warmly upon returning to his country was certainly serendipitous.

The young woman stamped his passport for reentry without going through the usual list of security and customs questions, then lowered her voice. "The Lord is risen," she said.

Again, Mordechai was taken aback.

"He is risen indeed," he whispered in return. "How long have you been a follower of *Yeshua*?"

"Almost three months," she said. "I kept seeing you on TV before everything happened. I read your memo on the Internet. At first I thought you were a lunatic. But then everything happened, just like you predicted."

"Just as Ezekiel predicted," Mordechai gently corrected.

"Yes, of course," the young woman conceded, still in a whisper. "Anyway, I just wanted to say thank you. I know it hasn't been easy for you. But most of my family now believes as I do. Not my father. He

THE COPPER SCROLL 45

thinks we're all nuts, but we're praying for him night and day, just like you tell us to do."

The woman had tears in her eyes, and Mordechai found himself moved by the passion of her new faith. Thousands of people had posted similar thank-you's on his weblog (while many others posted curses). But this was the first Israeli he had met with the courage to thank him face-to-face, and it meant more to him than he could possibly tell her.

"Don't forget Psalm 122:6—keep praying for the peace of Jerusalem," he told her. "And I'll be praying for your father."

"Thank you, Dr. Mordechai," she said. "Thank you so much."

"You're most welcome," he replied. "You've made an old man's day. God bless you." Then he scooped up his briefcase and bags and headed out front to find his driver.

9

★ ★
★

Security was tight around the Great Tower of the People.

Outside, dark clouds were rolling in and a cool breeze was picking up. The winter rains were coming, and the temperature, now hovering in the low sixties, would soon plummet. Inside the luxuriously appointed and newly completed Iraqi capitol, the National Assembly speaker called for order.

One by one, all 434 men and 16 women—some in finely tailored suits from London and Paris and New York, others in the traditional robes of the Arab sheikhs—took their seats and grew quiet, eager to understand why they had been summoned on such short notice and with such secrecy.

"Members of Parliament and distinguished guests and neighbors, I realize many of you have come a great distance at your own personal expense and with very little notice. It is my honor to welcome you to the city of Babylon," the speaker began to polite applause. "On behalf of our president and our people, I want to thank you personally for joining us for what I believe will prove to be a most historic event. For most of you, this is your first time inside the walls of this great city. We hope it will not be your last. Indeed, we will do everything we can to make your stay here as enjoyable as possible. Please do not hesitate to ask if there is anything you need.

"For many years, as you know, Baghdad was our capital, but as you can see, it is no longer. *Why?* you may ask. It is a reasonable question and there is a simple answer. Baghdad, my friends, was Saddam's capital, the capital of a past we wish to forget. Babylon, on the other hand, is our future—not just mine or my colleagues' but yours as well. President Al-Hassani and I firmly believe that together we can build something great, something enduring, something that will cause the whole world to stop and take notice, and this is why you have been invited here tonight."

★   ★   ★

From his seat, Mustafa Al-Hassani looked out over the packed chamber.

It was being used for the very first time, and even though he had approved every detail in the design phase, now that it was finished, he could not help but admire its marble pillars and crystal chandeliers and handsome mahogany desks. It was the perfect venue for this decisive event.

He scanned the crowd, taking special care to make eye contact with each and every one of the fifty VIPs who had accepted his personal invitation, assembled from across North Africa, the Middle East, Turkey, and the former Soviet Union. They were not heads of state, of course, for most of those had perished in the firestorm. But they were men and women of great respect and influence, a potpourri of ministers and deputy ministers and tribal leaders and CEOs who happened to have had the good fortune of being far from their capitals when the tragedy struck. Now their countrymen back home were looking to them to rebuild their devastated nation-states as they struggled to comprehend the loss of family members, friends, and business and political allies. But the question looming large over the heads of all those now assembled was, where—and how—could they begin?

As he surveyed the audience, Al-Hassani was a cauldron of mixed emotions. In many ways, he—like them—was still in shock. Tehran and Moscow were all but gone. So were Riyadh, Kuwait City, and Tripoli, and cities such as Beirut, Tunis, Ankara, and Tashkent had fared little better. Aside from Babylon itself, only Cairo, Amman, and Rabat seemed to have been spared the magnitude of destruction the other major Middle Eastern Islamic capitals had faced.

Yet at the same time, Al-Hassani privately found himself relishing the apocalyptic turn of events. In one single, horrifying, history-altering day, the leaders and military forces of all of his enemies—save the Israelis—had been wiped off the face of the earth. For the moment he didn't know how or why; nor did he care. All he knew for sure was that his initial assessment was as true today as it had been three months earlier.

He had been given a gift, an opportunity unparalleled, perhaps, since the days of the great Babylonian king Nebuchadnezzar. The ancient empire of his ancestors had once stretched from the mountains of Iran in the east to the western deserts of Egypt, from Saudi Arabia in the south to Georgia and lower Russia in the north. And now events were conspiring in his favor to rebuild it.

Who could now prevent him from consolidating his control over the same territory, a vast and wealthy region of more than half a billion people and two-thirds of the world's known energy supplies? The Americans? The European Union or the Chinese? Not likely. They all saw him as an ally, not an enemy.

Indeed, if he played his cards shrewdly, the U.S., the E.U., and the entire United Nations would soon all but beg him to take this enormous burden off their shoulders. After all, it was one thing to "nation build" in some poor, war-torn, despotic African jungle. It was quite another to rebuild the economic and political infrastructure of a region as vital to the global economy as the oil-rich Middle East.

Who else was going to do it? Iraq was the only major OPEC member left standing. The industrialized world was desperate to get oil flowing out of Saudi Arabia, Iran, the Gulf, and the Caspian Sea once again. And with the price of oil north of two hundred dollars a barrel since the Day of Devastation, hundreds of billions of dollars were already pouring into Iraqi coffers. Soon trillions would be. Why not offer the world Iraq's help in rebuilding the drilling, pumping, and refining facilities throughout the region needed to bring sanity back to global energy prices?

For a small price, of course.

10
★ ★
★

Al-Hassani suddenly heard his name echo through the hall.

He saw the gathering of dignitaries rise to give him a standing ovation. How far he had come, he now realized, further than he had ever imagined, and it was as intoxicating as it was surreal. He basked for a few moments in the warmth of his colleagues' affection, then slowly rose and made his way to the podium to share his vision with a people perishing without one.

Without the aid of notes, he greeted each of the visiting VIPs by name and expressed his condolences for their losses, and then he said, "The Iraqi people share in your suffering. We have seen the horror that has been inflicted upon you. We have heard the cries of the suffering. We have responded as quickly as we could, but this is only the beginning. You have my word, and that of the people of Iraq—we will move heaven and earth to help you recover and rebuild; you will not be left alone."

The crowd erupted with applause, but Al-Hassani barreled on.

"No nation on the face of the earth—not the Americans, nor any of the Europeans—have done as much as the Republic of Iraq to bring bread to the hungry, water to the thirsty, clothes to the naked, shelter to the homeless, and medical assistance to all those in pain. We have already paid out more than half a billion dollars in humanitarian aid and emergency relief. But it is not enough. I would like to announce right now that the people of Iraq pledge a billion dollars more, and we will double it again if need be, because you are our brothers and sisters and we must stand together in this critical hour."

The entire assembly was now on their feet again. There were tears in the eyes of many.

"We deserve no credit," Al-Hassani demurred. "We are merely repaying a great debt. You came to our side in our moment of need. You helped us get back on our feet after a devastating war and a brutal insurgency, and for this the Iraqi nation will always be grateful. Baghdad may have been the epicenter of evil. But Babylon will be the house of compassion, hospitality, and unity among all the peoples of North Africa and the Middle East."

Once again, the hall erupted. The standing ovation lasted for several minutes, and Al-Hassani stepped back from the podium and lowered his head, overcome with emotion.

When the crowd quieted and sat back down, he continued.

"A great terror has befallen us, my friends. Some call it the Day of Devastation. Some say it was the judgment of God. But this cannot be true. How can it be? How could any god be so cruel, so vengeful? Regardless, the deed is done. It has changed our region and forever changed our hearts. Of this there can be no doubt. The question is not *whether* we will be changed, but *how*. Will we be defeated and divided or inspired and united?

"In the last three months we have seen an outpouring of concern and care from the four corners of the earth. Beyond what has been provided by the people of Iraq, other nations have pledged enormous sums in relief assistance, and more is coming. But do not be deceived, my brothers and sisters. Such aid comes with strings attached."

A hush began to settle over the great hall.

"In the last century, the British and the French and the Americans carved up our region, and we did nothing," Al-Hassani continued. "We sat back and let it happen. We let them draw artificial boundary lines to create our borders. We let them exploit our resources without just compensation. Cash? Yes, they gave us cash for our oil. But what about our freedom? What about our right to govern ourselves and shape our own destinies? Were we not too quick to give up what was rightfully ours for mere trinkets from the West?

"And now we have come to another critical juncture in the history of our people. What will we do? How will our children and grandchildren judge us? How will they remember us? Will we sit back and let Washington and London and Brussels and the U.N. Security Council claim to have 'bought' the privilege to draw new maps simply because we have accepted their aid packages? Is this the best for which we can hope?

"I realize full well that you and the people you represent have had precious little time to think of such things. You and your colleagues have been consumed with thoughts of survival, which is only right and proper. But know this: larger questions are coming. The future of our entire region is at stake, and the imperialists are already sharpening their carving knives. Of this you can be certain.

"At the moment, those of you from the devastated nations have little or no political power, clout, or leverage. Most of you have no formal governments, elected or appointed. You have no capital cities. You have no militaries, nor the national treasuries with which to rebuild them. Your ambassadors have no instructions, no idea to whom they should report, and rapidly dwindling funds with which to operate. For all intents and purposes, you are occupied by U.S. and E.U. and U.N. military forces, cloaked in the disguise of humanitarian workers.

"How long can this last before you all once again become colonies of the West? Your only hope of resisting long-term Western occupation is to rapidly rebuild your oil and gas industries, as we in Iraq have done. But how are you supposed to accomplish this urgent task without desperately needed infusions of capital—large amounts of capital? And how can you raise capital if the banks are loath to lend you money? This, my friends, is a hard, cruel reality, and it leaves you dangerously vulnerable to the very imperialist forces you have long sought to resist.

"Distinguished colleagues, I submit that the only way we can survive is if we unify. Only if we combine our economic and political resources will our region ever be able to get back on its feet and give dignity to our people. We Iraqis have done it. After a long, hard struggle, we have come together as one—imperfectly, I concede. But who can argue that out of the ashes of war and insurgency and despair a new Iraq has emerged as one nation, with one voice—Sunnis and Shi'ites, Arabs and Kurds, north and south, east and west—able to defeat the forces of evil within and the forces of imperialism without? Let this be a model for all. Unity must be our aim. We cannot rebuild if we allow ancient passions and prejudices to divide us. We cannot achieve our destiny if we allow the Western powers to divide and conquer us.

"So I put these questions to you today: What if we seize the initiative and take our future into our own hands? What if a year from now there was a great power to rival the United States of America and the United States of Europe? What if there arose a single new nation, a single new economic and political force, encompassing the great peoples of southern Europe, the Mediterranean basin, North Africa, the Middle East, and the former Soviet republics of Central Asia? Perhaps it would be known as the United States of Eurasia, or perhaps the Republic of Namestan, or perhaps something else altogether. It is not a name to which I am wed. It is a single vision by which I am driven—a vision of one people, one government, one currency, one unified force with which the rest of the world must reckon.

"And I ask you tonight: who among you will share my vision?"

II

★ ★
★

"Tripwire to Dagger."

"Dagger, go."

"I've got a visual on the car. He's coming your way."

"Who's with him?"

"Just the driver."

"Anyone else?"

"Negative. You should have a clear shot."

"Roger that. Dagger to Wolf Pack, six minutes."

★ ★ ★

Mordechai hung up the phone and stared out his window.

Row upon row of oil wells blurred by as his car raced up Highway 1, trying to get him into Jerusalem in time for a BBC television interview scheduled just twenty-five minutes from now. Depending on traffic, they might just make it, thought Mordechai, but he wasn't worried. He had done more interviews than he could count since "The Ezekiel Option" memo had been splashed across the pages of the world's newspapers. Dozens of new requests came in every day. He couldn't possibly do them all.

Interest in his perspective on world events was growing exponentially. His weblog registered upward of 6 and even 7 million hits a day, and he was having trouble finding an ISP that was both willing and able to handle the actual volume, which several computer technicians estimated at north 15 million hits a day.

He leaned back in his seat and wondered what he would write about when he got home. He had already written extensively about the bombing in Washington on his flight home and uploaded all that at the airport. He couldn't write about Jon and Erin's wedding, of course. They hardly needed more publicity. But the truth was, that beautiful ceremony was what he was thinking about most.

Mordechai had particularly enjoyed his conversation with Ken Costello and his wife, Tracy, just before the service had begun. They had been intrigued by his memo and fascinated with his theory. But they still weren't sure they bought his conclusions. By their own admission, they had been agnostics before the world had taken a turn for the worse—"lapsed Catholics," in their words—whose trips to church in the past had been on Easter and Christmas, but rarely in between. Now they were searching for answers and attending a Bible church in Bethesda, Maryland. Mordechai had no doubt they would discover the truth. He just hoped it was in time.

★ ★ ★

"Dagger, this is Periscope, over."

"Go ahead, Periscope."

"We have eyes on the target. Just hit some traffic. Slowing a bit. But still headed your way."

"Roger that. All units stand by."

★ ★ ★

Something extraordinary was under way.

In Ezekiel 38 and 39, the God of Israel had declared, "I will magnify Myself, sanctify Myself, and make Myself known in the sight of many nations; and they will know that I am the Lord," and "I will not hide My face from them any longer, for I will have poured out My Spirit on the house of Israel."

And sure enough, these ancient prophecies were coming to pass.

Never in history had so many Jews and Gentiles declared themselves followers of Jesus Christ. Every day Mordechai received e-mails with news from around the globe that made him literally weep with joy. Churches and messianic Jewish congregations were exploding in numbers. The term *small-group Bible studies* was quickly becoming extinct from the evangelical lexicon. Nothing was small anymore. Once-deserted cathedrals throughout Europe were filled to capacity. Tiny country churches in rural America were having enormous camp meetings in cornfields. Thousands of Buddhist and Hindu temples in India, Pakistan, and Southeast Asia were being converted into Bible churches. In Korea and Japan and throughout the Pacific Rim, millions of new believers were meeting for worship in soccer stadiums.

Perhaps most extraordinary was word of hundreds of new Bible-believing, Bible-preaching congregations springing up throughout the Middle East, as well as news that once-clandestine house churches and underground gatherings of believers were now coming out into the warm Mediterranean sunshine. Muslims were turning to Christ in record numbers, and Mordechai could only shake his head to see former mullahs and imams on Al-Jazeera and other regional television and radio shows now preaching the gospel like modern-day apostles.

He wanted to go and see it all for himself, firsthand. He wanted to visit the people, the homes, the rapidly growing assemblies of new believers in Libya and Sudan and especially Iran. He had received invitations from all over the region from believers eager to hear his teaching after reading his words online. But time was running out. The Lord was coming back soon. How could he best invest his time until the end?

Mordechai scrolled through his Treo for new e-mails. As he did, he came across one from the pastor of Christ Our Shepherd Church, now the largest and fastest-growing congregation of Muslim converts to Christ on the Arabian Peninsula.

```
Dear Brother Mordechai—
    Greetings from Mecca, where Jesus is now the King!
Thank you so much for your very encouraging note,
and even more important, for your unceasing prayers.
I write to you with good news of great joy, an update
on how our risen Savior is blessing our little
```

congregation. Over the past thirty days, we have had
the privilege of baptizing another 2,206 members,
bringing the total followers of Jesus in our community
to just over 14,000. We face great hardships here. As
the shock of the earthquake and firestorm begins to
lessen slightly, persecution is intensifying—but not
from Muslims. Indeed, there are few true followers of
Mohammed anymore. Most Saudis are experiencing great
confusion over what they believe and where to go next.
They have seen their god shattered, like the prophets
of Baal, and now they are searching for the truth and
asking us many questions. We can barely keep up!

That said, the trials we face today come mostly from
the U.N. peacekeeping forces who recently arrived to
"keep order." They have shut down our church's food-
and-clothing-distribution efforts to families in need
and are accusing us of trying to bribe people into our
faith. They have denied us a building permit as well,
refusing to let us build a church amid the ashes of the
destroyed mosques. But we have not lost our joy! May
it never be! We will persevere by His grace.

Would you pray about coming to preach to us, to
encourage us, and to help us choose and anoint elders
who can guide us through these difficult times? We would
be most grateful. The Lord's family is growing so rapidly
here, and as you well know I have only been a believer
myself for a few years. I need all the wisdom and advice
you can supply. Thank you so much, and may God continue
to bless you and keep you in His mighty arms.

Yours in Christ,
Brother Faisal

☆　☆　☆

One by one, the four men rechecked their weapons.

And one by one they clicked off their safeties and eased into position.
Dagger would take the first shots from a rock ledge, using a high-power
sniper rifle smuggled in through Gaza from Egypt during all the chaos.

The rest would follow suit, then disappear into the hills, never to see one another again.

Their radios suddenly crackled to life.

"One minute," said Dagger.

* * *

Mordechai reread the e-mail.

He felt a lump forming in his throat. He had never been in Saudi Arabia, even while serving in the Mossad. He had certainly never been to Mecca. What an amazing privilege it would be to preach the gospel there and strengthen the new followers of Christ. But when would he have the time? His schedule was already packed with speaking opportunities for the better part of the next year. Still, he would pray about it, and perhaps the Lord of the harvest would make a way.

Mordechai's phone rang.

* * *

"Now!" Dagger shouted into his radio.

He took careful aim at the oncoming vehicle and pulled the trigger. His snipers immediately opened fire as well, blowing out the tires and riddling the doors with armor-piercing rounds. The car swerved violently. It veered into oncoming traffic, then came back again into its own lane, barely missing a tractor trailer, as the shooting continued without pause.

* * *

The windshield exploded.

Mordechai ducked below the seat as the cell phone, still ringing, fell to the floor. His driver abruptly slumped forward. He'd been hit in the face and chest multiple times.

The car again swerved violently. They were headed for the guardrail and a thirty-foot embankment. Mordechai reached over the front seat and tried to grab the wheel. But more machine-gun fire now erupted from both sides of the road. It was a classic ambush, and for the first time in his life, Mordechai was caught utterly unprepared.

Shattered glass flew all around him. Armor-piercing rounds penetrated the thick metal doors of his government-issue Volvo. He felt one rip through his arm. Another ripped into the small of his back, and Mordechai cried out in pain.

He felt the car crash through the twisted metal of the guardrail and plunge through the air, and for one brief moment, all was silent. No gunfire. No pain. Just the horrifying realization that he was about to die and then the sudden, unexpected joy that he was about to meet his Savior face-to-face.

Mordechai never saw his attackers run for the hills. He never heard his car smash on the rocks below. He did not feel the force of the explosion or the searing, roaring flames consuming his flesh. He felt nothing and heard only the echo of his wife's name as he drifted into darkness.

12
★ ★
★

Al-Hassani retired to his suite.

There, in the sprawling executive conference room adjacent to his almost equally spacious office on the sixtieth floor—overlooking the city of Babylon, which seemed to be rising like a phoenix from the ashes—the Iraqi president met privately with a dozen of his foreign guests over hot tea and sweet cakes.

"Mr. President, with all due respect, you have caught us all completely off guard," an Iranian CEO began when Al-Hassani opened the small meeting to questions. "If I understand you correctly, you are essentially proposing that we give up our sovereignty and turn over our oil assets to you."

Al-Hassani paused a moment and scanned the other faces. "Is that how you all see this—as a power grab?"

"On the contrary," said one of the few Saudi princes who had survived the near destruction of his country. "I believe you have been quite generous. You are proposing that we band together and maximize our economic and political clout rather than remain divided and thus defeated. I think it makes great sense."

"I agree," said the son of the Kuwaiti oil minister, who had lost his entire extended family. "Under the circumstances, it is the most hopeful news I have heard since this nightmare began."

The Iranian businessman could not believe what he was hearing. "After all the Iraqis have done to your countries—and to mine—how can you both sit there and say that with straight faces?" he demanded. "How can you be so naive? Can you not see what is going on here?"

"How dare you lecture me about Iraqi history?" said the young Kuwaiti man, his face turning red. "Don't let your passions blind you to the truth, my friend. The rape of our countries was not committed by Mustafa Al-Hassani. It was the act of a single madman, and President Al-Hassani is not Saddam Hussein. He is not about to invade my country or yours or fire Scud missiles into Saudi Arabia."

"He won't have to," the man from Isfahan shouted back as he jumped to his feet. "You'd gladly hand over your children on a silver platter."

"*Enough*," demanded Syria's former finance minister, who had been on vacation in Switzerland when the devastation occurred. "Enough. This is exactly our problem. We are in the midst of a terrible crisis. We must make decisions very quickly or have them made for us, and we haven't the luxury of feuding among ourselves.

"Look around you. Have you not noticed that even with oil at over two hundred dollars a barrel, our treasuries are all but empty? Have you not seen that OPEC essentially lies in ruins? And while we bicker over trivialities, our real enemy is rapidly becoming a global superpower. If we do not join forces and get our oil and gas industries back on line, we will be ceding the entire playing field to the true and ultimate enemy of our people. Wake up, brothers. Medexco now controls the flow of oil to the world and has suddenly become the wealthiest company on earth. President Al-Hassani is not the enemy. Iraq is not the enemy. The Jews are our real enemy."

The man from Isfahan sat down. The Syrian, an elderly man in his late seventies, asked Al-Hassani if he could make a few more points.

"By all means," said the Iraqi president, privately wondering if Khalid Tariq, his chief political advisor, had coached this man in advance.

"You are most kind, Your Excellency," said the Syrian. "My brothers, please, consider what the Europeans have done. They fought two world wars. They massacred tens of millions of their neighbors. Fifty years ago, no one in their right mind could ever have imagined the emergence of the European Union. Had someone predicted the rise of a common market, a common currency, a central government in Brussels, a unified foreign policy, or any of the rest of it, he would have been committed to an insane asylum."

He pulled a single euro coin from his pocket and tossed it into the center of the enormous conference table. "But there it is. The euro is crushing the dollar, the yen, and every other currency in the world. Don't you see it? It's a symbol that nothing is impossible if men of goodwill come together and unite under one banner, for one cause. Open your eyes, my brothers. Europe is rising. She is triumphing. Why? Because she has unified. She is competing with the Americans and she's winning—not divided, but together. We are witnessing the rebirth of the Roman Empire, and if we are not careful, we will be eaten alive."

The Syrian paused and looked around the room. "Which leaves us where?" he asked. "Divided, confused, bickering, feuding, and thus consigned to the ash heap of history? Is that what you want for your children and your children's children? Are you really so blind, so young, and so foolish as to miss the fact that what President Al-Hassani has just laid out for us is not only a brilliant vision of what our future could be, it is in fact our *only* hope?"

★　★　★

"Ken, it's Marsha Kirkpatrick. Sorry to bother you at home."

"No problem," Ken Costello lied. He was just back from a marathon few days at the White House and now coming down with a fever. "What's up?"

"I know you and Tracy are close to Eli Mordechai," Kirkpatrick said.

"Sure," said Costello. "We just saw him Saturday at Jon and Erin's wedding. Why?"

"Well," she said, "I'm afraid I have some bad news."

★　★　★

A different Iranian CEO rose to speak.

He was thirty-three and had been educated in the U.S. "I must say I agree with my brother from Damascus. Together, we could be a very powerful force, and it is not as though we have a lot of options on our own. The fact is, we need to raise reconstruction capital from somewhere, and President Al-Hassani is right. We can either join forces with him, or we can beg on our knees from our competitors—the Americans and the Europeans. I say we work together. We could create a new OPEC, a force the rest of the world would have to fear and respect. But, that said, Mr. President, we must have certain guarantees."

Every eye turned to Al-Hassani.

"Guarantees?" the elderly Iraqi leader asked, a glint in his eyes.

"Yes," said the young Iranian. "For one thing, everyone in this room must have real governing authority in our regions—the power to legislate, the power to tax, and so forth, like American governors and legislatures have over their states."

"Of course," said Al-Hassani. "It goes without question. I am proposing a republic, not a dictatorship."

"Good," said the Iranian. "And we would all need to share equally in the oil and gas profits, which will eventually be enormous."

"I don't see how this new republic could work any other way," Al-Hassani agreed.

"We would also need to create a national governing body," the Iranian continued, "a legislature with equal say in the decisions that are made over the currency, the tax laws, budgetary decisions, and so forth, like the American Senate."

"God help us," said Al-Hassani, to a round of laughter. "We will have to come up with something better than that."

"Fair enough," the Iranian conceded. "But that's not all. We will have to get the Egyptians and Jordanians involved, and the Moroccans, too. We could do all this without them, but it would be far better with them."

"I have already dispatched my foreign minister to Cairo and Amman. And I will speak with the Moroccan king by phone in the morning."

"We will need a way to keep the Europeans and Americans from feeling threatened by any of this," warned the Syrian.

Al-Hassani nodded. "The E.U. foreign minister is coming to Babylon this week," he noted. "Salvador Lucente and I worked very closely together during the reconstruction of Iraq. We have a good working relationship. I expect some very productive talks."

"Excellent," said the Iranian. "But there is one more thing."

"That's quite a shopping list already," Al-Hassani quipped.

His guests laughed.

The Iranian smiled and continued. "I am looking for a promise."

"What kind of promise?" asked Al-Hassani.

"I want your personal assurance that you will do everything in your power to stop the Jews from becoming a superpower."

"Isn't that, in part, what this whole discussion is about?" asked the Iraqi leader.

"No," said the Iranian. "It is not enough that *we* become a major economic and political force. You must prevent the Israelis from becoming an equal or greater force."

"And just how do you propose I do that?"

"To begin with, you must stop the Jews from building their Temple."

Al-Hassani looked around the room. Everyone was nodding.

"Personally," said the Iranian, "I was never that religious. But the Temple is a symbol. If the Jews rebuild it on the site of the Dome of the Rock, it will be a symbol of their power and our impotence."

"Yes," said the Syrian, "you must stop the Jews."

"The Jews must never be allowed back onto the Temple Mount," said another.

"Let me remind you all that we haven't much time," Al-Hassani warned. "The faster we unify into a single legal and political entity, the sooner we can request a seat on the U.N. Security Council. The sooner we can ask to become a member of the G8 conference of industrialized countries. The sooner we can begin coordinating international relief efforts and maximizing the resources being offered to us. But if we hesitate or demand more than we can achieve, we could lose everything."

At that point the Saudi prince stepped back into the fray. "I, for one, am ready to sign on to your plan right now, Your Excellency," he declared. "But my brother from Iran is right. We must first have written guarantees on each of the points we've discussed here today and your personal oath that the Jews will *never* be allowed to build their so-called Temple in the holy city of Al Quds."

Al-Hassani tried not to smile. Everything was going just as he had planned, and he knew something the others did not. He had already set in motion plans to stop the Jews in their tracks. Operation Black Box was well under way.

13

★ ★
★

The Bennetts finished a late dinner and strolled back to their hotel.

It was almost midnight when they picked up their keys from the front desk and found a message from Ken Costello waiting for them, marked "Urgent."

At first, Bennett was shocked simply by the presence of any message. Nobody was supposed to know where they were. Not the president and First Lady. Not even his mother. How could Ken have known? But then came the more important question: what could be so urgent as to interrupt them on their honeymoon?

"Are you going to call him back?" Erin asked as they got on the elevator.

"We had a pact, remember?"

"I know, but what if it's personal?" said Erin. "The only way Ken could have tracked us down is through the travel agency, and if he went to all that trouble, it must be important. What if something's wrong with your mom?"

Bennett winced. His mother had a long history of heart trouble. At the wedding, friends had remarked that they hadn't seen her so relaxed and so peaceful in years, but Erin was right. Anything was possible. So as soon as they got back to their room, he placed the call while Erin stepped into the bathroom to get ready for bed.

"White House operator. May I help you?"

"Yeah, hi, this is Jon Bennett. I got a message that Ken—"

"Yes, Mr. Bennett. The president is expecting your call. Please hold and I will put you right through."

The president? It had to be a mistake.

"No, I—"

But the call had already gone through.

"Situation Room, Marsha Kirkpatrick."

It had been months since he had heard the national security advisor's voice.

"Marsha, it's Jon Bennett. I'm just trying to return Ken Costello's call, but—"

"I know. I am sitting here with the president. Ken's here too. So are Corsetti and Chuck Murray. Hold on. The president would like to speak with you first."

Before Bennett could react, MacPherson was on the line. His voice was unusually subdued. Something was wrong.

"Jon, I'm so sorry to interrupt your honeymoon, but I'm afraid it couldn't be helped."

"I'm always happy to take a call from you, Mr. President."

"Jon, it's Mordechai. He's been attacked."

Bennett couldn't breathe.

"He's alive," MacPherson continued, "but probably not for long. The doctors believe it's only a matter of time. He's unconscious and barely hanging on. He's been shot at least a dozen times, and he's got third-degree burns over most of his body."

The president further explained that Mordechai was currently in emergency surgery and had been for the last few hours, but he was not expected to make it beyond the next few hours or days.

Bennett couldn't believe what he was hearing. He didn't know how to respond.

"Jon," MacPherson continued, "I don't have to tell you how involved Dr. Mordechai was as a back channel between the Israelis and the Palestinians. And as you know, under the radar he's also been instrumental in building ties between the Israelis and the Iraqis. I've just gotten off the phone with Prime Minister Doron, and given all the uncertainty in the region right now, we both agree we need to be very careful not to allow the peace process, fragile as it is, to become derailed once again. That said, I've asked Ken to head to Israel immediately. He lifts off from Andrews Air Force Base within the hour. He'll be meeting with Prime Minister Doron and the new Palestinian leadership to take everyone's temperature and see if we can get final status talks moving forward again. If you'd like, I can have Ken pick you and Erin up on the way and take you over there. I don't know if you can make it in time, but . . . well, it's up to you."

Jon was numb, but he thanked the president and accepted his gracious offer, then discussed the details with Ken. Just as he hung up, Erin stepped out of the bathroom.

"Is it your mom?" Erin asked, seeing the pain in his eyes. "Is she okay?"

"She's fine," Jon said flatly. "It wasn't that."

"Then what?"

He took her in his arms and held her tight.

☆   ☆   ☆

The next morning, they stood on the tarmac in Málaga.

Costello stepped off the plane and embraced them both, then welcomed them back on board the same State Department Gulfstream V that had practically been their home during their years of shuttle diplomacy.

"What's the latest, Ken?" Bennett asked as they lifted off.

Costello hesitated.

"Is he still alive?" asked Erin.

"Barely," Costello admitted. "One of the bullets nearly severed his spinal cord. His doctors say his pelvis, right arm, and shoulder were shattered when his car went off the road, and he lost most of his blood before medical teams were able to get to him. To be honest, it's a miracle he made it through the night."

The G5 touched down in Israel just after 4 p.m. local time. Costello and the Bennetts were met at the airport by Mossad chief Avi Zadok, who briefed them on the way to Hadassah Hospital in Jerusalem.

"We don't have many leads at the moment," Zadok said, "but we have two working theories. The first is that the assassination attempt was an act of Muslim retribution for Dr. Mordechai's 'Ezekiel Option' memo. The second is that the attack could have been carried out by ultra-Orthodox Jews because of Dr. Mordechai's public claims about Jesus."

Privately, Bennett wished there were evidence of Islamic extremism. But the truth was, most of the region's Muslim community was mourning its dead and was shell-shocked by the extraordinary losses of its holiest sites. To him, it strained credibility to believe active cells of jihadists were capable of a carefully orchestrated attack so quickly after such devastation. More likely was the Jewish angle. Israeli outrage at Mordechai's "betrayal" was widespread among the Orthodox, heated, and very public.

Zadok showed them copies of written death threats—letters and e-mails—that Mordechai had received in recent weeks. Even letters to the editor of major Israeli newspapers and callers on local radio shows had been warning Mordechai to watch his back.

But then another wave of questions flooded Bennett's thoughts. How exactly was it possible to gun down a former Mossad chief inside Israel? True, Mordechai had given up his full taxpayer-financed security detail. But that was because the Mossad and Shin Bet had told him all the threats were just talk, that he really had nothing to fear. They had assured him that they would keep an eye on him. Zadok had personally chosen Mordechai's driver, a former special-forces commando, and insisted he carry a sidearm and be with Mordechai at all times.

How, then, could this have happened? Was it possible someone in Doron's inner circle wanted Mordechai dead?

14

★ ★
★

They found Mordechai under heavy sedation.

According to his doctors, he was barely hanging on for his life. Bennett stared at his mentor through a glass window and silently pled with God to spare him.

All of a sudden a dozen security agents began taking up positions throughout the hallway. Bennett turned and looked at Erin and then at the elevator as the door opened and the prime minister and two of his top aides stepped off.

"It's good to see you both," David Doron said as he shook their hands. "I'm sorry it's under such tragic circumstances. I want you to know I'll do everything I can to bring the monsters that did this to justice."

The Bennetts thanked the prime minister, as did Costello.

"It can't be doing you any political good to be here right now," Bennett acknowledged.

"I don't care," said Doron. "He was my friend, no matter how much we disagreed."

A doctor stepped into the hall. He was startled to see the prime minister but addressed the Bennetts. "He just opened his eyes, and he asked for you. But he doesn't have long. Did you bring a rabbi—er, a priest?"

They had brought neither and didn't know any pastors in Israel. "I'm afraid we just got here from the airport," said Bennett.

"Very well," said the doctor. "You can have a few minutes with him. Follow me."

The Bennetts entered the dimly lit ICU room. They were immediately overwhelmed by the array of technology keeping their friend tethered to this world, and they were completely unprepared for the visual impact of Mordechai's broken body. His body was wrapped in gauze and bandages, as were his hands and feet, but it was his charred and blistered face that made Bennett wince and, for a moment, look away.

When he regained his composure, he looked back and saw casts on both of Mordechai's arms and legs and the tangled spaghetti of tubes and wires running in and out of his body. He scanned the various instruments, glowing and beeping in the dark. Mordechai's pulse and blood pressure were weak.

Bennett gathered his strength and said, "Dr. Mordechai, it's Jon and Erin."

Slowly, the old man opened his eyes. A nurse gave him some ice chips, and Bennett noticed that his lips were about the only part of his face not severely burned. But they were chapped and cracked and covered with dried blood.

It took a few moments, but in a raspy, faltering voice, Mordechai said his first words. "I'm sorry."

Bennett noticed tears trickling down Erin's cheeks. He fought back his own.

Then Mordechai spoke again. "I should have liked more time with you both."

"Hey, hey, don't talk like that," said Erin. "We'll have plenty of time together. You still need to teach us how to make that curry of yours."

"Erin sent an e-mail to everyone on your list serve, explaining what happened," Bennett added. "She posted it on your weblog as well. The response has been overwhelming. Millions are praying for you to recover, Dr. Mordechai, and I have no doubt you will."

A faint smile began to form on the old man's lips, and crinkles formed around his bloodshot eyes. "Jonathan, my son, you're a good boy, but you still have much to learn. . . . I'm afraid I no longer have the privilege of being your teacher."

"Don't say that, Dr. Mordechai," Bennett pleaded, his voice wavering. "You're going to pull through this."

"No. My time has come. The Lord blessed me with a long and full life, but now I'm ready . . . to meet my God face-to-face, and to see my beautiful Yael once more. . . . And I tell you both, I cannot think of anything I want more."

"But we need you here," said Bennett. "There's still so much we don't know, so much to be done."

"No, Jonathan," Mordechai said softly. "This is your time. Make the most of it."

"What if I'm not ready?" Bennett asked.

But Mordechai would have none of it. "You are, and so is Erin. But be on guard. A new evil is rising, more deadly than anything that has ever come before. I should have seen it coming, but I was so busy. I let my guard down, and then . . ."

There was a long pause. The old man's eyes were at half-mast. His strength was quickly fading. "You both must promise me something," he said at last.

"Anything," said Erin.

"You must find . . . them . . ."

"Who, Dr. Mordechai?"

". . . and stop . . . them . . ."

His hands were trembling. His pulse was becoming erratic.

"Who, Dr. Mordechai?" Bennett pressed. "Who did this to you?"

". . . before they . . ."

"Before they what?"

But Mordechai's eyes barely registered a response. He seemed to be drifting away, and there was another long, wrenching silence. Bennett saw tears streaming down Erin's face as she covered her mouth to keep from being heard. Then he looked back at the man who had been his spiritual father and put his ear close to his mouth. He thought Mordechai said something like "start with," but the next word was barely audible. *Break? Brock? Broke?* Mordechai was mumbling the same word over and over, but Bennett couldn't make sense of it.

Then suddenly, it was as though Mordechai had gained a second wind, if only for a moment. "I should have liked to have met my Lord in the clouds," he said finally.

And then he closed his eyes and breathed his last.

An alarm on the heart monitor went off. Then the ventilator alarm went off as well. Mordechai was flatlining. Doctors and nurses burst into the room, forcing Bennett and Erin to move aside. A nurse plunged a needle into Mordechai's chest. Another pulled electric shock paddles off the wall. A team of specialists raced through a series of emergency procedures, heroically battling to save a man most of them believed was a traitor. But it was too late. There was nothing they or anyone else could do.

Mordechai's heart had stopped, and at last he was home.

15

★ ★
★

The blood in Bennett's face began to drain away.

The colors in the room faded. The room spun. His mouth was dry. A shiver shot through his body. An aching, throbbing pain coursed through his veins and through his soul. He felt the warmth of Erin's hand, and for a moment, at least, it seemed to anchor him back to reality.

He blinked hard and turned to her as she began to sob, her body heaving, gasping for air amid her cries. He pulled her to him and wrapped his arms around her, and she buried her face in his chest and refused to let go. Soon his shirt was soaked through. But for some reason he couldn't join her. He couldn't cry. Not yet. It was all too sudden. He still didn't believe it was true.

In the hallway, Jon could hear muffled voices. Someone was telling the prime minister and then Ken Costello the news. He couldn't hear the words, but he could feel their effect. The shock of Mordechai's death was spreading through the ICU, as it would soon spread through the country and the world.

A nurse pulled a sheet up over Mordechai's head while another filled out a clipboard of paperwork. They said nothing. They were professionals, and they were respectful of the dead. But Jon couldn't help wondering what they thought of Eliezer Mordechai. Could they ever believe what he'd believed?

A moment later, Costello stepped into the room to pay his last respects. Then he gave both Jon and Erin a quiet hug and stepped back into the hallway, making way for Prime Minister Doron, who came in next, without his security detail.

"He was a good man," Doron said after a long, awkward pause.

"The best," said Bennett.

"He had such certainty about life and such a peace about dying," Doron observed as he stared at the shrouded body of his friend of nearly forty years. "I have to admit, I envied him."

Bennett was surprised to hear Doron say it. But in his grief, at least for now, he couldn't find the words to respond.

A Shin Bet agent popped her head into the room. "Mr. Prime Minister," she said quietly.

"Yes?"

"I'm afraid we need to clear this room for a few minutes."

"Yes, yes, of course," Doron said, noticing two orderlies waiting in the hallway, no doubt ready to take Mordechai's body to the morgue.

With his arms still around her, Bennett led his grieving bride out of the room and followed Doron, Costello, and several aides and bodyguards down the hallway and out of the orderlies' way.

"Jon, I know this is a very difficult time, but I wonder if I could speak with you for a moment," the prime minister whispered. "It's about Eli. I think it might shed some light on what happened."

Bennett hesitated, not wanting to leave Erin alone. But she wiped away her tears with the handkerchief he'd given her and motioned for him to go. "I'll be okay for a few minutes," she sniffled.

"You sure?" he whispered back.

"Don't be long."

"I won't."

Bennett caught Costello's eye, and Costello immediately came over and guided Erin to a lounge chair, sat her down, and offered to get her some hot tea, which she gratefully accepted.

Doron, meanwhile, motioned to his chief of staff and press secretary. "Would you both excuse us for a moment?"

The men took their leave, and with several security men in tow, the prime minister led Bennett to the stairwell and up to the roof.

* * *

Mustafa Al-Hassani needed some fresh air.

He stepped out onto the balcony of his presidential palace, built by Saddam and now his very own, and felt the cool evening breezes coming off the desert as he listened to the steady drilling of construction crews and saw the great cranes in motion as far as the eye could see. A moment later, his consigliere, Khalid Tariq, joined him.

"You were right, Your Excellency," said Tariq. "They were more pliable than I had expected."

"You expected more resistance?" asked Al-Hassani.

"I expected *some* resistance."

"Never underestimate the power of desperation, Khalid. Remember, these are men without homes, without hope, without the families and treasures they have always loved. They are adrift. They have no leaders, no direction, no sense of destiny. Like their great-great-grandfathers, they are, once again, nomads, wandering in the desert, and we are the shelter amid the storms."

"You were right about the Temple as well," Tariq noted.

"Always remember," Al-Hassani said, lighting his pipe, his white robes rippling in the desert breezes, "these men's faith in Islam may have shattered, but not their passion for Jerusalem. Jerusalem predates Islam. Indeed, it transcends Islam. Jerusalem has always been the temptress that draws men's souls. She is the jewel for which every ruler lusts. Men spilled their blood to possess her long before Mohammed was born, my friend. And with the right leadership, they will do so again. Our new alliance depends upon it."

"What if Operation Black Box fails?" asked Tariq.

"*It cannot be allowed to fail, Khalid,*" Al-Hassani said emphatically. "You must make sure of that. If we are to rebuild the empire of our fathers, we must stop the Jews—whatever it takes and whatever the cost. And we must do so carefully, without any of our actions ever being traced back to us. Did you tell me that pressure on Doron to build the Temple is growing?"

"I'm afraid so, Your Excellency," Tariq replied. "The *Jerusalem Post* has a new poll out just this morning—78 percent of Israelis want to see construction begin on the Temple within the next six months. That's up nine points since the first of the year. What's more, Israel's chief rabbi is quoted as saying he wants the government to put up all the funds."

"What more proof do you need?" asked Al-Hassani. "It no longer matters how much pressure the White House puts on the Israelis. Or whether the bureaucrats in Brussels stamp their feet. Or whether the U.N. decides to pass a resolution warning Israel not to move forward. All of that is irrelevant. The simple fact is, if Doron refuses to build the Temple, his government could very well collapse. Which means we are running out of time, Khalid. We must stop the Jews from moving forward before it's too late."

16

The night air was damp and chilly.

Bennett stepped onto the roof of the hospital and stared into the distance at the scorched surface of the Temple Mount. No matter how many times he'd seen the now-barren sacred site—wiped clean, as it were, by the great firestorm—it was still surreal.

The Dome of the Rock had been standing there day and night, rain or shine, since the seventh century AD. The Al-Aksa Mosque had been there in one form or another since early in the eighth century. Both had been modified, redesigned, and reconstructed several times over the years, to be sure. But they had been landmarks of history, emblems of culture, centers of learning and worship for Muslims nearly since the founding of Islam. Now they were no more. It was a fact the implications of which Bennett had not yet fully processed, given all else that had happened in the world and in his life.

"There is something you should know, Jonathan," the prime minister began, jarring Bennett back into the moment. "I know Avi Zadok shared with you several of the theories being bandied about in the press about who killed Eli and why. But there may be another explanation for why Eli died. Come, take a walk with me."

The concrete beneath their feet was wet from a late-afternoon shower, and as they walked they stepped carefully around the puddles.

"Last November," the prime minister began, "not long after the earthquake and the firestorm, I quietly asked Mordechai to come to my office. We talked about 'The Ezekiel Option,' about why he'd written it and about what he thought was coming next. As you can imagine, he did his best to convert—er, *persuade*—me to become a follower of Jesus. He warned me time was running short, that the Scriptures said 'now is the day of salvation,' and I asked him what he believed was next on the prophetic calendar."

"What did he say?" asked Bennett.

"He talked a lot about the Rapture—which, if I understand correctly, is when all of the followers of Jesus around the world disappear in the blink of an eye and are caught up in heaven to be with God forever."

Bennett nodded.

"Well, he gave me quite an earful on that."

"And you didn't buy it?" asked Bennett.

"Please, Jonathan. I'm the prime minister of Israel, for crying out loud. Eli's prescience was uncanny. I will grant you that. But just because he was right about Russia and Iran doesn't prove ipso facto that Jesus is the Messiah. Believe me, I've read Ezekiel 38 and 39. They don't say anything about Jesus. They're not in the New Testament. They're *Jewish* prophecies, written by a Hebrew prophet. While Eli loved to point out how many millions have become followers of Christ in the last few months, I would always remind him that we've also seen an unprecedented resurgence in Jews all over the world attending synagogue, buying Hebrew Bibles, wearing *tefillin*, enrolling their children in Hebrew school, and so on. The fact is, Jews are turning back to Judaism in record numbers, Jonathan. And why is that? Because they have seen the God of Israel—the God of Abraham, Isaac, and Jacob—show Himself in an amazing way."

"All true," Bennett conceded. "But I'm not sure I understand your point."

"My point," said Doron, "is that Christians and Jews have very different interpretations of what has just happened, and very different understandings of what is going to happen next. But Eli did say there's at least one thing that all of the Jewish and Christian prophets and teachers—ancient and modern—agree upon, and that is this: the next major prophetic event that will occur is the building of the Third Jewish Temple in Jerusalem. He pointed out that Ezekiel chapters 40 through 48 are all about the re-building of the Temple, right after the War of Gog and Magog. And he warned me how explosive the issue of the Temple would be. Specifically, he urged me to be on guard against a new evil that will rise and begin targeting anyone who tries to bring the Temple to completion."

"He used that phrase, *a new evil*?" Bennett asked.

"Yes, why?" asked Doron.

"Because he used that same phrase with Erin and me, just before he died."

"What do you mean?"

"He said, 'But be on guard, my children, for a new evil is rising, more deadly than anything that has ever come before.'"

"Yes, yes, that's what he said to me," said Doron.

"And then," Bennett added, "he told us to 'stop them before . . .'"

"Before what?"

"I don't know. He passed away before he could explain."

"This may all be my fault," Doron said suddenly, almost in a whisper.

"Why?" asked Bennett. "What do you mean?"

"When Eli told me his theories about the Temple and about this 'new evil' rising, I asked him to do one last mission for me. And now, I fear, it may have cost him his life."

Bennett's stomach tightened. "What kind of mission?"

Doron stopped and looked into Bennett's eyes, then turned away and leaned against the damp, cold metal railing along the edge of the roof. For a few moments he said nothing, just stared out over the twinkling lights of the Old City, and it struck Bennett that the prime minister was measuring his response carefully.

"I asked Eli to do what he did best," Doron began. "To think around corners, look over the horizon. I asked him to help me identify the forces behind this 'new evil' and how they might try to hit us when construction began."

"Construction?" asked Bennett. "Of what?"

Doron stared at him. "The Temple, of course."

Bennett was stunned. "You're actually going to let the Orthodox build the Third Temple?"

"Of course not," said Doron. "The government will take the lead."

"You're joking," said Bennett.

But Doron shook his head. "I've already pulled together a team of religious scholars, historians, archeologists, architects, artists, engineers—everyone we'll need. It's all been hush-hush. They've all signed strict nondisclosure forms. I should have final blueprints on my desk by the end of next week. The funds are already set aside. They've been part of the military budget for years. And barring anything unforeseen, we'll start construction when the winter rains stop, probably around March first."

In more than three years of peace talks between the Israelis, the Palestinians, and the Arab world, Bennett had never heard anything like this. To the contrary, the Israeli government had always taken extraordinary measures to protect the Dome of the Rock and the Al-Aksa Mosque from attack. They had long feared that any change in the status quo—especially an attack by an ultra-Orthodox Jewish extremist group—could unleash the wrath of a billion Muslims against the tiny State of Israel and instantly obliterate any hope of peace. And rightly so. Ariel Sharon had provoked three years of Palestinian riots and terrorist attacks just by taking a stroll across the Temple Mount in September of 2000. One could only imagine what a ground-breaking ceremony for a Jewish Temple would unleash.

17

★ ★
★

Bennett couldn't believe what he was hearing.

"You're not going to let the Muslims rebuild their holy sites?" he asked.

"What Muslims?" asked Doron. "Eli said it himself; Islam is finished."

"Actually, Mr. Prime Minister, that's not what he said. He said Ezekiel's War would be the 'end of radical Islam as we know it.' He was talking about the end of the jihadists. But there are still hundreds of millions of Muslims out there. They may be in a state of shock and disarray, but they still believe the Temple Mount is theirs, and this could be just the thing that unifies them and mobilizes them against you. Is that really what you want?"

"What are you talking about?" asked Doron. "I thought you and Eli were on the same page on all this. He was very clear. After the War of Gog and Magog would come the building of the Temple, and then the coming of the Messiah. Which means the sooner we get it done, the sooner we'll know who's right—you Christians or we Jews."

"Look," said Bennett, "Eli was the theologian, not me. I'm just telling you as a friend and a political ally that if you start building unilaterally, you're going to face international condemnation. You're not going to get a peace treaty with the Palestinians. You're not going to get a peace deal with Iraq or Syria or anyone else in the Arab world. Everything we've all worked for all these years will go up in flames."

"I beg to differ, Jonathan," Doron replied, pacing around the roof again. "Really, think about it. Who is going to stop us? All of our major enemies are gone. The world needs our oil. We're about to see the greatest era of peace and prosperity in the history of the Middle East. As soon as cleanup operations in Jordan, Lebanon, and Syria are completed, we will witness an unprecedented wave of tourism to the Holy Land, the likes of which no one has ever dreamed. We're already planning for it—new airports, new roads, new hotels, new theaters and convention centers, all financed by the petrodollars that are pouring in right now. The Third Temple will be the main attraction, for Christians and Jews alike. For everyone, really. And that's just the beginning."

"Meaning what?" asked Jon.

"Meaning I don't want us to simply rebuild the Temple. I want to fill it with the lost treasures from the First and Second Temple eras. I want pilgrims to come from all over the world and see ancient biblical history come alive, right before their eyes. I want them to be able to see the past—touch it, experience it—and thus have hope for the future.

"That's why immediately after the firestorm, I authorized funding for a team of the world's leading archeologists and experts on the First and Second Temple periods. I asked them to search heaven and earth for the greatest Jewish treasures of the ages. I figured if Eli was right about even a small fraction of what he was saying—if we really are living in what the Scriptures call 'last days'—then anything's possible. Maybe the God of Israel is about to reveal that which has been hidden for centuries."

Bennett's head swam as he tried to make sense of all that Doron was telling him. "But how is all this related to Dr. Mordechai's death?" he asked.

"Well, that's just it," Doron continued. "About a month ago, I got an update from Mordechai and the team of archeologists I'd put together. They told me they had new leads. The team seemed excited about the progress they were making. And then . . ." Doron paused. He shoulders seemed to slump a bit.

"Then what?" asked Bennett.

"And then one by one, the team started dying, starting with Lionel Mansfield, then George Murray, then Barry Jaspers, and now Eli himself."

Mansfield. The name surprised Bennett, but it registered instantly.

Professor Lionel Mansfield was the famed British archeologist from Oxford who had died in a mysterious car accident in London a few weeks earlier. That was the story he'd been trying to remember when he heard about Murray's death in Washington.

"You think their deaths are related?"

"I'm absolutely sure of it," said Doron. "They were all part of this clandestine archeological team I put together, and now they're all dead."

"What was Dr. Mordechai's take, before he died?"

"We actually talked about the Mansfield and Murray deaths by phone while he was at your reception," Doron replied. "He had no doubt the murders were related. He just couldn't figure out how anyone could have known that both men were part of this team I'd assembled. There's been no publicity about the Temple project, or the team, or anything. Not yet. Even now, only a handful of people know what we're up to."

"Then you've got a leak," said Bennett.

Doron shook his head. "That's what I said. But Eli said, 'No, it's worse than that. It's not only a leak. People are dying. You've got a mole.' It didn't seem possible. I personally selected each member of the team. Only a handful of my senior aides knew anything about it. But what else could it be? So I asked Eli to launch a mole hunt the minute he got back from Washington. And now look what's happened."

"Was anyone else on this team of archeologists?" asked Bennett.

"Just one," said Doron. "Yossi Barak over at the Israel Museum."

"Did you say *Barak*?"

"Yes, do you know him?" asked Doron.

Break. Brock. Broke. Could that be it—Yossi *Barak*?

"I've never heard of him until now," said Bennett. "But just before Dr. Mordechai died, he was trying to tell me something. It was hard to hear him. At the time I wasn't sure what he was saying, but that may have been it. Yossi Barak."

"That would make sense," said Doron. "They've been friends for years."

"And who is he?"

"Yossi is the chief archeologist at the Israel Museum. He's also the head of the Archeology Department at Hebrew University and the world's leading expert on the Copper Scroll."

"The what?" asked Bennett.

"The Copper Scroll," Doron repeated. "Eli never told you about it?"

"No, why? What is it?"

The prime minister pulled out a pen and a small piece of paper, wrote down Barak's name and private phone numbers, and handed it to Bennett. "Call him. Tell him you need to see him immediately and that I said it's urgent. He'll know who you are and why you're coming. I'll have a car meet you downstairs."

Bennett wasn't sure how to respond. He was still in shock over his mentor's death. He had a grieving wife to care for, and he was supposed to be on his honeymoon. The last thing he needed to be doing was tracking down a serial killer. But Mordechai's dying request was that they find whoever was responsible and stop him before something far worse happened, and something told him he'd better move quickly.

18

★ ★
★

TUESDAY, JANUARY 13 – 7:32 P.M. – BABYLON, IRAQ

Khalid Tariq poked his head into the darkened office.

He expected to find President Al-Hassani reviewing his stack of briefing books for the upcoming visit of European Union foreign minister Salvador Lucente. The trip was shaping up to be a critical one. Lucente's aides were hinting that their boss was bringing a new proposal to discuss but had no other details, and given that Al-Hassani's own plans were likely to cause a great deal of anxiety in Brussels, they had to be ready.

But Al-Hassani was no longer sitting at his desk. Rather, he had settled into a rocking chair by a crackling fireplace, surrounded by his beloved books. Among them were Churchill's *The Gathering Storm*, Gibbon's *The Decline and Fall of the Roman Empire*, Tuchman's *The Guns of August*, and *The United States of Europe: The New Superpower and the End of American Supremacy* by former *Washington Post* reporter T.R. Reid, which Al-Hassani had become fond of quoting of late. Each was dog-eared and on the verge of falling apart, having not just been read but thoroughly devoured by a man desperate to make up for the years Saddam Hussein and his thugs had stolen.

Tonight Al-Hassani's head was buried in yet another thousand-page tome of some kind, and while Tariq from his vantage point could not see the title, he could see the ubiquitous yellow highlighter in Al-Hassani's left hand and the steaming cup of cardamom tea in his right. It was an all-too-rare moment of literary solace for a onetime professor so long deprived in prison of the reading materials that had once been his life and who was now once again increasingly deprived of the time with which to enjoy them.

Tariq cleared his throat. "Forgive me, Your Excellency."

Al-Hassani motioned for his aide to enter, though he remained fixated on the book in his lap. "Khalid, how much do you know of the British monarchs?"

"Not much, I'm afraid."

"Then you must read this when I am finished. Did you know, for example, that at the funeral of England's King Edward VII in 1910, nine of the kings and queens in attendance were actually related to him?"

"I did not."

"It's true," said Al-Hassani, with a long-dormant passion rising in his voice. "His son, George V, was the new king of England. One of his daughters was the queen of Norway. His nephew Wilhelm II was the kaiser of the rising German empire. His nephew Nicholas II was the czar of Russia. One of his nieces was the czarina of Russia. Another niece was the queen of Spain, and yet another niece would soon become the queen of Romania."

Al-Hassani looked up from his book and removed his reading glasses. "The secret of success is successors, Khalid. It is not enough merely to rule an empire. You must raise up future emperors who will expand and enlarge your borders long after you have rested with your fathers."

"I concur, Your Excellency, but was it not shortly after King Edward's death that the sun began to set on the British Empire and on the whole of Europe?"

"It was, Khalid," said Al-Hassani. "Mistakes we shall not revisit. To paraphrase Santayana, we must learn from history, particularly the history of Europe, lest we be doomed to repeat it."

"Forgive me, Your Excellency, but I have Viggo Mariano on the line. I passed on your message, but he would still like to talk with you personally."

"Is the call secure?" Al-Hassani asked instinctively.

"It is, Your Excellency. We ran a trace. It's clean."

"Where is he calling from?"

"Rome."

"Very well," said Al-Hassani. He waved Tariq out of the room and waited for him to transfer the call.

☆ ☆ ☆

Viggo Mariano was a killer for hire.

And to Mustafa Al-Hassani, the Sicilian would be worth every penny—$2 million up front, $3 million upon completion, and half the treasure, if it was ever recovered—if he could actually deliver what he promised on time.

The youngest son of one of the founding members of the Red Brigades that had struck fear in the hearts of Europeans throughout the 1970s and 1980s, Mariano, now forty-six, had cut his teeth in the world of international terror. Living in the shadows, off the grid, always on offense, had simply become part of his DNA in his earliest years. If everything Al-Hassani had heard from friends and associates was true, no one in the underworld had a better track record of success.

It was said that Mariano and his small team of associates had personally been involved in the assassinations of twenty-three of the thirty-seven highest-profile CEOs and parliamentarians killed in Europe and the Middle East over the past decade. They were wanted by police in every country in Europe—and by different names in each country.

Al-Hassani had first met Mariano as Bernardo Carlucci, operating under the cover of a cell-phone dealer in Palermo. They had been introduced by Tariq on a trip to Sicily almost a year before. Mariano and Tariq had been roommates during their undergraduate studies in Milan, but few who knew them at the time would have ever imagined the partnership they had forged more than twenty-five years later or the role they would play in Al-Hassani's rise to power.

"I just heard from my team," said Mariano when the call was patched through to the Iraqi president. "Mordechai is dead."

"Good," said Al-Hassani. "That makes four?"

"Correct. Operation Black Box is proceeding as planned and on schedule."

"What about number five?"

"You should hear something tomorrow. Thursday at the latest."

"And the other matters?"

"My team is working on the location of the treasure as we speak."

"How much longer?"

"There are no guarantees," said Mariano. "We still don't know for sure if it even exists or if the information we have is accurate."

"You assured me it was."

"No. I said *if* it was accurate, we would find it."

"Don't play games with me, Viggo. I don't have the luxury of time."

"I'm not playing games, Your Excellency. I just want to be clear about our agreement. I cannot deliver what doesn't exist."

"It exists, all right. You told me yourself that Murray and Jaspers were sure of it. So was Mordechai."

"Then perhaps we should have let them live a little longer, until they led us to it."

"No," said Al-Hassani, his patience growing thin. "We discussed that. It was too risky. We can't risk the treasure falling into the hands of the Jews. I cannot stress that enough."

"Then with all due respect, Your Excellency, I am not sure what more I can do but update you on our progress as often as I can."

"Push your men harder."

"I cannot push them any harder than I already am."

"Yes, you can, Viggo," Al-Hassani demanded. "And you will."

19

★ ★
★

Bennett found his wife resting in a lounge off the ICU.

She was quiet now and eager to get back to the King David to rest and deal with everything that had just happened, and so was he. He thanked Costello for keeping an eye on her and promised to call him the next day. Then he briefed Erin on his conversation with the prime minister, conceding that for now, all he had were questions, not answers. Had Mordechai been killed for his faith or because of Doron's assignment? Who was Yossi Barak? Another target? A coconspirator? What in the world was the Copper Scroll, and how did it relate to any of this?

"So what do you want to do?" asked Erin when he'd laid it all out.

"Take you back to Ronda and pretend this never happened."

She tried to smile through weary eyes, and he took her in his arms. Every fiber of his being screamed run. He had already seen so much violence and so much evil, and the last thing he wanted to do was face any of it again.

He had nearly lost Erin to terrorists in Moscow, and neither of them could bear the thought of going through that again. Why couldn't they just live a quiet, peaceful life with a house in the country, maybe have a few dogs to run with, kids they could take fishing and hiking in the mountains? He had never signed up for any of this. He'd been dragged into it by a president who had betrayed him, and he wanted out. For good. Yet even now, months after his resignation, he still couldn't seem to break free.

"But I have a hard time saying no to a man's dying request," he continued at last.

"Me too," she said. "I think we'd dishonor his memory—and his sacrifice for us—if we walked away now."

"So you think we should stay here?" Bennett asked, just to be sure.

Erin nodded slowly. "I don't think we have a choice."

Bennett pulled her closer to him and silently thanked God for her. He didn't deserve this woman, but for the life of him, he couldn't imagine living without her.

He pulled out his BlackBerry and the slip of paper Doron had given him and dialed Barak's private number.

After three rings, a young woman picked up. "Hello?"

"Uh, yeah, my name is Jon Bennett. I am looking for a Yossi Barak."

"Hi, Mr. Bennett, my name is Natasha. Dr. Barak is my grandfather. He just spoke to the prime minister. We were expecting your call. But let me say I am so sorry for your loss. Dr. Mordechai was a dear friend of both of ours."

"That's very kind," said Bennett. "It's a hard moment for all of us."

"It is indeed," said the woman.

"And, I'm sorry," Bennett added, eager to change the subject, "is this Dr. Barak's home, or . . ."

"No, no, this is his Hebrew University office at Mount Scopus."

"And you work there as well?"

"I do. I'm an associate professor of Near East archeology. Normally there's a secretary here, but she's already gone home for the day. That's how you got me."

"So may I speak to your grandfather?"

"Actually, I'm afraid that's not possible right now."

"I don't understand," said Bennett. "I was under the impression that—"

"I realize the urgency, as does my grandfather. But he wanted to arrange some things before meeting with you. I explained all this to the prime minister. He understands. My grandfather and I can meet you and your wife tomorrow morning at ten o'clock. I hope that is acceptable, under the circumstances."

Bennett wasn't sure what was going on but he didn't have the emotional energy to argue. He and Erin both needed rest and some time alone anyway.

"Very well," he said. "Ten o'clock tomorrow it is. Should we come to campus?"

"No," said Natasha. "My grandfather would like to meet you in his private office at the Israel Museum. I understand you'll have a car and driver."

"Yes," said Bennett. "The prime minister was very generous."

"Have the driver bring you to the entrance of the Shrine of the Book. I'll meet you there and guide you through security."

★   ★   ★

The phone startled Bennett awake.

Rubbing the sleep out of his eyes, he checked his watch as the phone kept ringing. It was barely four-thirty in the morning. He grabbed the receiver and found Ken Costello on the other end.

"Sorry to wake you, Jon."

"Who died?" Jon said, without a trace of humor in his voice.

"No one—not today," Costello replied.

"Then why are you calling me so early?"

"It's Lucente."

Bennett's brain scrambled to catch up. E.U. foreign minister Salvador Lucente was set to arrive in Israel later this morning to tour the region with Costello and Prime Minister Doron. An exclusive in *Yediot Aharonot*, the leading Israeli daily, had reported the day before that Lucente was set to offer the Jewish state billions of euros in aid for continuing disaster-relief efforts. It was the first such offer of its kind in the rocky history between the E.U. and Israel, and the country was buzzing. *But so what?* thought Jon. What did that have to do with him?

"What about him?" he asked, trying hard not to sound as upset as he felt for a wake-up call at such an hour.

"He's cutting his trip to Israel short to go to Babylon."

"What for?" Bennett whispered, trying not to wake Erin.

"I have no idea," said Costello. "I was hoping you'd know."

"I don't, Ken. And don't take this the wrong way, but what exactly does this have to do with me? I don't work for you guys anymore, remember?"

"I know. I'm sorry. But Lucente's chief of staff just called me from the plane. Lucente wants to meet with you and Erin tonight, before he leaves for Babylon."

"What are you talking about? Why?"

"He didn't say."

"But you just said he's only here for the day."

"That's right. He flies out around nine. But he'd like to meet for dinner."

"Would you be there?"

"No, just you and Erin."

"Where?"

"Right there at the King David. His advance team is already there, doing a security sweep."

"And you don't have any idea what this is about?" Bennett asked.

"No."

"Even off the record?"

"Sorry, my friend. But I need to get back to them with an answer right away. Apparently he'd rather have dinner with you than with Prime Minister Doron and his wife. That's who's on the schedule right now."

"I'm out of the game, Ken. Do they know that?"

"Of course, but his people say it's urgent. He's up to something, Jon. He's angling for something, and I'm not sure what. But the president would like you to say yes and report back to him."

"President MacPherson knows about this?"

"Of course," said Costello. "I called him before I called you."

Bennett sighed. "What time does Lucente want to meet?"

"At 6 p.m., downstairs at La Regence. You'll have the whole place to yourselves."

Bennett laid his head back on the pillow and closed his eyes. This was a mistake. He was getting sucked back into a job he'd just quit. But he told Costello yes, hung up the phone, and immediately hoped he wouldn't regret it.

★   ★   ★

Mordechai's death was big news in Israel.

Over breakfast, Erin called Indira Rajiv back at CIA headquarters in Langley, Virginia, to check in while Jon scanned the morning papers. Rajiv offered her condolences.

Erin thanked her but quickly moved on to the business at hand. "You guys hearing anything on Dr. Mordechai's murder?" she asked Rajiv.

"Too much, actually," said Rajiv, to Erin's surprise. "We're picking up chatter about Mordechai all over the world. It's going to take a while to sort through. He certainly engendered strong feelings on both sides."

"I guess so," Erin said, stirring cream into her coffee. "What are you thinking?"

"It's too early to say anything conclusive," Rajiv replied. "But speaking purely on instinct, I'd say it was a team of Israelis—former special forces, probably religious, almost certainly with inside access to Israeli police and intel files."

"Why do you say that?" asked Erin.

"Because the hit team clearly knew what flight Mordechai was on. They knew when he'd land, how he was getting home, and what route he'd be on, and they were waiting for him. That's not easy to do—not without help or access. I checked the El Al flight manifest myself. Mordechai wasn't even listed as a passenger."

"He goes by an alias," said Erin.

"A man of his position would," said Rajiv. "But somebody knew. They were watching him. What's more, they knew that he'd dropped his security detail."

A chill ran down Erin's spine.

So there *was* a mole inside Doron's team and a team of assassins inside Israel's borders, and God only knew whom they might go after next.

20

WEDNESDAY, JANUARY 14 – 8:17 A.M. – TEL AVIV, ISRAEL

The blue-and-gold Airbus A320 landed just after breakfast.

With almost a hundred members of the international press corps watching, the E.U. foreign minister's jumbo jet taxied across the runway at Ben Gurion International to its designated tarmac, where Prime Minister David Doron and Special White House Envoy Ken Costello waited to greet Mr. Lucente as he came down the ramp. The three shook hands and smiled for the cameras. Then aides guided them to an Israeli military helicopter, and soon they were airborne and headed north toward the Lebanon border.

Fifteen minutes later, they crossed a mountain ridge and began descending into a valley where some of the worst of the devastation from the firestorm had occurred.

The scene so revolted Costello that he had to grab two airsickness bags, both of which were quickly filled. It was the first time he had seen any of the carnage in person. In an unprecedented show of tact, television networks back home had refused to show such gruesome images to Americans in their homes during the dinner hour, and though Costello had read all the intelligence reports and press accounts emanating from the region, neither the printed word nor dozens of still photos began to capture the magnitude of the disaster he now saw firsthand.

Even all these weeks after the fact, tens of thousands of putrefying, nearly completely decomposed corpses lay strewn throughout the hills, alongside piles of bones scattered as far as the eye could see. Yet even if one had wanted an unobstructed view of the carnage, it wasn't easy to get given the swarms of vultures and rodents and dogs and animals of all kinds that had gathered to feast upon the bodies.

"Why has so little been done to clean all this up?" Lucente shouted over the roar of the chopper's rotors.

"This is actually a dramatic improvement," Doron responded over his headset. "You should have been here the day after the firestorm. I've never seen such a horrific sight in my life. We have three thousand soldiers working sixteen hours a day burying bodies and remains. At night our air force sprays disinfectants, trying to keep disease from spreading. But it hasn't been easy, and our experts are worried the chemicals could soon contaminate our water supply."

They came over another ridge and found a dozen IDF bulldozers pushing bodies into mass graves.

"I know it looks bad," Doron said before the question could be asked, "but there is no time to dig individual graves, gentlemen. As you know, U.N. disaster teams started arriving a few weeks ago to help, but with the winter rains it's been hard to get all their heavy equipment in. And, of course, every airport in Lebanon was destroyed, so everything has to come in through Israeli military bases near the border and be driven up here on trucks. It's very time consuming, very labor intensive, and very expensive."

"And very slow," Lucente added. "How much longer until you're finished?"

"It's hard to say," said Doron.

"Best guess?" asked Lucente.

"Three or four months, maybe more," said Doron. "It all depends on how much the international community will help, and on whether the weather cooperates."

"What is being done for the local populations?" Lucente asked.

"Everything possible," Doron responded. "As I stated in the report I sent to you, we've been airlifting in food, water, tents, clothing, electric generators, medical supplies, and as many doctors and nurses as we can spare. But the fact is, we're only scratching the surface. We simply don't have the money or the manpower to do more. That's why I wanted you both to see for yourselves what the situation is. These dead were enemies of ours, but they deserve the dignity of a proper burial. Yet that's impossible right now. And time is of the essence. Diseases like the avian flu are beginning to spread to the local communities. It's a miracle that a full-blown plague hasn't broken out yet. But it's a very real possibility, gentlemen. It could happen at any moment."

★   ★   ★

Words failed Costello.

He had never witnessed anything so horrible, and all he could think of were the words of the Hebrew prophet Ezekiel, cited by Dr. Mordechai in his now-infamous memo, describing not just a supernatural judgment of Israel's enemies but its grisly aftermath.

As for you, son of man,
thus says the Lord God,
"Speak to every kind of bird
and to every beast
of the field, 'Assemble and come,
gather from every side
to My sacrifice which I am
going to sacrifice for you,
as a great sacrifice
on the mountains of Israel,
that you may eat flesh
and drink blood.
You will eat the flesh
of mighty men and drink
the blood of the princes
of the earth, as though
they were rams, lambs,
goats and bulls,
all of them fatlings of Bashan.
So you will eat fat until
you are glutted, and drink blood

until you are drunk,
from My sacrifice which I have
sacrificed for you.'"

Was this not happening right in front of him? Weren't the birds of the air and the beasts of the fields gorging themselves on the flesh of the slain enemies of Israel, as they had been for months?

Costello had never tried to memorize the words of Ezekiel. Yet the words were now welling up from somewhere, and with them came a thought: how was it possible for someone writing 2,500 years ago to have predicted modern events with such eerie precision unless there really was a God, unless it was, in fact, actually possible for man to know Him and hear His voice and be guided by His words? Even for someone as irreligious as he, thought Costello, no other explanation seemed to fit.

★　★　★

The prime minister's helicopter banked left.

Soon they came up over another ridge, where more IDF bulldozers were digging more mass graves.

Off in the distance Salvador Lucente saw a huge convoy of several hundred flatbed trucks heading south toward Israel. "Mr. Prime Minister," he asked, "what are all those trucks over there?"

"They're hauling abandoned Russian and Iranian and Turkish military equipment back to Israel so none of it falls into enemy hands," Doron replied.

"Given all the pressing humanitarian needs, is that really a wise use of manpower right now?" Lucente asked.

"With all due respect, Mr. Foreign Minister, we have no choice."

"What are you talking about, David?" Lucente countered. "Israel hardly needs more weaponry. Your situation has changed quite dramatically. You have no more enemies. I would think now would be the time to dismantle some of your military, not add to it."

"Salvador, our forces have just captured six thousand Russian missiles, each of which is armed with tactical nuclear warheads. Do you really think it wise for us to just leave those lying around on the battlefield unsecured?"

21
★ ★
★

Natasha Barak met the Bennetts as scheduled.

But she was not who Erin had imagined. She was taller than most Israeli women, almost Erin's own height of five feet ten inches, with a slim, athletic build that suggested she spent quite a bit of time out of doors. She was also significantly more attractive than Erin pictured most professors of archeology to be. Natasha was in her early thrities and had shoulder-length jet-black hair, warm brown eyes, a slender nose, and a healthy tan that didn't seem consistent with long hours cooped up in a museum. When they shook hands, Erin noticed Natasha was not wearing a wedding ring.

Natasha directed their driver to a VIP parking lot, then guided the Bennetts down a stone path and asked, "Have you ever seen the Shrine of the Book?"

"I'm afraid not," Erin said as she held Jon's hand.

"Ever been to the rest of the museum?"

"No, this is the first time for both of us."

"My goodness, and you've been to Israel so many times," Natasha exclaimed. "I've followed your work with the peace process for years, not to mention your romance and your wedding—*mazel tov.*"

"Thank you," said Erin softly, allowing the hint of a smile for the first time in twenty-four hours. "Yes, Jon and I have been to Israel many times, but always on business, I'm afraid, never for pleasure."

"Well then," Natasha said as they approached the large white-dome structure of the Shrine and a set of stairs descending into a courtyard. "You're in for a treat. It's Wednesday. The museum is not yet open to visitors. You'll have it all to yourselves."

Erin traded glances with her husband.

"The prime minister asked us to come, so we have, but I'm afraid we're not here for a tour," Jon said as graciously as he could. "It's our understanding your grandfather may be able to shed some light on why Dr. Mordechai was killed. That's our only interest today."

"Yes, of course, forgive me," Natasha said quickly. "I meant no disrespect. I know you have suffered a great loss."

"No apology is needed," Erin replied. "We understand you were both close to Dr. Mordechai as well."

The young woman stopped abruptly, turned, and looked them both in the eye. "My parents were killed by terrorists when I was seven. My grandmother died of cancer when I was nine. I was raised by my grandfather and Uncle Eli. That's what I called him. He was my grandfather's best friend, and mine. I can't believe he's really gone."

There was a moment of awkward silence, and then Natasha turned and continued.

☆　☆　☆

Bennett looked around as they entered the Shrine.

"The building in which you are standing was opened on April 20, 1965," Natasha said. "I wasn't born yet, but my grandfather was here for the big inaugural gala. He actually helped design it, along with two American Jewish architects, and they based it on an ancient interpretation of the War of Gog and Magog."

"Really," said Bennett, suddenly intrigued. "How so?"

"Well, you see, the Shrine of the Book is similar, in a sense, to your National Archives Building in Washington," Natasha explained. "It protects and displays some of Israel's most important founding documents, namely the Dead Sea Scrolls. Most of the scrolls were written by a Jewish sect called the Essenes, who lived near the Dead Sea around 200 BCE. Now, what's interesting about the Essenes is that they were convinced that the War of Gog and Magog was imminent. They saw themselves as the Sons of Light squaring off against the Sons of Darkness, and they believed that as soon as the war was over, a new Temple would be erected, and the Messiah would come. So when the architects were looking for a theme for this building, my grandfather suggested this war between good and evil, this War of Gog and Magog. The dome we saw outside symbolizes the lids of the jars in which some of the scrolls were found, and it is painted white to represent the Sons of Light. That large wall you saw upstairs, the one directly opposite the dome, is black to represent the Sons of Darkness, to convey the spiritual tension between the two warring camps."

Natasha led them down the dark, cavernous hallway to the main exhibits. The air was cool and dry. An ever-so-slight breeze was coming from a state-of-the-art air-conditioning and dehumidification system, and the farther they went, the more intrigued Bennett became. In one display were the actual clay jars in which several of the scrolls had been found, and sure enough, the lids looked exactly like the curvaceous dome they had just seen. In another display were small, ink-stained quills, the very ones used by the Essenes to write the scrolls so many centuries ago.

And then they entered the main exhibit hall, a circular room—directly underneath the great dome—in the center of which was a large, drumlike glass display case lit from within and designed in part, it seemed, to look like the end of a scroll handle.

Bennett let go of his wife's hand for a moment and bounded up the six steps leading to the curious display. He was stunned by what he found. Inside the case, unfurled and carefully mounted on a large internal drum, was a nine-foot portion of the Isaiah Scroll. Like a kid outside of Macy's at Christmas, Bennett pressed his face against the glass to see it for himself.

"You are looking at the oldest Bible manuscript ever found," Natasha said reverently, almost in a whisper. "Written at least two centuries before the birth of Christ, it's at least one thousand years older than any previously known copy of the book of Isaiah."

"And this is the real thing?" asked Erin.

"We usually put a replica on display, for security," Natasha replied, "but we knew you were coming, so we bent the rules a bit. Yes, that's the real thing."

"That's incredible," said Bennett, peering through the glass at parchment so incredibly well preserved. Here was a scroll penned two hundred years before the birth, death, and resurrection of Jesus. Yet it contained the words of the very Hebrew prophet who had said the Messiah would be born of a virgin, live in Galilee, be a light to the nations, suffer and die for the sins of mankind, and yet rise again and "prolong His days, and the good pleasure of the Lord will prosper." And Bennett was less than two inches away from it. He could scarcely take it in.

Natasha then led them over to a smaller display case to one side of the rotunda. "This one is called the War Scroll, laying out the Essenes' vision of the War of Gog and Magog." She translated a passage from the ancient Hebrew:

> *"Thou hast revealed to us the times*
> *of the battles of Thy hands that Thou*
> *mayest glorify Thyself in our enemies*
> *by leveling the hordes. . . . Make for Thyself*
> *an everlasting Name among the people . . .*
> *when Thou chastisest Gog and all his assembly*
> *gathered about him . . . for Thou wilt*
> *fight them from heaven."*

"And that's not all," said Natasha. "Follow me."

Now she led them to another case in which a white card mounted in the corner said "4Q285, fragment 4—from The Rule of War."

Again Natasha translated from the Hebrew:

> *". . . wickedness will be smitten . . .*
> *the Prince of the Congregation*
> *and all Israel . . . which was written*
> *in the Book of Ezekiel the Prophet,*
> *I will strike your bow from your*
> *left hand and make your*
> *arrows drop from your right hand.*
> *On the mountains of Israel*
> *you will fall."*

"Sound familiar?" Natasha asked.

It certainly did, Bennett realized. The words had been seared into his memory in the weeks leading up to their fulfillment. "Ezekiel 39:3 and part of verse 4," he said in amazement. "Did Dr. Mordechai know these were here?"

"Absolutely," said Natasha. "These aren't usually the scrolls and fragments we have on display. But when Uncle Eli published his 'Ezekiel Option' memo on the Web, my grandfather called him and invited him over to see these. They've been here ever since."

"They were on display when the firestorm happened?" Erin asked.

"They were," Natasha confirmed. "My grandfather believed Ezekiel's prophecy was about to come true and that the War of Gog and Magog would trigger the coming of the Messiah. He and Uncle Eli only disagreed about which coming that would be—the first or the second."

"How about you?" Bennett asked. "What do you think?"

But they were interrupted by a door they hadn't even seen opening behind them, and there stood Natasha's grandfather, motioning them to follow.

22

★ ★
★

Now in his eighties, Yossi Barak still had a young man's zeal.

He wore small a yarmulke, or *kipah*, atop a shock of silver hair; he had a neatly trimmed salt-and-pepper beard. His wrinkled, wizened face betrayed a lifetime of struggle in a land that had seldom known peace. Standing there in baggy trousers and a slightly frayed blue Oxford button-down shirt covered by a brown cardigan sweater, he was a bit stooped, and he steadied himself on a beautifully carved wooden cane. But it was his green eyes, shining full of passion and curiosity even behind gold-rimmed spectacles, that drew Bennett's interest.

"Come, follow me," Dr. Barak said in a thick, gravelly voice that suggested a pipe or cigar was rarely far from his lips.

Natasha waved them forward, and together they slipped out of the Shrine's main exhibit hall, through the doorway, and down a dim hallway to a cluster of small offices attached to a conference room and a lab of some kind, marked with signs that read Authorized Personnel Only in English and Hebrew. A moment later, the foursome entered a wood-paneled conference room, where Dr. Barak directed them all to take a seat in any of the dozen leather executive chairs that surrounded the large, rectangular mahogany table.

"Coffee anyone?" he asked, already pouring himself a mug at a drink station at the far end of the room.

Both Bennetts accepted the offer. Natasha asked for water. Barak fixed the drinks and then joined them at the table.

"It is so good to finally meet you both," he said after taking a moment to catch his breath and wipe his forehead with a clean handkerchief he kept in his trouser pocket. "Eli spoke so much about you I feel like you're practically my own grandchildren. I suspect, however, he told you little, if anything, about me."

"I'm afraid not," Bennett said, though he'd been racking his brain for the past few minutes, trying to think of any reference Mordechai may have made to him or Natasha.

"He was a man of his word," Barak sighed. "A real class act."

"I'm afraid I don't understand," said Erin.

"Well, we've been friends for almost fifty years," the old man explained. "We served in military intelligence together. We served in the reserves together. Our wives—God rest their souls—were close when they were alive. We even vacationed together once. But when he became—how do you say it, 'born again'?—I'm afraid we had a falling out. We didn't speak for several years, and when we did, when we tried to patch things up between us and get together from time to time, I asked him not to mention it to anyone."

"Why not?" asked Bennett.

"Well, you must understand that I come from a very strict religious community, and to them, any time I spent with Eliezer Mordechai was fraternizing with the enemy. But, God bless him, he was a man of his word, even to the end. He said he wouldn't tell anyone about our friendship, and he didn't. I'm really going to miss him."

Barak took a deep breath, dabbed his eyes with his handkerchief, and shifted gears, just as Natasha had a while earlier. "So, you are probably wondering," he said, staring into his coffee, "what brought us back together."

The Bennetts nodded, but he didn't see them. Not that it would have mattered. It was obvious he was going to tell the story anyway.

"A treasure hunt," Barak said softly.

"I'm afraid I don't follow," said Bennett.

"Well, it's like this. After so many years of not speaking, Eli called me out of the blue one day and said he'd found a clue—a big clue—to a puzzle

I'd been trying to solve for decades. And then he made me an offer I couldn't refuse: if I would talk to him again, he would help find the greatest treasure the world has ever known."

The old man had their full attention now—Natasha's, too, though Bennett was sure she had heard this story a thousand times before.

"Is everything ready?" Barak then asked, turning to his granddaughter.

"Whenever you are," Natasha replied.

"Very well then," said Barak. "What are we waiting for? Let's go."

"Go where?" asked Bennett.

"Let's go for a little ride."

★ ★ ★

Five minutes later they were on the museum's roof.

Boarding a helicopter. Donning headphones. Lifting off—Natasha at the controls, Barak playing copilot—and banking eastward into the sun, though Jon and Erin had no idea where. Out the left-rear window, Bennett could see the Israeli Knesset building, not far from the museum grounds. Soon they were flying over the Temple Mount and the Mount of Olives, before making a slight course correction to the south.

"Dr. Barak, do you mind letting us in on our destination?" Jon asked, adjusting the volume on his headset and trying to hear over the roar of the rotors.

"What, and spoil all the fun?" asked Barak, clearly enjoying himself.

"Let me guess," said Erin. "Qumran, where the scrolls were found."

"Good try," Barak replied, his eyes still fixed on the horizon ahead. "But not even close."

"Masada?" asked Jon.

"What for?" said Barak. "Great place to visit, but irrelevant to the treasure hunt I'm taking you on."

"Then where?" Erin pressed.

Barak mumbled something in Hebrew they couldn't understand, and then—when he seemed confident Natasha had the flight under control—he turned back, as best he could, to address them both face-to-face.

"It will all make sense in a moment," he insisted. "But first I must tell you a little story. Okay?"

They hardly had a choice, so they leaned back, enjoyed the flight and the view, and let the old man tell his tale.

"The year is 1947," Barak began. "The Nazis have been defeated. Europe has been liberated. The concentration camps have been shut down. The British are preparing to pull out of Palestine. The U.N. is carving up the Holy Land between the Arabs and the Jews. We Jews are about to declare our independence, and five Arab nations are preparing to attack us and wipe us off the face of the earth.

"Meanwhile, a few miles east of Jerusalem, two shepherds—Bedouins, actually—begin tossing stones into a distant mountain cave. Suddenly, they hear something shatter, like pottery or glass. Their first thought: *buried treasure!* So they return at night with friends, ropes, torches, and a plan to scale the sheer rock face and enter the remote cavern. They're electrified by the hope that what is waiting for them is gold or silver or precious jewels. To their dismay, that's not what they find. But in time it will become clear that they have stumbled upon a treasure much greater by far: the Dead Sea Scrolls."

Barak stopped for a moment, fished several bottles of water out of a cooler, offered two to the Bennetts, and then took a swig of his own. A moment later, he was back to his story, his voice low and mysterious.

"Over the next few years, more than eight hundred scrolls and more than 100,000 fragments were discovered," he explained. "Whole books of the Bible—such as the Isaiah Scroll Natasha showed you—emerged from the caves of Qumran. Sections of nearly every Old Testament book were found, along with religious commentaries and detailed descriptions of the day-to-day lives of religious Jews under Roman occupation."

He stopped abruptly and pointed out the window, off to their right. "We're flying through the Jordan Valley," he explained. "That's the Dead Sea down there. Can you see it?"

"Yes," they said.

"Good—now look over there, to the west," Barak instructed as he urged Natasha to bank a bit so Jon and Erin could get a good look.

All Bennett could see were mountains—dusty, barren, and bleak.

"Now, you see those foothills? those caves?" Barak asked.

They did.

"Well that, my friends, is Qumran. That's where the scrolls were found, where history was made."

"Wow," said Erin. "You'd never suspect something important would be hidden away in something so nondescript."

"That's often the case with archeology," said Barak. "Where you least expect it, expect it."

Erin pointed at a cluster of buildings and a parking lot. "What's that?"

"That's the visitor center and the offices that run the excavations at Qumran."

"They're still digging there?"

"A bit, yes," said Barak. "Plus there's a little theater and museum there, a gift shop, a snack bar, some restrooms—that kind of thing."

"And that's where we're headed?" asked Bennett.

"No, no," said Barak, pointing eastward. "Qumran was a big story in its day—the biggest archeological discovery in history to that point. But believe me, Jonathan, based on the research Eli and I did, I can tell you it pales in comparison with what is coming next."

23

★ ★
★

The prime minister's helicopter landed on the Temple Mount.

Surrounded by their protective details and flanked by a traveling pool of reporters, producers, cameramen, and sound technicians, Doron and his distinguished guests exited the chopper and began touring the ash and charred debris. Aside from firemen and security personnel, they were actually the first to walk this historic ground since the Day of Devastation, and in so doing they were making headlines.

The battle over the future of the Temple Mount was already well under way. The president of Egypt and the king of Jordan had just launched a massive lobbying operation aimed at Washington, Brussels, and the U.N. Security Council in New York. Their clear objective was to build international pressure on Israel not to take any steps that would change the status quo—such as building the Temple—until peace talks with the Palestinians and the rest of the Arab world were completed.

Just two days before, however, the American Israel Public Affairs Committee—the largest and most powerful Jewish lobby in the United States—had cranked up its own operation to counter the Egyptian and Jordanian campaign. The status quo had already been changed, they argued, and not by Israel but by an act of God. What's more, it was time once and for all for the U.S. to acknowledge Jerusalem as the "eternal and undivided capital of the Jewish State of Israel," to move the U.S. Embassy to Jerusalem, and to allow Israeli democracy to govern the future of the Temple Mount.

As he walked across the ruins of what had long been one of the holiest sites in Islam, Ken Costello was acutely aware of the political and religious land mines that lay ahead. It was his job to listen to all sides and bring back a firsthand report to the president. And now here he was, at the vortex of the debate, in the eye of the hurricane.

It would be hard to convey to MacPherson the visceral sense of loss and devastation he had seen throughout the day, and this moment was no different. But for the soot and ash of the once-great historic landmarks that had stood here, there was absolutely no physical evidence that the Dome of the Rock or the Al-Aksa Mosque had ever existed.

Such was the power of an almighty God, Costello mused, *able to create the world in six days and destroy it in one.*

When they finished their tour, Salvador Lucente gathered reporters around him and held an impromptu press conference at the dead center of the Mount. He began by praising Doron and the Israeli people as well as the entire world community for banding together to provide medical care, food, and drinking water for those affected by the devastation. He thanked them for their commitment and dedication to working around the clock to bury the dead, despite the enormity of the task. Then he announced that the E.U. was willing to contribute an additional one billion euros to Israel's emergency relief efforts, on top of the 250 million euros the E.U. had already divided among Israel, Jordan, Syria, and Lebanon over the past three months. But then Lucente caught Doron and Costello completely off guard by laying down three conditions for the distribution of such aid.

"The European Union is ready to exceed anything we have ever given before, including to the tsunami relief campaign in Asia a number of years ago," Lucente said to the cameras now beaming the breaking news to the world. "But we also believe the time for peace and reconciliation between Israel and her neighbors has come at last, and we are determined to see a comprehensive resolution of the Arab-Israeli conflict as rapidly as humanly possible. We must, therefore, be careful that such large infusions of aid not be allowed to complicate the peace process. As such, we will provide the funds only if my good friend, Prime Minister Doron, and his government commit themselves to three peacemaking steps of goodwill."

Costello could only look on with a smile plastered on his face, acting as though he were fully prepared for what was about to happen. But he was not and expected his cell phone to ring any moment with the president or his chief of staff demanding to know what in the world was going on.

"First," Lucente continued, "the E.U. requests that the State of Israel agree to block any and all efforts by Jews—or by Christians, for that matter—to build a Jewish Temple on this site, at least for now. This site is, of course, sacred to all three monotheistic religions who call this city home, and its future should be decided in negotiations with all the parties, not unilaterally by one side or another."

Costello could feel his phone vibrating in his jacket pocket.

"Second," Lucente went on, "the E.U. requests that the State of Israel allow the United Nations to assume interim control of the Temple Mount until such final peace talks are complete, so that Jews, Muslims, and Christians can rest assured that their interests in this historically volatile site can and will be handled fairly, impartially, and expeditiously.

"Third, the E.U. requests that the State of Israel and the Palestinian Authority, along with their Arab neighbors, commit themselves to completing and signing a final peace treaty within the next twelve months. As the Jewish Scriptures say, there is 'a time for war and a time for peace.' There is 'a time to tear down and a time to build up.' There is 'a time to be silent and a time to speak.' And now, I believe, is the time to speak as one world, one voice, for peace, for unity, and for working together to rebuild what was lost. I invite all civilized nations—and particularly our friends in the United States—to join us in ensuring a full and comprehensive settlement to one of the world's most enduring conflicts."

Costello knew he was about to be asked to comment on Lucente's demands. The last thing the White House needed was another foreign-policy fight with Europe. But was the president prepared to join the E.U. in blocking emergency aid to Israel unless they knuckled under on an issue as sensitive as the Temple Mount? The only good news for Costello was that Doron would have to answer first, and he knew the Israeli prime minister must be just as startled by Lucente's sucker punch.

"Mr. Prime Minister," shouted a reporter, "how do you respond to the E.U.'s demands?"

Costello found himself impressed by Doron's answer.

"I don't see the foreign minister's remarks as demands but rather a proposal, and I appreciate it a great deal," the prime minister replied. "Israel remains as committed as always to making peace with our neighbors. We are grateful for the friendship and support of the European Union during this difficult hour, and I look forward to discussing these issues with Mr. Lucente in more detail."

"But, Mr. Prime Minister," shouted another reporter, "polls show that more than seven in ten Israelis want you to move forward and build the Temple, and to do so quickly. In your mind, which is the higher priority—the aid or the Temple?"

"I have made no final decision on the future of the Temple Mount," Doron replied calmly. "That's why we are here today, touring the site, discussing options, listening to opinions and proposals from all sides. We will announce our decisions in due course, but let me just say this: There have been two great Jewish Temples on this site. The Hebrew prophets tell us there will be another, and I for one look forward to that day. It was a European power that destroyed the last Temple in AD 70, and Jews throughout world have been praying for almost two thousand years that such an injustice would be remedied. Today is not the day to decide such questions, but I do believe such a day is not far off."

24

★ ★
★

They were about thirty kilometers from Amman.

But why? With the exception of its largest mosques, which had been consumed by the firestorm, the Jordanian capital had largely been spared the wholesale destruction visited upon other Arab capitals like Damascus and Tehran. What could be there to see that was worth all this effort?

Dr. Barak soon answered this question.

"In the spring of 1952, something very curious happened," he said, his eyes twinkling with the glee of a professor with a captive and uninitiated audience. "A new scroll was found in Cave Three in the hills above Qumran, unlike any of the scrolls that had been found before. I was not part of the team that found it, but as a young research assistant, I had the extraordinary privilege of being part of the team that studied it. And believe me, no one had ever seen anything like this scroll.

"It was not written with ink on animal skins or parchments, as were the others. It was, instead, engraved on metal—on copper, to be precise. But whatever for? If the book of Isaiah—*the Holy Scriptures*, mind you— could be written on something so fragile as parchment, what message could the Copper Scroll possibly contain that was so precious it had to be engraved on metal to be preserved for the ages? This was the first big question we had but only one of many. Another was, how do we open the blasted thing? It was encrusted with nineteen hundred years of oxidation.

It was so brittle we feared it might disintegrate in our hands. Indeed, unlike any of the other scrolls, it took us four years to figure out how to get it open."

"So how did you?" asked Erin, leaning forward in her seat.

"Interesting, but not critical," Barak replied. "I'll explain that later, if you'd like. But the point is we did get it open, in the spring of 1956, and from there the mystery only deepened. You see, the language of the text was very odd. It wasn't conventional Hebrew or the colloquial Aramaic of the day, but an obscure version of ancient Hebrew laced with Greek cryptograms, seemingly without purpose. As if that weren't enough, the text itself bore no resemblance to other scrolls. It wasn't a copy of the Jewish Scriptures, or a set of religious commentaries, or a journal of daily life in the religious community at Qumran like we'd found in the other scrolls. This only baffled us further.

"Nor was the text of the Copper Scroll even a narrative, as the others are. Instead, it contained sixty-four individual lines or entries, each of which seemed to take us forever to decipher. But as we did, a shock wave began to shake this elite team of archeologists, linguists, and cryptographers. For each entry described a cache of gold, silver, jewels, or ancient religious artifacts hidden in the surrounding hills. A hundred talents of gold here. Fifty talents there. Five hundred talents over there. And so forth. When we tallied it all up—line by line—and translated it into modern weights and measures, *the total came to almost two hundred tons of treasure!* We could hardly believe our eyes!"

"Was it real, or a legend?" asked Bennett, still unclear how any of this had anything to do with Mordechai's death but captivated by the tale.

"Ah, that's the question, isn't it?" said Barak. "Some of the team immediately dismissed it all as ancient folklore. How could it be anything but? There was no way, they argued, that a band of monastic Jews living in the Judean wilderness during the first century could possibly have possessed nearly two hundred tons of gold and silver—one quarter of all the known gold and silver in the entire world at the time!

"But others on the team were convinced it was real. There were certainly massive quantities of gold and silver in Palestine at the time. Biblical and other historical records indicate that the ancient Hebrews had built up enormous reserves of gold and silver and other treasures over the years, all of which they stored in the Temple in Jerusalem. Second Chronicles 9 says: 'The weight of the gold that Solomon received yearly was 666 talents, not including the revenues brought in by merchants and traders. Also all the kings of Arabia and the governors of the land brought gold and silver to Solomon.' Now, just to put that into perspective, 666 talents is about *twenty-five tons* of gold and silver, and that came into the Temple treasury *every year*."

"But wasn't Solomon's Temple destroyed by the Babylonians?" asked Erin. "And didn't Nebuchadnezzer cart off all the treasure?"

"True," said Barak. "But remember, seventy years later Nehemiah and Ezra were allowed to return from Babylon to rebuild the walls of Jerusalem, restore the Temple, and bring back the treasures. They also took up an offering to resupply the Temple treasury, and in the process, Ezra collected 18,125 ounces of gold—about half a ton—and 100,000 ounces of silver—roughly three tons. Then Ezra chapter 7 notes that the Persian king Artaxerxes issued a decree authorizing that up to 120,000 ounces of silver—almost four tons—be given to the Israelites to rebuild 'the house of the God of heaven.'"

"That's a lot of treasure," said Bennett.

"It certainly is," Barak agreed. "And the treasures of the Second Temple only grew. King Herod, as you know, dramatically expanded the size of the Temple, and Jews annually brought enormous sums of gold, silver, and precious jewels into the Temple as part of their tithes and offerings to God. In fact, as you probably know, Jesus Himself spoke of the enormity of the Temple treasures in Matthew 23: 'Woe to you, blind guides! You say, "If anyone swears by the temple, it means nothing; but if anyone swears by the gold of the temple, he is bound by his oath." You blind fools! Which is greater: the gold, or the temple that makes the gold sacred?'

"Bottom line: everybody in Israel knew how great were the treasures of the Second Temple. What's interesting to me is that in the years following Jesus' crucifixion, the Jewish leaders in Jerusalem grew more and more worried that the Romans were going to destroy their Holy City and take the Temple treasures back to Rome, like the Babylonians had done with Solomon's Temple. That's what makes the dating of the Copper Scroll so intriguing."

Natasha was on approach to Queen Alia International Airport, but no one else in the chopper seemed to notice or care.

"As best we can tell," Barak continued, "the Copper Scroll was written in AD 68 or 69."

"That's just a year or two before the Romans burned Jerusalem and destroyed the Temple," said Bennett.

"Exactly," said Barak. "And that's when our theory of the Copper Scroll began to take shape. What if the Temple priests had a premonition of what the Romans were about to do? What if they feared the Temple treasures would be lost forever if they did not act? What if they began to smuggle the treasures out of the Temple at night, in small batches, secreting them out of Jerusalem and burying them in the desert sands and the mountain caves to protect them from the coming apocalypse, from what some believed was the coming War of Gog and Magog?"

A moment later they were back on the ground, stretching their legs. The January air was cool. A slight breeze crossed the desert, and thick winter rain clouds formed overhead.

"Come," Natasha said, directing them to a Land Rover parked on the edge of the tarmac. "We should go before the rains begin."

They quickly departed the airport grounds and headed to a dusty hill in a suburb of Amman. To their left were the remains of a once-great Roman structure of some kind. Six enormous, ancient stone pillars stood side by side. The tallest two in the center were capped by ornate pieces of carved stone, forming an archway of sorts. But this held little interest for the Baraks. They were already making their way toward an unimpressive little building that seemed more like a small-town post office back in the U.S. than the Jordan Archaeological Museum, indicated by a large blue sign over the doorway.

"Finally," Dr. Barak said, using his carved wooden cane and Natasha's assistance to make it up the stone stairway to the front door. "We are here."

The Bennetts followed their hosts into the building and were struck immediately by how different it was from the Israel Museum and the Shrine of the Book.

"Modest, to be sure," Natasha whispered after paying the small entrance fee for them all. "The Jordanians are excellent archeologists. But unfortunately, they've never had access to the resources necessary to put on a more impressive display."

"I'm not sure I understand," Bennett said. "Why exactly did you bring us here?"

"Because," Natasha whispered, even more quietly this time, "the Jordanians possess one of the greatest artifacts ever found, and they have no idea of its significance."

Dr. Barak was ambling toward the back of the museum. He turned back and motioned that he was about to turn off the main corridor into a smaller exhibit room and that the rest should follow. They did so, and Bennett soon found himself standing amid several glass display cases, none of which appeared to be bulletproof. There were no guards, no surveillance cameras, nor any other monitoring equipment Jon could detect. Indeed, there was nothing that would indicate that something in this particular room—much less in this entire museum—could even remotely be considered "one of the greatest artifacts ever found."

Then they turned another corner and Bennett suddenly realized what he was looking at—the Copper Scroll itself.

25

★ ★
★

It looked nothing like he had expected.

For one thing, it didn't look like a scroll at all. Instead of a long sheet or a roll, the scroll was divided into numerous sections, or strips, each of which looked to Bennett like a shin guard a child might wear when playing soccer.

The segments were each roughly a foot in length and curved upward, evidence that they had once been rolled like a parchment scroll. Each was green with twenty centuries of oxidation, and each rested on a plastic tray inside these inexpensive glass display cases that would have taken all of about two seconds to smash to pieces, had they so intended.

"Why is it cut up like that?" Bennett asked.

"Remember, when the scroll was first discovered, the whole thing was fused together from oxidation," Barak said. "It took us four years, but eventually it was decided that the safest way to open it was to subdivide it."

In a case along the back wall was a wood-framed copper reconstruction of the scroll to give visitors a sense of what the original may have looked like when it was first made. Beside it were two large, reconstructed pottery jars.

"Those jars were found in pieces in the same cave as the Copper Scroll," Natasha pointed out.

Mounted to each of the cases being used to display the pieces of the scroll were several black-and-white photographs. One showed the wrapped sheet of engraved copper as it had originally looked before being cut into strips. Another showed the entrance to the cave where it was found, guarded by a Jordanian soldier. Yet another showed a picture of the shattered clay jars before they had been reconstructed.

On another wall hung a fairly bland description of the Copper Scroll and of the Dead Sea Scrolls in general. It certainly didn't capture the sense of mystery the Baraks had evoked, but there was one curious line that Bennett read aloud to the others.

"'The Copper Scroll gives detailed descriptions of sixty-three treasure troves hidden in Palestine, weighing a total of 160 tons (10 tons of gold, 80 tons of silver, gold and silver ingots and vases, ritual implements, priestly vestments, etc.). All attempts to find this treasure have failed. Some scholars interpret the text as a fable or having symbolic significance.'"

Bennett stopped reading and turned to Dr. Barak. "Question."

"Yes?" the old man replied.

"It says 160 tons of treasure," Jon noted. "I thought you said there was close to 200 tons."

"Good point," Barak explained. "The scroll itself measures the treasure in *talents*. The question is, which definition of talent was the writer of the scroll using? Many scholars peg the amount at somewhere between 160 and 175 tons. Others say it's closer to 200. But the truth is no one knows for sure because, as the Jordanians note, 'all attempts to find this treasure have failed.'"

"Either way, that's a boatload of loot," Bennett quipped.

"It is indeed," Barak agreed. "If anyone were to find it all, the gold and silver alone could be worth at least two *billion* dollars in today's market value. But, of course, its actual religious and historic value is absolutely priceless."

"Okay," said Erin, peering through the glass, studying the scroll as closely as she could. "I've got a question as well."

"Yes, my dear."

"This says there are sixty-three locations where the treasure is buried. But you said the scroll contains sixty-four lines of text."

"Ah," Barak sighed. "Now we've come to it. Of all the mysteries surrounding the Copper Scroll, the most fascinating is line 64, for rather than speaking of more treasure, it seems to speak of yet another scroll, one that may unlock the secrets of the first."

Barak reached into his breast pocket and pulled out a photocopy of several pages from a book, an English translation of each line of the Copper Scroll. He handed it to Erin, who found line 64 and began to read aloud:

> *"In the tunnel*
> *which is in Sechab,*
> *to the north*
> *of Kochlit,*
> *which opens*
> *towards the north,*
> *and has graves*
> *in its entrance:*
> *a copy of this text*
> *and its explanation*
> *and their measurements*
> *and the inventory*
> *. . . item by item."*

"Ever since we first opened and translated the Copper Scroll in 1956, there has been a raging debate among scholars about the meaning of line 64. Some believe this second scroll is merely a duplicate, an insurance policy of sorts, lest the original was lost or destroyed. But others—myself included—believe the second scroll could actually be the more important of the two. I call it the Key Scroll because I believe it alone can unlock the mystery of the Copper Scroll. If I'm right, whoever finds the Key Scroll will find the Second Temple treasures, and not a few Jewish scholars believe that when the Second Temple treasures are discovered, it will be time to build the Third Temple."

"Does that include you?" asked Erin.

"It does indeed," Barak said.

"Which means you believe their discovery is imminent?" Erin added.

"Exactly, and I'm not alone," said Barak, lowering his voice to a whisper. "Barry Jaspers believed that as well. So did Lionel Mansfield and George Murray. So did Eli. That's why we were working together again after all these years. For just after the earthquake and the firestorm, something remarkable happened. I can't say what—not here, at least—not in Jordan. But new information came to us, startling information, and we all believed we were just days away from finding the Key Scroll and thus the treasure. And . . . that's when people started dying."

"You think someone is systematically assassinating everyone connected to the Copper Scroll?" Erin asked.

"I do," said Barak.

"For the money?" asked Bennett

"In part, perhaps," said Barak. "As I said, it would be quite a fortune in the hands of any one man or organization. But that's not the most important thing. Something else is at work here."

"Like what?" Bennett pressed.

Barak's eyes scanned the rest of the museum for any sign that someone was listening in on their conversation. Finally he whispered, "Fear."

26
★ ★
★

"Mr. President, do you have a moment?"

Al-Hassani looked up from a stack of cables he was sifting through and found Khalid Tariq poking his head in the door of his private office.

"What is it, Khalid?"

"Foreign Minister Zeng Zou has just arrived."

"Ah yes," said Al-Hassani. "Show him in."

Al-Hassani greeted the Chinese leader warmly, along with the Chinese ambassador and their translator.

"You are very kind to see me, Mr. President. I am very humbled."

"It is my pleasure, Mr. Foreign Minister. And please, please, come have a seat. You are among friends here. Have you been offered any tea?"

"Thank you. You are most kind. I understand it is on the way."

"Excellent," said Al-Hassani, taking a seat beside Tariq. "Now, what can I do for you gentlemen? I understand you have a problem."

"We prefer to think of it as a challenge."

"Of course," said Al-Hassani. "And an enormous challenge it is. You have just passed Japan as the second-largest consumer of petroleum products in the world, and you're catching up to the Americans quite fast."

"This is true," Mr. Zou replied.

"In 1990, I believe you built 700,000 cars," Al-Hassani continued as he lit his pipe. "In 2000, you produced 2 million. This year you'll produce almost 5 million. In just a few short years, you will need 600 million tons of crude oil a year just to keep up with your current economic and population growth rates. And you're wondering where all that oil is going to come from."

"I am most impressed, Mr. President. You have certainly done your homework."

"You once did business with my country, but then came the U.N. sanctions, and then came the wars," Al-Hassani explained, waving off the compliment. "You cut huge deals with the Iranians, but they suddenly find themselves out of business. You signed a massive deal with Russia, but they, too, are no longer of any help. The Canadians are a possibility, and you've been courting them for years, with some success. But the brutal truth is they aren't producing fast enough, and the oil companies there are in constant battles with environmental groups that seem to care more about porcupine caribou than commerce. Which leaves you with two options—the Israelis or us."

"We want a deal," the Chinese foreign minister said flatly. "And we are prepared to pay handsomely for it."

"Very well," said Al-Hassani. "Please enlighten me."

"Mr. President, I am prepared to talk about more than oil," came Mr. Zou's reply. "I have come to explore the possibilities of forming a military and strategic alliance between China and Iraq."

Al-Hassani's eyes lit up. The Chinese foreign minister finally had his full attention.

☆   ☆   ☆

"What did you mean, fear?" Bennett asked.

The foursome had been mostly quiet since leaving the museum. Now Barak looked out the helicopter window at the Jordan Valley below, then back at the Bennetts.

"Someone out there is deathly afraid that the Temple treasures are about to be discovered, and they should be," he explained. "Why? Because finding the treasures would provide conclusive historical proof that a Jewish Temple once existed, thus sealing not only Israel's legal and historic claim to the Temple Mount but to Jerusalem as her capital. What's more, if the Temple treasures are actually found on land the world calls the

West Bank but which the Bible calls Judea and Samaria, it would power-
fully demonstrate that the land was once, in fact, Jewish land—our land—
thus undermining the Palestinians' claim to have a state there. Moreover,
such a discovery would end any doubt once and for all over whether Israel
would rebuild her Temple on the site of the first two. We would, and
quickly. But that's not all.

"Religious Jews like myself believe that building the next Temple is
the prerequisite to the coming of the Messiah, and that when the Messiah
finally comes, the judgment of all the nations will begin in full. In other
words, we believe what Russia and her allies just went through will pale in
comparison to what is coming next. Jewish theology says the worst is yet
to come. You Christians believe the same thing, don't you? Don't you believe that building the Third Temple will trigger the rise of the Antichrist
and unleash the Great Tribulation? And then Armageddon? And then the
so-called Second Coming?"

He was leaving out some important details, but he wasn't that far off.

"That's pretty close," Bennett agreed.

"Well, there you have it," said Barak. "No matter how you look at it,
the Third Jewish Temple brings with it the end of days."

"No wonder there are people out there who will do anything to prevent it from being built," said Erin.

"Indeed," said Barak. "You know, for four years after the Copper
Scroll was found, the Jordanian government did everything it could to
keep its very existence under wraps. Even when the New York Times finally
broke the story in 1956, Jordanian archeologists and the royal family insisted that the scroll was a myth, a legend, that there was no treasure and
thus no link whatsoever to any Jewish Temple. In fact, the main reason we
haven't rebuilt the Temple until now was out of fear that by doing so we'd
unleash a jihad of a billion Muslims attacking us for desecrating the Dome
of the Rock and the Al-Aksa Mosque. But all that has changed, you see?
And now somebody out there is terrified that with the dome and the
mosque both gone, plans to rebuild the Temple may finally proceed."

"Okay, I'm following you," Bennett said, "but why kill all these Copper Scroll experts now, and why kill Mordechai? Given all that's happened, isn't Israel likely to rebuild the Temple now whether the Temple
treasures are found or not?"

"Perhaps," said Barak, "but there is one other issue I have not yet mentioned."

"What's that?" asked Erin.

"I hesitate to bring it up because it's very speculative."

"Dr. Barak, please," said Erin. "We need to know everything you know if we're going to help track down Dr. Mordechai's killers."

Natasha was bringing the helicopter down on the roof of the Israel Museum.

"Well," Barak said finally, "there are some who believe the Copper Scroll will not only lead us to the Second Temple treasures but to something far greater as well."

"Which is what?" asked Bennett.

Barak pulled out his handkerchief again.

"The Ark," he whispered. "The Ark of the Covenant."

27

★ ★
★

Bennett had no interest in dining with Salvador Lucente.

His mind was whirring with all he had heard from the Baraks, and he still had so many questions. Had Mordechai, Barak, and the others really been on the verge of finding the Second Temple treasures? Had they actually found a clue that would have led them to the Ark of the Covenant? Was that really why they had all been murdered?

On its face, it all seemed crazy. But in Bennett's experience, anything was possible if it involved Eliezer Mordechai. This wasn't, after all, some cockamamy theory they'd just read in the *National Enquirer*. It was coming from Israel's highly respected chief archeologist. It involved three of the world's most renowned archeologists, each of whom had been murdered or died mysteriously in the span of just a few weeks. What's more, Barak hadn't come to them with his tale. The prime minister of Israel had sent them to Barak. Each man involved in the story was advising Doron, and Bennett knew Doron did not suffer fools gladly.

But even if it was all true, what exactly was he supposed to do about it? Neither he nor Erin had time to gather more answers now, so they arranged to meet the Baraks after dinner.

Bennett just prayed they would all live that long.

★   ★   ★

It was a strange meeting.

The Bennetts had worked with Lucente over the years on the Oil-for-Peace plan. Together they had hammered out an interim peace deal between the Israelis and the Palestinians and had cut a deal by which the U.S. and E.U. would buy a growing percentage of their oil and natural gas from Medexco.

But since the Russian-led attack on Israel, they had not spoken to each other at all. It had, after all, been Lucente—now in his seventies—who had helped Russian leader Yuri Gogolov muscle his anti-Israel resolution through the United Nations, trying to force Israel to give up its strategic weapons in return for NATO membership. What's more, it was Lucente, Bennett had learned recently, who had pressured President MacPherson not to come to Israel's defense during the midst of the crisis, and in so doing Salvador Lucente had earned Bennett's disdain, if not his contempt.

"Jonathan, Erin, thank you for seeing me—I am so sorry for your loss," Lucente said upon seeing them enter La Regence, the five-star restaurant on the lower level of the King David Hotel. He stood and hugged and kissed them both, though he didn't receive a particularly warm response. "I want you to know I have spoken personally with the head of Interpol and demanded they do whatever possible to hunt down Eli's killers."

"Thank you," said Erin. "That's very kind."

"It's the least I can do," he said. "I understand you were both with Eli when he passed away. I can only imagine how difficult that must have been."

"We were glad to be able to say good-bye," Bennett said softly as they all took their seats at a small table at the far end of the dining hall. The large room was deserted but for the foreign minister's security detail.

"Prime Minister Doron told me you had a few minutes to speak with Eli before he died. Is that true?"

Bennett nodded.

"Was he lucid?" Lucente asked. "Did he know it was you?"

Bennett took Erin's hand under the table and squeezed it gently.

"He did," said Bennett. "The doctors were as surprised as we were."

"Could he talk?"

"A little."

"What did he say, if you don't mind me asking?"

A waiter came over, poured each a glass of water, and set down a basket of warm rolls, then stepped away.

Bennett was grateful for a spare moment to gather his thoughts. He wanted to unleash on this guy for cozying up to Gogolov while Erin was being tortured in some gulag in Moscow. But something in Erin's eyes gave him pause. She was trying to remind him that Costello and the president had asked them to take Lucente's temperature and find out what he was up to, and they shouldn't let them down.

Bennett shifted in his seat. His personal problems with Lucente would have to wait. "Remarkably, he seemed to be thinking quite clearly, given the circumstances," he answered, pacing himself.

"Really? How so?" asked Lucente.

Bennett took a sip of water, then looked Lucente in the eye and said, "Actually, he told me to watch for the first guy to pressure Israel not to build her Temple. Guess he meant you."

That raised Lucente's bushy gray eyebrows in a hurry.

"You don't say," the foreign minister replied, scrambling for a comeback. "Actually, I would think you would be the first one to agree with me, Jonathan."

"Why?" asked Bennett.

"Well, to be quite candid, I'm not opposed to the Jews building their Temple—not per se," said Lucente, splitting open a freshly baked roll. "But my main interest, as I thought was yours, is finding a way to conclude a peace treaty between Israel and her neighbors once and for all. And toward that end, a unilateral move like seizing the Temple Mount doesn't seem very peace-inducing, does it?"

In his previous job as the president's senior advisor on the Arab-Israeli peace process, Bennett very likely would have agreed, or been required to by his boss back at 1600 Pennsylvania Avenue. But his perspective—and thus his allegiances—had been shifting, and not toward Europe.

Before he could answer, however, Erin cut in.

"To what exactly do we owe the honor of a meal with you, Mr. Foreign Minister?" she asked, cool though not quite impolite.

Lucente, however, was startled. "Well, I thought we might ease into the pool a bit more, but if you would like to dive in . . ."

He reached down to open his briefcase and fished out a letter-sized envelope. Bennett noticed it had the distinctive blue-and-white United Nations logo on the front.

"Well then, yes . . . ," Lucente began, clearly thrown off his game plan by Erin's abrupt question. "Yes, well, as you both no doubt know, the secretary-general's term in office expired on the first of January."

"We know," said Erin. "And President Mogande of South Africa is set to replace him, if I'm not mistaken."

"Actually, I'm afraid you are," said Lucente.

"What do you mean?"

"There's been a change."

"I haven't heard anything," Bennett said.

"Then again, you've been on your honeymoon." Lucente smiled.

"Nevertheless," said Erin, "we would have heard about a change like that."

"Which is why we're breaking bread together tonight," Lucente said. "It has just come up."

He handed over the sealed envelope, labeled "Private and Confidential for the President of the United States."

"What is this?" asked Jon.

"It is a handwritten letter from Secretary-General Pipilo. It explains that President Mogande has been diagnosed with liver cancer. It appears to be terminal. That is why he has been in the hospital the past few weeks, delaying the January first transition. President Mogande has, therefore, changed his mind. He is not going to serve, and the secretary-general intends to nominate me to be his replacement."

Neither of the Bennetts could believe what they were hearing.

For the last several years, Lucente had been engineering a new foreign policy for the European Union that diverged sharply from American interests and threatened to rip the NATO alliance to shreds. He had been bad enough to deal with in his current role. As secretary-general, he could make life extremely difficult for Washington.

"I have the votes," Lucente said after a moment, sensing their reactions. "It would be a mistake for the president to oppose me."

"It is no longer our concern," said Bennett. "We don't work for the president, and we no longer advise him on such matters. But you know that. You could have told him directly, or Secretary Warner, or Marsha Kirkpatrick. Why us? Why tonight?"

"Because I'd like to hire you," Lucente replied.

"Both of us?" Bennett asked, taken aback.

"I want both of you to serve on my senior team."

"To do what?" asked Erin.

"To help me finalize the peace deal between Israel and the Palestinians," Lucente explained. "It's almost done, as you know, but we need to finish it off quickly."

"And?"

"And I want you to hammer out a treaty between Israel and Iraq."

Bennett looked at Erin. "What kind of treaty?"

"Full peace, full recognition, full economic and diplomatic ties," said Lucente. "Think about it. The Israelis and Iraqis are now the biggest oil producers in the world. They're making money hand over fist. The last thing we need is for either of them to start an arms race or square off against the other. One more price spike and the entire global economy will collapse."

Bennett mulled that over for a moment. "I imagine Doron would love to cut a peace deal with Iraq," he agreed. "But would Al-Hassani agree? I don't know."

"I think he would, Jonathan," said Lucente. "Al-Hassani is poised to become the oil kingpin of the Middle East. He wants permission to rebuild the oil infrastructure in Iran, Saudi Arabia, the Gulf states, and the former Soviet republics and to run it himself. He also wants Russia's seat on the U.N. Security Council. I'll give him both tomorrow, but not unless he signs a full peace treaty with Israel. That's why I'm headed to Babylon. I just wish you two were coming with me. Think about it, and I'll call you when I get back to Brussels."

28

★ ★
★

It was just after eleven when they finally reconnected.

The two Bennetts and the two Baraks met at a little café called Keshet in the heart of the Jewish Quarter of the Old City. Normally the café closed at nine, but the couple who owned it was meeting with their accountant to go over their tax returns, and when Dr. Barak, an old friend, showed up, they happily put on some coffee and brought out baklava.

It was a quiet, charming little place with wooden tables and chairs. On a hot summer night they could probably accommodate upward of fifty patrons, but this, of course, was the middle of January, and though it was unseasonably mild, the Quarter was deserted. Bennett suggested they meet inside, but Barak insisted he needed the fresh air. Besides, he said, he saw no point in letting the owners or their accountant overhear their discussion. So the four of them dragged chairs out to one of the outdoor tables and made themselves at home.

Barak rested his cane against the table and took a seat with his back to the café, eager to enjoy the quiet of a large courtyard to his left, typically filled with the laughter of little children, mothers chatting with neighbors, and Yeshiva students arguing over some obscure Torah passage. Natasha took a seat beside him while Jon and Erin sat across from them, soaking up their surroundings as well. For all their travels to this Holy City, they had never had the time to be tourists and thus had never strolled along these stone streets like so many young lovers had through the ages.

Behind them was a branch of the Mizraim Bank, Bennett noticed, which was good because he needed to use the ATM before they headed back to the King David. A sign next to the bank pointed the way to a short walk to the Western Wall. He thought he might like to take Erin down there if they didn't finish up too late. They certainly had a lot to pray about, and what better place than the wall?

To Bennett's immediate right was a colonnade that led to the Cardo Center, the Arab market, and the heart of the Moslem Quarter, not a route he thought would be best tonight but one that would actually be quite interesting during the day. For now, though, they were being served piping hot Turkish coffee and a generous spread of fruit and nuts and sweets.

Barak was clearly itching to pick up his story where he'd left off. "Ever hear of a man named Abdullah Farouk?" the old man said when they were alone again.

Neither Jon nor Erin had.

"He's a Saudi prince," Barak explained. "He's been hunting for the Ark for years and has poured millions of dollars into the quest. He's absolutely obsessed with the idea that the Copper Scroll is the key to finding the Ark, and he's terrified that the Jews will get to it first. His family thinks he's crazy. But that's what makes him so dangerous. He's rich and he's driven and he simply won't give up. According to Eli, Farouk has had ties with all kinds of terrorist groups over the years—Hezbollah, Hamas, Al-Qaeda, and more recently, Al-Nakbah. Basically, he'll give enormous sums of money to anyone committed to driving the Jews into the sea and to keeping Israel from ever finding the Ark."

Barak reached into his briefcase and pulled out a clipping from a London-based, Saudi-financed newspaper. He handed it to Bennett. "Prince Pledges Millions to Ark Quest" read the headline, dated six years earlier.

With Erin looking over his shoulder, Jon scanned the story and came to a quote, highlighted in yellow, which he read aloud.

"'People don't understand,' Farouk explained over a cup of tea in a mosque outside of London. 'This isn't about finding some dusty old relic

for a museum. It's about finding the first weapon of mass destruction. Laugh if you want, but what if the legends are true? Have you read the ancient manuscripts? In their original languages? The Ark killed tens of thousands. It shattered enemy cities. It leveled entire armies. What if the Zionists find it first? It would make them invincible. They could control all of Palestine. They could seize Mecca and Medina. They could dominate all of the Muslim lands, and there would be nothing we could do to stop them. Then again, imagine if I found it first. What if the very power of Allah was in our hands? It is we who would be unstoppable. Not only could we destroy the Jews, but we could build an Islamic caliphate that could rule the world.'"

Bennett took another sip of coffee.

"This Farouk guy has been watching a little too much *Raiders of the Lost Ark*, don't you think?"

"I'll say," Erin laughed. "A classic fanatic."

Bennett noticed the old man's hesitation.

"You don't think he's nuts?"

"I said he's obsessed, but not crazy," Barak explained. "There's a difference. But either way, it makes him dangerous."

"So you think he might be behind these killings?" said Erin.

"I do," Barak confirmed.

There was something in the way he answered that made Bennett uncomfortable.

"It's more than that, isn't it?" he asked, setting his coffee down and staring into Barak's eyes. "You believe him, don't you?"

"I didn't say that," Barak demurred.

"You think the Ark actually has some sort of supernatural powers, don't you?" Bennett pressed.

"Don't *you*?" Barak replied.

Bennett said nothing for a moment. Nor did Natasha or Erin.

"Look, Jonathan," Barak explained. "There is no one in Israel who has studied the history of the Ark more carefully than I have. Yet there is so much we don't know. No one has seen the Ark in almost three thousand years. It is surrounded by mysteries and legends. Who among us can separate fact from fiction at this point? But there is one point upon which the

Holy Scriptures could not be more clear: the Ark is an object of tremendous power, mystical power. It is to be feared, not dismissed. Men who were careless about its fearsome power died instantly. Those who touched it improperly died instantly."

"Come on, Dr. Barak, really," said Bennett. "I'm a Christian. I believe what the Bible says about the Ark. But as you said yourself, that was thousands of years ago."

"Jonathan, you are new to all this, I realize. Thus you have a luxury I dare not share—cynicism. But you should know that Eli Mordechai understood the significance of the Ark. What's more, he understood the stakes should the Ark fall into the hands of a man like Abdullah Farouk. Eli gave up his life to prevent that from happening. So perhaps you should not be so cavalier. Perhaps you should—"

A shot rang out.

Barak snapped back in his chair and fell to the ground. Natasha screamed as blood oozed from the old man's mouth. Another shot went wild, shattering the café's plate-glass window. Jon and Erin dove for cover as more shots ripped through windows and walls. Natasha was on the ground, her arms wrapped around her grandfather. She was still screaming, her hands shaking uncontrollably.

For a split second, the shooting stopped. Bennett guessed the shooter was reloading. Erin grabbed Natasha and pulled her to safety while Bennett rushed to Barak's side and checked his pulse. There was none.

Suddenly, he heard Erin shouting. *"Jon, get down!"*

He could see a shadow moving on a fourth-floor balcony across the courtyard.

Then Erin was there, Beretta in hand. She opened fire. *"Jon, now, go,"* she yelled.

Bennett made his move. He grabbed Natasha by her arms and literally dragged her into the stone colonnade, behind the café and out of the line of fire. She was kicking and swinging at him and stronger than Bennett had expected.

"Let me go," she screamed. *"Let me die with him!"*

But there was no way Bennett was going to let that happen. Natasha Barak was now the only link they had to the secrets of the scrolls and the men willing to kill for them.

29

★ ★
★

Bennett shielded Natasha with his own body.

Erin shot back at their assailants until she had fired her last round. A moment later, she dove into the colonnade as more automatic gunfire tore up the café. The shooters didn't have a clear shot at them now, but they didn't seem to care. They were firing at anything and everything that moved.

Erin glanced into the café through a side door as she reloaded her Beretta. Then she disappeared inside.

Bennett had no idea what she was doing, but he didn't dare call out to ask. Instead, he grabbed Natasha's chin and squeezed until her frightened eyes focused on his. "You can't stay here," he said through gritted teeth. "They'll kill you, and we need you."

Natasha was shaking, but she had not slipped into shock. Not yet.

Erin reemerged from the café with an Uzi in her hand. It was covered with blood. "Everyone in there is dead," she said as she handed over the machine gun and some ammo. "I found this inside."

Suddenly, they could hear men running and shouting in Arabic. Whoever was hunting them, they were coming fast.

"We need to move—*now*," Bennett ordered. "Follow me."

He held the gun in one hand, grabbed Natasha with the other, and sprinted down the colonnade toward the Moslem Quarter. They scrambled down some stairs, took a sharp left, and entered the Arab market. During the day, these narrow stone streets were bustling with shoppers buying spices or electronics or shoes or bread and old men haggling over prices, playing backgammon, and smoking their water pipes. But the streets were deserted now. The shoppers were gone. The shops were closed, their metal shutters pulled down and locked for the night.

A burst of automatic gunfire let loose over Bennett's shoulder as they whipped around another corner and headed deeper into the souk. He could hear the rounds pelting into the stone walls behind him but didn't dare look back.

He hugged the Uzi tight to his chest and wrapped the strap around his neck and shoulder. He would use it only as a last resort, he decided. Then he realized he'd never checked the magazine. Was it even loaded? How many rounds did he have left, if any?

Another burst of gunfire. The shooters were gaining ground.

Bennett rounded another corner, quickly handed Natasha off to Erin, and told them to keep running. Then he backed into the shadows and dropped to the ground. He could see two masked men coming at him, full steam. But for the moment, they couldn't see him.

He steadied the Uzi, took aim, and when they got close, he pulled the trigger and didn't let go. Fire poured from the end of the weapon. The two men dropped to the ground, careening down the narrow passageway and coming to a stop not far from where he was hiding.

And suddenly, all was quiet.

Bennett could hear his heart pounding. He knew how close to death he had just come. He climbed to his feet and carefully peered around the corner. No one else was coming, and he breathed a sigh of relief.

Until he heard Erin scream, *"Jon, look out."*

Startled, Bennett swung around to see one of his injured assailants groping for his AK-47. But before Jon could fire, Erin kicked away the man's gun and smashed his head against the stones. Then she ripped off his mask, jammed her Beretta in his left temple, and growled at him in Arabic. He smiled but said nothing. She slammed his head against the rock a second time and again jammed her Beretta into his temple.

It wasn't working. Blood was running from the man's ears and mouth. His eyes were glassy. What little life was still within was quickly draining away. She wasn't going to get whatever information she had hoped to extract from him. Sure enough, a moment later he was dead.

Bennett peeked back around the corner. They were still alone, but they wouldn't be for long.

Erin, meanwhile, moved to the second man and checked his pulse. He, too, was dead. She checked their pockets for any bit of identification but came up empty.

"Two John Does," she said. "But they knew right where to find us."

"How?" asked Natasha, her body trembling and covered with sweat.

That wasn't a topic Bennett wanted to cover just yet.

"We need to keep moving," he insisted. "Whoever these guys are, they've got better intel than we do. We're sitting ducks if we stay here."

"Where should we go?" Erin asked. "We can't take her back to her flat. They'll kill her. And we can't go back to the King David either. They obviously know we're with her."

"What are you two talking about?" Natasha demanded. "Just call the police. Tell them what happened. Call the prime minister. He'll give us anything we need."

"We can't," said Erin. She stuffed her Beretta into her back pocket and put her arm around Natasha, trying to calm her down. "We think there's a mole in Doron's office. No one else knew we'd be meeting you tonight but Doron and his top staff."

"Why? Why are they doing this to us?" Natasha cried.

Erin's hand shot to Natasha's mouth, trying to keep her quiet without terrifying her all the more. "Your grandfather just told us why. But now you've got to believe us. You're not safe in Israel—not anymore. And neither are we. We've got to find a way to get you out of the country. It's too dangerous."

"Erin, really, we need to get moving," said Bennett.

Erin turned to Natasha and stared into her eyes. "Think, Natasha. Do you know anyone in the Old City? anyone we could stay with overnight until we sort things out?"

Natasha tried, but it was clear her emotions were getting the best of her. "My sister-in-law . . . she and my brother . . . they . . ."

"No," said Erin. "No family. No close friends. Somewhere no one would know to look. It has to be someone you know but not well. Someone who will take us in without turning us in."

Natasha said suddenly, "I've got it. Come on. This way."

Bennett and Erin looked at each other but did not say a word. They could hear sirens rapidly approaching. They had no choice and no time. They had to trust Natasha and hope for the best. So they each grabbed an AK-47 and extra ammo and followed Natasha deeper inside the Moslem Quarter.

Dogs were barking. People were awakening to the commotion. Lights were coming on in every home, and Bennett knew if they did not get off the streets quickly, they could easily get cornered by an angry mob or by an Israeli patrol, and for the moment, he wasn't sure which was worse. Were they really being hunted by forces bought and paid for by Abdullah Farouk or by a fifth column inside the Israeli government, possibly run by a mole deep inside Prime Minister Doron's own office? Who were their allies? Whom could they trust?

Cautiously they worked their way down Aqabat El-Saryia Street, expecting an ambush at every door and alleyway, but so far it had been clear. When they got to El-Wad Road, Natasha poked her head around the corner. She turned back and motioned that they were taking a left; no sooner had they done this than they came upon a set of stairs leading to a small apartment. It was surrounded by fencing and barbed wire, and an Israeli flag was draped over one window. Natasha headed up, two steps at a time.

"Where are we?" Bennett whispered, scanning the rooftops around them for any signs of danger.

"My friends Ori and Lila Shochat live here," Natasha whispered back. "Their daughter, Sara, was a student of mine at the university."

"How long ago?"

"Three, four years maybe."

"You trust them?"

"They're *political* Zionists, not religious ones," Natasha replied. "Believe me, if they hate you, it'll be over your peace deal with the Arabs, not over Jesus."

"And you're sure they still live here?"

"Absolutely," said Natasha. "When Jews move into the Moslem Quarter, they don't leave unless they're in a body bag."

Natasha turned and buzzed the intercom. She spoke for a moment with a man in Hebrew, then held her breath. Seconds passed. Then a minute. No reply.

Bennett's heart was racing. Whoever was in there was (a) consulting with his family, (b) finding his gun, or (c) calling the police. Whichever, time was running out. He could hear people spilling out onto the streets, shouting in Arabic. He wiped his hands on his pants, then tightened his grip on the machine gun and checked on Erin, now guarding Natasha's back. She was okay for the moment, but he didn't want her out in the open a minute more than necessary.

And then the electronic locks on the door clicked open.

They were in.

30

★ ★
★

The Shochats didn't know what to say at first.

They were obviously surprised to see Natasha at their door at this late hour, but they were clearly worried about her too. Natasha suddenly seemed dazed and incoherent, and Bennett realized she was going into shock.

Erin quickly explained that they were friends of Natasha's from the U.S., that there had been a series of shootings in the Arab market, and that they weren't convinced there was a safe way out of the Quarter just now. She also explained that Natasha thought the Shochats were the only people they could all turn to, and that's why they were here. For now, Bennett noticed, she chose not to tell them Natasha's grandfather had just been shot or that they were on the run. It was just as well.

Erin apologized for inconveniencing them, but the Shochats wouldn't hear of it. They had seen Jon's and Erin's faces on the news for years, they said. It would be an honor to protect them for the night.

"You'll be safe with us," said Mr. Shochat, his Uzi in hand. "I'll make sure of it."

"Thank you, Mr. Shochat," Bennett replied, shaking his hand. "We really appreciate it."

"Please, please, call me Ori."

Natasha began to worsen. She slumped down on the living-room couch and started to shake. Mrs. Shochat ran to get blankets to wrap around her, and then she led them all into the basement, opened two fold-out couches, and gave them clean sheets, towels, blankets, and pillows. Erin tucked Natasha in and took her vital signs. After a few minutes, Natasha began to relax a bit, and soon she was fast asleep.

"Perhaps I should let you all get some rest," said Mrs. Shochat. "We can talk more in the morning. Is there anything else you need?"

"Actually there is," said Bennett apologetically. "You wouldn't happen to have a computer we could use for a few minutes, would you?"

"Of course, in the corner," the woman replied, "with wireless access, if you need it."

She showed them how to get it started, then gave Natasha a kiss on the forehead, said good night, and went back upstairs to bed.

☆　☆　☆

Bennett stepped into the bathroom.

He closed the door and pulled out his cell phone. The first thing he did was call his mom. He got voice mail and breathed a guilty sigh of relief. They had much to talk about, but now was not the time.

"You're going to hear some terrible things on the news," he explained. "We're okay. We're safe. I can't tell you everything now. I just need you to pray for us, Mom. That would mean a lot to me. I'll call you when I can. I love you. Bye."

Next, he speed-dialed Ken Costello.

"Ken, it's Jon. I'm sorry if I woke you up."

"Are you kidding?" asked Costello. "I've been on the phone the last half hour with the ambassador, Langley, Foggy Bottom, the Situation Room. I'm watching the coverage right now on Channel 2."

"Are you still at the King David?"

"For a few more minutes," Costello replied. "They're sending a car from the consulate in East Jerusalem. Kirkpatrick wants me to monitor the situation from there. But what about you? Where are you? Are you okay?"

"I'm fine," said Bennett, "but I need a favor."

"Sure, what's up?"

"Ever heard of a guy named Abdullah Farouk?"

"Can't say I have."

"Get whatever State and the FBI have on this guy and e-mail it to my BlackBerry."

"Why? Is he involved in this thing?"

"I'll explain later. But it's urgent—fast as you can."

"No problem," said Costello. "What about Rajiv at CIA?"

"Erin's about to call her," Bennett said.

"And Avi Zadok at Mossad?" asked Costello.

"No, we haven't tried him yet."

"Why not?"

Bennett hesitated for a moment, but then realized he didn't have much choice. He explained their growing fears of a high-level penetration inside the Doron inner circle.

"A double agent inside the prime minister's office?" said Costello. "Come on, Jon. That's crazy."

Bennett conceded that he'd thought so at first. But then he gave Costello a rundown of all the recent deaths and how all of them were linked back to Doron and his team in one way or another. Costello still couldn't believe it. He, like Jon and Erin, knew each member of the prime minister's team on a first-name basis. They'd worked together for years. It seemed impossible that any of them could be involved in anything like this. But Costello agreed that the whole chain of events was suspicious, and he promised to proceed with caution and get back to him in a few hours.

"How's Tracy doing?" Bennett asked before saying good-bye.

"You won't believe it," said Costello.

"What's that?"

"She just called me an hour ago with news."

"What?"

"We're expecting."

★   ★   ★

Erin speed-dialed Indira Rajiv at Langley.

Fortunately, Washington was seven hours behind them, and it was now only six-thirty in the evening there. Rajiv picked up on the second ring.

"Tell me you're not in the middle of this thing," Rajiv said immediately.

"It's made the news there already?" Erin asked, surprised, even by the standards of American cable news.

"No, not yet," said Rajiv. "I got a priority flash traffic from our consulate and dialed up Israeli TV off our satellite. The whole section is watching it. It's the first violence in the Moslem Quarter since the firestorm. And you're in it, aren't you?"

"I'm afraid so," Erin conceded, glad to find a sympathetic voice.

"What happened?" asked Rajiv. "You guys okay?"

"We're fine," said Erin. "I'll explain later. Right now I need some help."

"Of course," said Rajiv. "What do you need?"

"Two things," Erin explained. "First, I need you to track down everything the agency has on a guy named Abdullah Farouk and get it to me overnight."

There was a long pause on the other end of the line.

"Who is Abdullah Farouk?" Rajiv finally asked.

"I'm not sure," Erin conceded. "It might be a rabbit trail, but I need to follow it for a bit and see where it leads."

"Okay," Rajiv said, an edge of reluctance in her voice. "Let me see what I can do. Was there something else?"

Now Erin paused. She had just asked one of her closest friends to break about six different federal laws by giving her classified information on Farouk when she was no longer working for the CIA. Was she really about to ask for more? She had no choice. Someone was hunting for them, and she needed to regain the initiative. She swallowed hard and said to Rajiv, "Yeah, actually there is."

*　*　*

Exasperated, Bennett ran his hands through his hair.

"I don't believe you," he said at last. "I really don't believe you."

"I know it looks bad, Jon, but I—"

"Looks bad? Erin, are you crazy? Have you completely lost your mind? You're going to send us all to prison for the rest of our lives!"

"That wasn't my first concern," she said.

"What was?"

"Surviving."

Bennett was beside himself. He wanted to scream at her, but he couldn't afford to wake up Natasha or the rest of the house, much less the neighborhood.

"So let me get this straight," he said, his mind still reeling. "You actually asked Indira Rajiv to log on to a secure CIA satellite account, zoom into Jerusalem, map out a secure route from the apartment where we're staying to Dr. Mordechai's house and back, and then feed that imagery to a password-protected Web account that we can access on our Black-Berrys?"

"Pretty much," said Erin.

"So despite the fact that we have a warm bed to sleep in, and a family willing to protect us, and access to friends in the White House and CIA who can help us out of this thing, you're actually proposing that we leave this house, sneak back through the Moslem Quarter, and find our way to Dr. Mordechai's house?"

"Right."

"Because you have a death wish?"

"No," Erin shot back, "because someone has one for us."

"And what exactly are we supposed to find at Dr. Mordechai's place?"

"I don't know," said Erin. "Not exactly."

"Oh, great, that's helpful."

"Look, Jon, I'm exhausted. We both are. But we don't have a lot of choices right now, do we? We've got a lot of pieces to this puzzle, but I can't seem to make them fit. Can you?"

Bennett said nothing, so Erin continued. "When the sun comes up we're going to be pinned down here for another night unless you want to go traipsing through the Moslem Quarter in broad daylight."

"Not with what tomorrow's headlines are going to bring," he said.

"Precisely my point," said Erin. "If we're going to make a move, we have to make it now. I'm just hoping that if we can hack into Mordechai's files, we might come across something helpful, something we can use to figure this all out, before it's too late."

31

★ ★
★

An hour later, they were standing outside Mordechai's house.

Officially, the house was under investigation and would be until the circumstances of Mordechai's death had been thoroughly studied, but most of the detective work here had been done already. The question now was whether there remained any clues to Mordechai's death that may not have been obvious to the Mossad or Shin Bet.

Bennett followed his bride up the cobblestone path and realized this might very well be the last time they visited this remarkable home. He wondered how much this house carved into the hills would sell for—six, eight million? Ten?

He recalled how intrigued he'd been the first time he visited. He'd been struck at the time by an almost overpowering sense that the house was a reflection of the man inside, eclectic and unconventional, shrouded in mystery, infused with a hint of magic. Tonight was no different. For old times' sake, he wished they could ring the doorbell and once again hear the chimes echoing through the valley, as beautiful as those in the Church of the Holy Sepulchre not far away. Instead, he punched in the nine-digit security code Mordechai had taught them. To their surprise, it was still active, and they entered the front door. But this time they were not greeted by armed Mossad agents. They were greeted, instead, by an eerie silence.

As they climbed the circular staircase into the great room—its walls covered with Jackson Pollock paintings, its shelves adorned with archeological relics from all over the Near East—Bennett thought he could still pick up the faint smell of the curry and coriander and turmeric with which Mordechai so often cooked, and the memories began to well up within him. It was on these very couches that he'd first heard the Ezekiel 38 and 39 prophecies. It was out there on the stone porch overlooking the Old City that Erin had first shared her faith in Christ with him. Below his feet were the thick Persian rugs once covered with the blood of Iraqi terrorists who had come in the middle of the night to hunt them down. And when he closed his eyes he could still see the chalk outlines around the bodies, all these years later.

Erin made a right toward the kitchen and Mordechai's bedroom and private study. Bennett, on the other hand, turned left to look through the guest rooms where they had so often stayed. The beds were all made with fresh linens no one would ever use. Clean bath towels and washcloths were stacked neatly in wicker baskets at the foot of each bed, and as always, each room had a collection of small soaps and bottles of shampoo, along with new toothbrushes and unused tubes of toothpaste, always prepared for another guest, though no more would ever come.

He stopped over the section of hallway where his friend and colleague Dietrich Black had been killed, and where he had almost been, as well. So much had happened since that night, yet the memories were still vivid, still painful, and he wondered when, if ever, they would begin to fade. He wondered, too, how Deek's family was holding up. He'd set up a scholarship fund for the girls and helped Katrina land a job outside of Philly as the executive secretary to a bank VP he'd known from Harvard. But it had been way too long since they had all seen each other. Erin and Katrina still e-mailed each other occasionally, but less often than they had, and less often than Bennett wished. They had sent Katrina an invitation to their wedding but had never received a reply. He made mental note to give her a call when he got back to the States.

Since the day he had been hired by the president of the United States to help bring about an Arab-Israeli peace treaty, he had known personally fifty-three people who were now dead. Funny how the mind kept track of the details. Most deaths he had witnessed firsthand. But of all of them, Mordechai's was by far the most painful. Already Bennett missed him more than he had thought possible, more even than his own father, and though he knew with great certainty that he would see his old friend once again one day, it wasn't the same, and there was no use pretending that it was. There would be no more talks late into the night about politics and prophecy, no more marathon Scrabble tournaments that Bennett would always lose and Erin would sometimes win. All that was over, and over too quickly. The only way to redeem it was to figure out why.

His BlackBerry began to vibrate. He glanced at the screen. It was his mother. He gritted his teeth. She had the most incredible timing.

"Hey, Mom, now is not the best time," he said, cupping his hand over his mouth to keep as quiet as possible.

"Why are you whispering? Is everything all right?" asked Ruth Bennett from her town house in Orlando.

"I'm actually in the middle of something right now. Can I call you back?"

"Will you?"

"Of course I will."

"You promise?"

"Of course I promise," he sighed. "Every Saturday morning, 9 a.m.— have I missed one yet?"

"You're a good boy. I'm so, so sorry about Dr. Mordechai. Are you going to the funeral?"

"There's not going to be a funeral, Mom."

"What are you talking about? There has to be a funeral. He was a great man."

"They don't think of him that way here. But look, I really need to go. I'll call you tonight."

"You know, I think I've settled on a church," his mother continued, oblivious to the urgency in his voice. "It's a big one, about fifteen minutes from me. The pastor is wonderful. You and Erin really need to come down and hear him. He's doing a series on the End Times right now. Fascinating. Absolutely fascinating. He actually quoted Dr. Mordechai last week. I just about fell out of my chair. I wanted to stand up and shout, '*I know that guy. I know him!*'"

Bennett had to bite his tongue. He loved his mother dearly. The last thing he wanted was to communicate any disrespect. But sometimes . . .

"Anyway, the pastor said Dr. Mordechai had an intriguing theory. Since nobody knows when Jesus is going to return—Jesus said even He didn't know; He said only His Father knew—that would mean that Satan doesn't know either. Which means Satan has always had to be prepared for any eventuality. That means that for almost two thousand years, he's had to have at least one Antichrist on the earth, in position, ready to go, in every generation since the Resurrection. Which is why there have been so many evil dictators throughout history. So there has to be someone out there, right now, walking around the planet at this very minute. Waiting. Preparing. Plotting. It could be somebody you know. It could be someone *I* know. It's scary, don't you think?"

Bennett took a deep breath. That was enough for now. He again told his mother how much he loved her and promised to call her the moment he had the chance. Then he went looking for Erin, whom he found in Mordechai's private study.

32

★ ★
★

The room had been stripped bare.

All the books of every shelf were gone. So were the papers and the file cabinets. A PC still sat on the old man's desk, but its hard drive had been ripped out. Even his favorite swivel chair was gone.

"You think Mossad took it all?" Bennett asked, putting his arm around Erin.

"I guess," said Erin, still trying to make sense of it.

"What do you think they were looking for?"

"Same thing we are," Erin replied. "Any scrap that could point in the right direction."

Bennett noticed something under the desk. He bent down to see what it was only to find a shattered picture frame. He carefully picked through the shards of glass and pulled out a small black-and-white photograph. It was Mordechai and his wife, Yael, on their wedding day at a synagogue in west Jerusalem.

He dusted it off and handed it to Erin, angered by what he was seeing. A murder investigation was one thing; the wholesale removal of a man's most personal possessions from his own home was another thing entirely.

"Didn't Dr. Barak tell us that Mordechai had come to him with new information about the Copper Scroll sometime shortly after the firestorm?" Bennett suddenly asked.

"Yes," Erin replied.

"And isn't that new information what prompted Mordechai to go to Doron and urge him to put together the whole group with Murray and Jaspers?"

Erin nodded.

"And he said that Murray had been meeting with a literary agent the day he died."

"I don't remember that," said Erin.

"You don't?"

"No," she said. "Is that what you and Dr. Barak were talking about when we got back from Amman?"

"Yeah."

"Well, I was talking to Natasha, remember? I didn't hear what you guys were saying."

Bennett strained to recall the details of the conversation. "Barak said something about how Jaspers had called him and told him Murray was shopping a book proposal around New York, something about the Copper Scroll. Barak was furious with Murray and called him up and said he was jeopardizing everything. Murray told him they had nothing to worry about."

"Okay, so . . . ?"

"So what was Mordechai's lead? What did he have? Where did he get it from, and where is it now?"

"I don't know," said Erin. "Nobody knows. Natasha said she didn't even know. Her grandfather never told her."

"But someone thought the answer lay in this room," said Bennett.

"Which is why they took everything," Erin agreed. "The big question is, would they know what they were looking for?"

"I've got a bigger question than that," said Bennett.

"What's that?"

"Shouldn't there be a backup of all the files that were on Mordechai's PC?"

They both thought about that for a moment.

The war room, said Erin.

They bolted for Mordechai's closet, pushed through the racks of clothes, and found the hidden elevator that had once saved their lives when Saddam Hussein had ordered Operation Last Jihad. Erin entered the passcode from memory, and thirty seconds later they were in the subterranean chamber that once had been used as a clandestine Mossad operations center. It was here that Erin and Mordechai had worked so feverishly to keep Bennett alive after that ferocious gun battle with Iraqi terrorists, and it was here that they had watched the U.S. launch its massive attack on Saddam Hussein and his Republican Guard. But this, too, was now all cleaned out.

Gone were all the video monitors and the computers, once cross-linked to the Mossad and CIA mainframes. Gone were the mini-medical center and the weapons-storage closet and the data-storage system that had helped Mordechai track the latest world developments and do all the analysis for which he'd become so famous. It had all been ripped out. The room was now just a ghost of what it had been, filled with nothing more than frayed wiring and bittersweet memories. They had hit a dead end.

As frustrated as they were exhausted, they made their way back to the elevator and headed up. Erin checked her watch. They had only a few minutes before the neighborhood security patrol would finish its rounds and come back to check Mordechai's house.

"What now?" Bennett asked as the door slid open and they stepped back into Mordechai's closet.

But Erin didn't answer. She stuck out her arm to block him from moving forward, then pulled out her Beretta.

Down the hallway, someone was whispering.

Erin carefully slid off her shoes, moved to the door, and motioned for him to stay put for a moment. Bennett's pulse was racing. His palms were sweaty. Who was out there, and why? It couldn't be the security patrol. There would be no reason for them to whisper. But why else would anybody be in the house? Unless they were hunting the same clue—or hunting for them.

Bennett had no weapon. He did, however, have access to the best intel money could buy. He quickly put his BlackBerry on silence mode, then used the tracking wheel to find the live CIA satellite downlink that had helped them get here in the first place. He double-clicked and waited for the connection to kick in. It never did. He got an error message instead: *Server connection lost*. That was strange, Bennett thought. It had worked just moments earlier. Now, when they needed it most, it went down?

Erin took a quick peek into the hallway, then darted across the hall to the master bedroom. She cleared that room and caught Jon's eye again.

Downstairs, she signaled, *then come back up on the other side.*

He climbed into the elevator and headed down. When the doors reopened, he crossed through the former ops center and found the other elevator shaft on the opposite wing. He climbed in and pressed the button.

Nothing happened.

He pressed it again. Still nothing. It was out of order, and suddenly he could feel perspiration running down his back.

★ ★ ★

The main floor was now stone silent.

The whispers had ceased. Whoever was out there knew she was here too.

Erin did another quick peek down the hallway. That's when they unleashed. She pulled back and pressed herself against the bedroom wall, only to see the wall at the end of the hallway torn to shreds by twenty or thirty rounds of automatic-weapons fire.

As soon as the shooting stopped for a moment, she pivoted around, squeezed off six rounds, and dove back into the walk-in closet. She hit the elevator button and waited. Gunfire erupted again in the hall. There were two of them, she realized. One would fire a short burst, then the other. They were tag teaming down the hallway. They were coming for her, and they could be only eight or ten yards away at most by now.

Erin pressed the elevator button again. She could hear the muffled sounds of the motor kicking in, but it was still a good ten seconds away. She didn't have that long.

33

THURSDAY, JANUARY 15 – 4:02 A.M. – JERUSALEM, ISRAEL

Bennett could hear the gunfire above him.

It was moving east to west, toward Erin. Should he go back up the west elevator? And do what? He still had no weapon. If Erin was pinned down, the only good he could do would be to try to ambush these guys from behind. But how?

Desperate, he checked every door for a stairway to the main floor, but found none. Instead, he ducked back into the broken elevator and noticed an access panel in the ceiling. He grabbed an old wooden chair, set it in the elevator, climbed on top of it, and pushed the access panel free, then pulled himself up onto the top of the elevator.

The shaft was nearly pitch-black, pierced only by the lights inside the elevator carriage itself. It wasn't much, but it was enough to find the metal maintenance ladder bolted to the side of the back wall, and that's all he needed. A moment later, Bennett reached the top of the ladder. He pried open the elevator door, climbed onto the main floor, and found himself in a closet in one of the east-wing guest rooms. That put him at the far end of the house. Now the shooting stopped, but the gunman let fly a storm of profanities.

Bennett's only solace: if Erin were dead, he had no doubt the cursing would stop.

* * *

Despite the cursing, Erin could hear the elevator rising behind her.

She could also hear both men ejecting spent magazines. It was her only chance and she took it. She pumped five shots through the closet wall into the hallway and hit pay dirt. Someone dropped to the floor. She lowered her aim and fired five more shots through the drywall into the hallway. The screaming ceased, but now someone else was approaching, and he was coming fast.

Just then the elevator door opened behind her. She dove in, hit the down button, and dropped to the floor as a barrage of AK-47 fire filled the closet.

* * *

Bennett knew he had to move quickly.

He rummaged through the closet looking for a weapon, but all he found were clothes Mordechai hadn't worn in years and would never wear again. He scanned the guest room but found nothing. The kitchen was on the other side of the house—with knives, a meat cleaver—but he'd never reach it in time. He glanced into the hallway. No one was there. He slid off his shoes, then eased open the guest-room door and worked his way toward the great room, terrified of making a sound and drawing gunfire he couldn't return. He found no one there or on the stairs. Nor could he see anyone outdoors on the deck overlooking the Old City. For the moment, at least, the coast was clear.

He made his move, darting behind one of the leather couches and then working his way around to the fireplace. There he stopped for a moment to slow his breathing. He could hear one of the intruders probing room by room. Whoever it was, he obviously had never been in the house before, Bennett realized. He had no idea about the secret elevator. Was that where Erin had gone?

Bennett glanced at his watch. The sun would be coming up before long, and they desperately needed to be able to make their way back to their temporary residence in the Moslem Quarter before daybreak, or there would be no place for them to hide. If he was going to do anything, it had to be now.

Slowly, carefully, Bennett removed one of the cast-iron pokers from the stand beside Mordechai's fireplace. Then he moved toward the hallway leading to the west wing and tried to steady his breathing. A few moments later, as he'd anticipated, he heard footsteps. They were heavy and determined and were coming quickly down the hall toward him. He raised the poker like a baseball bat and waited. When the gunman came through the archway into the great room, Bennett swung for the fences.

The man was huge, at least six feet six, maybe 250 pounds, but he was caught completely off guard by the force of the poker, which struck him square across the upper lip, just below the nose. His head snapped back. He lost his footing and crashed onto his back. His weapon skidded across the hardwood floor toward the stairs.

Bennett leaped for it. Seconds later, he had the AK-47 in his hands. He pivoted quickly to face his assailant, but it was too late. The man was already on top of him, knocking the gun away and pounding him with his fists. Bennett was stunned. He had no idea how the man could have recovered so quickly, but it hardly mattered. The two of them were now hurtling down the stairs, and soon they hit the floor with a bone-crunching thud.

The man's hands closed like a vise around Bennett's neck. They were squeezing, squeezing. Bennett couldn't break free. He was gagging and choking, but there was nothing he could do to wrest himself from the man's grip. A wave of panic washed over him. He couldn't breathe, couldn't see, couldn't think, and then—without warning—a single gunshot exploded in his ears. Bennett saw the man's life drain from his eyes. He watched the man slump to the floor, blood pouring out of his mouth, and an involuntary shudder rippled through Bennett's system.

He shoved the body off of him and rolled away to safety. When he looked up, he saw his wife at the top of the stairs, the Beretta still pointed at the fallen man's head, the acrid stench of gunpowder once again thick in the air. They stared at each other for a moment, and Bennett realized how close they had both once again come to dying in this house.

Erin lowered her gun, scanned the great room behind her one last time, then made her way down the stairway. Bennett got up and went to embrace her but Erin stopped him abruptly.

"Your BlackBerry," she said as she pulled out her own.

"What about it?" asked Jon.

"Do you have it on you?"

"Of course," he replied. "Why?"

"Quick, turn it off," she replied as she did the same. "They must have tracked us here. That's how they found us. They triangulated the signals from our phones. We need to get out of here—fast."

She was right. How could they not have thought of it sooner? Bennett turned off his Blackberry and pulled out his SIM card. On it were the addresses, phone numbers, and e-mail accounts of everybody he knew on Wall Street, in Washington, and in all of the capitals he and Erin had been to around the world over the last few years. It was not something he dared lose.

"I checked the guys upstairs," Erin said, rifling through the pockets of the man she'd just shot. "Nothing—no ID, no passport."

But this time was different. On him, she found a set of car keys and a cell phone—a cell phone with a built-in camera. She snapped a few shots of all three men before Bennett insisted they get out while they still could. Then they raced outside, found the men's black Mercedes, and "borrowed" it, at least for a while.

34

★ ★
★

To their relief, everyone in the Shochat house was still asleep.

They snuck down to the basement, and while Bennett took a quick shower, Erin booted up the desktop computer. She quickly logged back on to the CIA satellite account, reentered the coordinates for Mordechai's house, and soon had a live, wide shot of his entire neighborhood. For the moment, all appeared calm—no police cars, no ambulances, no media. By daybreak, that would change. But at least they had a few hours' head start.

Next she hacked into the Israeli police department's database, using a back door she had learned in her years with the CIA. She immediately uploaded the photos of the men who had tried to kill them and ran a trace. It came back negative. The men weren't locals. She entered the license plate of the Mercedes they had used. Not surprisingly, it was stolen.

Then she logged on to the Interpol database and tried again. This time she got hits on all three attackers. They were Italians—two from Rome, one from Milan. They were members of an underground radical faction known as the Legion, wanted for bombings, bank robberies, and assassinations in France, Spain, Holland, and Germany. The Interpol files had vital stats on all of the men—when and where they'd been born, names of their parents, criminal records, etc.—but little on the Legion itself. It was believed to be a splinter group of the Red Brigades, but that was about all Erin could glean without a higher clearance code.

She e-mailed images of each man to Indira Rajiv at Langley, along with a brief note explaining what had just happened at Mordechai's house.

can you trace this and get back to me, raj? i need info on the legion asap . . . thanks—erin.

She hit *Send* and closed her eyes for a few minutes. She was exhausted, but the attack must mean they were doing something right. The very fact that someone was gunning for them meant Mordechai and Barak and their little band of treasure hunters had been on to something. Someone *was* systematically hunting down anyone trying to solve the mystery of the Copper Scroll. It didn't prove the Cracker Jack box contained a prize. But it did prove that someone somewhere was rattled by the thought.

Suddenly, Erin opened her eyes, sat up straight in her chair, and began typing on the computer again. She brought up the Yahoo! home page, clicked on *Mail*, and typed in Mordechai's ID. She guessed at his password. She was wrong.

Invalid ID or password, came the response in bright red letters. *Please try again.*

So she did. She tried every password she could think of—his name, his wife's name, the numbers of his birthday, the numbers of his birthday backward, his wife's name backward, and so forth. But she struck out every time.

The door opened behind her.

"Mordechai's password," Erin called over her shoulder. "Do you know it?"

"To what?" Bennett asked as he dried and combed his hair.

"His Yahoo! account."

"I don't know. Why?"

Erin swiveled around in her chair. "Come on. You know the passcodes to get into his house, onto his elevators. You're telling me you don't know how to break into his e-mail account?"

Bennett shook his head. "He never asked me to read his mail."

"Well, think, Jon, think."

"Why? What are you after?"

"It's just a hunch," Erin demurred. "I could be wrong, but . . ."

"A hunch about what?" Bennett pressed.

"Just help me break in."

* * *

Bennett was still at it as the sun came up.

Erin stepped out of the shower, wrapped a towel around herself, and came to check on his progress. He had three pages of possible passwords that he had written down, entered into the Yahoo! system, and then crossed off as rejected.

"How's it going?" she asked, oddly refreshed though she hadn't slept a wink. She leaned over his shoulder and gave him a kiss on the cheek.

"It's no use," he said, his eyes at half-mast, desperate to crawl back into bed and take her with him. "Spymaster Rule #1—you can't break into a Mossad chief's e-mail account. It simply can't be done. Period. End of sentence. It's impossible. You should know that better than anyone."

"Wait a minute—that's it," she said.

"What's it?"

"Can I sit there a moment?" said Erin.

"Sure, if you tell me what's going on." Nevertheless, he got up and let her have the chair, looking on over her shoulder.

She did a quick search for English translations of the Bible. From there she narrowed the search to New Testament translations online. Then she picked one and typed in the word *impossible*. Thirteen results popped up. She scanned the list.

There it was. Luke 1:37—"For nothing is impossible with God." It was Mordechai's life creed. She found the log-in page again and tried *Luke1:37* as the password. It didn't work. She tried *Luke137*. Nothing.

"Come on, we need some sleep," Bennett insisted. "We'll try again later."

Erin sighed. "I know, you're right," she whispered and began shutting off the lights. "I just can't believe I can't crack this thing."

"You will," he promised her as he headed over to the couch to lie down. "Just for a few minutes," he insisted. "You just need some rest. We both do, and then I promise we'll get up and pray about it and I'm sure God will show us something. Jeremiah 33:3—isn't that what Mordechai was always quoting to us?"

That was it, Erin realized. *"Call to Me and I will answer you, and I will tell you great and mighty things, which you do not know."*

She turned the lights back on, logged back on, entered *Jeremiah33:3* and waited. Again she got an error message. She tried *Jeremiah333*, but that didn't work either. Finally, in desperation, she tried *J333* and gasped.

"We're in!" she declared, only to find her husband already fast asleep.

★   ★   ★

Hundreds of e-mails were sitting there unopened.

They were waiting for replies that would never come. Erin had no idea where to begin. She wasn't even entirely sure what she was looking for. All she had was a hunch—perhaps the "clue" that had stirred up this hornet's nest had come in by e-mail. Perhaps Mordechai had written to Doron or Barak or the rest of the team about the clue. This was a man, after all, who had communicated with most people most of the time by e-mail. It was inconceivable to her that there wouldn't be something useful here. And the huge number of unopened e-mails was an encouraging sign. Maybe she'd gotten there first.

She quickly sorted the in-box by date received, then isolated all the e-mails that had come in during the first two weeks after the firestorm. As best as she could recall, that was roughly the time Mordechai had first come across the clue, according to Doron.

But the more she hunted for the proverbial needle in the haystack, the more Erin was taken aback by the enormous number of e-mails she found that Mordechai had written and received that had to do with her—with finding her, with letting the White House and CIA know she had been found, with organizing an extraction to get her and Jon out of Russia after the firestorm had hit. There were e-mails to senior officials in the Mossad, to Ken Costello, to Indira Rajiv, to Ruth Bennett, and to dozens of colleagues and associates of Mordechai's located throughout Iran and the former USSR.

Until now, Erin had had no idea just how involved Mordechai had been with their extraction. She knew he was a key player, of course. She and Jon had, after all, been flown not to Washington after leaving Russian airspace but to Jerusalem. They'd spent weeks recovering from their ordeal in Mordechai's guest rooms. Only now did it suddenly dawn on her how much Jon and Mordechai had shielded her from the specifics of her rescue so she could focus solely on the rest and medical care she so badly needed after being held by Gogolov's forces.

What's more, she had unexpectedly uncovered a treasure trove of Mordechai's thinking on all kinds of political and spiritual issues, issues about which he was corresponding with people all over the world. She was eager to explore more, but there was one e-mail that now caught her eye.

A gift, was all the subject heading said.

It was from someone named Kenneth Donovan. It was not a name she recognized, but she was curious about what might be inside.

35

★ ★
★

"Jon, get up—you need to see this."

He heard the words, and the urgency in Erin's voice, but it took a moment to make sense of it all. He stared at the ceiling and at the ceiling fan he'd been too busy to notice earlier, but he dreaded the notion of being awake so soon.

"What have you got?" he groaned.

"Black gold," Erin replied. "Texas tea."

"What are you talking about?"

He forced himself off the couch and stumbled over to her. His bleary eyes took a while to adjust to the words on the screen, but when they did, he was suddenly and completely awake.

```
Dear Dr. Mordechai—
    Please don't toss this into your spam file.
    You don't know me. In fact, you'll never meet me.
But you know my kid brother. Or rather, you did, until
his death in October 1996.
    My brother was Raymond S. Donovan. Most of his family
and friends believed (and still do, to this day), that
Ray was a pilot for Continental. But you were among a
handful of people who knew the truth—that he was a NOC
officer in the CIA's Directorate of Operations.
```

I only learned the truth upon being informed of his death by a phone call from the director of Central Intelligence and becoming executor of his will. That's when I gained access to his safe-deposit box and to the secrets it contained.

I am writing to you now because in the box was a large, sealed envelope with your name on it. I assumed Ray wanted me to get this to you, but frankly, I didn't know how. I had no idea who you were. The CIA proved to be no help. I couldn't find a shred of information about you on the Internet. So I finally gave up.

But now your "Ezekiel Option" memo has hit the news, and suddenly the whole world knows who you are. I see you have a Web site and an e-mail address. So I'm passing this whole mess on to you.

But first, a confession: When I couldn't track you down back in '96, I decided to open the envelope and see what was inside. It was the most foolish thing I've ever done, and I've done some pretty stupid things in my day. Inside was an audiocassette, made by Ray. There was also a copy of an old leather journal he bought somewhere in southern Syria. It's all in Arabic. It makes no sense to me. But the tape is pretty clear, and it has shattered my life.

I thought I knew my brother. But the more I learn of the life he was really living, the more I realize how little I knew. We weren't as close as I thought. Little Ray was living a lie. It turns out he was a felon and a traitor, and I don't know how I could have failed him so badly.

As I don't have a mailing address for you, I've converted the audiocassette to an MP3 file and the journal into a PDF file. I've been living with this nightmare for too long. It's yours now. May you have more strength than I.

Sincerely,
Kenneth J. Donovan

Erin double-clicked on the audio file, and suddenly they were listening to the voice of Ray Donovan.

"Dr. Mordechai, greetings from the hereafter. If you are listening to this, it can only be for one reason. I have failed, and thus I am dead, and my brother, Kenny, has found a way to track you down and get you this tape and the accompanying journal.

"You and I first met at the Farm nine years ago, when you addressed my class of new Agency recruits. We met again three years ago when you were helping my colleague Craig Harkin and me train Kurdish rebels to run sabotage missions in northern Iraq. Ring any bells? Remember me now? If not, perhaps this will jog your memory. About eighteen months ago, you took Craig and me to meet with some Bedouin trackers you thought we should hire. We were scheduled to meet them at that archeological museum in Qumran, and while we were waiting for them to show up, you and I got into a big argument over the Dead Sea Scrolls.

"You said they were proof that the Bible we have today is the exact same one people had two thousand years ago. No changes. No alterations. Word for word, the same. I said religion was fine for old people who needed a crutch but had no serious basis in science and history. You were very gracious about the 'old people' crack, for which I want to apologize again. But I'll never forget the story you told me next, the story of the Copper Scroll. You insisted that one day the Key Scroll would be found as well, that the Second Temple treasures would be found, that the Ark of the Covenant would be found, and that all these would be further proof— if more were needed—that the Bible is not a myth, not a legend, not some sort of superstitious fiction, but rock-solid history, history that one day would explode into the headlines.

"To your face, I suggested we just agree to disagree. Inside, I was laughing at you all the way back to my hotel. But I have to admit, I was intrigued by what you'd said—not about the religious part, mind you. What intrigued me was the idea of buried treasure—billions of dollars of buried treasure—scattered throughout the West Bank.

"And then something unexpected happened.

"It was around Christmas 1995. Craig and I were in Syria. We were set to meet the economic attaché from the Iraqi embassy whom we were running as a double agent. He was feeding us intel on Saddam's ties to

Hafez al-Assad. We were supposed to meet him that afternoon in a book-store on the east side of Damascus.

"As we waited for the guy to show up, I was browsing through a wooden crate of used books, and I came across an old leather journal that caught my eye. It was handwritten in colloquial Arabic but had originally been written by a rabbi. The first entry was dated December 9, 1924. The last entry was June 9, 1967. How the bookstore got it, I have no idea. Why the store was selling it rather than burning it, I have no idea. Clearly the store owner hadn't ever read it. But there it was. I didn't ask any questions. I just bought it and stuffed it in my briefcase until after our meeting with the Iraqi.

"But when I got back to the safe house we were using, I showed the journal to Craig. What immediately caught his attention, as it had mine, was the rabbi's description of a network of ancient smuggling tunnels south of Damascus, running under the Golan Heights. According to local legends, the tunnels were dug in the first century BC by local merchants trying to smuggle goods in and out of Palestine without getting hit by Ro-man taxes. According to the rabbi's journal, Arab groups were using the tunnels by the late 1920s and early 1930s to smuggle arms and explosives into Palestine to fight the Jews, and as you read through the journal, the rabbi wrote urgent letters to Jewish leaders in Jerusalem, warning them of the old smuggling routes. Then we came to a passage on page 55, in which the rabbi explains that the routes run through territory that used to be home to his great-great-grandparents, an area known to locals as *Sechab*."

Erin paused the audio file. Bennett looked at her in disbelief. She'd done it. This was it. This was the clue Mordechai had been talking about.

36

★ ★
★

Erin pulled up the PDF file.

She scrolled down to page 55, found the passage to which Donovan referred, and read it aloud, translating from the Arabic.

> *"Sechab runs right along*
> *the edge of the Syrian border,*
> *near a place some local Arabs*
> *call Tel Shihab.*
> *It's a sacred place to my family.*
> *My grandfather calls it Kochlit,*
> *and speaks of it with*
> *almost mystical reverence."*

Erin hit *Play* again. Donovan actually read the passage aloud, and then continued his analysis.

"Dr. Mordechai, I have to tell you, no sooner did I finish reading that than the hair on the back of my neck began standing on end. I knew those names. I'd heard them before. Finally I realized where. After you told me the story of the Copper Scroll, I went back to the States and did as much research as I possibly could, and I remembered line 64: 'In the tunnel which is in Sechab, to the north of Kochlit, which opens towards the north, and has graves in its entrance: a copy of this text and its explanation and their measurements and the inventory . . . item by item.'

"Now, as I understand it, scholars long believed the name *Sechab* referred to plots of land owned by the religious commune that wrote the Dead Sea Scrolls and thus was a place where the group could easily have hidden the Temple treasures without attracting undue attention. Some said the plots were in the Qumran area, where the other scrolls were found. Others said it had to be farther north, perhaps near Tiberias. But the truth is, no one was ever sure where *Sechab* was. In my research, though, I found a quote by Father Bargil Pixner. As you no doubt recall, Pixner was a member of the original team of archeologists from L'Ecole Biblique and the American School of Oriental Research who discovered the Copper Scroll, and he said, and I quote:

> "'*They [the Essenes] had treasures hidden away and I think that those [hiding] places are the ones mentioned in the Copper Scroll. [I have deduced that] they must have owned these areas in order to have had access to them [to hide the treasures]. These hiding places were called Kochlit, monastic centers of the community. One Kochlit was in Qumran itself, although it was not called Qumran since this is an Arabic word, but was called Saccacah, a place mentioned in the Bible. A second [Kochlit] was on Mount Zion, and a third one, in my opinion, was in an area of the Yarmuk River, south of Damascus.*'

"On the map on page 60 of the journal," Donovan continued, "you'll see the Sea of Galilee on the west, the Golan Heights dead center, and the Yarmuk River to the east, running down the mountains and through a place called Wadi Shihab. The river, as you can see, supposedly leads to a waterfall, which lies just to the north of Tel Shihab."

"Stop the tape," Bennett said.

Erin did. "What is it?" she asked.

"Scroll through the PDF file a bit farther," he said. "I want to find that map."

Sure enough, on page 60, she found the map drawn by the rabbi. She started the recording again.

"To be honest, Craig and I couldn't resist the temptation to verify the map. So under the guise of needing more intel for our project with the Kurds—Operation November Thunder—we requested updated, high-resolution satellite photography of the Golan Heights and the Yarmuk River. Sure enough, using thermal imaging, we could clearly see traces of a tunnel running from a cave on the Israeli side of the Golan, through the mountain, across the demilitarized zone, and winding up in a cave at the base of the waterfall. The opening of the cave is not that far from a forward Syrian monitoring post, but since the cave itself is inside the DMZ, we doubt it's ever been explored by the Syrians, much less the Israelis.

"Now here's my point, Dr. Mordechai—I am absolutely convinced the Key Scroll is hidden at the end of that tunnel. So is Craig. We know the CIA would never let us explore it. The whole place is guarded by barbed wire, land mines, and impressive electronic surveillance, not to mention ten thousand crack Syrian troops, all on a hair trigger to go to war with the Israelis on a moment's notice. One wrong move and *kaboom*! But we can't help it. We're going to find a way into that tunnel, even if it kills us.

"Which obviously it has. Craig and I are dead now. That's the only reason you're hearing this tape and reading this journal. Perhaps we died in the tunnels. Perhaps someone found out what we were up to and tried to stop us. Perhaps the Israelis or the Syrians captured us along the way and we've died in prison or by firing squad. It doesn't really matter. All that matters is that someone finds the treasure. I believe it should be you. All the best. Maybe I will see you on the other side."

And with that, the audio file came to an end.

Bennett was stunned. So was Erin.

"No wonder Mordechai was so sure he was on the verge of a major breakthrough," she said. "He was."

"He was," Bennett echoed, staring at the computer monitor and wondering if Barak had heard this. Had the others? Had they read the journal as well?

"Did you know these guys?" he asked instead.

"Who, Harkin and Donovan?" said Erin.

"Right."

"No, not personally. But I'd heard of them—rumors really. People said they went rogue. As far as I know, the Agency never did find their bodies. They just listed them as missing and presumed dead. But there was always something a bit fishy about it. I'm not sure if their files were ever formally closed."

"What about this brother?" said Bennett. "Do a search. If we can find him, we might be able to learn more."

Erin swiveled back around in her chair and typed the name *Kenneth J. Donovan* into a news search engine and hit Enter. A second later, a headline popped up from the *Rocky Mountain News:* "Local Man Commits Suicide on Thanksgiving."

Bennett shook his head. That had been just weeks after the firestorm. Everywhere they turned, the death toll kept rising. He got up and paced the room.

"What are you thinking?" asked Erin.

"I'm thinking we may not be the only people who have this journal," he replied, the anxiety showing on his face. "If we are, it won't be for long. The original is still out there somewhere. Who knows who got ahold of it after Donovan committed suicide?"

"If it really was a suicide," Erin noted.

"You think he might have been murdered?"

"It would certainly fit with everything else we've found."

"You may be right," said Bennett, mulling over their options. "What about sending an e-mail to Rajiv? Maybe she knew Donovan and Harkin. She might have something that could help us."

"Good idea," said Erin. "Give me a few minutes."

"We need to move fast," Bennett insisted. "When you're done with that, get Natasha up. Have her listen to the tape and see what she thinks. Then print out a copy of the journal and delete the file. I'm going to get the car. I'll meet you at the Damascus Gate in one hour. If for whatever reason I don't show, don't wait. Go without me."

"What are you talking about?" Erin asked. "Go where?"

"To the DMZ," Bennett said as he headed up the stairs. "We need to find the Key Scroll before anyone else does."

37

★ ★
★

It was Salvador Lucente's first visit to the new Iraqi capital.

He had met President Al-Hassani on numerous occasions, including a weekend at Camp David with President MacPherson and at the opening session of the United Nations General Assembly the previous September. The Iraqi president had also been a guest of the E.U. leadership in Brussels twice before, and they spoke together by phone or video-conference at least once a week.

But there was something different about actually landing at the dazzling new Babylon International Airport and being driven to the Great Tower of the People in a twenty-vehicle screaming motorcade down massive new highways, all paid for by U.S. and E.U. taxpayers.

How quickly the world could change, Lucente realized.

It hadn't been that long since Saddam Hussein had brutalized these people and forced them to live in such squalor. Nor had it been that long since America destroyed Saddam's regime and fought a brutal war of attrition with Iraqi insurgents. Who could have imagined in those dark days when the entire country teetered on the brink of civil war that Iraq would finally crush the rebellion, see order restored to its streets, and become a magnet for capitalists rather than car bombers?

The motorcade passed a sign announcing the upcoming opening of the famed Hanging Gardens. They passed the dazzling new Iraqi

Museum of Archeology and Antiquities, complete with its own IMAX theater bringing the ancient history of Babylonia to life in 3-D and THX surround sound. Lucente was stunned by how much construction was under way in the city, by how much progress had been made in just a few short years, and it suddenly struck him how powerful a force Al-Hassani and his people were rapidly becoming.

☆ ☆ ☆

"Welcome, my friend. How wonderful to see you again."

"It is an honor to be here, Your Excellency," Lucente responded, receiving from Al-Hassani the traditional Arab kiss on each cheek.

"Come, come, let us enjoy the morning sunshine," the Iraqi president insisted, leading Lucente through his private office to the balcony overlooking the city. "Have a seat. Make yourself comfortable. Breakfast will be served to us in a few minutes, but first some coffee? Fresh-squeezed orange juice? What would you like?"

The two men settled in, exchanged pleasantries, and ate their breakfasts, admiring the views and sharing tidbits of news about the relief efforts ongoing across the region. But when their plates were cleared, they finally turned to the business at hand.

"Mr. President," Lucente began at last, "as you know I have just come from Jerusalem, where I toured the areas of the worst devastation and had some very frank conversations with Prime Minister Doron. And as you requested, I insisted that he forestall any plans to build a Jewish Temple until, at the very least, we can all reengage in final status negotiations and hammer out a peace treaty between the Israelis and Palestinians once and for all."

"And how did the prime minister respond?" asked Al-Hassani as he began lighting up his pipe.

"Let's just say he was noncommittal," Lucente explained.

"You don't think the aid package you offered will be enough?"

"Frankly, I doubt it."

"Why?"

"It's simple, really," said Lucente. "At the moment, Europe is getting 60 percent of our oil from Medexco. Doron acts like he needs our aid. He'd love as much international assistance as possible. Who wouldn't?

But with oil topping 175 euros a barrel, he knows full well that he doesn't need us as much as we need him right now."

"Which, I assume, is why you are here."

"It is, Mr. President. Our economies are choking. Unemployment is soaring. We can't operate with oil prices this high. We have got to get oil flowing out of the Gulf states again within the next few months. My advisors tell me that's possible, but it will take an enormous effort, and it's one that we simply cannot take on by ourselves."

Lucente noted that Iraq was in a far better position to take the lead in bringing the petroleum facilities in Saudi Arabia, Kuwait, Iran, and the other regional OPEC players online, and doing it quickly.

"Right now you and the Israelis are experiencing a great windfall," Lucente noted. "But you know as well as I do that if the global economy slips into a depression, everyone loses. That's why I have been asked by the various leaders of the E.U. to make our position very plain: you must get oil prices down below a hundred euros a barrel by summer, or I am afraid we will have to consider some unpleasant scenarios."

Startled, Al-Hassani stared into Lucente's eyes. Had he heard the man correctly?

"Mr. Foreign Minister, did you just threaten me?"

"Of course not, Mr. President," Lucente replied coolly. "You know how much Europe has done to rebuild your country. I have no doubt you will now help us in our time of need."

"Or else?" asked Al-Hassani.

"I wouldn't put it that way," Lucente replied.

"Didn't you just?"

Lucente paused a moment, then leaned toward Al-Hassani and spoke almost in a whisper. "You have a formidable military, Mr. President. Two hundred thousand troops, armed with the latest weaponry. I know. Because we—NATO and the Americans—recruited them, trained them, equipped them, and helped them gain combat experience in crushing the insurgency. But do not deceive yourself. Your forces are not yet ready to face the combined forces of a unified Western alliance determined to achieve energy security at all costs. And who might your allies be? You think I don't know about the little conclave you held here the other day? Did you think you could shuttle in leaders from all over the region without our notice? They cannot help you now. Do not miscalculate as Iraqi leaders are wont to do. Your country cannot afford a misstep."

＊　＊　＊

The black Mercedes headed north on Highway 90.

If they weren't stopped and arrested first, they would be in Tiberias in less than an hour. Natasha's cousin had a house up there, in the hills overlooking the Sea of Galilee. They would go there first, Bennett had decided, hunker down until dark, then head for the Golan Heights. Time was not on their side, but none of them thought it wise to be seen in the mountains in daylight.

＊　＊　＊

"We want Russia's seat," Al-Hassani began.

"So does Israel," Lucente countered.

He could tell by the look in Al-Hassani's eyes that he had caught him by surprise.

"They have not made that public," Al-Hassani noted cautiously.

"Nor have you," said Lucente. "Doron just told me yesterday. By now he has talked to the Americans."

"Nevertheless," said Al-Hassani, "if you want our oil, we want a permanent seat on the Security Council. It can be Russia's. It can be new. But it is nonnegotiable. We want assurances that neither the E.U. or the U.S. or the U.N. will interfere with our efforts to unify the region's political and economic structures.".

"In other words, you want carte blanche to rebuild the Babylonian Empire."

"We have the same right to reorganize our region of the world as you had in reorganizing Europe. We are not asking for your permission. We are looking for assurances that no one will interfere."

"Such as?"

"Withdrawal of foreign troops from the region. Coordination of all relief and reconstruction efforts through my office, not through the U.N. Guaranteed accession to the WTO. A few others. I will give you a list."

Lucente took it all in without tipping his hand one way or the other.

"There is one thing more," said Al-Hassani.

Lucente waited. Al-Hassani said nothing.

"Let me guess," Lucente said at last. "Jerusalem."

Al-Hassani nodded. "The U.N. must seize control of the Temple Mount. The Jews must not be allowed to build anything there—not a Temple, not a visitor center, not a falafel stand, nothing. Ever. Period."

"Or else?" asked Lucente.

"I wouldn't put it that way," said Al-Hassani, a slight twinkle in his eye. "Didn't you just?"

38
★ ★
★

"Mr. Prime Minister, we have a situation developing."

Doron looked up to see a very agitated Avi Zadok, flanked by the heads of the Shin Bet and the Border Patrol along with the chief of police.

"What have you got?" Doron asked, removing his reading glasses and setting them on the desk.

"Three more murders," Zadok explained.

"Where?"

"Eli Mordechai's house."

"*What?* When?" asked Doron, standing.

"We just found them, but the bodies have been there most of the night."

"Are they connected to the other killings last night?"

"Ballistics is running tests right now. We should know soon. But yes, we believe they're connected to the killings at the café in the Jewish Quarter and to the others in the Arab market a short while later. We're just not sure how yet."

"Have you found any witnesses?"

"The police are canvassing the neighborhood, but nothing so far."

"Keep me up to speed, Avi. I want reports every fifteen minutes."

★ ★ ★

Lucente looked the Iraqi president in the eye.

"I'm not sure if I can deliver on the Temple Mount."

But Al-Hassani didn't believe him. "Do not take me for a fool, Salvador. I know Mogande is dying. I know you're angling for the secretary-general position. And I know you have almost all the votes you need to be nominated—*almost*. But my sources tell me that China is threatening to veto you unless you get oil flowing out of the Middle East again. Which means you need a deal with me, and you need it quick."

"And you trust these sources?" Lucente asked.

"With my life," Al-Hassani said firmly.

Lucente turned and looked out across Babylon, glowing in the morning sun. "Very well, you are correct," he confirmed. "China would be more supportive if I can help them with their energy needs."

"So, no deal with me, no job for you?" asked Al-Hassani.

"Not quite, my friend," Lucente countered. "As I said before, if you don't cut a deal favorable to the global powers, I assure you, I will be the least of your worries. But on one thing you are correct: I am in more of a bargaining mood than the rest of the Security Council. So let me be clear: if you cut a deal with me, one that I can announce to the rest of the world, I will guarantee you Russia's seat on the Security Council."

Al-Hassani leaned back in his seat. "And the rest?"

"Everything but the Temple Mount."

"Come, come, Salvador," said Al-Hassani, lighting his pipe again. "You can do better than that."

"I cannot guarantee the internationalization of the Temple Mount, Mr. President," Lucente responded. "In case you hadn't noticed, Israel has just become an economic superpower. Even if you can get oil flowing out of the Gulf again in the next three to six months, most of the world will still be buying most of their oil from Medexco. They have us over a barrel, Mustafa, literally. My hands are tied."

Al-Hassani grew angry. "You want to be the secretary-general? You want to bring about global peace and prosperity? Then how can you, of all people, even consider for one moment the notion of the Jews building the

Temple on land sacred to all Middle Easterners? Do you not know what that will unleash?"

"I never said I favored the idea," Lucente insisted. "I'm just being honest with you. I don't know if I can stop it. But I can promise you this: I will try."

★   ★   ★

As soon as Lucente left, Khalid Tariq rushed into the room.

"Your Excellency, it's Mariano. He says it's urgent."

Al-Hassani accepted the call. "What is it, Viggo?"

"Sir, we have a problem."

"What is it?"

"Alonzo and Scarpetti are dead. So is Miletto. Bennett and his wife killed them and took their car."

"What about the Barak girl? Did they get her, at least?"

"No, I don't think so."

"*What?* How could this have happened? You assured me both Baraks would be dead by now, did you not?"

"I said it might take a few days."

"And it's been a few days," countered Al-Hassani. "Where are they now?"

"They're on the run," said Mariano. "I don't know where. But at this point there are only two realistic options."

"I'm listening."

"First, they're fleeing the country, in which case they'll go dark and we won't find them until they choose to pop back up on the grid."

"And the other?"

"They know where the Key Scroll is, and they're on their way to get it."

Al-Hassani's face turned dark red. "*You cannot let that happen, Viggo. You must stop them, whatever it takes.*"

"Yes, Your Excellency," said Mariano. "I've got another team in Cyprus. I've already called them. They should be in Tel Aviv by nightfall. In the meantime, I'll try to contact our mole and see if I can pick up their trail."

"You had better, Viggo. Or I will have your head on a platter."

39

Bennett glanced back in his rearview mirror.

Natasha was staring out the window. Her eyes were red and there were smudges of mascara on her cheeks.

He looked at Erin, who was poring over a map, no doubt planning a route to the Golan and several escape routes back. The three of them had been driving in near silence for almost forty-five minutes. They would be in Tiberias any minute. Perhaps it was time to break the ice.

"You okay?" he asked, again looking into the rearview mirror.

Natasha wiped her eyes but did not look up. "I guess."

"You want to talk about it?"

"Not particularly."

Erin set her map down and turned to Natasha. "I would like to have gotten to know your grandfather more."

Natasha nodded. "You would have liked him."

"I already did."

They drove in silence another few minutes. Then, still gazing out the window at farmland covered with oil wells, Natasha said, "He was convinced he was going to live to see the Temple rebuilt. For most of my life, I thought he was crazy. Even when I was studying to follow in his footsteps, I thought his obsession with the Temple and the Ark was all a little much."

It was quiet again for a few minutes; then Natasha picked up the thought.

"It's funny," she said softly. "I thought of archeology as the study of the past, but my grandfather always said it was about the future. 'What good is digging up relics today if it doesn't affect how we live tomorrow?' he used to say. To him, finding the Temple treasures wasn't simply about proving that the Jews controlled Jerusalem thousands of years ago. It was about setting into motion the building of the Third Temple and thus fulfilling the words of the Hebrew prophets."

"But you didn't buy it?" asked Erin.

"He was the zealot in the family, not me. After my parents died, I decided there couldn't be a God so capricious that He would leave me and millions of other children around the world orphaned. But my grandfather never gave up on me. He wanted me to be a believer."

☆   ☆   ☆

Again they drove for a while in silence.

Then Jon spoke up. "Forgive me, Natasha, but I'm curious. What exactly do Jewish people believe when it comes to rebuilding the Temple?"

In some ways, Natasha dreaded the question. It had been a mistake to say anything. She would have preferred to suffer in silence. But then again, her grandfather had taught her well, and perhaps the chance to pass along some of his knowledge would help keep her mind off of how utterly alone she felt without him.

"That's like asking Christians what they think about the pope," she replied. "Ask a Catholic and you'll get one answer. Ask the Greek or Russian Orthodox, and you'll get quite another. Everything depends on your point of view."

"I've heard some people say the building of the Temple will precede the coming of the Messiah," Erin said. "Others say the Messiah will build it Himself."

"Well, you're right about that," Natasha replied. "It's been an age-old debate. Even some of our wisest sages were confused. Read Maimonides. At various points, he made the case for both sides. But the truth is, until the last few months, most Israelis—secular ones, anyway—didn't believe the Temple would *ever* be rebuilt, nor did they much care. With the Dome of the Rock and the Al-Aksa Mosque there, it just seemed impossible. Obviously, religious Jews—particularly the Orthodox and ultra-Orthodox—believed it would happen, though most couldn't imagine how.

"That said, ever since we reunified Jerusalem and took control of the Temple Mount in 1967, the movement to rebuild has certainly been growing from just a handful of true believers into a very powerful force. They've been publishing books and holding conferences about it. They've been making implements for Temple service and training priests in Temple rituals. And then came October 13, 2004."

"What happened then?" asked Bennett.

They were now approaching the outskirts of the city, and Natasha could see the Sea of Galilee glistening in the morning sun.

"That was the day the Sanhedrin was reconvened—right here in Tiberias, actually—for the first time in over 1,600 years."

"*The* Sanhedrin?" Erin asked, astonished. "The same one that condemned Jesus and sent Him to Pilate, hoping the Romans would execute Him?"

"Well, most Jews don't exactly think of *that* as the group's defining moment, but yes, that's the one," said Natasha. "The original Sanhedrin was the governing religious council of the Temple, made up of the seventy-one most prominent rabbis in the country. They met in the Temple. They oversaw its daily life and practice. After Jerusalem was sacked and the Temple destroyed in the year 70, the Sanhedrin went underground. They were convinced the city and the sanctuary would be rebuilt. They were convinced the Messiah would come and make it all right, and they believed it would all happen soon. But years turned into decades and decades into centuries, and around the year 425, those who were running the council finally gave up hope, and the Sanhedrin disbanded."

"Until 2004," said Erin.

"That's right," said Natasha. "That's when the Sanhedrin was reconvened. But that was only the beginning. On June 6, 2005, the Sanhedrin made news again—big news, actually, at least in our house. I remember their statement verbatim because my grandfather drilled it into my head, night and day. 'The Sanhedrin calls upon all groups who work in the area of Temple and Temple Mount–related research and activity to begin to prepare detailed architectural plans for the construction of the Holy

Temple, towards the goal of its establishment in its proper place. The Sanhedrin will establish a forum of architects and engineers whose goal will be to implement this decision, so that detailed working plans are effectively brought to an operational stage.'

"That's when I began to sit up and take notice of all this Temple talk," Natasha confided. "Because it suddenly seemed like the train was really leaving the station. Now remember, this was all long before the War of Gog and Magog. Few people in Israel realized what was coming or that the Muslim holy sites were going to be destroyed in a firestorm. But we still knew the rebirth of the Sanhedrin and the call to prepare detailed plans for the Temple were dramatic developments. Even me. And in my grandfather's eyes, they were prophetic ones. Why? Because it meant a significant shift had occurred in Jewish thinking. No longer did the majority of rabbis in Israel believe the Messiah would come and build the Temple. Now they believed that they were required to build the Temple themselves, in the last days, *and then* the Messiah would come."

A few moments later, they found Ehad Ha'am Street, and Natasha tapped Bennett on the shoulder and pointed. "That one," she said. "That's my cousin's house—the big one on the left."

40

★ ★
★

They pulled into the driveway.

"What did you say your cousin does?" Erin asked.

It was an enormous house, with gardens surrounding it and a spacious two-car garage, all newly built on a cliff overlooking the Sea of Galilee.

"She's the new VP of marketing for Medexco," said Natasha. "Miriam Gozal. Do you know her?"

Neither Jon nor Erin did, but it reminded them both that they ought to give Dmitri Galishnikov a call when the coast was clear. They had just seen him at the wedding, and he would no doubt be mourning Mordechai's death.

"It doesn't look like anyone is here," said Bennett after ringing the doorbell several times and peering in the vestibule window and seeing no one.

"She might be in Europe," Natasha said. "For the life of me I don't know why she bought this place. She's never here."

They pulled the Mercedes into the garage and began poking around the enormous, three-level home. It had seven bedrooms, four bathrooms, a gorgeous new Italian kitchen, a huge office on the top floor, and no sign that anyone lived there but the cousin. Each floor had a wrap-around balcony. On one of them Natasha paused, staring out over the small but growing city of Tiberias below them and the Golan Heights on the other side of the sea. Not wanting to leave her alone, the Bennetts remained with her for a while, trying to enjoy the view despite all that had happened.

"You look like you have another question, Jon," Natasha said softly.

"I'm fine."

"Really, it's okay. I'd rather answer your questions than wallow in my grief."

"Well, it's just that I'm still curious about the Temple treasures and the Ark."

"What do you mean?"

"I mean, besides all these theories that you and your grandfather and these ex-CIA guys have about the Copper Scroll, does the Bible actually *say* they'll ever be found? Is that in any of the prophecies, or is this just . . . ?"

"Just what?" Natasha asked. "A fool's errand?"

Bennett shrugged.

"You mean, is this thing really worth risking your life for?" said Natasha.

"Right."

"Ever read Jeremiah 27:21-22?" she asked.

"I don't remember," said Bennett.

"I have a Bible," Erin said. She pulled one out of her purse and looked up the passage.

> *Yes, thus says the LORD of hosts,*
> *the God of Israel, concerning*
> *the vessels that are left*
> *in the house of the LORD*
> *and in the house of the*
> *king of Judah and in Jerusalem,*
> *"They will be carried to Babylon*
> *and they will be there*
> *until the day I visit them,"*
> *declares the LORD.*

> *"Then I will bring them back*
> *and restore them to this place."*

"See that?" said Natasha, looking out over the water. "God promised to watch over the Temple treasures and 'restore them' to the Jewish people when the next Temple was to be rebuilt. What's more, He kept that promise."

"You're saying if God restored the treasures once, He'll do it again?" asked Erin.

"That's what most rabbis believe," said Natasha. "That's certainly what my grandfather believed. So did Uncle Eli."

"And the Ark?" asked Bennett. "Is that all Hollywood, or is there really a snowball's chance somebody's going to find it someday?"

"I think we're really going to find it," said Natasha.

"Is the Ark mentioned in the Copper Scroll?" Erin wondered.

"Actually, no, not once," said Natasha. "Most scholars would tell you there's no connection. After all, you have to remember that the Ark was never in the Second Temple, so it seems unlikely that it would have been hidden away with the other Temple treasures."

"Then why are you so confident?"

"A few reasons," said Natasha. "Remember the Temple Scroll we saw back at the museum? The really long one?"

The Bennetts nodded.

"It's actually the longest of the Dead Sea Scrolls. But more important, it lays out remarkably detailed plans for the Third Temple and describes the First and Second Temple vessels and furnishings all being present and accounted for, including the Ark."

"Really?" asked Bennett. "What does it say?"

Natasha closed her eyes and drew up the words from deep within her soul.

> *"And two cherubim you shall make*
> *at both ends of the cover,*
> *the one cherub on this end,*
> *and the other end the second,*
> *spreading their wings over*

the place of the Ark,
and shielding the cover with
their wings above the Ark,
with their faces one to the other."

"That's fascinating," said Erin. "Are there any Scriptures to back that up?"

"There are," said Natasha, "Take a look at 2 Chronicles 35:3."

Erin quickly found the passage and read it aloud.

"King Josiah also said to the Levites,
who taught all Israel and
who were holy to the LORD:
'Put the holy ark in the house
which Solomon the son of David
king of Israel built; it will be
a burden on your shoulders no longer.
Now serve the LORD your God
and His people Israel.'"

"Now, what does that tell us?" asked Natasha. "It tells us that when men did evil in the sight of the Lord—like erecting an idol in the Holy of Holies, which King Manasseh did in 2 Chronicles 33—the priests who were still faithful to God actually removed the Ark from the Temple to keep it from being desecrated. They kept it hidden, possibly on the move, for years, until it was safe to bring it back. And then, when Josiah cleaned up the corruption of the Temple and turned the people's hearts back to God, he ordered the Ark brought back to the Temple, and the priests readily complied.

"Many Jewish scholars, and not a few Christian ones, see this passage as a precedent, proof that if God once protected the Ark and then made way for it to be 'rediscovered,' as it were, then He will do it again when the time for the Third Temple has come. But the passage that really got Uncle Eli excited a few weeks ago was Haggai 2:6-9."

Bennett looked over Erin's shoulder as she found the right page.

"You probably haven't spent much time studying the book of

Haggai," Natasha said. "Join the crowd. I haven't either. But about a month ago, Uncle Eli called us around one in the morning. He said he couldn't sleep. He was reading the ancient prophets, and suddenly became convinced that he'd hit the jackpot."

Erin read the passage aloud.

> *"For thus says the LORD of hosts,*
> *'Once more in a little while,*
> *I am going to shake the heavens*
> *and the earth, the sea also*
> *and the dry land. I will shake*
> *all the nations; and they will*
> *come with the wealth of all nations,*
> *and I will fill this house with glory,'*
> *says the LORD of hosts.*
> *'The silver is Mine and the gold is Mine,'*
> *declares the LORD of hosts.*
> *'The latter glory of this house*
> *will be greater than the former,'*
> *says the LORD of hosts,*
> *'and in this place I will give peace,'*
> *declares the LORD of hosts."*

"I have to admit," said Natasha, "I didn't see it at first. But as Uncle Eli explained it, it began to make too much sense. Look closely."

The Bennetts reread the verses.

"You see?" asked Natasha. "The Lord says He's going to 'shake the heavens and the earth.' In fact, He says He's going to 'shake all the nations.' As Uncle Eli pointed out, that's exactly what He did last October in fulfilling Ezekiel 38 and 39. Then, look what happens next. The Lord says He will bring 'the wealth of the nations' to Israel. That's happening too. Oil is over $200 a barrel. We've never had more money pouring in here. But, of course, that's not all. According to Haggai, the Lord will then 'fill this house with glory.'"

"A rebuilt Temple," said Bennett.

"Exactly," said Natasha. "The Third Temple, to be precise. Now look a bit farther. The Lord says He's going to fill the Temple with gold and silver, which He says are His."

"The Temple treasures," said Erin, amazed.

Natasha nodded and said, "Now look at verse 9. 'The latter glory of this house will be greater than the former,'" she noted. "I asked Uncle Eli what that meant, and I have to admit, skeptic though I am, his answer intrigued me. He reminded me that the Second Temple, which King Herod helped construct, was an incredible physical structure—far grander and more impressive than the Temple Solomon had built. But it certainly didn't have more glory than the first. Why? Because the First Temple had the Ark of the Covenant. The Ark was the resting place of God's glory. The Temple was originally built to be a home for the Ark, a home for God's glory. So while the Second Temple was remarkable in every way, it couldn't have more glory than the First Temple since it didn't have the Ark."

"Okay, keep going," said Bennett, beginning to see where she was headed.

"Well, just think about it, Jon," said Natasha. "Haggai was prophesying about a future Temple—a 'latter' Temple—that would have more glory than the Second Temple. There's only one way the Third Temple could have more glory than the Second."

She paused to let Bennett finish her thought, and he did.

"If it actually housed the original Ark of the Covenant."

41

★ ★
★

Later that afternoon, Bennett turned to Natasha.

"Your cousin wouldn't by any chance have a satellite phone, would she?"

"Actually, she does, but it's probably with her," said Natasha. "But I've got one. I keep it with all my gear."

"Gear?"

"I do a lot of digs in this area," said Natasha. "Miriam used to join me when she could, before she got the new Medexco gig. Anyway, she lets me keep a lot of my junk stored here so I don't always have to schlep it up here from Jerusalem."

"You guys are close?" asked Erin.

"We used to be closer," said Natasha. "After my parents died, I spent a lot of time with her, and we both adored my grandfather. But I guess we ended up developing two very different concepts of buried treasure. She wanted to find oil in Israel and make a fortune. That's how she got hooked up with Dmitri Galishnikov and the whole Medexco crowd. We drifted apart for a while in college, but once she started making serious money she was certainly very generous. She started buying me all kinds of gear—for me and my best students, actually. She let me use her place as a base camp. She usually joins me on a dig for a week or two each summer. And I never know what high-tech gizmo she'll order next."

She got up and led them to a storage area off the master bedroom. In addition to shovels, trowels, brushes of all shapes and sizes, and a half dozen metal detectors, it was a spelunker's treasure trove—helmets, gloves, kneepads, ropes, harnesses, lights, a rack of night-vision goggles, and even an array of pistols and submachine guns. It was still Israel, after all. One never knew when the next attack might come.

"Ah, here it is," said Natasha, and she handed Bennett the phone.

*   *   *

"American Consulate, may I help you?"

"Jon Bennett for Ken Costello."

"Yes sir, Mr. Bennett. One moment. I'll put you right through."

"Thanks."

As he sat at the kitchen table, Natasha set up Miriam Gozal's laptop computer in front of him and helped him log on to the Internet to download his latest e-mails. There were five from his mother. She was worried sick about them and begged them to get back to her as soon as possible. He dashed off a quick note saying he would call as soon as he could, but things were not going well.

Keep praying, Mom, he concluded. *And get some of your friends at that new church praying too. We could use all the air cover we can get. Thanks. I love you, Jon.*

Costello came on the line. "Jon, thank God. Are you and Erin okay?"

"We're fine, thanks."

"You know there's an APB out for your arrest—for both of you."

"What? What are you talking about?"

"I just heard it from Rajiv," Costello explained. "The Israeli police say three bodies were found murdered in Dr. Mordechai's house. Ballistics says the slugs they pulled out of them came from Erin's Beretta."

"That was self-defense," said Bennett.

"You might have mentioned that to somebody before fleeing the scene."

"They're not the only ones after us."

"You're telling me," Costello said. "You've got the whole country after you."

Erin and Natasha now turned to listen. They were only getting one side of the conversation, of course, but it was enough to make them realize they were in serious trouble.

"Look, I'll call Avi Zadok," Costello offered. "We'll bring you into the consulate and arrange a deal for you guys to turn yourselves in. Where are you right now?"

"Ken, I can't," said Bennett.

"Jon, you have to."

"I can't."

"Why not?"

"How do we know Avi isn't part of this thing?"

"Avi Zadok? Are you crazy? He's the head of the Mossad, for crying out loud. You think he's a terrorist?"

"I don't know what's going on right now, but the bottom line is that someone out there is trying to kill us, and Avi can't guarantee our safety and, frankly, Ken, neither can you."

"What, you think I'm in on this too?" Costello asked.

"No, of course not. I'm just saying—"

"I'm not sure you understand the gravity of the situation, Jon," Costello insisted. "At least let me call the prime minister. I'm sure I can work out something with him."

"No, Ken, you're not hearing me. I'm not coming in. Not yet."

"Jon, what are you saying? You can't run. How do you think that looks? Israel's a pretty small country. You know they're going to catch you, and then what? You're on your own. At least if you guys turn yourselves in now, the embassy will come to your defense. I'll talk to the president. He'll make sure you're okay. He owes you one, remember?"

"I'm not looking for a deal," said Bennett. "I'm looking for the people who killed my friend. That's what Mordechai asked me to do, and I gave him my word. Now you can hunt me down, or you can help me. Besides Erin, you're about the only friend I've got right now, Ken. I could really use your help."

There was a pause on the other end of the line.

"What do you need?" asked Costello.

"Two things," said Bennett. "First, there's an envelope on my dresser back at the King David. It's a private letter from Salvador Lucente to the president. Can you get it and make sure the president sees it?"

"Sure. What's it about?"

"Lucente thinks he's about to get a promotion."

"To what?"

"Secretary-general."

"Of the U.N.? Are you kidding?"

"No, but as you can imagine, there is a boatload of implications to that," Bennett continued. "The president and NSC need to know ASAP so they can start war-gaming their response."

"Okay, I'll get the letter to him. What's the second thing?"

"Erin asked Rajiv for intel on Abdullah Farouk," said Bennett. "Do you happen to know if she found anything?"

Costello hesitated for a moment, then said, "Yeah, I do, Jon. She told me about the request, and I helped her look. It's not good."

42

★ ★
★

Viggo Mariano had just landed in Tel Aviv.

"Dr. Guillaume, welcome to Israel," said a voice behind him.

For a moment Mariano didn't react to the unfamiliar alias, but then he turned and smiled at the young Israeli woman from the airport's VIP office who had been assigned to greet Mariano upon his arrival from Paris.

"Forgive me," she said, "but I just learned you were coming less than an hour ago. I understand you and your team are here from the World Health Organization?"

"*Oui, oui*, but we want no special attention, *s'il vous plait*," Mariano said, sporting a light French accent with ease. "We just want to do our work as unobtrusively as possible, and then we will be on our way."

"We are delighted to have you here," said the young woman. "In fact, I just called our health minister. I'm afraid he was not aware you were coming. But he asked me to make sure you were taken care of and asked if you could join him for dinner in Jerusalem tonight."

For a moment, Mariano felt a flash of panic. That was the last thing he wanted. "You are most kind, most kind. But I am afraid my colleagues and I have a very tight schedule. We must conduct our tests and get back to Paris immediately. I am afraid under the circumstances we must respectfully request a rain check with the minister."

With a polite smile and a quick handshake, Mariano and his four "colleagues" walked briskly to the doors, jumped into a waiting WHO van, and sped off.

☆ ☆ ☆

Bennett hung up quickly and turned to Erin and Natasha.

"We have to leave now."

"Why? What is it?" asked Erin.

"I'll explain on the way. Natasha, does your cousin have a car we could borrow?"

"Why can't we use the Mercedes?"

"Every cop in Israel is looking for it."

"She's got an SUV," said Natasha. "A Navigator—it's in the garage."

"Where does she keep the keys?"

"In a dish by the back door."

"See if they're still there," said Bennett. "Erin and I will get the gear."

Ten minutes later they were on the road, headed north around the lake, through Capernaum, and around to the eastern shores.

"So why the rush?" asked Natasha. "I thought we were going to wait until dark."

"Costello said Abdullah Farouk is on the move. He may be coming here."

"To Israel?"

"To the Golan Heights, at least, through Jordan."

"What? Wait a minute," said Erin. "Go back. What exactly did Ken say?"

"He and Rajiv did some checking on Prince Farouk, like you asked. Rajiv said he's someone the intelligence world is beginning to get very worried about. Two weeks ago Lee James added Farouk to Homeland Security's watch list of suspected terrorists."

"Why?"

"Apparently Farouk recently moved his money and his men from Saudi Arabia to somewhere in southern Europe. They're not sure where, but they believe he is actively recruiting terrorists for the Legion. The same group behind the bombing in Washington that killed George

Murray. The same group the guys who attacked us at Eli's house belonged to. Then Ken called your old buddy Danny Tracker."

"What did Danny say?" asked Erin.

"Who's Danny Tracker?" Natasha interjected, trying to keep up.

"Sorry," said Erin. "He's the deputy director of operations at CIA."

"Got it. Sorry. Go on."

"Anyway," Bennett continued, "Danny had good news and bad news. The good news was that an Agency operative spotted Farouk three weeks ago, arriving at the Kuwait City airport on a flight from Rome. Two days later, Danny's financial unit spotted $25 million being routed into a Cayman Islands bank account believed to be controlled by one of Farouk's sons. The money changed hands at least a half dozen times before arriving in the Caymans, but Danny said as best as they could tell, its origin was an Iraqi-owned shipping company. What's more, a friend of Danny's at NSA said a few days ago they intercepted a cell-phone call between a senior aide to President Al-Hassani and the CEO of that Iraqi shipping company. On the call, the CEO mentioned something called Operation Black Box; then the call was cut off."

"Operation Black Box? What's that?" asked Erin.

"Actually, Danny was hoping you'd know."

"I've never heard of it. Have you, Natasha?"

"No."

"Your grandfather never mentioned it? or maybe Mordechai?"

"No—not with me around, at least."

"Could it be a plan to find the Ark?" said Bennett.

"Maybe," said Natasha. "Or a plan to kill everyone looking for the Ark."

"Either way, Danny says Farouk's private jet landed in Amman this morning," Bennett continued. "A CIA operative assigned to our embassy there says twelve men got off the plane, including a man matching the prince's description. They got into two vans with U.N. markings and went to the Jordan Archaeological Museum."

Erin gasped. "The same place we were yesterday!"

"Right. An hour later, they were headed north to the border of Syria."

"So what's the problem?" asked Natasha. "Can't they just move in and get them?"

Bennett shook his head. "That's the bad news. You know how many U.N. relief trucks are in Jordan right now? Our guy lost them in the crowd."

"Which means he's on the loose, just across the border," said Erin. "And he may be heading straight for us."

✯   ✯   ✯

The phone rang and he answered it immediately.

"Ken Costello."

"Mr. Costello, this is the White House operator. Please hold for the national security advisor."

A moment later, Marsha Kirkpatrick was on the line. "Any luck finding Jon and Erin?"

Costello explained the situation.

"They're making a terrible mistake," said Kirkpatrick. "But it sounds like there's nothing more you can do. The president wants you back in Washington right away. He wants a briefing on your meetings with Doron and Lucente, and he wants to see that letter Lucente gave Jon."

✯   ✯   ✯

The sun had not yet set, but they couldn't wait.

Bennett knew they had to get into those tunnels before Farouk and his team did. He just prayed they weren't already too late.

"There, take a left," Erin said suddenly.

Bennett pulled off onto a dirt road. He came to a stop and cut the lights. Just over the ridge, Israeli and U.N. peacekeeping forces were busy burying the dead and trying to keep deadly diseases from triggering a global pandemic. Here—for now, at least—all was quiet. But they dared not attract attention.

Natasha's night-vision equipment was designed to be used inside caves, not off-roading through old mine fields, but it would do.

They proceeded up the side of the mountain for another twenty minutes.

It was agreed that Bennett and Erin would be the "scroll hunters." Natasha would take the SUV back down the mountain to avoid suspicion, monitor police and military frequencies, stay in constant communication with the Bennetts via encrypted wireless radios, and come back for them when the time was right.

"How much farther?" Bennett asked.

Erin used a penlight to double-check the coordinates from Ray Donovan's message, then took another GPS reading. "Another half mile on the left," she said.

A few moments later, she tapped Jon on the shoulder.

"Pull over," she said. "We'll have to walk from here."

43

★ ★
★

The sun was gone and the moon had not taken its place.

Thick clouds covered the night sky, and a strong breeze swept through the mountains. Bennett and Erin hiked for another fifteen minutes, and then began hunting through the thick brush for the cave opening Donovan had described in such detail in his notes. They never would have found it without the GPS coordinates, Bennett realized. The small opening was completely concealed. When they finally found it, the opening was just large enough to squeeze through.

Bennett lowered his equipment first, then strapped on the MP5 machine gun Natasha had given him and lowered himself into the cave. There was no telling who or what was already in there. But he was not about to let Erin go first into the unknown.

The air inside was cold and moist. The walls were damp and mossy. The granite floor was thick with mud.

"You okay?" he asked when Erin joined him, also outfitted with an MP5.

"Yeah, I guess," she said. "How about you?"

"I'd rather be back in that honeymoon suite in Ronda; that's for sure."

"Me too," she said wistfully. "Me too."

They helped each other put on the hefty backpacks full of gadgets and supplies, then flicked on the flashlights atop their weapons and began moving forward, weaving through stalagmites and stalactites. The tunnel was narrower than Bennett had expected, without much headroom, giving him a feeling of claustrophobia he had never experienced before.

The farther they walked, the colder it became. Bennett's mind began wandering as they probed deeper into the tunnel. He wondered what had happened to Donovan and Harkin. How far had they gone? How close had they come? How had they died?

The cobwebs were thick in his face, suggesting that no one had been down here in quite some time. With any luck they had beat Farouk and his minions to the punch. On the other hand, they had no guarantee they were on the right track. All they really had to go on were the scribblings of a dead Syrian rabbi and the testimony of two rogue CIA agents willing to sell out their country for buried treasure that might not even be real.

Soon the granite below his feet began sloping downward at a fairly steep angle. Bennett steadied himself against the cold, wet walls, but behind him he heard Erin lose her balance and slam onto her back. With nothing to grab on to, nothing to break her fall, she began sliding, picking up speed as she plunged into the icy darkness. Instinctively, he reached out to grab her, but she was moving too fast. Her screams echoed through the tunnel chambers, silenced only by an enormous splash as she hit the surface of the springs below.

☆   ☆   ☆

Erin gasped for air, but she needed more.

The bone-chilling waters seemed to suck all energy from her body. She thrashed around, desperately trying to regain her footing, but the weight of her pack began pulling her under. She was sinking—sinking fast—and she had no idea what to do. She expected to touch bottom any moment, but there was nothing there, nothing to grab on to, nothing to push off of.

Terrified, she wrestled with the backpack, trying to unhook it and get it off her back before she drowned. She finally managed to pry it loose and slip away, but she was still going down. She tried to kick off her boots, heavy and now waterlogged, but they were tied too tightly. She couldn't get them off. The gun was gone. The pack was gone. Tens of thousands of dollars of Natasha's gear was gone. And she was still sinking.

* * *

Bennett expected Erin to resurface any moment.

But there was no sign of her, just a mass of bubbles that were fading quickly.

With his adrenaline pumping, he moved with desperate caution, working his way down the sloped tunnel floor, trying to get to the water's edge without slipping in himself. When he got to the bottom, he made his way around the edge of the pool to another tunnel that shot off to one side. He tore off his backpack and gloves and tossed them into the side tunnel, along with his gun. Then he quickly untied his boots, ripped them and his socks off his feet, and plunged in headfirst. The frigid water instantly numbed his hands and feet, and a shock of pain shot through his skull. The icy temperatures stung his eyes, and he was forced to close them. But it wouldn't have mattered anyway. The water was pitch-black. He wouldn't have been able to see Erin if she had been just inches way.

His lungs screamed for oxygen. His hands grasped for his wife. Though he could barely feel his legs now, he kicked as hard he could, trying to close the gap.

* * *

Suddenly, finally, Erin felt her feet hit rock.

She bent her knees to cushion her landing and then sprang back up with all the force she could muster. Up, up she crawled, her legs flailing, her lungs burning, her body freezing, her heart racing. Out of nowhere, she felt Jon's hand and felt hope jolt through her body like a charge of electrical current.

* * *

Bennett's hands clamped on to Erin's.

He had her and he would never let her go. But now he had another problem: how to stop his descent. He had to reverse course and pull her and himself back to the surface. But his weight and the added weight of their soaked clothing were making it almost impossible to gain upward momentum.

Suddenly, as they thrashed about in the murky darkness, they slammed against something. He felt a jagged shard of rock slice deep into his knee. He had almost no air left in his lungs. It was everything he could do not to scream out in pain. But instead, he wedged his foot into the side of the razor-sharp crag and used it as leverage to push his way up.

The pain in his foot shot through him like a knife. It was unlike anything he had ever felt before, worse even than when he had been shot a few years before. But it worked. A moment later, he felt Erin pushing off the edge as well, and soon they both burst to the surface, gasping for air.

But there was no time for rejoicing. Erin suddenly went limp. He dragged her to the side and scrambled up onto the rocky edge while still holding fast to her shirt and arms. Then, using every last ounce of energy he had, he pulled her out of the water and into the side tunnel and rolled her onto her back.

To his horror, he realized she wasn't breathing.

44

★ ★
★

An Israeli Apache gunship rose over the ridge.

It made a low sweep over the western slopes, its spotlight on and directed toward the ground. *Was this a normal patrol*, Natasha wondered, *or were they hunting for someone? Were they hunting for* them? *Were the authorities on to them already?*

Natasha was almost a mile from the tunnel opening. She was parked in a roadside rest area near Kibbutz Ein Gev, on the eastern shores of the Sea of Galilee. But she had a clear view of the Golan Heights, and she watched as the chopper made one pass and then another.

Forgetting the code words they had agreed upon, she grabbed the radio and whispered, "Guys, you there? We have a little situation up here. Come in, over."

She waited a moment, but there was no response.

"Guys, seriously, we've got a problem. There's an Apache sweeping back and forth over your location. I repeat, an Israeli gunship over your location. How much longer are you guys going to be?"

★ ★ ★

Bennett was now giving his wife mouth-to-mouth.

But nothing was working.

A minute went by, then another, but it felt like an hour. Bennett was begging God to let Erin live. She couldn't die. She couldn't leave him. Not here. Not like this. They'd only been married a few days. It wasn't fair, he argued. Why would God do this to them? Why would He give them a taste of the happiness of being together and then rip them apart forever?

★　★　★

"Hey, guys, are you there?"

Natasha checked the frequency and the batteries and tried again. "Base Camp to Angel One, Angel Two, are you okay? Come in, over."

But there was still no response, and now she began to fear the worst.

★　★　★

Suddenly Erin gagged.

Bennett turned her head, and she began vomiting uncontrollably.

But she was back. She was breathing. And he began to sob. He held her in his arms for what seemed like an eternity, rubbing her face and hands, trying to get her warm. His mind reeled. What was he supposed to do now? She obviously couldn't keep going forward. But how in the world was he going to get her back to the surface?

He grabbed the radio. "Base Camp, this is Angel One, do you read me? Over."

"Jon, it's me," responded a startled Natasha. "Are you okay?"

"Hey, hey, no names," he insisted.

"Right, I'm sorry. I forgot. But where are you guys? I've been calling you forever."

Bennett explained what happened.

"I'm afraid she's slipping into hypothermia," he said. "I need to get her out."

"Jon, listen to me. If she's hypothermic, you have to stabilize her. You can't move her yet."

There was silence for a moment; then Bennett said, "Did you hear what I just said? She's unconscious. We need to get her out of here, and fast."

"If you move her in this condition, she could get worse or die," said Natasha urgently. "You need to raise her core temperature right away."

"What do I do?" Bennett asked.

"Do you still have your backpacks?" asked Natasha.

"Erin's is gone. But I've still got mine."

"Open it. Tell me what's in there."

"Why? What are you talking about?"

"It's either archeological gear or medical supplies," Natasha said. "I don't remember which of you had which."

Bennett set down the radio and scrambled to find the pack. He dragged it over to Erin's side and quickly rifled through its contents. "Okay, got it," he told Natasha. "I see several blankets and a large first-aid kit."

"Okay, good. Put the blankets over her," Natasha instructed. "Then dig to the bottom of the pack."

"What am I looking for?"

"A tan pouch, about the size of a small transistor radio."

"Yeah, I see it."

"Unzip it. It's an IV warmer. Put a bag of fluid in there and turn it on."

Natasha waited until Bennett's voice came back over the radio.

"Okay, done. Now what?"

"There's an LED reading on the top. Do you see it?"

"Yes."

"What's it say?"

"101."

"Good," said Natasha. "When it hits 104, give her the IV. It'll bring up her core temperature. Do you see a long, narrow, black-canvas bag right there?"

"Yes."

"Open it. There's a special thermometer for taking core temperature readings."

"I see it. Now what?"

Natasha quickly explained how to use it. "What kind of reading are you getting?"

"She's at 92.1," Bennett said.

"Do you have a flashlight handy?"

"Yes."

"Check her pupils."

"They're constricted."

"But are they reacting to the light?"

"A little, yes."

"How's her pulse?"

"Weak, but she's hanging in there."

"Okay, check the IV warmer."

"105."

"Perfect. Give it to her now."

With Erin's blood vessels so constricted, Bennett had trouble finding a good vein. When he finally did and breathed a sigh of relief, Erin suddenly went into convulsions.

"Oh no! Erin!" Bennett shouted.

"What's happening?" came Natasha's voice over the radio.

Bennett couldn't answer. He was terrified. Erin's back arched. She shook violently. Then as quickly as she began, she stopped.

"She was convulsing," Bennett reported, "but now she's stopped."

Immediately Erin's body started shaking again.

"Now she's convulsing again! What do I do?"

"Don't worry," Natasha said. "Her body is reacting to the temperature change. Just keep her stable and make sure the IV doesn't come loose."

Bennett did as Natasha instructed, praying aloud the whole time, asking Jesus to heal and comfort the woman he loved so much. He didn't care what Natasha thought. He didn't even realize the radio was still on. He just couldn't bear the thought of living without Erin, the woman who had saved his life again and again.

"Jon, do you see another canvas case in there?"

"I do."

"That's a special ventilator," said Natasha. "It pumps in heated air. There should be a twelve-volt battery pack in there."

"Yeah, it's right here."

"Good. Hook it up, turn it on, and get it on her right away."

It seemed to work. After eight or ten minutes, the convulsions subsided, and Bennett began to relax. Erin's temperature was up to 96.4. Her pulse was stronger. And after a few more minutes, her eyes began to flutter open.

"*Jon?*" she asked, her voice weak and groggy.

"I'm right here, sweetheart," he replied, putting his hand on her forehead.

She mumbled something else, but it was barely a whisper.

"Just rest, Erin," he told her. "It's okay. Everything's going to be all right."

But again she tried to speak.

"What's that?" he asked. "What did you say?"

"*Did we get it?*" she asked, barely audible.

Bennett was stunned at the question. "What, the scroll?"

Erin couldn't seem to nod. She barely had enough energy to speak. But she blinked hard, as if she was trying to say yes.

Bennett shook his head, amazed at her focus, even now, with all that she had just been through. "I'm afraid that's going to have to wait, Erin. We need to get you out of here and find a hospital."

"*No,*" she whispered back emphatically. "*You . . . go . . .*"

A moment later, however, she had slipped back into unconsciousness.

Bennett radioed Natasha, his voice thick with emotion. "She just blacked out."

"That's 'after drop,'" Natasha explained. "It's normal. It's part of the process. She's going to be out for a while, but she'll be fine. I promise."

Bennett took a deep breath and tried to believe that. He rechecked Erin's temperature every five minutes, and sure enough, it slowly began to rise, as did her pulse.

He thought about what Erin had said. It was a crazy thought. He couldn't bear the idea of leaving her here all by herself, even for a little while. Who knew what lay ahead? But then again, given all that they had been through already, how could they give up now?

45

★ ★
★

Viggo Mariano and his men sped up Highway 90.

Unless they hit traffic or police roadblocks, neither of which he expected, they would be in Tiberias in the next ten to fifteen minutes. Mariano pulled out a satellite phone and hit speed-dial.

Abdullah Farouk's voice came on the line. *"Where are you?"* he demanded.

"We're almost there," Mariano assured him. "How about you?"

"I'm safe in Amman. The rest of the team is in position in the north. They just called. You were right. The U.N. vans worked like a charm. The hills are swarming with blue helmets. They blend right in. No one has even asked for ID. Perhaps I should have gone with them."

"No," said Mariano. "You need to stick with the plan and keep out of sight. What about the communications equipment I sent them?"

"They got it, and they're sweeping every frequency, as you requested," said Farouk. "They've found nothing yet, but they promised to call the moment they do."

"Don't worry, Mr. Farouk," Mariano said. "These guys are very good. If Bennett and his wife and the Barak girl are up there, they'll find them and neutralize them. On that you have my word."

★ ★ ★

Erin wasn't the only one battling hypothermia.

It was pure adrenaline—and the grace of God—that had kept Bennett from slipping into shock as well. But he couldn't just sit there. Shivering and soaked to the bone, he checked on Erin again. She was out—cold, as it were.

He picked up the radio and pressed send. "Angel One to Base Camp, do you copy? Over."

An instant later, Natasha came on the line. "Base Camp to Angel One. How's she doing?"

"She seems to have stabilized."

"Should I come back up there to get you guys?"

Bennett hesitated, but only for a moment. He knew the stakes, and he knew time was running out. But he also knew that if the scroll was still here, it wouldn't be for long.

"No, not yet," he replied.

"Why?" asked Natasha, worry rising in her voice. "What's the matter?"

Bennett paused to catch his breath, then said, "I'm going for it."

"You're gonna do what?"

But Bennett didn't respond. He stuffed the radio back into his coat and checked Erin's temperature again. It was 97.1. Her pulse was improving. Her head was resting on his backpack, and she was wrapped in two thick wool blankets. He gave her a kiss on the forehead and said a brief prayer. Then he scooped up his MP5, double-checked Donovan's map, and proceeded as rapidly as he could down the tunnel.

Ten minutes later, as he raced through an ever-narrowing passageway, a cruel thought crossed his mind: Erin's backpack had had the shovels and the metal detector. So even if he found his way to the right place, even if he found the scroll—which still seemed highly unlikely—what was he supposed to do then? How was he supposed to dig it up? It had been buried for more than two thousand years.

He shook off the thought and kept moving. He would simply have to blow up that bridge when he came to it.

The good news: the farther he went, the drier the tunnel got.

The bad news: it was getting colder—much colder—and his hands and feet were already numb. His gloves were soaked, so he'd left them behind. At least his socks and boots were dry. But he was shivering uncontrollably. He could feel his reflexes growing sluggish, and his head was throbbing.

And then more bad news: the tunnel abruptly branched off in four directions. Which route did he want? Which route had Donovan and Harkin taken, if they had even made it this far? He pulled the map from his pocket and studied it carefully, but there was no indication of a fork. He had hit another wall. Erin was waiting for him. He didn't have time to check all these tunnels. He barely had time to check one.

"Call to Me and I will answer you, and I will tell you great and mighty things, which you do not know." Mordechai's verse came back to mind. It had worked before. Maybe the Lord would bless him again. God certainly knew where the scroll was. And didn't Jesus say, "Seek and you will find"? There was no time like the present.

He set the gun down and got on his knees to pray. When he opened his eyes again, he noticed dead ahead of him small bits of dried mud in almost a zigzag pattern. Curious, he picked up several pieces and examined them more closely. They were from the tread of a boot. Someone *had* been here before. Not in the last few minutes, but a whole lot more recently than two thousand years ago. Could Donovan and Harkin have made it this far? Could these be their boot prints? Who else could possibly have been down here? A smile crossed his face for the first time in days.

"Thank you, Father," he whispered.

Then he grabbed the MP5 again and followed the prints. He heard the noise of a helicopter overhead. It sounded military—an Apache. Were the Israelis on to them? It didn't really matter, he realized. There was nothing he could do about it now. He had to keep moving.

Bennett pressed ahead another two hundred yards before coming to another fork. He stopped again, caught his breath, and double-checked the map and his watch. None of these forks were marked, but the map did indicate that the spring waters of the Yarmuk River were nearby, and the markings on the map seemed to indicate that the ancient smuggler tunnels followed the path of the underground springs to the river itself.

He closed his eyes and strained to listen to every sound. The helicopter had briefly passed out of range, and now he noticed that through the smaller of the two tunnel branches he could hear the ever-so-faint sound of water trickling in the distance. That had to be it. He crawled into the small tunnel and before long was scrambling down a muddy embankment. The only way forward was through more icy waters. But at least he'd found the river, and his heart was racing. He had to be incredibly close now.

☆   ☆   ☆

"Angel One to Base Camp, over."

"Base Camp, over," said Natasha. She heard the strain in her voice. She was increasingly fearful of getting caught.

"You still with me?" asked Bennett.

"Absolutely. What do you need?"

"What's it looking like up there?"

"Not good," she admitted. "There are now three choppers in the air—no, wait, there's a fourth. They're passing by every few minutes. I think they're on to us. You need to get Er—Angel Two out of there now."

"Any boots on the ground?"

Natasha picked up her pair of night-vision binoculars and scanned the horizon.

"There was a patrol that went by about forty-five minutes ago. I don't see anything else at the moment."

"What about the radios?"

"They're using encrypted channels. The police bands have been pretty quiet. How much longer?"

"I don't know," said Bennett. "Just start thinking about how we get Angel Two out of here."

"Will do," she said, but the truth was, she had no idea.

☆   ☆   ☆

It suddenly dawned on Bennett how much danger he was in.

His wife was battling hypothermia, as was he. But rather than getting either of them back to safety, he was advancing deep into the demilitarized zone between Israel and Syria, moving under an active minefield, almost to a waterfall on the border with Syria, with Israeli gunships buzzing overhead, hunting a treasure that almost no one on the planet believed actually existed.

Some honeymoon.

The tunnel now narrowed sharply to a small hole in the granite floor. Bennett tossed a rock into the hole to gauge its depth, then pointed the flashlight of the MP5 to see what was down there.

No rodents. No vipers. Just a claustrophobic's nightmare.

He lowered himself into the hole, then dropped to his belly and crawled forward about twenty or thirty yards. He soon found himself crawling through a partially collapsed tunnel, and when he came around the next corner, he thought his heart would stop.

He was staring into a man's eyes.

46

Eye sockets, to be more precise.

Bennett shuddered. Not six inches from his face a skull stared back at him, and scattered behind it were shattered pieces of bone and electronics and small shreds of clothing. He pushed the skull aside and pulled himself into the slightly larger tunnel. To one side, he found a CIA-issue sidearm. A few feet away he found the dead man's wallet. He took a deep breath and opened it.

The credit cards and the Continental Airlines ID gave the name Marcus T. Morelli, as did the Virginia driver's license. But the face was Ray Donovan's. He recognized Donovan immediately from the photo his brother had included in the materials he'd sent to Mordechai, and shuddered. No wonder the Agency had never found him. He'd been blown up by an underground land mine.

Bennett picked through the mangled metal device and scorched pieces of wiring scattered about. Might there be more mines down here?

He stuffed the wallet into his pocket and kept moving, crawling into an antechamber another dozen yards ahead. This room seemed much bigger than the last one, and the sound of the distant helicopter was much louder here. Looking around, Bennett realized that this once-hidden antechamber was now partially exposed to the northeast. The far side of the room had collapsed at some point, leaving a small mountain of rock and dirt in the center of the room. He would have to move fast. He couldn't stay exposed here for long.

He looked at the floor again and found more bones. Unlike the first pile, though, these formed an intact skeleton.

The man's clothes had largely been eaten away by rats and other rodents, as had, presumably, his flesh. But Bennett had no doubt who it was.

Sure enough, he quickly found a moldy leather wallet. Again the credit cards and various IDs were all in the names of an alias. But it was Harkin, all right. How had he died? Bennett wondered. He knelt down to examine the remains and found two bullet holes in the skull—one in the back down by the base of the neck, the other dead center in the deceased's forehead. Harkin had been murdered, senselessly killed at the age of twenty-five. But by whom? Had somebody known they were coming, or had Harkin been cut down by a Syrian sniper? Bennett wondered whether the tunnel had been partially collapsed when Donovan and Harkin had come here. Maybe a sniper had seen Harkin, his attention drawn by the sound of the land mine exploding.

Thunder rumbled through the night sky, and again Bennett realized he would have to hurry if he wanted to avoid Harkin's fate. There were two shovels near the mound of dirt and rock in the center of the room, undisturbed by time. That must be where they had been digging.

His heart accelerated. As terrible as he felt for what had happened to these two men, he was suddenly oddly grateful for their sacrifice and for the clues they had left behind for Mordechai and thus for him. They had come so far and gotten so close, and now he was about to discover what they had not—whether this really was the final resting place of the Key Scroll.

He peeked out the gaping hole to the northeast and scanned for signs of life but saw nothing. He could hear the choppers not far away, and he knew that U.N. relief forces were operating nearby. But the chances that they would hear him had to be minimal, he figured, so he grabbed a shovel and began to dig.

* * *

"Jack Knife to Black Box."

"Black Box, go."

"I've got something."

Excitement spread through Mariano's team.

"What is it?"

"Movement to the southwest, half a click from the old Syrian bunker."

"How many?"

"Looks like just one, sir. He's inside the collapsed tunnel. Hold on. Let me see if I can get a better angle."

"No, don't move," Mariano ordered. "Nothing that could attract attention. Nomad, can you see anything from your position?"

"No, sir."

"What about—?"

But before Mariano could finish the thought, his lead sniper broke back in.

"Jack Knife to Black Box, he just moved into plain view."

"Who is it? Can you see?"

"Negative. It's too dark."

"Is it Bennett?" Mariano pressed.

"I can't tell. But he's definitely alone—and he's digging."

Mariano couldn't believe it. Their inside source had come through for them again, giving them exact coordinates of where the Bennetts were headed, and just in time.

Then Jack Knife radioed again. "I've got a clear shot," he told Mariano. "Should I take it?"

"What's he doing now?" Mariano asked.

"Digging furiously," came the reply. "But I've still got a shot. Should I take it?"

* * *

Bennett struck metal.

Exhausted, he nevertheless dug faster. The exercise was, after all, helping to warm his frozen body a little, and he was thrilled beyond belief at the possibility of what he was about to find. Soon he had uncovered a small trunk, which he promptly yanked from the ground. The lid was stuck. Bennett pulled a knife from his pocket.

☆ ☆ ☆

Again Mariano's radio crackled to life.

"I have the shot," said Jack Knife. "I repeat, I have the shot. Can I take it?"

"Hold one, Jack Knife, hold one," Mariano barked into the radio.

He pulled out his satphone and speed-dialed Farouk.

"We've got him," he said the moment Farouk answered.

"Who?"

"*Bennett*. One of my men has him in his sights. What do you want to do?"

"Are you with him?"

"No, no, he's on the Syrian side. I'm on the Israeli side. But I've got him on the other line, and he needs authorization, *fast.*"

Mariano's radio came to life. It was Jack Knife again.

"He's got something."

"Hold on, Mr. Farouk," said Mariano, grabbing the radio. "What have you got, Jack Knife?"

"He's got something—it's in his hands."

"*What*—what is it?"

"It's a box of some kind."

"What's he doing?"

"He's trying to pry it open."

Farouk was screaming on the other end of the line, demanding to know what was happening. Mariano explained while Jack Knife fed him second-by-second updates.

"He's got it open," said the sniper.

"He's got it open," Mariano repeated into the phone. "What do you want me to do, Mr. Farouk? Do we take him out? *I need to know now.*"

☆ ☆ ☆

Bennett had no idea that his head was centered in a sniper's scope.

All he could think of was the scroll in his hands. It was small and metal—probably copper, like the other—oxidized and encrusted with twenty centuries of dirt and filth. He had no idea how they were going to get it open. It felt as though it could disintegrate into a fine powder at any moment. Something to worry about later. For now he had to get back to Erin and get both of them out of there alive.

☆　☆　☆

"Where are you?" asked Farouk.

"Tiberias."

"How long will it take you and your team to get into the Golan?"

"Another twenty or thirty minutes—why?"

"Get moving, now," said Farouk. "I'll explain while you're en route."

Mariano was beside himself. *"Fine, but what do I tell my man? He's got the shot. I say he should take it."*

☆　☆　☆

"Angel One to Base Camp, the eagle has landed."

Natasha heard the words but couldn't believe them.

"Base Camp to Angel One, come again?" Natasha asked, her voice trembling with emotion.

"The eagle has landed," Bennett repeated. "I'm coming home."

☆　☆　☆

Jack Knife steadied his rifle and adjusted his scope.

He had to account for the strong breeze now picking up through the valley. He would likely have only one shot, and he had to get it right.

☆　☆　☆

Farouk finally made the call.

"Tell your man to hold his fire," he ordered.

"What?" said Mariano, apoplectic.

"Tell your man not to shoot."

"Why not? We may not get another chance like this."

"It's the scroll I want, not the Bennetts," Farouk growled.

"We can do both," Mariano insisted. "Let me take this guy out, and I'll go into the tunnel and recover the scroll myself."

"No," said Farouk. "It's too risky. You start shooting and that whole mountain is going to be teeming with special forces. You'll never get another chance to get in there."

Mariano couldn't believe what he was hearing. "But if they get it—"

Farouk cut him off. "Then we'll follow them."

"What if they take the scroll to the authorities?" asked Mariano, nearly ready to authorize Jack Knife to take the shot anyway.

"Haven't you been listening to the news?" Farouk demanded. "The Bennetts are wanted for murder. They're not going to the authorities."

"They could cut a deal."

"Then we'll cut their throats."

"When?" Mariano wanted to know, eager to do the job himself.

"After they lead us to the treasures," said Farouk. "Let them get the scroll out of the tunnels. Then follow them. If they head to the police station, kill them. But I guarantee you, that's not going to happen. They want the treasure. That's what they're going after. After all, it's the only leverage they can use to stay out of prison."

There was silence on the other end of the line.

"And think about it, Viggo," Farouk added. "Who is more likely to decode the scroll—the Barak woman and the Bennetts, or you?"

47

★ ★
★

Erin had no idea where she was.

She stared up at a ceiling fan for almost five minutes before she noticed it wasn't spinning. Slowly, painfully, she turned her head to the right. All she found was wallpaper she didn't recognize. When she finally turned all the way to the left, she found a small night table, a lamp that was off, and a digital alarm clock that told her it was morning, though of what day she hadn't the foggiest idea.

A few minutes later, she noticed the electric blankets wrapped around her and the needle stuck in her arm, attached by a tube to a bag of fluid hanging from the bedpost. She noticed that her feet were wrapped in thick bandages. Slowly she began to remember flashes of the cave, the water, Jon's face, Jon and Natasha pulling her out of the tunnel and putting her in the back of the SUV. But no sooner did it all register than she once again drifted away into a long and dreamless sleep.

★　　★　　★

Bennett stepped out of another long, hot shower.

As he dressed, he tried to clear his head and think about the next steps, but it was still almost impossible to believe that they had all made it this far. He checked in on Erin. Her pulse and temperature were both back to normal. Breathing a sigh of relief, he kissed her on the cheek and went down to the kitchen to make some coffee.

It was going to be a long day.

Downstairs, Bennett found Natasha hard at work at the kitchen table, tools and brushes and bottles of solvent spread everywhere.

"How's it going?" he asked.

"Slow," said Natasha. "I've been up all night with it."

"Well, not to put any pressure on you or anything, but you are aware that the entire Israeli police force is hunting us down, right?"

Natasha was not amused. She set down the small toothbrush she was using to clean the outside of the scroll and looked Bennett in the eye. "We only get one shot at this, you know? One wrong move and this thing will turn to chalk dust faster than you can blink. Okay?"

"I'm sorry," he said. "I'm just worried about Erin, for starters."

"Me too," said Natasha, accepting his apology. "I'm going as fast as I can."

"I know," he said, rifling through the cabinets to find something to eat.

"Third door on your right," Natasha said as she focused again on her work.

Bennett opened the cupboard door and found a box of granola. "Thanks."

"Don't mention it. But there's no milk."

"No milk?"

"No. Well, there was, but it had gone bad. I poured it out."

His stomach growled.

"There are some eggs in the fridge," Natasha added.

"Any bacon?" he asked, pulling the refrigerator door open.

"Very funny," said Natasha. "You're in Israel, remember? Not a big market for bacon here, you know?"

"Sorry," he said, shaking his head. He couldn't let the stress eat him alive. There was too much at stake. "How about if I make us some fried eggs and toast?"

Natasha looked up. "That'd be nice. Thanks."

"No problem," he said, pulling out pans and firing up the stove. "So how much more time do you think you'll need?"

"You'd better pray that I'm faster than Baker was," Natasha replied.

"Who?"

"Dr. H. Wright Baker."

"Who's that?"

"He was a professor of mechanical engineering at the University of Manchester Institute of Science and Technology in England. He was the one who finally came up with the solution to opening the Copper Scroll without destroying it."

"Oh, right," said Bennett, remembering Dr. Barak's words in the Jordan Archaeological Museum. "It took three years or something."

"Four."

Bennett turned and looked back at Natasha. "You're right. I do hope you're faster than Baker. Why did it take so long to open the Copper Scroll anyway?"

"It didn't," she explained, still hard at work. "What took so long was figuring out *how* to open it. When they actually got around to doing it, it didn't take long at all. Once they had a plan, Baker and his team cleaned away as much of the external oxidation as they could. Then they X-rayed the scroll to see where the letters were positioned inside. After that, they built a high-speed circular saw, like something a jeweler would use to cut diamonds, and they sliced the scroll into twenty-three segments."

Bennett remembered the copper segments in the flimsy display cases in the museum.

"And they did this all the while attempting to cut only *between* the various columns of text so as to avoid destroying any of the letters," Natasha said.

A few minutes later, Bennett walked over to the table and set down two plates of food. "How long would it take to build a saw like that?" he asked.

"We already did it," she replied.

"What are you talking about?"

"We already built one," Natasha said again. "It's in my grandfather's office in Jerusalem. Don't forget, he was absolutely sure we were going to find the Key Scroll. So he had the engineers at the museum make one for him. There's just one problem."

"What's that?" asked Bennett.

"We can't go back to his office without getting caught."

"Good point," he said, wondering again if any of this had been worth it. "So now what do we do?"

"I have an idea." She smiled. "You'll see."

48

★ ★
★

"The president will see you now, Mr. Costello."

Costello thanked the president's military assistant and waited for a Marine guard to enter the passcode into the Situation Room. Once inside, he shook Bob Corsetti's hand and was directed to take a seat beside Indira Rajiv. Already seated were President MacPherson, Vice President Bill Oaks, Homeland Security Secretary Lee James, CIA Director Jack Mitchell, Secretary of State Nicholas Warner, and National Security Advisor Marsha Kirkpatrick.

"Good morning, Mr. President."

"Good morning, Ken. Thanks for getting back here so quickly. I want to talk about Lucente and the U.N. in a moment. But first I understand we have a serious situation developing in Israel."

"We do, Mr. President," Costello confirmed.

"I've just read the memo you sent to Marsha and the update you e-mailed from the plane on the way home," MacPherson continued. "But just to clarify, Ken, most of this is based on your phone call with Jon?"

"Several calls, actually, but yes, Mr. President, that is correct."

"So Jon actually told you that the men found dead in Mordechai's house were killed by Erin?"

"In self-defense, sir."

"He said that himself?"

"He did, sir."

"Those exact words?"

"Yes, sir."

"'*Self-defense*'?"

"Yes, sir."

"What about the four people the Israelis found dead in the café in the Jewish Quarter?"

"It didn't come up, sir."

"And you didn't ask?"

"No, sir. But the Israelis are saying those three—the café owners and their accountant—were killed by a different gun—a sniper rifle, I believe."

"Not a Beretta?"

"Correct, sir."

"And Jon told you he couldn't turn himself in because he fears a penetration of Doron's inner circle?"

Costello nodded. "Yes, sir."

"Didn't he expect you would have to pass that on to me?"

"I wouldn't presume to know exactly what Jon's thinking at the moment, sir. But yes, I think that's a pretty safe assumption. He certainly knows how this office works."

"Have you talked to anyone in the Israeli government since you spoke with Jon?"

"No, sir. I thought it best to bring this to Ms. Kirkpatrick's attention first, and then to yours."

MacPherson nodded and turned to CIA Director Jack Mitchell. "What do you make of all this, Jack?

"Mr. President, I'm tempted to say Jon's gone off the deep end this time," said Mitchell, whose own history with Bennett was long and complicated. "But in this case there is a lot of circumstantial evidence to suggest some sort of conspiracy is unfolding."

"Such as?"

"There's the bombing at the Willard that resulted in Dr. Murray's death. There's the car bombing in L.A. that took Barry Jaspers' life. There's Eli Mordechai's assassination to account for, the unsolved mystery of Lionel Mansfield's death in London, and now the murder of Dr.

Barak in Jerusalem. I never thought of archeology as such a dangerous profession, but it's clear that somebody's on a killing spree."

"But how can you be sure all those deaths are linked?" the president asked.

"Because every one of those men was working on a project for Prime Minister Doron."

The president gave Mitchell a hard look. "What project?"

Mitchell didn't blink. "Doron put together a team of archeologists to look into the possibility of recovering Israel's ancient Temple treasures and rebuilding the Temple."

"And you knew about this?" MacPherson demanded.

"Yes, sir."

"Who else knew?"

Every eye in the room volleyed back to the DCI.

Mitchell opened a folder and handed out a single sheet stamped "Top Secret—Eyes Only" to everyone in the room, beginning with the president. Costello did a double take when he got his copy. Listed, of course, were the names of the Israeli prime minister and his closest advisors. Dr. Yossi Barak's name was also there, as was Natasha Barak's, along with Dr. Barry Jaspers, Dr. Lionel Mansfield, Dr. George Murray of the Smithsonian, his literary agent, and each of the men's wives. But there were other names on the list as well.

* Dr. Larry McKenzie, Director, National Security Agency
* Dr. Christopher Watkins, Director of Analysis, NSA
* Col. Tanya Freeling, Hebrew Analyst, NSA
* Dr. John Mitchell, Director of Central Intelligence
* Dr. Alex Valetta, DDI, CIA
* Daniel J. Tracker, DDO, CIA
* Dr. Indira Rajiv, Director, NAMESTAN Desk, CIA

Costello looked to the president. The shock in MacPherson's eyes mirrored the shock in his own.

"Indira, what is this?" asked the president. "You knew about Doron's Temple project too?"

"I did, sir."

"How?"

"Electronic intercepts," Mitchell explained.

"What are you talking about?" asked the president.

"Sir, last fall, after Bennett gave you a copy of Dr. Mordechai's 'Ezekiel Option' memo, I asked NSA to wiretap Mordechai's phones and pay extra close attention to Doron and his inner circle."

"Why?" MacPherson wanted to know.

Vice President Oaks took a crack at that. "Let me guess, Jack. You wanted to know where Mordechai was getting his information?"

"In part, of course," Mitchell conceded. "Mordechai was projecting events none of us in the Agency had foreseen, and every day that went by, he was being proven right. I found that extraordinary, and I found it hard to believe that the Bible was the source of his prescience. I was sure he had other sources, and I wanted to track them down and tap them myself."

"But that wasn't all?" the vice president asked.

"No, it wasn't," said Mitchell. "I also needed to know how Prime Minister Doron and his team were using Mordechai's information."

"You were afraid they might strike at Russia and Iran first?" asked Kirkpatrick.

"Weren't we all?" asked Mitchell. "And we were right to be concerned. Doron almost did launch first."

"But it was Mordechai who stopped him," MacPherson noted.

"It was a number of factors, Mr. President," said Mitchell. "But the point is, I needed to know precisely what was happening in Israel, and who was influencing whom, and what might happen next so that I could brief you and the rest of the NSC as accurately as possible. Given the circumstances, I would do it again."

"You would tap the phones of the Israeli prime minister, the head of the Mossad, and the former head of the Mossad without my authorization?" MacPherson asked.

"Yes, sir—given the uniquely dangerous situation we were in, on the brink of a worldwide nuclear war."

"I will deal with all that in a moment, but this still doesn't explain how you knew about Doron's Temple project."

"That's true, Mr. President," Mitchell said, "but I'll explain. The truth of the matter is that there was so much happening in the days and weeks after the firestorm that I never called Larry McKenzie at NSA to shut the operation down."

"You're saying we just kept gathering intel on Eli and Doron?" asked the VP.

"Yes, sir."

"And then?"

"And then," Mitchell continued, "about a month ago, Larry and his team—Chris and Tanya—came over to Langley and told us what they had."

"Why didn't you shut it down right then?" asked MacPherson.

"I'll admit," said Mitchell, "by then I was curious. Indira here reminded me about rumors that had been floating around the Agency for years that two CIA officers had died back in the nineties trying to track down the Temple treasures and the Ark. And then Larry and his team began picking up strange chatter out of Italy, Kuwait, and Iraq about something called Operation Black Box, but we didn't know what that was. I thought they might be connected. But so much else was happening, I couldn't give it much time."

The president leaned in toward Mitchell and lowered his voice. "When George Murray was killed, why didn't you say anything?"

The DCI said nothing.

"When Barry Jaspers was killed, why didn't you say something to me then?"

"I don't know, Mr. President. It was just a working theory, one of many. I didn't think it was ready to bring to your level just yet."

Costello watched the president lean back in his chair, mulling it all over.

After a moment, MacPherson said, "You mentioned Operation Black Box. What is that?"

"We don't know at this point, sir," admitted Mitchell. "But one possibility is it's an operation to take out the people involved with Prime Minister Doron's project. That's why I think it's just possible that Bennett may be right. Someone may be after him."

The president turned to his Homeland Security secretary. "What about you, Lee? You buy it?"

"No, I don't buy it, Mr. President," James said without hesitation.

"With all due respect to Jack here, I just can't see anyone on Doron's team betraying him like that."

"Can't or won't?" asked Mitchell.

Costello watched James turn to the DCI. He expected him to fire back hard, but James was too much of a gentleman for that.

"Jack, be serious," James replied. "You really think someone in David Doron's office is feeding inside intel to Israel's enemies? You think someone inside Doron's office is trying to keep Doron from rebuilding the Temple? There's no evidence of that."

"Except for the list of dead bodies," replied Mitchell. "And the fact that someone does seem to be tracking Jon and Erin Bennett."

MacPherson looked back down at the names typed, single-spaced, on CIA letterhead. "There's another possibility here. If there *is* a mole, it's possible that it's not in Doron's office at all," he said to no one in particular. "Theoretically, it could be one of our own."

The room grew icy and still.

Mitchell shifted in his seat. "Yes, sir," the DCI said at last. "I guess it could."

MacPherson turned to his chief of staff. "Bob, get the attorney general and the director of the FBI on the phone. I want a lie-detector test given to every American on this list by close of business tomorrow. I want to know who leaked this thing, and if anyone in my government was involved, I promise you, heads will roll."

49

Natasha led Bennett into the basement.

They flicked on some lights and then entered a storage room, and there in the far corner was a strange machine with all kinds of wires and tubes running in and out of it.

"What is that?" Bennett asked as his eyes adjusted to the harshness of the fluorescent bulbs overhead.

"A laser," Natasha said as she went over and turned it on.

"It's huge."

"It's industrial strength, top-of-the-line."

"But why's it so big?"

"Copper is one of the toughest metals to cut with a laser," said Natasha. "It's highly reflective and highly conductive, meaning it can absorb a truckload of heat without melting or cracking, both of which slow down the cutting process. Typically, the less copper an alloy contains, the faster it will cut. But in this case, we're dealing with extremely pure copper, which means we needed a laser that could operate at 400 watts, rather than the typical 100 to 250 watts. The problem is, 400 watts is a whole lot of energy and creates a whole lot of heat. Making sure the laser—and the scroll—are stable and keeping the laser well cooled and ventilated takes a bit of space."

"I guess so," said Bennett. "And you just happened to have one lying around?"

"I told you already," said Natasha. "My grandfather and I have been making preparations for this for almost three months."

"Right, but I thought that's why he had the special saw built at the museum."

"He did."

"Then why this?"

"It was my idea," said Natasha. "I thought I'd play around with it a bit and see if it would work. I asked Miriam if she would get me one, and she agreed."

"Did you tell her why you needed it?"

"Not exactly."

"Did you tell her about the Key Scroll?"

"Of course not. I just said I needed it for an upcoming project. She said yes. End of story."

"Did your grandfather know about it?"

"No, I never told him."

"Why not?"

"You met him," said Natasha. "He was old-fashioned. He had a certain way of doing things, and that was that. He was in the room when Dr. Baker opened the Copper Scroll in Manchester in 1956. He saw how it *was* done, so he decided that's how it *should* be done. He wasn't exactly open to new ideas about the latest technology."

"Not big into lasers, huh?" asked Bennett.

Natasha shook her head. "He never even saw *Star Wars*."

★   ★   ★

Ken Costello kept tossing and turning.

It was only 2 a.m. in Washington, but his body was still on Israel time, and there it was nine in the morning. He was glad to finally be back in his own bed after several wrenching days in Israel, back with his wife, whose pregnancy was just beginning to show. But as she slept soundly, he couldn't sleep at all. He kept replaying the meeting in the Situation Room over and over in his mind.

How in the world could Mitchell have authorized wiretaps and other electronic surveillance on Israel's top leaders? How could he have kept all that from the president? Costello could only imagine the political firestorm that would erupt if such information leaked out. Any leverage MacPherson might have over Doron to keep the Temple from being built would fly right out the window.

But the more he thought about it, the more he realized that it wasn't shock he was feeling so much as anger. *Had* someone at the CIA or NSA leaked Doron's Temple project? To whom? For what reason? And as much as he wished it weren't true, Costello couldn't shake the feeling that it was.

There was no shortage of officials in the American intelligence community opposed to Israel's plans to rebuild their ancient Temple in Jerusalem. Some opposed the idea for geopolitical reasons, fearing it could trigger another regional war or impede the peace process. Others opposed it on ideological grounds, convinced as they were that religious fundamentalism was at the root of most of the world's conflicts and thus suspicious if not outright hostile to those who held strong spiritual convictions.

As for himself, Costello didn't know where he stood. He and Tracy had quietly been studying End Times prophecies for weeks, drawing much of their information from Eli Mordechai's Web site, as did millions of other curious souls. Though he could never admit it at work, he found himself intrigued by the possibility that major prophecies were coming true in their lifetime and that even bigger ones could be on the way.

Mordechai had taught that the War of Gog and Magog was just the beginning. The Temple would be built next, he explained, whether world leaders wanted it to be or not. And the Rapture could happen at any moment, he warned, followed by the rise of the Antichrist and then the Tribulation. Is that what was really about to happen?

In some ways it seemed so ludicrous. Yet so much of what Mordechai had predicted had already come true. What if the old man was right about the rest, too? And then there was the big question: when Jesus came, would Costello be allowed to meet Him in the air, or was he in danger of being lost? Costello wondered. And what about Tracy? Would they go to heaven together or suffer seven years of hell on earth, if they even made it that long?

Such were the questions that weighed on him these days, but he could not make up his mind. As much as he wanted to, he couldn't seem to take the leap of faith required to become a true, devoted follower of Christ. The notion of being "born again" was just a little too much for him. And yet the words of the Bible seemed to haunt him. *"He who has the Son, has eternal life; he who does not have the Son of God does not have the life. . . . Now is the day of salvation. . . . Behold, I stand at the door and knock; if anyone hears My voice and opens the door, I will come in to him and will dine with him, and he with Me."*

Suddenly, Costello heard someone pounding downstairs. Then the doorbell rang. It wasn't spiritual. It wasn't metaphoric. There was actually someone at his front door. Startled, he put on his glasses and ran downstairs in his boxer shorts and T-shirt. He peered through the curtains. It was a courier. *At this hour?* He opened the door.

The courier was a tall black man in a large blue parka. "Are you Mr. Kenneth Costello?"

"I am."

"You ordered a 'rush' job from the Library of Congress?"

"I did."

"Sorry it's so late, but I got here as fast as I could," said the man. "Sign here."

Costello scribbled his name, took the large sealed envelope, and closed the door. Next, he went into the kitchen, flicked on some lights, turned on the coffeepot, and ripped open the package. Inside was a note from the chief librarian—"As requested"—along with a first edition of the book that Costello had a hunch was going to occupy the rest of his day. He stared at the cover.

THE TREASURE OF THE COPPER SCROLL
The opening and decipherment of the most
mysterious of the Dead Sea Scrolls,
a unique inventory of buried treasure
by John Marco Allegro

Costello opened the book to the title page and found it copyrighted in 1960, then began slowly flipping through its pages, trying to get a brief overview before reading it cover to cover. On page 33, he came across Allegro's translation of the now-notorious Copper Scroll.

> *ITEM 1: In the fortress which is in the Vale of Achor, forty cubits under the steps entering to the east: a money chest and its contents, of a weight of seventeen talents.*
>
> *ITEM 2: In the sepulchral monument, in the third course of stones:—light bars of gold.*
>
> *ITEM 3: In the Great Cistern which is in the Court of Peristyle, in the plaster of its floor, concealed in a hole in front of the upper opening: nine hundred talents.*

And so it went, for page after page.

> *ITEM 47: In the reservoir which is in Beth Kerem, ten cubits on its left as you enter: sixty-two talents of silver.*
>
> *ITEM 48: In the vat of the olive press, in its western side, a plug-stone of two cubits (it is the opening): three hundred talents of gold and ten serving vessels.*

Costello had never read anything like it. Nor had he ever planned to. But now people were apparently being killed, and he had to know more. He skipped ahead to chapter 3, "The Treasure." One passage in particular caught his eye.

"Tales of buried treasure are to be found in any folklore, and Jewish literature has them in full measure," wrote Allegro, who went on to summarize some of the more popular versions from the Bible, as well as from extrabiblical literature, like the second book of Maccabees, which said that the prophet Jeremiah once "commanded the Tabernacle and the Ark to accompany him" to Mount Nebo on the shores of the Dead Sea. "There he found a cave in which he placed the Tabernacle, the Ark, and the incense altar, and then sealed its entrance," Allegro explained. "Even the prophet's followers did not know its whereabouts, but he promised that it would be revealed when 'God shall gather His people together again, and receive them unto His mercy.'

"Most of these traditions look to the time when the Messiah would restore the glory and the Temple and its treasures," Allegro concluded, adding that "all such stories bear the obvious marks of fiction either in the manner and place of concealment or in the nature of the treasure concerned."

But what intrigued Costello most was that Allegro explained that he believed the Copper Scroll was no legend. He believed that it was real and fully expected the treasures to one day be found.

Is that what Jon and Erin are really doing, hunting for the Temple treasures and the Ark of the Covenant? Whatever they were doing, someone was trying to kill them before they succeeded. Someone was killing *everyone* connected to the Copper Scroll. And for all Costello knew, it might actually be someone in his own government.

50
★ ★
★

It was almost 3 a.m. when Rajiv finally got home.

She quietly closed and locked the front door behind her, then checked on her husband. He was sound asleep. Next she tiptoed into her closet, pulled out a small carry-on suitcase, and took it back down to the kitchen of their Tysons Corner town house. There was no time to pack clothes, but she wouldn't need them anyway. With the money she was being paid, she could buy anything she wanted when she reached her destination.

Rajiv crawled under the sink, pulled up the linoleum, and pried away two wood panels. Inside was a steel box sealed shut with a combination lock. Inside the box were six fake passports, six different credit cards—each tied to the aliases on the passports—and nine thousand dollars in cash, all in well-worn twenty- and fifty-dollar bills. She stuffed it all in the suitcase, zipped it up, and replaced the wood panels under the sink. Then she took one last look around at a home she had loved but always known she'd one day flee.

She would actually miss her husband, she suddenly realized. He had been better to her than she had expected. Indeed, he had turned out to be a very sweet man—attentive, doting, the kind of man she might have enjoyed growing old with, if she had ever planned to stay married to begin with. It had never dawned on Peter Mohan Rajiv that his arranged marriage to Indira Visaloo Parajee had been a sham from the beginning, and in a way, she loved him for that. But it was over now. She hoped it would not destroy him, but she feared it would.

Rajiv jumped in her BMW Z4 and took off; then came the hard part: which airport, which alias, which getaway city? Dulles and Reagan National were out. It was too likely she'd run into someone she knew. The same was true with BWI. Even JFK was risky. She got on the beltway and headed north to 95. She could be in Boston in eight hours, nine at the most, and in London by morning.

It was a gamble. But it was the only chance she had.

51

★ ★
★

"Erin? Can you hear me?"

She could hear the words. She knew it was Jon. She was just having trouble actually getting her eyes open. She found his hand and squeezed it gently, and a moment later, she was looking into his beautiful green eyes.

"Hey, welcome back," she heard her husband say.

She smiled and tried to speak.

"You need some water?" he asked, apparently not sure if he had heard her right.

Erin nodded, almost imperceptibly.

Jon quickly poured her a glass from the carafe on the bedside table. He held her head up as she took a few sips and then gently lowered her head back onto the pillow.

"You had me worried for a while there," he said as his eyes filled with tears. "You've gotta stop doing that to me."

"I'm sorry," Erin whispered back.

"It's okay. I forgive you," he replied. "Just don't let it happen again."

He put another pillow under her head to prop her up a bit. "How about some good news?" he asked.

Erin nodded eagerly.

"It's pretty big," he said, smiling. "You might want to lie down for this."

She loved to see those crinkles form around his eyes.

"I found the Key Scroll."

Erin gasped. *"You're kidding,"* she whispered as she tried to sit up.

"I'm not," he replied, his eyes telling the story.

"In the tunnel?" she asked.

"Absolutely," he confirmed. "Right where Donovan thought it was all the time. Unfortunately, I found him as well. His bones at least. Harkin's too. It was pretty grim."

"How did they die?" she asked of the men who had once been her colleagues.

"Land mine, snipers—I doubt they even knew what hit them."

Erin winced and squeezed his hand again. It was amazing they hadn't been killed as well.

There was a knock at the bedroom door.

"Come in," Bennett replied.

Natasha entered the room. She pulled up a chair next to the bed, a yellow legal pad and a pen in her hands.

"You done?" Bennett asked, clearly surprised to see her.

"Yes!" she said, her face showing the relief. "I just finished. It went faster than I'd expected."

"It's done?" asked Erin, her voice still barely a whisper. "Can we see it?"

"Right now?" asked Natasha.

"No, next week," Erin quipped.

"Good to see you've still got a sense of humor," Natasha noted. "I'll show it to you in a moment. First, let me read you what it says."

There was an electricity of anticipation in the room as Natasha flipped back through her notes, cleared her throat, and started to read.

> *"The word of the LORD came to me:*
> *'Son of man, this is what the*
> *Sovereign LORD says to the*
> *land of Israel: The end!*
> *The end is now upon you*
> *and I will unleash*
> *my anger against you.*
> *I will judge you*
> *according to your conduct*

and repay you for all
your detestable practices.
I will not look on you
with pity or spare you.
Then you will know
that I am the LORD.
This is what the
Sovereign LORD says:
Disaster!
An unheard-of disaster
is coming.
Doom has come upon you—
you who dwell in the land.
Outside is the sword,
inside are the plague
and famine.
All who survive and escape
will be in the mountains.
Their silver and gold
will not be able to save them
in the day of the LORD's wrath.
See, I am setting before you
today a blessing and a curse—
the blessing if you obey
the commands of the LORD your God
that I am giving you today;
the curse if you disobey
the commands of the LORD your God
and turn from the way
that I command you today
by following other gods,
which you have not known.
When the LORD your God
has brought you into the land
you are entering to possess,
you are to proclaim

the blessings, and
the curses
as you know.'"

"That's it?" asked Bennett.

"That's everything," said Natasha.

"I don't understand," he continued. "The Copper Scroll pointed to-ward sixty-four different locations. Line 64 said that the Key Scroll would decode it all and lead us to the treasure. So what's this? Are we sure this is even the right scroll?"

"What are the chances of you finding *anything* in those tunnels— a million to one?" asked Natasha. "And what are the chances of you finding a scroll also engraved on copper if it's not connected to the first Copper Scroll? A billion to one?"

"But what good is it?" Bennett countered. "It doesn't tell us any-thing."

"Maybe it does," said Natasha. "Look at line 5."

The end is now upon you.

"See, that's interesting," said Natasha, now up and pacing about the room. "That's certainly consistent with the thinking of the Essenes. They definitely believed the end was upon them."

"So what?" Bennett complained. "That doesn't mean that—"

Bennett stopped in midsentence. Erin was whispering something.

"Read a few lines down," she said. *"Something about silver and gold."*

Bennett looked at Natasha, who scanned the text again and read the lines aloud.

"Their silver and gold
will not be able to save them
in the day of the LORD's wrath."

"You think that could refer to the Temple treasures?" Natasha asked. Erin nodded.

"She may be right," said Natasha, looking at Bennett.

"Maybe," he said. "But, Erin, sweetheart, that's pretty thin evidence, you've got to admit, especially compared to the Copper Scroll. You said it yourself, Natasha. The first one lists over three thousand talents of silver, almost thirteen hundred talents of gold, more than sixty-five gold bars, some six hundred silver pitchers—all of which are said to contain silver—and over six hundred other vessels made of silver and gold. And you said the Key Scroll would explain it all."

"Maybe it does," said Erin.

"What do you mean?" asked Bennett.

"Maybe it does, and we're just not seeing it clearly."

"How so?"

"It's in the mountains."

"What is?"

"The treasure—read it again—the silver and gold won't save them, but . . ."

Again, Bennett and Natasha looked back at the text.

> *All who survive and escape*
> *will be in the mountains.*
> *Their silver and gold*
> *will not be able to save them*
> *in the day of the LORD's wrath.*

Was she right? Bennett wondered. Was the treasure hidden in the mountains, and if so, which ones?

52

★ ★
★

"How many mountains are there in Israel?" Bennett asked.

Natasha looked at him with a pained expression. "Where do you want to start? There's the Mount of Olives, Mount Hermon, Mount Zion of course, Masada—"

"Masada," Bennett broke in. "Could that be it? That bit about 'surviving and escaping in the mountains'? Masada is a fortress, right?"

Masada towered some fifteen hundred feet over the Dead Sea. It was the site where the last band of Jewish rebels—more than a thousand men, women, and children—held off the Roman army for four years as the Romans sought to conquer every square inch of the Holy Land for their caesar and themselves. Was it possible the Jews had taken the Second Temple treasures there? Had that been why the Romans had been so determined to seize Masada? When the Roman forces finally stormed the mountaintop fortress, they found that the entire band of Jewish insurgents had already committed suicide. Could they have killed themselves to keep the Romans from ever finding the gold and silver of their beloved Temple?

Natasha suddenly ran out of the room without saying a word. Bennett and Erin just looked at each other, perplexed. But a moment later Natasha was back with her laptop. She logged on to Miriam's wireless Internet system and pulled up a Hebrew Bible site. Then she typed in the text from their mystery scroll and ran a search.

"What is it?" asked Bennett. "What are you looking for?"

"The language of this scroll is so curious," Natasha explained. "I'm wondering if . . ." She leaned toward her computer screen. "I knew it," she said at last.

"Knew what?" asked Bennett.

"This first section is Scripture," she exclaimed. "In fact, it's an excerpt from Ezekiel, chapter 7."

Natasha punched some keys and ran another search. "The next portion is from the book of Deuteronomy, chapter 11."

"Does either book mention Masada?" asked Erin.

"That's what I'm checking right now," said Natasha as her fingers flew across the keyboard.

"And?"

Natasha looked disappointed. "Masada isn't mentioned in either Ezekiel or Deuteronomy," she sighed.

"Check the rest of the Bible," Bennett suggested.

Natasha did but came up with nothing. Disappointment settled over the room.

"What about the other mountains you mentioned?" asked Bennett.

"I don't see how that helps us," said Natasha. "If Erin's right—if the treasure is buried in the mountains—then there must be a clue that we're missing."

Again she went to work on the computer as Bennett and Erin waited impatiently.

"That's strange," she said after a moment.

"What's that?"

"The passage from Deuteronomy . . . it's not complete."

"What do you mean?"

"I mean it begins in chapter 11, verse 26, and runs through the first phrase of verse 30. But in between, it's missing several key words and phrases."

Again Natasha bolted out of the room.

"Where are you going?" Bennett shouted after her.

"Hold on! I'll be right back," Natasha yelled back.

A minute later, she was back with Miriam's personal laptop. She set the two computers side by side. On one, she pulled up a portion of the scroll text.

> *When the LORD your God*
> *has brought you into the land*
> *you are entering to possess,*
> *you are to proclaim*
> *the blessings, and*
> *the curses*
> *as you know.*

On the other computer, she pulled up Deuteronomy 11:29-30.

> *When the LORD your God*
> *has brought you into the land*
> *you are entering to possess,*
> *you are to proclaim*
> *on Mount Gerizim*
> *the blessings, and*
> *on Mount Ebal*
> *the curses.*
>
> *As you know,*
> *these mountains are across*
> *the Jordan, west of the road,*
> *toward the setting sun,*
> *near the great trees of Moreh,*
> *in the territory of those*
> *Canaanites living in the Arabah*
> *in the vicinity of Gilgal.*

Natasha pointed to the English text on the first screen, and then to her notes on the second. "See where the scroll's author writes 'you are to pro-claim'—then there's an extra space—'the blessings, and'—then there's another extra space—'the curses'—then another extra space—then the phrase 'as you know.'"

The Bennetts nodded.

"Now look at the actual biblical text," said Natasha. "The full sentence should read, 'You are to proclaim on Mount Gerizim the blessings, and on Mount Ebal the curses.' But in the scroll version, the words *'on Mount Gerizim'* and *'on Mount Ebal'* are missing from the text."

"That *is* odd," said Bennett, studying the passage more closely.

Then Erin said, "Wait a minute. *Gerizim* and *Ebal*—those are mentioned in the Copper Scroll."

"They are?" asked Bennett, surprised but pleased that Erin was thinking clearly enough to recall such an obscure detail.

Natasha nodded and looked impressed. "Somebody was doing her homework. You studied the translation my grandfather gave you and Jon back at the Jordan Archaeological Museum in Amman, didn't you?"

Erin nodded.

"Gerizim and Ebal are two mountains north of Jerusalem and due west of where we just discovered the Key Scroll," Natasha said. "Line 61 of the Copper Scroll refers directly to Mount Gerizim."

She pulled up a digital image of the Copper Scroll on one laptop screen and the English translation of line 61 on the other. Bennett read it aloud.

"On Mount Garizin,
underneath the staircase
of the upper tunnel:
a chest and all its contents,
and sixty talents of silver."

"You're sure it's talking about the same mountain?" he asked.

"The spelling is different," Natasha noted. "But yes, that's it."

"So could those be the mountains where the treasure is buried?" he pressed.

They all looked at each other with anticipation. They were on to something.

"They could be," said Natasha. "After all, if what we've got really is the Key Scroll, then whoever wrote it came up with a pretty ingenious code for keeping the treasures secret."

Bennett wasn't sure he followed. "Meaning?"

"Meaning it would take someone who has a tremendous knowledge and understanding of the Holy Scriptures to break this code," Natasha explained. "They would have to be able to find this scroll. Then they'd have to be able to read it, which means they would have to be able to read Hebrew, and not many Romans could. Then they'd have to know that the words in the scroll were actually Scripture. And even if they did realize that the text was Scripture, they would still have to figure out that each paragraph was a different portion of Scripture and that certain phrases of those Scriptures were missing. Then they'd have to know where each portion of Scripture was found so they could accurately identify the missing phrases. And, of course, they'd have to do it all without the aid of computers."

She was right, Bennett realized, and his anticipation began to grow.

53

★ ★
★

"Code in."

"Sigma delta niner, alpha five sigma."

"Stand by for authentification. . . . Okay, go ahead. You are connected."

"Viggo, we have a problem," said Indira Rajiv as she headed toward Boston.

"No, we don't," said Mariano. "We've got them."

"What are you talking about?" asked Rajiv.

"The Bennetts and the Barak girl—I'm telling you we found them."

"Where?"

"They're holed up in a house in Tiberias," said Mariano. "We picked up their trail as they were coming out of the tunnel in the Golan Heights. My team and I followed them here. We've got them under surveillance. I just got off the phone with Farouk and Al-Hassani. They want me to camp out here until the Bennetts make their next move."

Golan. So her hunch had been correct. "Did they find the Key Scroll?" she asked.

"They did," Mariano confirmed. "They're decoding it now. We've got laser microphones trained on the windows. We're listening to everything they're saying."

"Have they figured out where the treasures are yet?" asked Rajiv. "Or the Ark?"

"No, not yet, but they seem to be getting close," he assured her. "By the way, thanks for the tip. I still can't believe they actually asked you about Donovan and Harkin. The timing couldn't have been more perfect."

"I know," said Rajiv. "Once I got the e-mail, I knew they were headed to the Golan. I didn't know exactly where, of course, but I guess you guys took care of that."

"When do you think they'll contact you?" Mariano asked. "They may need your help again."

"That may be a problem," said Rajiv.

"Why?"

"I'm on the run."

"*What?* What are you talking about?"

"They're on to me," Rajiv explained. "The president found out yesterday morning that I'm one of only seven people within our government who knew about Doron's Temple project. He doesn't know it's me. None of them do. But it was only a matter of time."

"How much time?"

"If I'd stayed, I'd have been in jail by nightfall."

"Where are you now?"

"Trying to get out of the country."

"Can you make it?"

"I think so," she said. "I've got a decent head start. I left a message for my boss that I wasn't feeling well and was going to a doctor's appointment at noon. I said I'd be in sometime in the afternoon."

"But it's Saturday," said Mariano.

"They don't care," said Rajiv. "It's the CIA."

"What about your husband?"

"He'll think I got home late, left early. Happens all the time. I left him a note reminding him to meet me at the Kennedy Center tonight for a concert. I'll leave him a message on his cell phone in a few hours, tell him I love him. I doubt he'll be suspicious until nightfall."

"You'd better be right," said Mariano.

"Where do you want me?" asked Rajiv, changing the subject.

"Head for Rome."

"Why not Milan?"

"Rome is better. We have more assets there. I'll have someone meet you at the airport. Don't worry. We'll take care of everything. Do you have the files we asked for with you?"

"Of course."

"Perfect."

"But I want to meet him," said Rajiv.

"What, face-to-face?"

"Of course."

"When?"

"By the end of the week."

"No, that's impossible."

"Do you want the files or don't you?"

"Of course we want them, but . . ."

"Then I want a meeting—face-to-face—just me and him."

"And you'll get one, but not right now. Too much is happening, and we can't afford for you to be out in the open for long. Just get to Rome and we'll make sure you're safe. I'll meet with you as soon as I can, probably a couple of days at most."

"You didn't recruit me," said Rajiv, defiantly. "He did."

"It doesn't matter. I'm running this operation, not him."

"Don't play games with me, Viggo," Rajv shot back. "I know too much."

"Are you threatening me?" he asked.

"You'd have nothing without me, and you know it. Now I want to see him before the week is out. Alone. I don't care how you do it. Just make it happen."

54

★ ★
★

Natasha had been working around the clock.

Exhausted and edgy, she had steered clear of both Bennetts for the last day or so as she continued trying to crack the code. But now she called them both to the kitchen.

"Whoever wrote this stuff was absolutely brilliant," she said, her eyes weary and bloodshot, when the Bennetts sat down with her at the table where her computers, notebooks, maps, and Bibles were all spread out. "Obviously, they kept the Romans from ever even finding the Copper Scroll. But even if the Romans had found and deciphered it, they'd never have found the treasure. They'd have been on a wild-goose chase. The treasure isn't buried in sixty-three different locations. It's only buried in one."

"You're sure?" asked Bennett.

"As sure as I can be," said Natasha. "I've studied the scroll Jon found in the tunnel from every possible angle, and I am now convinced, beyond the shadow of a doubt, that it is the Key Scroll. This is the real thing."

Bennett breathed a sigh of relief and turned to Erin. Over the past several hours her strength had been returning, and now a beautiful smile broke out across her face.

"What clinched it for you?" he asked.

"Pontius Pilate," Natasha replied.

"The guy who condemned Jesus to die?"

"Exactly."

"What are you talking about?"

"Do you know how Pilate left office?" Natasha asked.

"No," Jon and Erin admitted.

"He was forced out."

"Why?" asked Erin.

"Because he ordered the slaughter of a group of Samaritans who believed a great treasure was buried on Mount Gerizim."

"Really?" said Bennett. "I've never heard that."

"Josephus tells the story in *The Antiquities of the Jews*," Natasha explained. "Look, I'll show you."

She pulled up a Web site with the complete works of Josephus and did a search for Pilate. A moment later, she found book 18, chapter 4, section 1.

> *But the nation of the Samaritans did not escape without tumults. The man who excited them to it, was one who thought lying a thing of little consequence, and who contrived everything so that the multitude might be pleased; so he bade them get together upon Mount Gerizzim, which is by them looked upon as the most holy of all mountains, and assured them that, when they were come thither, he would show them those sacred vessels which were laid under that place, because Moses put them there. So they came thither armed. . . . But Pilate prevented their going up, by seizing upon the roads with a great band of horsemen and footmen. . . . and Pilate ordered [them] to be slain.*

They went on to read about how Pilate was reprimanded by his superiors for the massacre and forced to leave his post in Jerusalem. Then Natasha said, "Moses never crossed the Jordan, so obviously he could never have buried 'those sacred vessels' on Mount Gerizim. But what's interesting about Josephus's account is how strong the tradition was in the region that Temple treasures, perhaps even including the Ark, were buried on that mountain. And if that weren't enough, there are still some six hundred or so Samaritans living in Israel today, and they are convinced that the Messiah will come one day and show them where that great treasure is buried on Mount Gerizim."

They were getting closer.

"That's the good news," said Natasha. "Now the bad news."

Confused, Jon and Erin followed Natasha as she abruptly left the kitchen and sat down on the balcony, staring out across the Sea of Galilee as storm clouds gathered over the Golan Heights in the distance.

"What bad news?" Erin asked, taking a seat on one of the cushioned lounge chairs and wrapping herself with a wool blanket.

"Gerizim was the site of a Samaritan temple—a temple long considered heretical by the Jews," said Natasha. "What's more, at the time the Copper Scroll and the Key Scroll were written and hidden, Mount Gerizim was the site of a Roman military stronghold, as well as a major Roman palace. The ruins are still there today."

"And?"

"Well, why would the Jews risk burying the entire Temple treasure so close to their worst enemy? It doesn't fit."

"What about Mount Ebal?" Bennett asked.

Natasha sighed. "The problem there is that the Scriptures refer to Mount Ebal as a mountain of curses. It seems unlikely that the Jews who wrote this scroll would hide the Temple treasures in a mountain of curses."

It was quiet for a few minutes, save for the sound of some birds flying over the sea. Bennett leaned back and watched the storm moving in.

Erin, meanwhile, pulled out her Bible and began studying it carefully. "Natasha, with all due respect, I think you might be mistaken about Mount Ebal," she said a few minutes later.

"How so?"

"Well, look, you're the expert in all these archeology matters, and I don't pretend to understand it all—certainly not like you do," Erin said, as diplomatically as she could. "But I'm in a women's Bible study back in Washington, and we've been studying the book of Joshua. And if I remember correctly, Mount Ebal itself was never cursed."

"Go on," said Natasha, obviously curious.

"Well, from what I understand—and again, I realize you've got a lot more training and experience than I do—the Scriptures simply say that Mount Ebal is the location where the Hebrews were supposed to *explain* God's curses on those who disobey. It doesn't actually say the mountain itself is cursed."

"Where are you getting this from?" asked Natasha.

"Joshua 8:30-34. Should I read it out loud?"

"Absolutely," said Bennett.

"Then Joshua built
on Mount Ebal
an altar to the LORD,
the God of Israel,
as Moses the servant of the LORD
had commanded the Israelites.
He built it according to
what is written in the
Book of the Law of Moses—
an altar of uncut stones,
on which no iron tool
had been used.
On it they offered
to the LORD
burnt offerings and
sacrificed fellowship offerings.
There, in the presence
of the Israelites,
Joshua copied on stones
the law of Moses,
which he had written.
All Israel, aliens
and citizens alike, . . .
were standing on both sides of
the ark of the covenant of the LORD,
facing those who carried it—
the priests, who were Levites.
Half of the people stood
in front of Mount Gerizim
and half of them
in front of Mount Ebal,
as Moses the servant

of the LORD
had formerly commanded
when he gave
instructions to bless
the people of Israel.
Afterward, Joshua read all
the words of the law—
the blessings and the curses—
just as it is written
in the Book of the Law."

"Did the Romans ever have a fortress or palace on Mount Ebal?" asked Erin.

Natasha shook her head. "Not that I'm aware of," she said. "Why?"

"Humor me for a moment," Erin replied, "but I'm just thinking, if Mount Ebal were really cursed, why would Joshua have built an altar there? Why would he have offered sacrifices to God there? Or chiseled the Word of God into stone on Mount Ebal?"

Natasha didn't reply.

"He wouldn't have," Erin continued. "Which means Mount Ebal couldn't have been cursed."

"Where are you going with this?" Bennett asked.

"I'm just saying, what if the author of the Copper Scroll mentioned Gerizim to throw people off track, knowing full well that the Samaritans had a temple there and that the Romans had a fortress there? What if that's why no one's ever found anything in the caves of Gerizim—because the treasure was actually buried on Mount Ebal instead?"

55

★ ★
★

MONDAY, JANUARY 19 – 8:00 P.M. – BABYLON, IRAQ

The press conference began promptly at noon Eastern Standard Time.

Halfway around the world, Iraqi president Al-Hassani watched with great interest.

"Ladies and gentlemen, good afternoon, and thank you for coming," began U.N. Secretary-General Luis Pipilo. "As you know, I did not seek a second term. Indeed, I had hoped to step out of this job on January first and turn over the reins of this great institution to the president of South Africa. President Mogande has been in the hospital for the past few weeks, and I have stayed on in an interim capacity until he could assume his duties here. Sadly, I must inform you that President Mogande has just been diagnosed with an inoperable cancer, and he believes that he will not be able to serve as he had hoped. He has, therefore, asked me to help find someone who will bring the necessary energy and passion to the job. After careful consideration, it is my great pleasure to nominate Dr. Salvador Ciro Lucente."

Two hundred flashes and autoadvancers went off as cameramen captured the moment. It was being hailed as breaking news on television networks around the world. But it was old news to Al-Hassani, and he studied the scene carefully, waiting for a signal that his fate and Lucente's were now inextricably linked.

"Dr. Lucente is not simply exceptionally well qualified for this position," the secretary-general continued. "In so many ways his life represents the vision of the U.N. He was born in Barcelona on June 6, 1942, to parents who came from two different countries, two different languages, two different ethnic backgrounds. His father, Ciro Lucente, was born and raised just outside of Rome. His mother, Juanita, was born in Madrid. But when they met in the spring of 1940, they did not let their differences stand between them. They were married six weeks from the day they met.

"When the war was over, young Salvador went to school in Spain and summered in Sicily. He went on to graduate from the University of Barcelona and from Harvard. He worked for AT&T and then started his own company . . ."

Al-Hassani lit his pipe. He had the foreign minister of India waiting to see him, followed by another six hours of meetings with various leaders from what was left of Syria, Iran, Saudi Arabia, and the several Central Asian republics. So far, everything was on schedule. Terms were being negotiated. Deals were being cut. He hoped to have his own announcement to make to the world soon. But so much depended upon Lucente.

". . . and, of course, for the last several years he has served ably as the European Union foreign minister where he has helped improve relations between India and Pakistan, assisted in defusing tensions between North and South Korea, and helped manage the crisis we had between Russia and Israel last year. Personally, I cannot think of a better man to lead the United Nations in this critical hour, and it is my hope . . ."

Enough, thought Al-Hassani. *Let the man speak.*

Several minutes later, Lucente finally took his place behind the podium and bank of microphones.

"What a tremendous honor to be considered for this position," he began. "It is one that I take very seriously, and should I be acceptable to the nations of this esteemed body, I will do everything in my power to continue the important structural and institutional reforms Secretary-General Pipilo has begun to implement and to bring peace and prosperity to the developing nations of our world. Out of respect for the process, I will not take any questions until I have had the opportunity to meet personally with each representative on the Security Council. I promise, however, to hold a press conference very soon so I can answer your questions, of which I am sure there are many.

"That said, I do want to say that my top two priorities as secretary-general would be, number one, to accelerate both the relief and reconstruction efforts in those countries devastated by the firestorm and earthquake of a few months ago, and number two, to get oil flowing out of the Middle East once again, so we can bring down prices and reinvigorate the global economy.

"Neither of these tasks will be easy, of course. They will require an enormous degree of cooperation, particularly with countries such as Israel and Iraq. As you know, I have just come from meetings with leaders in those countries, and I can tell you that both Prime Minister Doron and President Al-Hassani have personally assured me that they will do everything possible to reduce tensions in the region and get Middle Eastern oil back on the market. Indeed, to that end, I hope to have a major announcement for you very shortly. Thank you all very much."

56

★ ★
★

The three of them pored over every map they could find.

Mount Ebal was south of them, about halfway between Tiberias and Jerusalem, not far from the Palestinian town of Nablus, known in ancient times as Shechem. Yet according to Natasha, very few serious archeological excavations had ever been done there. Most scholars focused on the Roman and Samaritan ruins on Gerizim. Thus the kind of access roads found on Gerizim simply didn't exist on Ebal.

What's more, they had neither the time nor the manpower to scour the entire mountain. One wrong move could mean being arrested by Israeli forces or shot by one of Farouk's men.

Bennett turned to his wife. "What do you think?"

"With what we've got?" she asked. "I don't think we'll make it. We don't even know where to start."

"Any suggestions?"

"We need satellite photos," said Erin. "Plain and simple. These maps simply aren't good enough. We need to study every nook and cranny of the mountain, look for cave openings, do thermal imaging, hunt for underground tunnels—that kind of thing."

"What about Rajiv?" Bennett suggested. "She helped us before. Maybe you could call her again."

"Who's Rajiv?" asked Natasha.

"A friend of mine at CIA," said Erin. "She's the one who helped us get into Mordechai's house the other night."

"So what do you think?" asked Bennett.

Erin looked uneasy. "To do it, she'd have to retask the satellite again."

"She did it once for you."

"I know, but I can't ask her again. It wouldn't be fair to her."

"You really think she'd turn us in?"

"No, but it's not just her. Claire at the National Recon Office, Bobby at NGA, maybe a few more, would have to be involved. We'd be putting Rajiv in a terrible position. She could lose her job. She could go to prison."

Bennett sighed. "It's not like our cup of options runneth over," he noted. "Call her. The worst that can happen is she'll say no."

☆　☆　☆

Mariano called with another update.

Al-Hassani said good-bye to the Indian foreign minister and took the secure call.

"We've had a complication," Mariano began.

"Don't tell me you lost them," said Al-Hassani.

"No, no, it's Doron," said Mariano. "He's appointed a government commission to finalize a design for the Third Temple."

"Tell me you're joking."

"I wish I were," said Mariano. "But the news just broke here, and Farouk is going nuts. I'm telling you, he's lost it, Your Excellency. He just called to say he wants me to kill the Bennetts, take the Barak girl hostage, and force her to lead us to the Ark. And if I don't do it, he'll find someone who will."

"*The fool!*" snapped Al-Hassani. "He'll ruin everything. I don't want them touched until we see how far they can take us or unless they turn themselves in."

"But Farouk is threatening to pull his money," said Mariano.

"I don't need his money," Al-Hassani fumed. "I don't need him at all."

"This was his idea," Mariano recalled. "And he has gotten us this far."

"And he's becoming a liability. Where is he now?"

"In a house outside of Amman, sir."

"You know what to do, Viggo," Al-Hassani said calmly. "Just make it look like a suicide."

☆   ☆   ☆

"Rajiv isn't answering."

"Did you try her cell phone?" Bennett asked.

"Twice," said Erin. "All I got was voice mail."

Bennett glanced out the window. It was already dark. If they were going to move, it would have to be soon. "Any suggestions?" he asked, not expecting any.

"Actually, one," said Erin.

"What is it?"

"Come here," she said as she logged on to the Internet and went to earth.google.com.

"What is that?" asked Natasha.

"Open-source satellite imagery. I'll need to download the software and install it, but it's free, and it just might help," Erin said.

Moments later the download was complete. Erin quickly executed the installation procedures and launched the application.

"What is this going to do for us, exactly?" Natasha asked.

Erin clicked on *More Information*, which Natasha read aloud.

> *"Point and zoom to anyplace on the planet that you want to explore. Satellite images and local facts zoom into view. Tap into Google search to show local points of interest and facts. Zoom to a specific address to check out an apartment or hotel. View driving directions and even fly along your route."*

On the screen, a star field appeared with a small image of planet Earth in the center, as seen from 39,189.76 miles up. Next, Erin typed in *Tiberias, Israel*. Instantly, the computer began to take them on a guided flight from outer space to a remarkably clear view of the seaside city from 13,044 feet up. The image was all blurry until she hit Control F6 followed by a cheat code she'd learned from her days at Langley. This enabled her to bypass the scrambling software that Israel had demanded Google include so enemies of the Jewish state couldn't use the site to target missile or bomber strikes.

Suddenly the topography was crystal clear.

"That's incredible," Natasha marveled.

"What street are we on again?" asked Erin.

"Ehad Ha'am Street," said Natasha.

Erin clicked a small icon called *Roads*, and suddenly bright red lines marked every road in and around Tiberias, small and large, showing street names in bright white letters. She found the right street, manipulated the controls a bit further, and they were zooming in to five thousand feet, then a thousand feet, then just a few hundred feet until they were looking through the kitchen windows of the very house they were sitting in.

"Pretty cool, huh?"

Natasha gasped. "It's amazing! If I walk out on the balcony, will you be able to see me?"

Erin laughed. "Sorry, it's not real time. But the resolution is actually quite extraordinary for a nonmilitary satellite."

"I'll say," said Natasha, examining the picture more closely.

"And check this out," said Erin. "You can rotate it to see the other side of the house as well."

"Look, you can even read the number on the front door," said Natasha.

"Can you pull up Mount Ebal?" said Bennett, checking his watch again.

"Absolutely," said Erin. "That's where I'm headed."

She zoomed out for a moment, panned southward to Nablus, and found the distinctive slopes of Mount Ebal. For the next twenty minutes, the three of them scoured every square inch of the "mountain of curses." Sure enough, there were no roads of any kind. But they did find nine cave openings—six on the south and east fronts, one on the north side, and two on the west.

"So what should we do?" asked Erin. "We don't have time to explore all nine. We barely have enough time to explore one."

"And we need to get moving if we've got any prayer of getting something done tonight," said Natasha.

Erin turned to her husband. "Want to just pick one at random?"

But Bennett was chewing on something. "What was that verse again? The one that begins, 'as you know'?"

"Deuteronomy 11:30," said Natasha.

"Can you look it up again?"

"What are you thinking?"

"I'm not sure, but . . ." His voice trailed off.

Natasha found the verse and began reading it aloud.

> *"As you know,*
> *these mountains are*
> *across the Jordan,*
> *west of the road,*
> *toward the setting sun,*
> *near the giant trees of—"*

"There, that's it," said Bennett, apologizing for cutting her off. "*West of the road*. That's what we're looking for. Caves on the west side. I know it's thin. But it's the only geographic reference in the whole scroll. I say we go with it and pray for mercy."

57

★ ★
★

"They're moving."

Mariano realized he had drifted off. "Who's moving?" he asked, trying to shake off his fatigue.

"The Bennetts and the Barak girl."

"When?"

"They just pulled out. Rosetti's got two vehicles following them. We've got another car waiting for you."

"Have they got radios?"

"Yes, sir."

"Make sure they don't get too close. If they spot them, we're dead. They'll vanish and we may never pick them up again."

"I'm on it, sir. And we're ready to roll when you are."

"No," said Mariano. "Let Rosetti handle it. Get me into that house. I want to see everything they've been doing and get it all to Al-Hassani."

★ ★ ★

They raced to Mount Ebal in the dark of night.

By eleven local time, with the help of the Navigator's GPS, they reached the outskirts of the Palestinian stronghold of Nablus, and in another fifteen minutes, they reached the base of Mount Ebal and realized anew what a long climb they had ahead. After hiding the SUV in a patch of brush, they gathered their equipment and began working their way up the north face.

Natasha's maps put the summit at about three thousand feet above sea level, but they weren't going to have to go quite that far. The two caves they had seen on the mountain's west side in the satellite imagery were located two-thirds of the way up, and roughly a hundred and fifty yards apart. For tonight, at least, these were the targets, and they quickly began their ascent.

☆　☆　☆

Mariano crept up the stairs of the Gozal house.

He held a .45 in one hand, a flashlight in the other. He didn't expect trouble, but he hated surprises. Having already found the maps and the laptops and a dozen unwashed coffee mugs spread across the kitchen, he headed for the master bedroom and soon came across the medical supplies that had helped Erin Bennett recover over the past few days.

"Put one over there and another in the lamp," he said, directing two of his men as they planted microphones throughout the house.

They had been listening to the Bennetts' conversations for days using laser microphones aimed at Miriam Gozal's windows, but they had been imperfect at best and hadn't worked at all when their subjects had been in the basement.

Mariano's phone began vibrating.

"Rosetti?" Mariano whispered into a headset.

"Yes, sir. We're about a mile and a half from the base."

"Do you have a visual?"

"Affirmative. The Barak girl is about halfway up. Mr. Bennett is close behind. Mrs. Bennett is a ways back. She's struggling quite a bit."

I bet she is, thought Mariano, still surprised that Erin hadn't died from hypothermia under the DMZ.

"Stay on them," he said, "and stay out of sight."

☆　☆　☆

He was going in alone.

Bennett doubled-checked his harness and helmet. He took another few minutes to check over the rest of his equipment as well and to make sure Erin and Natasha were ready. Then he turned on his headlamp and eased toward the edge of the cave.

Bennett could that tell his wife wasn't enthusiastic about his doing this without her, but there was no other way. Erin had barely recovered, and Bennett didn't feel right about sending Natasha in by herself, no matter how experienced she was.

"All set?" he asked as he donned gloves and took hold of the nylon rope.

"Ready when you are," Natasha replied.

"Just be more careful than me in there," Erin said.

"Don't worry," he said. "I will." He gave Erin such a long kiss that Natasha had to turn away in embarrassment.

"I love you," Erin whispered into his ear.

"I love you, too."

"All right, you two," Natasha groaned, "move it along."

Erin apologized and Bennett wondered if Natasha could see him blush in the dark. He didn't wait to find out. A moment later, he was rappelling into the cave. As best they could tell, the descent was rougly sixty-five or seventy feet down into the mountain. Where it went from there, he had no idea.

Bennett took his time, lowering himself a few yards, checking his equipment, letting Erin and Natasha adjust to his weight, then dropping another few yards. At the bottom, he finally remembered to turn on his radio.

"Testing, one, two, three—can you guys hear me?"

"Loud and clear," said Erin. "What can you see?"

"Not much. But, man, it stinks down here. What in the world is—?"

Suddenly there was a high-pitched screeching sound and a rush of wind. Before he knew it hundreds of bats were swarming all around him. He dropped to the ground and covered his head and face, but he could feel them everywhere—on his back and legs and hands and flapping around his ears. From the deepest recesses of the cave they just kept coming. After what seemed like an eternity, the horrifying cacophony tapered off, and all was quiet again.

Only then did he realize that what he was lying in wasn't mud but a huge pool of bat guano. He radioed to the top that he was fine, but he could feel his heart pounding and the humidity rising, and he was beginning to perspire in all his gear.

☆ ☆ ☆

No one tells a billionaire he snores.

So Abdullah Farouk had no idea. None of his wives or concubines back in Riyadh had ever told him. Nor had any of his lovers around the globe. And unbeknownst to him, both of his bodyguards used earplugs at night so they wouldn't have to suffer his horrible racket.

Tonight, they would suffer far worse.

The guard by the back door was the first to die. He was shot in the chest with a silencer, then dragged out of the house and loaded into a stolen bakery truck. The guard by the front door got a steel pipe over the head and a knife across his throat.

Before Farouk realized what was happening, four men were upon him. Two held him down while a third stuffed a rag down his throat. The fourth jammed a needle into his wrist, injecting a lethal but traceless toxin. Farouk twisted and writhed in pain, but a minute later, both the snoring and the muffled screams had ceased. The four men stripped his body, carried him into the bathroom, and set him in the tub. Then they drew a nice, hot bath, waited for the tub to fill, and slit Farouk's wrists, leaving the razor blade on the bloody tiled floor.

Sixty seconds later, a baker's truck rolled through the streets of Amman, attracting no attention at all.

58

Nearly three hours had passed.

Bennett had found nothing yet. He wanted to make sure he would be able to find his way back through the labyrinthine series of tunnels and small corridors branching off the main passageway, so he dropped glow sticks every twenty yards or so. He pressed onward.

At the beginning, the tunnel had been about four feet from one side to another. Now, as he continued his descent, the walls narrowed steadily. At the same time, the tunnel began to shrink from six or seven feet high near the entrance to a point where it was less than three feet high, forcing him to crawl on his hands and knees through more bat droppings and who knew what else.

Bennett noticed that the stench didn't seem as bad. Or perhaps he'd just gotten used to it. He also noticed that his radio was no longer working. He quickly changed batteries, but it didn't help. He had gone too deep to get any reception. But he couldn't stop now, so he dropped another glow stick and continued his journey into the subterranean maze.

☆   ☆   ☆

Back on the surface, Erin was panicking.

"I'm sure he's fine," said Natasha. "He knows what he's doing."

"How do you know?" Erin shot back, more aggressively than she'd meant. "You barely know him."

"I know more than you think," Natasha replied. "Uncle Eli used to go on and on about you guys until I thought I was going to be sick."

"Really?" said Erin. "He never mentioned you at all." She suddenly realized how cold that sounded. "I'm sorry. I didn't mean to be rude."

"It's all right," Natasha said. "I know what it's like to worry about someone you love."

"Your grandfather?" Erin asked.

"Actually," said Natasha, "I was thinking about my husband."

Erin was startled, to say the least. "Your husband?"

"Binyamin," Natasha said softly. "He was in the navy—a SEAL, you'd call him. Anyway, he went out on a mission off the coast of Beirut and he never came back."

"I'm so sorry," said Erin. "I had no idea."

"It was a long time ago," said Natasha. "Almost ten years."

Still, to Erin, the pain in her new friend's eyes looked fresh. "First your parents, and then your husband?"

"All the luck, huh?" said Natasha, her bottom lip beginning to quiver.

☆   ☆   ☆

Just a little farther, Bennett decided.

It was foolish, he knew. He was now at least three miles into the mountain. He must be nearing its core, he thought. But he couldn't go back without knowing for sure. He took a gulp of water and squeezed around a tight corner and through a narrow crevice, dripping with water. A minute went by, then two, then five. All of a sudden the tunnel opened up into a large cavern. He could finally stand again, and when he did, he found himself at a dead end.

And then he noticed something odd.

Scattered about the floor of the cavern were six large piles of rocks. Where had they come from? They were obviously not natural formations, but who had put them there? And why?

Bennett's heart rate began to rise. He set down his backpack, pulled out a digital camera, and snapped a few pictures. Then he stuffed the camera back in its bag and got started.

It was excruciating, backbreaking work. But after fifteen minutes, Bennett had cleared most of the rocks off the first pile. He pulled a spade from his pack and was preparing to dig when he realized he had already hit solid granite. There was nothing buried under the stones. Absolutely nothing.

Bennett repeated the process with the second pile, and the third, but each time he found nothing, and what little hope he had left quickly began to fade. It was now three-thirty in the morning. By the time he got back to the cave entrance, it would be at least five, and then he'd have to climb his way out. There would be no time left to explore another cave. At that point, they'd barely have enough time to get home before sunrise. But the thought of turning back with nothing to show for it made him physically ill, and he pled with God to show him favor.

* * *

"Why are you here, Erin?" Natasha asked.

The question came without warning, and Erin wasn't sure what she meant.

"Why are you doing this—you and Jon?" Natasha pressed. "Why risk your life for something that means nothing to you? I mean, this is my life. And it was my grandfather's. But you've got no stake in this thing. Sure, it was important to Uncle Eli, and maybe you'll track down his killers. But maybe not. Maybe they'll get you first."

Erin looked in Natasha's eyes. She was serious, and she was waiting for an answer Erin didn't feel comfortable giving. But it was the truth, and she was too tired to come up with anything different.

"Have you ever heard the expression 'The safest place to be is in the center of God's will'?"

"No," said Natasha.

"It just means if God wants you to do something, you'd better do it, even if it sounds a little crazy. Jesus said, 'If you love Me, you will keep My commandments.' And I love Him more than I can possibly explain. So I try to be faithful to whatever He asks of me."

"And if He told you to jump off a bridge . . ."

"No, no, it's not like that," said Erin. "But it is a little hard to explain if you've never—" She paused abruptly, then shifted gears. "How many languages do you speak, Natasha?"

"Speak or read?"

"Whatever."

"Seven," said Natasha.

"Wow, that's amazing."

"How about you?" Natasha demurred.

"Three," said Erin. "English, Arabic, and Russian. A little Farsi, I guess, but not much. But my point is that regardless of how many languages I could speak, if you were talking to me in Hebrew right now, I'd have absolutely no idea what you were saying. You could be telling me exactly where the treasure is, and I wouldn't know it. You could be telling me how you met your husband and fell in love, but I'd have no idea. Why? Because I don't know Hebrew. I haven't studied it, much less become fluent. It would mean nothing to me, and I'd miss everything you were trying to say to me.

"And you know, the same is true with God. He says He loves us 'with an everlasting love.' He has plans to give us 'a hope and a future.' He says He wants to adopt us into His family and have a personal relationship with us, to walk with us and talk to us and tell us great and mighty things we do not know. But unless we become true followers of His and learn to speak His language, we'll completely miss what He's trying to say. How did King Solomon put it? 'He is intimate with the upright.' And Jesus said, 'My sheep hear My voice, and I know them, and they follow Me; and I give eternal life to them.'

"For most of my life I didn't get that. I wasn't an atheist, mind you. Intellectually, I believed God existed, of course. But I just didn't care. He seemed irrelevant to me—distant, removed, far away, and unconcerned with my life and my problems. And I think that was partly because I had no idea what I was missing."

"And you think God wants you to be out here," asked Natasha, "in the heart of the West Bank, in the deep of the night, in bitter cold and whipping winds, hoping your husband finds some ancient Jewish treasure, or at least comes out alive?"

"I wouldn't be here if I didn't," said Erin. "And besides, what if God has more than one reason for me to be out here?"

"Like what?" asked Natasha.

"Like giving you the chance to know the Messiah and hear His voice as well."

59

★ ★
★

It wouldn't be long until daylight.

Erin and Natasha were growing increasingly worried about Jon Bennett. He wasn't back. He hadn't checked in for hours, and there was no way for them to contact him unless they went in after him. But if he didn't get back soon—with or without good news—they would have to drive back in daylight, and that meant the chances of getting caught or killed would rise dramatically.

"I'm going in," Erin said at last. She began fishing through one of the backpacks to find the gear she'd need.

"Oh no you're not," insisted Natasha. "Not in your condition."

"I can't leave him in there by himself," Erin replied. "What if something terrible has happened to him?"

"You're not well enough, Erin. Not yet. And you've been up all night."

"I'll be fine," Erin insisted.

But Natasha obviously wasn't convinced. "Maybe we need to think about turning ourselves in. Didn't your friend—that Costello guy—say he could talk to the prime minister for you? I'm sure they'd send out a team to help us."

"We're not turning ourselves in to Doron."

"Why not?"

"Because I don't know who I can trust in that office, and neither do you," said Erin. "You know as well as I do that the only chance we have of finding the people who killed Mordechai and your grandfather is finding the treasure. And we can't do that if we're in prison or dead."

But Natasha wouldn't let it go. "What about your friend at CIA—Rajiv somebody?"

"Indira Rajiv?"

"Right," said Natasha. "Didn't Jon want you to enlist her help?"

"I called her—several times. I never heard back."

"So call her again."

"For what?"

"I don't know," said Natasha. "For satellite coverage. An extraction team. Advice. Something. Anything. She helped you before. I'm sure she'd help you again, especially if she knew you and Jon were in danger."

Erin considered that for a moment. Maybe Natasha was right. They were flying solo and it wasn't going well. If there was anyone she could trust, she figured it was Rajiv. And even if she couldn't help them directly, perhaps Rajiv could point them to someone who could help.

Erin powered up the satellite phone and called Rajiv's cell phone. There was no answer. She tried the home number but again got voice mail. She closed her eyes and tried to think. Rajiv had a satellite phone as well, but what was the number? Finally it came to her and she dialed.

"Hi, this is Indira. I'm sorry I can't take your call right now. But please leave a message and I'll get right back to you."

Her anxiety about Jon rising quickly, Erin decided to leave a message. It was a risk, to be sure, but for the moment she couldn't think of what else to do.

"Indira, it's me, Erin. I really need your help. We're in the West Bank, near Nablus. Jon's missing. He went into a cave on Mount Ebal and never came back. Call me back as soon as you can. Please. It's urgent." Then she gave Rajiv their satphone number and hung up.

"No luck?" asked Natasha.

"No," said Erin. She donned her gear and prepared to head into the cave.

Natasha stepped in front of her, blocking the way. "I can't let you go in there. You'll just hurt yourself. Isn't there anyone else you can call?"

"No," said Erin. "I'm sorry. There just isn't. Now I'm going in. I'll call you as soon as I find him, and we'll figure out what to do then." She started forward again.

Natasha didn't move. "You think something's really happened to him?"

"Why else would he be taking so long?"

"Maybe he found something."

"Then he'd call in."

"Maybe he's out of range. Look, if something *has* happened to him—and believe me, I hope to God that nothing has—but if it has, you're not going to be able to get him out of there alone. Even together we couldn't do it. We need more bodies, and we're going to need a helicopter."

Erin thought about that. "What about yours?" she asked.

"Not possible."

"Why not?"

"Well, first of all, it's not mine," said Natasha. "Second, there's no way to get it out of Jerusalem with all the police and border patrol out looking for us. How about you? Know anyone else with a helicopter?"

"Someone who won't turn us in?"

"Narrows it down, doesn't it?" asked Natasha.

"A bit, yeah," said Erin. She thought a moment. "Actually," she said, "there is somebody."

"Who?"

"Dmitri Galishnikov."

Natasha raised her eyebrows. "Miriam's boss?"

Erin nodded.

"The founder and CEO of Medexco—the richest man in Israel?"

"That's him," said Erin. "He's got a fleet of choppers. Better yet, he's got a license to fly all of them. When he was younger—much younger, before he struck oil—he used to run commando missions for the IDF."

"Really?" asked Natasha. "I had no idea."

Erin pulled out the phone again and dialed.

"It's ringing," she said a moment later. "Hello, Mr. Galishnikov? It's Erin Bennett. I am so, so sorry to wake you, but I'm afraid Jon and I very much need your help."

★   ★   ★

Under the fourth rock pile, Bennett hit pay dirt.

Buried in the center of the stones was a large clay pot, not unlike the ones he had seen in the Shrine of the Book. His hands began to tremble with excitement. He carefully tipped the pot and shined his headlamp inside. And there, waiting, undisturbed for the past two thousand years, was yet another scroll.

★   ★   ★

Natasha was not about to let Erin go into the tunnel alone.

But they were both becoming more and more concerned. Natasha was almost to the point of going in herself to look for Bennett when there came a shout from the bottom of the cave shaft.

A few minutes later, Jon's filthy face appeared.

"Thank God you're okay," Erin exclaimed, giving her husband a huge embrace. "You had me freaking out up here."

"I'm sorry—I'm okay, really. I'm fine," he promised, giving her a long and tender kiss.

"What happened?" she asked, coming up for air. "What took you so long?"

"It's a long story," said Bennett.

He pulled off his backpack and unzipped it. Then he pulled out a blanket and slowly, carefully unwrapped it. And there, in its center, was the scroll.

"No treasure in there," Bennett said as he handed Natasha their latest clue, "but it wasn't a complete waste of time. At least I come bearing gifts."

But there was no time to examine the scroll. All three lifted their heads as a distant rumble, almost like thunder, grew nearer and intensified.

"What is that?" Bennett asked.

"Probably our ride," said Erin, glancing at her watch. "Right on time."

"What are you talking about?"

"Natasha and I were getting worried about you," she said. "So I decided to call in some backup."

"Erin, you didn't," Bennett said, still looking around for the source of the growing noise. "Tell me you didn't call Doron."

"I didn't call Doron."

"Erin . . ."

"I *didn't* call Doron, Jon," she insisted. "Ye of little faith!"

Erin and Natasha both stood and together helped the exhausted Bennett to his feet as a Bell 430 executive helicopter began descending a few yards away. Bennett peered into the cockpit just as the morning sun began to peek over the eastern mountains, only to find a familiar face at the controls.

"You called Dmitri?" he yelled over the roar of the rotors.

"I couldn't think of anyone else," Erin shouted back.

"You're amazing!"

"Thanks. Now let's go, before someone figures out what we're doing up here."

☆   ☆   ☆

Mariano's team stared in shock.

They watched in stunned silence as the jet helicopter touched down halfway up the western face of Mount Ebal. They thought they had prepared for every eventuality. But they hadn't prepared for this.

"What do we do?" one of the men radioed to his team leader.

"Take them out. I repeat, take them out."

☆   ☆   ☆

The back door of the chopper swung open.

There were three large men in the back—security types, Erin figured, probably working for Medexco—and they eagerly helped Bennett and the women scramble aboard with all of their gear, then quickly closed the door behind them.

"Welcome to Air Jerusalem," Galishnikov said over the intercom as the chopper began to gain altitude. "It is an honor to have you aboard this morning. Please buckle your seat belts and make yourselves comfortable. We'll be flying today at—"

A gunshot suddenly shattered the side window. Two more shots ripped into the fuselage. Natasha was screaming. Blood covered her face.

Another shot shattered the copilot's window, though fortunately there was no one in that seat.

Bennett instinctively pushed Erin and Natasha to the floor and covered their bodies with his own.

One of the men near Bennett smashed out one of the back windows with the butt of a rifle and began returning fire. A moment later, another did as well.

Galishnikov swung the bird around, and they began to climb rapidly. They could still hear rounds smashing into metal all around them, but before they knew it, they had cleared the mountain and were racing westward, trembling, wounded, and wondering who had found them and how.

60
★ ★
★

Eventually they landed at Galishnikov's seaside estate in Netanya.

Perhaps someday, thought Bennett, they'd be able to relax on the grounds of the palatial, five-acre, $19 million compound, with its tennis courts, swimming pool, and fountains, all overlooking the glistening Mediterranean. But today, he knew, wasn't going to be that day.

Dmitri's wife, Katya, met them on the landing pad and hurried them inside and into the spacious living room as Dmitri explained what had just happened. Then Katya wrapped Erin in blankets, got her tucked in on a couch, and began treating Natasha's facial lacerations, while Dmitri made coffee and brought in some rolls and fruit.

"How about you?" Katya asked Bennett when she had finished with the others. "Are you okay?"

"Just a little rattled," he said, grateful for the hot mug in his cold hands, "and worried about those two."

"I'd imagine so," she replied. "I just feel sick about what's happening to the three of you—Eli, then Yossi, and now this. It's madness. I don't know how you three are still functioning."

"Adrenaline," said Bennett.

"Caffeine," said Erin, peeking out from the blankets.

"Revenge," said Natasha.

A chill settled over the room, despite the fire now crackling in the fireplace.

"Yes, well, how can we help?" asked Dmitri. "What do you need now?"

Bennett looked at Erin, then at Natasha. "A lawyer, for starters," he said.

"I guess so," said Dmitri. "Well, I'm afraid Katya here doesn't practice much anymore, but I could make some calls. . . ."

"No, no," said Bennett. "You'd be perfect, Mrs. Galishnikov. Do you still have your license?"

"Please, Jonathan," she replied. "We've known each other too long. Call me Katya. But yes, I still have a valid law license."

"And everything we say from this point forward would be covered by attorney-client privilege?"

"Of course," she said. "And from what I can tell, you've got an airtight case for self-defense."

"Actually, that's not our main concern right now," said Bennett.

"What is?" asked Dmitri.

Again Bennett looked at Erin and Natasha. Both nodded, though each a bit reluctantly. So he opened his backpack, pulled out the blanket, and set it on the coffee table in front of them, where he unwrapped it until the scroll he had found deep inside Mount Ebal was visible.

The Galishnikovs stared in disbelief.

"What is it?" asked Dmitri.

"Bait," Bennett replied.

☆　☆　☆

Mariano slammed down the phone and unleashed.

He threw a plate across the kitchen. When it smashed against the refrigerator, he began heaving everything on the table across the room—plates, glasses, silverware. Then he flipped the table over and stormed around Miriam Gozal's house, cursing at the top of his lungs. *Lost them? His team had actually lost the Bennetts and the Barak girl? It was unbelievable. It was impossible. Now what was he supposed to do? Someone would pay for this failure.*

* * *

Bennett laid out the whole story.

The serial killings. Mordechai's last words. How they had met the Baraks and learned about Abdullah Farouk. Finding the Key Scroll. Their emerging theory that perhaps the Copper Scroll was an elaborate ruse, designed to cause people to look in dozens of different locations when the treasures—if they were, in fact, real—could be hidden in just a single location.

Bennett's new theory was that now that they had the Key Scroll and the scroll from Mount Ebal, they had the initiative. If they could only find the treasure, Mordechai's killers would find them and the conspiracy that had left a trail of blood from London to Los Angeles would soon unravel.

"And that gunfire back there?" asked Dmitri.

Bennett nodded. "The bait is working."

"And you think this scroll will lead you to the treasures?"

"It better," he said. "It's the only hope we've got."

* * *

An hour later, Mariano's team pulled into the driveway.

They gathered in the living room of Miriam Gozal's house, their heads hung low. The team leader explained what had happened as Mariano paced the thick Persian carpets, barely able to contain the rage seething within. He didn't ask questions. He didn't ask for clarifications. The team leader just continued talking, and Mariano finally could take it no longer. Before anyone realized what he was doing, he drew his silenced pistol and fired two bullets into the man's head.

Everyone got the message. Mariano didn't want excuses. He wanted the Bennetts and whatever they had found in that cave.

* * *

Natasha excused herself from the discussion.

She was still in pain, still battling shock, but she knew full well that none of them were going anywhere until she cleaned and translated the scroll they'd just found. The longer she waited, the more danger they were in. So she requested a toothbrush, baking soda, a glass of water, and a washcloth and headed for the dining room as Katya went to gather the items.

But Dmitri still had more questions.

"You're certain this Abdullah Farouk fellow is behind all this killing?" he asked.

"I'm not sure if it'd hold up in court, but yes, we're sure," said Bennett.

"And you think that's who opened fire at you?"

"I doubt it was Farouk personally. But his people? Sure."

"How much do you know about him?"

"Not much," Bennett conceded. "Obviously, an heir to an enormous fortune, said to be worth several billion dollars, but Farouk is also believed to be a shrewd investor. For the past several years he's been concentrating most of his assets in Iraqi oil and real estate. But his real passion is collecting antiquities. He apparently owns one of the world's largest private collections of Babylonian, Persian, and Roman artifacts and keeps most of it at his summer estate in Jiddah, Saudi Arabia, overlooking the Red Sea. Fancies himself an amateur archeologist but has obtained most of his collection through auctions and on the black market."

"And you said he's obsessed with hunting the Ark?" asked Dmitri.

"That's putting it mildly," Bennett replied. "He once told a London paper that the Ark wasn't some 'relic' to be put in a museum but 'a weapon of mass destruction' that would help Arab leaders build a caliphate from Morocco to Pakistan."

"Then I doubt he's working alone," said Dmitri.

"What do you mean?"

"I mean it doesn't sound like he wants the Ark sitting on his mantel, if he finds it. He's an ideologue. He thinks the Ark can help someone build a new Arab empire. The question is, who is the someone he's working with?"

Bennett suddenly realized just how tired he and Erin were. They hadn't been thinking through the larger geopolitical picture. They'd been in pure survival mode.

"Farouk has had a great deal of contact with Iraqi officials of late, though I'm not sure exactly who," said Bennett, considering the implications. "You don't think there's an Al-Hassani connection to all this, do you?"

"After the firestorm, who else is standing?" said Dmitri.

"Whoa, whoa, wait a minute," said Erin, pulling herself up to a sitting position. "Aren't we getting a little ahead of ourselves?"

"Maybe," Bennett conceded. "But Dmitri has a point. Farouk has money, and influence, and a vision of a new Arab empire. But he couldn't build it on his own, even with the Ark in hand. He'd need a partner, someone with land, oil, and an army and an air force."

"But, Jon, really, *Mustafa Al-Hassani?*" Erin countered. "Do you hear what you're saying? Al-Hassani was a philosophy professor, for crying out loud. Saddam threw him into the gulag for being a reformer. If we hadn't invaded Iraq, he'd still be rotting in prison. You really think the morning after he won 63 percent of the vote he woke up and thought, *Forget Thomas Jefferson. I think I'll pattern myself after Joseph Stalin?*"

"I don't know," said Bennett. "But be honest—neither do you."

"Maybe not," said Erin. "But I know a few things. I know Al-Hassani invited Eli Mordechai, the former head of the Israeli Mossad, to visit him in Iraq. I know he gave Mordechai classified Iraqi documents that exposed a conspiracy to overthrow the Russian government—a conspiracy that proved to be real, mind you. I know that Al-Hassani has quietly confided to you and me that he might be open to a peace treaty with Israel. And I just don't see this guy hiring Abdullah Farouk to play Indiana Jones for him, then ordering his thugs to gun down Mordechai in broad daylight. The whole notion is ridiculous, Jon. Al-Hassani isn't crazy. Farouk is. It's him we should be looking for. Period."

"You don't think Al-Hassani could be trying to capitalize on the firestorm to rebuild the Babylonian Empire?" asked Jon.

"Rebuild the region? Yes. But rebuild an empire? I doubt it. Even if he is, I highly doubt he's sending out hit teams to get it done."

"What if he is?" asked Bennett.

"Jon, how stupid do you think Al-Hassani is? You think he would really gamble everything he's got, after all we've done for him and his people, to turn Iraq back into a base camp for a whole new wave of global terrorism?"

"Actually, I think that is precisely what Eli believed," said Dmitri.

Jon and Erin both looked at him.

"As you know, Eli was quite skeptical of your country's efforts to rebuild Iraq—not a critic, mind you, but a skeptic, to be sure. Remember what he said at your reception? He said the War of Gog and Magog wasn't the end; it was just the beginning. He said evil was regathering, that something worse is coming. And that last posting on his weblog—how did he put it again?"

Bennett reluctantly finished Galishnikov's thought, for those very words had been ringing in his ears ever since he had first read them.

I supported the war in Iraq, Mordechai had written. *I believed Saddam Hussein was a serious threat to the region and the world, and I believed in the cause of regime change. Removing Saddam was not as easy as we had hoped, nor as quick. But the question isn't whether we should have gone to war in Iraq. The real question is, what exactly are we building there? Are we making Iraq safe for democracy, or safe for the Antichrist?*

61
★ ★
★

It was time to change the subject.

"It won't be long until they track us here," said Erin.

"What do you mean?" asked Dmitri.

"The tail numbers," Erin explained. "Once they trace those, they'll know it was your helicopter."

"That's not public information," said Dmitri.

"Maybe not. But like Jon said, we think they're working with someone inside the prime minister's office."

Dmitri shook his head. "I can't believe that. A traitor in David Doron's inner circle? It's impossible, I tell you."

"Yet people keep dying, don't they?" said Erin. "With all due respect, sir, the question isn't whether there is a mole. It's how easily Farouk and his men can contact him and how quickly Farouk can figure out where we are. That gives us only a few hours, at best."

"Maybe you're right," said Dmitri. "But I have three homes, ninety-two drill sites, and the refineries. What are the chances they'll look here first?"

"These guys are pros. They won't think for one minute we're all hanging out at some oil well. They're coming here—believe me—and I'd suggest we not be here when they arrive."

* * *

Al-Hassani exploded.

"What do you mean you lost them?"

Viggo Mariano swallowed hard. He knew what was coming. He was just glad he and the Iraqi leader were separated by several hundred miles.

"We're doing everything we can, Your Excellency," Mariano insisted. "My team from Jordan just landed in Tel Aviv."

"How many?"

"There are three of them, plus the four of us."

"How'd they get in?"

"Does it matter? I told you, I'm taking care of it."

"Why doesn't that reassure me?" sniffed Al-Hassani.

"Fine," said Mariano. "They're journalists. They're posing as an Italian television crew. They just rented a car. They're meeting me in Jerusalem in an hour."

"Weapons?"

"We'll give them what we can."

"And then what?"

Mariano stalled. The truth was, he had no idea.

* * *

Technically, what Bennett had found wasn't a scroll.

Not in the classic sense of the word, anyway. It was copper, like the others. But it was not rolled up as scrolls typically are. Thus it had no need to be sliced into pieces with a laser or a special circular saw. It actually looked more like a copper tablet. It was rectangular in shape—about a foot long and a foot and a half wide—and engraved with an ancient form of Hebrew lettering.

Exhausted and still in pain from her wounds, Natasha took longer on the translation than might otherwise have been usual, but she was determined to get it right. Finally, after more than two hours, she finished typing her notes into the laptop she had borrowed from the Galishnikovs and called the group into the dining room, where she had been working without a break.

"What have you got?" asked Bennett. "Are we on the right track?

"I think so," said Natasha. "This may be the most intriguing one of all. Let me take it section by section."

She pulled up a split-screen image with a digital photograph of the first paragraph in the scroll on the left side and the English translation on the right. Then she read the English aloud.

"All the commandments that I am
commanding you today you shall
be careful to do, that you may
live and multiply, and go in and
possess the land which the LORD
swore to give to your forefathers.
You shall remember all the way
which the LORD your God has led you
in the wilderness these forty years,
that He might humble you, testing you,
to know what was in your heart,
whether you would keep
His commandments or not.
He humbled you and let you be hungry,
and fed you with manna
which you did not know,
nor did your fathers know,
that He might make you understand
that man does not live
by bread alone, but man lives
by everything that proceeds
out of the mouth of the LORD."

"I ran a search," said Natasha. "That's Deuteronomy 8:1-3. Now, watch this."

"For the LORD your God
is bringing you into a good land,
a land of brooks of water,
of fountains and springs,

flowing forth in valleys and hills;
a land of wheat and barley,
of vines and fig trees and pomegranates,
a land of olive oil and honey;
a land where you will eat
food without scarcity, in which
you will not lack anything.
When you have eaten and are satisfied,
you shall bless the LORD your God
for the good land which He has given you."

"That's also Deuteronomy 8," Natasha noted. "But only verses 7, 8, part of 9, and all of 10."

Bennett quickly explained to the Galishnikovs the "missing link" theory they'd been using to crack the scroll codes, then asked Natasha what was missing this time.

"I think the second half of verse 9 is the clue," said Natasha. She pulled up a new screen with the full verse.

". . . a land where you will eat food without scarcity,
in which you will not lack anything;
a land whose stones are iron,
and out of whose hills you can dig copper."

"'Out of whose hills you can dig copper,'" she repeated. "That's it. That, I think, links it conclusively to the others."

"Go on," said Erin. "Show us the next section."

Natasha flashed a new image on the screen and read the text aloud.

"It came about
in the sixth year,
on the fifth day
of the sixth month,
as I was sitting in my house
with the elders of Judah
sitting before me, that the

hand of the Lord God
fell on me there. Then I looked,
and behold, a likeness
as the appearance of a man;
from His loins and downward
there was the appearance of fire,
and from His loins and upward
the appearance
of brightness, like the appearance
of glowing metal.
Then He brought me to
the entrance of the court,
and when I looked, behold,
Shallum the son of Col-hozeh,
the official of the district
of Mizpah, repaired the Fountain Gate.
He built it, covered it and
hung its doors with its bolts
and its bars.
After him, Nehemiah son of Azbuk,
official of half the district
of Beth-zur, made repairs as far as
a point opposite the tombs."

"I'm not sure I could follow any of that," said Bennett.

They were all thoroughly confused.

Natasha did her best to walk them through it. "What's interesting is that it's all Scripture," she began. "What's odd is that it's a real mishmash. The first part comes from the book of Ezekiel. Then it shifts abruptly to Nehemiah. The key, remember, is in finding the passages of Scripture that are *missing* from the scroll. In this case, I think the most interesting missing portion is Ezekiel 8:7-8."

She pulled up the translation of those verses on the laptop.

Then He brought me
to the entrance

of the court, and
when I looked, behold,
a hole in the wall.
He said to me,
"Son of man,
now dig through the wall."
So I dug through the wall,
and behold, an entrance.

"You think the scroll's author is telling us to dig through a wall?" asked Bennett.

"Yes, that's exactly what I think," Natasha replied.

"But what wall?"

"That's where the next missing passage seems to come in."

Shallum the son of Col-hozeh,
the official of the district
of Mizpah, repaired the Fountain Gate.
He built it, covered it and
hung its doors with its bolts
and its bars, and the wall of
the Pool of Shelah at
the King's Garden as far as
the steps that descend from
the City of David.

"The words in capital letters were missing from the scroll?" asked Dmitri.

"Exactly," said Natasha.

"What's the Pool of Shelah?" asked Erin.

"Oh, that's easy," said Katya. "*Shelah* is a Hebrew variant of *Shiloah*, or *Siloam*," said Katya. "That could be the Pool of Siloam in Jerusalem."

Bennett was stunned. "The pool near Hezekiah's Tunnel?" he asked. "Where Jesus told the blind man to go wash and he would be healed?"

"Yes, that's the one," Katya confirmed.

All eyes turned to Natasha.

"Mrs. Galishnikov is 100 percent correct," she said. "And what's intriguing to me is that according to John Marco Allegro, the first member of the Copper Scroll team to actually publish the original text in Hebrew and English, Lines 50 and 51 of the Copper Scroll actually point to the Pool of Siloam."

She quickly did a Google search for Allegro's translation and read it to the group.

"In the settling tank of the Bathhouse of running water, under the gutter: seventeen talents. In its four inner corner buttresses: tithe vessels, and inside them figured coins."

Then Natasha added, "Other translators have put it a little differently. One has it, 'In the basin of the latrines, beneath the water outlet: seventeen talents. In its pool, at its four corners, tithe vessels and marked coins.' Either way, a number of scholars—Allegro, my grandfather, and Uncle Eli included—believe the 'Bathhouse' or 'latrines' and the 'pool' nearby were direct references to the Pool of Siloam and the area around Hezekiah's Tunnel. Now, the scroll that Jon has found may actually confirm that theory."

"Wait a minute," said Bennett, at the edge of his seat. "Are you saying the Temple treasures might actually be buried as close as the City of David?"

"I can't say I know for sure, of course," said Natasha. "But that does seem to be where this scroll is pointing."

"That's just a five-minute walk from the Temple Mount," Erin gasped.

62

A shock of anticipation moved through the team.

Could they really be that close? Or was this another massive, time-consuming diversion? And even if it was true, what exactly were they supposed to do—march into Jerusalem with a few bags of explosives and blast their way to the Temple treasures?

Natasha tried to keep everyone's expectations in check. She cautioned that over the decades, numerous archeologists had prospected around the pool, to no avail. A few had even been arrested. There was also the very real possibility that the reference to the Pool of Siloam was, in fact, another decoy. After all, none of the locations directly mentioned in the Copper Scroll had yet borne out to be true. Why should this one?

"Could the treasures be hidden behind a wall *inside* Hezekiah's Tunnel?" Bennett wondered.

Natasha chewed on that for a little while. "It would certainly be consistent with the text and with the location," she agreed. The Pool of Siloam was an open-air water garden—no roof, no covering, and directly visible from at least three sides. The tunnel, on the other hand, was a perfect hiding place—long, dark, narrow, and waist deep with often-freezing running water from the Gihon Spring. It certainly would have been hidden from the prying eyes of Roman soldiers two thousand years ago, not to mention the watchful eye of Israeli soldiers today. Natasha went back and examined several other missing verses, then zeroed in on verse 16 from the Ezekiel passage.

> *He then brought me*
> *into the inner court of*
> *the house of the LORD,*
> *and there at the entrance*
> *to the temple,*
> *between the portico*
> *and the altar,*
> *were about twenty-five men.*
> *With their backs toward*
> *the temple of the LORD*
> *and their faces*
> *toward the east,*
> *they were bowing down*
> *to the sun in the east.*

"I think that's it," said Natasha at last.

"What?" asked Bennett, as Erin checked her watch.

"I think that's the clue we're looking for!" Natasha said excitedly.

"Which one?"

"'He then brought me into the inner court,'" Natasha explained. "I think we're supposed to go into Hezekiah's Tunnel, into the exact center."

"You're sure?" Erin pressed, noting that they had to move soon if they were going to move at all.

"Wait, wait, there's something else," said Natasha. "'Between the portico and the altar.' That's another clue. We need to go halfway into the tunnel and then move twenty-five paces from the precise center."

"How would we know which way?" asked Bennett.

"Well," said Natasha, "in the passage it says the men were doing something evil. They had turned their backs toward the Temple of the Lord and bowed east, toward the sun. I say we do the opposite. We'll go twenty-five paces west and try to break through the tunnel wall on the side facing the Temple, digging toward the Temple Mount."

Bennett's heart was pounding. Everyone's was. He didn't fully understand it, but he trusted Natasha's experience. It had, after all, gotten them this far. Now all they needed was a plan.

"How can we help?" asked Dmitri.

"Can we borrow your helicopter?" asked Natasha.

"You're kidding, right?"

"No," said Natasha. "I'm fully rated."

"Not my point," Dmitri replied. "I'm going with you."

Natasha looked to Bennett.

"Dmitri, you know we'd love to have you with us," he said as tactfully as he could. "But I think you've discovered enough treasure for one lifetime."

Dmitri didn't bat an eye. "And what exactly are you planning to do, Jon? Fly into Jerusalem, land near Hezekiah's Tunnel, and just leave the helicopter there? You really think that's not going to attract attention?"

"He's right, Jon," said Erin.

"Of course I'm right," said Dmitri. "Besides, there's no manhunt under way for me. I'll be able to get clearance to land in Jerusalem. None of you can. I'll fly you in, drop you off, and then hightail it out of there until you call me to come back for you. That's it. That's my final offer."

Bennett looked at Erin and then at Natasha. It wasn't like they had a lot of leverage. "We'll take it," he said. "But we could also use some men to guard the tunnel."

"As many as you need," said Dmitri.

"And some weapons," said Erin.

"No problem."

"And we'll need some other equipment, too," Natasha reminded them.

"What kind?" asked Dmitri.

"Something to blast through those walls would be nice."

"Done," said Dmitri. "Now, if you're all out of excuses, I suggest we get going."

☆   ☆   ☆

When they were in the air, Bennett called Ken Costello.

"Hello?"

"Ken, it's Jon. You got a minute?"

"Jon! Are you all right?"

"We're fine."

"I just got a call from the Palestinian interior minister," Costello explained. "He said there's been some kind of shooting incident outside of Nablus."

"No comment," said Bennett.

"Where are you now?"

"I can't say. Not yet. But—"

Costello cut him off. "Jon, seriously, I'm telling you this as a friend. If you want the president to go to bat for you, you guys have got to come in *now*."

"I need a few more hours."

"Right now."

"Ken, I'm only asking for a few more hours."

"And if you get caught? Or killed?"

"Look, Ken, I give you my word. We'll come in today. But I need your help."

"Are you crazy? You're going to get us all thrown in prison."

"We found it, Ken."

"What?"

"We think we've found the treasures of the Copper Scroll."

"You're kidding."

"I'm not."

"And the Ark?"

"I don't know."

"What do you mean you don't know?"

"I mean we haven't found the treasures yet. But we're pretty sure we know where they are now."

"And that's where you're headed?"

"Exactly."

"But you're not going to tell me where, are you?"

"Not yet," Bennett admitted. "But look, if something goes wrong, I'll call you. I'll tell you officially that Erin, Natasha, and I are ready to come in. And then I'll need you to send me as much backup as you possibly can. And reporters."

"Reporters?"

"Lots of them, with cameras, satellite trucks—the whole nine yards."

"Why?" asked Costello.

"Let's call it an insurance policy," said Bennett. "Just promise me you'll be there for me if I need it."

"Just promise *me* you'll turn yourself in by the end of the day," Costello replied.

"I promise," said Bennett.

"Then so do I," said Costello.

☆ ☆ ☆

Indira Rajiv tried to remember where she was.

She tried to remember what day it was. But it was all a blur. She blinked hard and stared at the phone next to her. A label on the handset read *The Rome Cavalieri Hilton.* She glanced at the alarm clock. Was it already Tuesday? Had she really slept so long? It didn't seem possible. She suddenly realized the phone next to her wasn't the one that was ringing. She got up, stumbled across the penthouse suite, and grabbed her satellite phone, answering it on the tenth ring.

"Hello?" she mumbled. "Rajiv."

"Indira, it's Erin—got a minute?"

Rajiv was instantly awake. "Erin? Is that you? I've been worried sick about you."

"Then where have you been?" Erin replied. "I've been calling you for days."

Rajiv froze. She couldn't tell her she'd been escaping a mole hunt, of course. Nor could she tell her "best friend" that she'd actually gotten her voice mail and immediately relayed their location on Mount Ebal to Viggo Mariano's team, though they'd been too stupid to kill them when they had the chance. Come to think of it, Rajiv wondered, what *could* she tell her? When nothing came to mind, she quickly changed the subject.

"It's a long story. I'll tell you later. The point is, where are you right now?"

Erin paused. "First promise me you won't turn me in," she insisted.

"Are you kidding?" asked Rajiv. "You know me better than that."

"You could lose your job if you don't," Erin warned.

If you only knew, thought Rajiv, wondering how much longer it would be before Langley told the media she was on the run, wanted on charges of espionage.

"Actually," said Rajiv, "they'll probably give me a promotion."

"Seriously, Indira," Erin insisted. "You could go to jail."

"No one's going to jail," said Rajiv.

"Then promise me."

"Erin, really, you've got to—"

"*Promise.*"

"Fine," Rajiv lied. "I promise. Now what do you need?"

There was a long pause. Rajiv feared Erin wouldn't believe her, but then she said, "I think we've found it, Indira."

"What?"

"The Temple treasures."

"Really?" asked Rajiv. "How? Where?"

"I'll explain later," said Erin. "Right now, I don't have much time."

"Why? Where are you headed?" Rajiv pressed.

"Hezekiah's Tunnel," said Erin. "We're in Dmitri's helicopter."

"Dmitri Galishnikov?"

"Yeah. We should touch down in about five minutes."

"How can I help?" asked Rajiv.

"I need satellite coverage over the tunnel."

"Expecting trouble?"

"Hoping for it, actually," said Erin. "We'll have guys watching both ends of the tunnel, but we need to buy as much time as possible."

"Who's helping you?"

"Dmitri's security team will be guarding the tunnel," said Erin. "So you'll do this for me?"

"For you? Anything," Rajiv answered. "Where should I route the feed?"

Rajiv no longer had access to American spy satellites. But Erin didn't know that. And this phone call was the break she needed. Now she just had to get the Bennetts' location to Mariano and his men.

63

★ ★
★

They landed in the Kidron Valley, about a mile away.

Any closer and Bennett feared they would attract too much attention. But that meant they had quite a hike ahead of them—uphill no less—with much gear and not much time. As they touched down, two of Galishnikov's security men jumped out of the chopper, armed with MP5 machine guns and communications gear to keep everyone connected. Bennett, Erin, and Natasha were right behind them. Each grabbed an Uzi, ammo, and a backpack stuffed with sledgehammers, picks, flashlights, batteries, and bottles of drinking water, and began racing up the hill, through the Arab village of Silwan, toward the Old City. When they looked back, Dmitri and the chopper were gone.

Ten minutes later, they had reached the Gihon Spring. For thousands of years the spring had been the only source of freshwater for Jerusalemites, who would exit the city gates each morning, fill pails with water, and bring them back to their homes. Now Bennett prayed it would somehow quench their thirst for justice.

The key, Natasha had convinced him, was Hezekiah's Tunnel. In 701 BCE, the Israelite king Hezekiah—fearing an imminent siege by the Assyrians—ordered his advisors to find a way to channel the water directly into the walled city in such a way that the Assyrians could neither find Jerusalem's water supply and cut it off nor use it to sustain their own troops.

But in order to complete the vital task before Sennacherib and his forces arrived, Hezekiah divided his men into two teams. One began digging from deep underneath the city toward the spring. The other began at the spring and chiseled their way toward the city. The result was a marvel of ancient engineering—a 1,750-foot-long, S-shaped tunnel, snaking its way through the limestone mountains to the Pool of Siloam, which at the time was located inside the walls of Jerusalem.

And according to the Scriptures, it was finished just in time. Israel's enemies were driven back, and the city and its Temple were saved. How history would play out this time, Bennett had no idea.

He glanced at his watch. On Tuesdays, the tunnel was only open to tourists from eight in the morning until two in the afternoon. It was now 2:47. He held the Uzi tight to his chest and peeked around a stone wall, then across the courtyard. There was no one there. The ticket booth was closed. The door leading to the tunnel was padlocked.

Bennett turned and nodded to the others, and they made their move. While Arik and Roni—Galishnikov's security men—scanned the grounds for signs of movement, Bennett cut the lock and waved the others through. Everyone entered except for Roni. He would stay and watch their backs.

"Miss Erin?"

"Yes, Roni," she whispered back.

"I still can't log on to the satellite feed you were telling me about."

"Neither can I," said Arik.

"Don't worry," said Erin. "I just talked to my friend. I'm sure it will come online any minute. Keep trying. And call us on the radios if anything comes up."

"Will do," said Roni. "Godspeed."

"Thanks."

With that, the rest of the group scrambled down the stairs to the tunnel entrance, turned on their flashlights, and began their journey, with Bennett in the lead, and Erin right behind him.

☆　☆　☆

Mariano's satphone rang again.

He instantly recognized the number. It was Rajiv, and he was furious. "I told you to stay put and not make any more calls."

"I don't take orders from you," Rajiv shot back.

"He'll meet you," Mariano countered. "I told you he would. But I don't know when, and quite frankly, I'm in the middle of something right now."

"That's not why I'm calling."

"Then why?"

"Just shut up and listen," Rajiv barked. "Where are you?"

"Why does it matter?"

"It just does. Now where are you?"

Mariano didn't have time to play games. But given all Rajiv had given them so far—and the fact that she had left the CIA and her husband and was holed up in his hotel room in Rome—she probably deserved to be listened to for a few more minutes.

"We just left Tiberias."

"Headed where?" she asked.

"Jerusalem."

"What's your ETA?"

"Thirty, forty minutes tops. Why?"

"What about the team in Jordan?"

"In Tel Aviv, waiting for orders. Why? What's all this about?"

"Erin Bennett."

"What about her?"

"She just called."

★ ★ ★

The water was knee-deep and freezing cold.

It was January, after all. But at least it kept the team moving. The bigger problem was the fact that though the tunnel rose to a height of some sixteen feet at the other end, in this stretch it was barely five feet high, making it all but impossible to run. They were moving as quickly as they could, but for Bennett it wasn't nearly fast enough.

"Why didn't these guys just dig in a straight line?" he asked, hunched over and trying not to smack his head as he followed the serpentine route through the mountain.

"Most archeologists say it was just the imperfections of their engineering knowledge at the time," said Natasha, having to raise her voice to be heard over all their sloshing. "But I think the more compelling theory is a more recent one."

"What's that?"

"It seems that there was actually a series of small, natural, limestone caves riddled through the mountain like Swiss cheese. Hezekiah's people were basically digging from cave to cave to connect them all into one long pipeline."

"You're saying they were playing connect-the-dots down here?" asked Bennett.

"Yes," said Natasha. "You could say that."

The team kept advancing toward their objective. They were almost to the halfway point of the tunnel.

Even as he tried not to think about the possibility of losing all his toes to frostbite, it struck Bennett that they were moving through 2,700 years of history. Every chisel mark his flashlight pointed to had been carved out by men who had lived a full seven centuries before Jesus. Somewhere along the way, perhaps during the Middle Ages—though no one seemed to know for sure—the tunnel had fallen into disuse and disrepair. According to Natasha, it had been all but forgotten until an American by the name of Edward Robinson stumbled upon it in 1838.

Then, in 1880, a young boy living in Jerusalem literally stumbled upon a remarkable discovery. While playing around the Pool of Siloam at the mouth of the tunnel, he slipped on some rocks and bumped his head. When he opened his eyes, he looked up and realized he was looking up at a Hebrew inscription, carved into one of the tunnel's walls. After he told his parents and teachers, a group of archeologists arrived to check out the boy's story. It turned out he had, quite by accident, found a description of how the tunnel was made—incribed there *by the workers who had made it.*

Most intriguing to Bennett, however, was Natasha's description of the work of a British officer named Montague Parker. In 1909, Parker brought a team to Palestine and began a two-year process of cleaning out the tunnel and excavating its vicinity. The interesting thing was why.

It turns out Parker had been hired by a Finnish philosopher and poet named Valter H. Juvelius, who had become absolutely convinced from studying the writings of the Jewish prophets—particularly the book of Ezekiel—that the Temple treasures and the Ark of the Covenant would be found in or around Hezekiah's Tunnel. Unfortunately, Natasha explained, Parker and his team hadn't paid off enough of the locals. Muslim leaders caught wind of what they were trying to do and ran them out of town, almost killing them in the process.

Now Bennett wondered, *Would they fare any better?*

64

★ ★
★

"Hold here for a moment," said Natasha.

"Why? What's the problem?" asked Bennett.

"Nothing," she insisted. "Just look up."

Bennett, Erin, and Arik all pointed their flashlights toward the ceiling, now between eight and ten feet above the floor.

"I don't see anything," said Erin.

"It's hard to see without stronger lights," Natasha explained. "But the ceiling above us isn't natural limestone. It's part of an artificial wall. If you were to break through it, you'd find a vertical shaft about a meter and a half wide, running some twelve meters straight up. That's connected to a larger vaulted cistern, which is connected to another series of tunnels and shafts. All told, the system extends some seventy meters to a secret well opening at the top, inside the Old City of Jerusalem. It's called Warren's Shaft. Archeologists believe that's how Jerusalemites got water up to the city before this tunnel was built."

"Never heard of it," said Erin.

"Charles Warren, British military officer, 1867," said Natasha. "Look him up online when you get home."

"*If* we get home," said Bennett, his tactical pessimism rising to the fore.

"Why was it walled off?" asked Erin.

"It's not clear, exactly," said Natasha. "Some say the system dates back to the tenth century BCE, some three centuries before this tunnel was built. Eventually, of course, the tunnel moved the water more efficiently than the shaft system. So it's believed the Israelites sealed it up to keep all the water moving from the spring to the Pool of Siloam."

"Guys, we really need to keep moving," said Bennett.

"Actually, we're already here," said Natasha. "Arik, you can keep going. But we're just a few yards away."

Arik passed by and kept hustling toward the other end of the tunnel. Natasha, meanwhile, rechecked her map until she was sure they had found the precise center of the tunnel, then turned west and marched another twenty-five yards, based on her interpretation of the Mount Ebal Scroll. Then she turned her flashlight against the right side wall, drawing Jon's and Erin's flashlights as well.

"That's not limestone," said Bennett, pointing to a small, square patch maybe three feet by three feet.

"No, it's plaster," said Natasha. "And it's old. Very old. When the tunnel was first built, they sealed it up with plaster so none of the water could leak out of the natural cracks and holes in the limestone. Every few centuries they would replaster it, just to be sure, but obviously it's been a long time since it was done last."

Bennett tapped it with the butt of his Uzi. Some pieces began to flake off. Was this really it? Was there really something behind that wall?

"Give me your packs," said Natasha. "I'll hold them for you."

First Jon and Erin put on miner helmets and turned on their lamps. Then they gave their backpacks and Uzis to Natasha and grabbed sledgehammers.

"On my count," said Bennett. "One, two, three!"

And with that, they attacked their target with all the strength they had left.

★ ★ ★

"I'm so sorry to bother you again," Mariano began.

"You'd better have good news," said Al-Hassani.

"We do, Your Excellency. The Bennetts and the Barak girl are in Jerusalem. We know where, and our teams are converging on them even as we speak."

☆ ☆ ☆

Progress was maddeningly slow.

Their work was made all the more difficult by the fact that the tunnel itself was no more than two and a half feet across, giving them precious little leverage with which to wield their hammers. But bit by bit, piece by piece, the plaster was falling away, and after another fifteen minutes, it became clear that they were really on to something, for the wall behind the plaster had long ago been chiseled away.

☆ ☆ ☆

Mariano peered through the sniper scope.

He could see Roni Migdal, an Uzi dangling at his side, pacing nervously and puffing away on yet another cigarette. Mariano took a deep breath, adjusted for the chilly breeze blowing through the valley, and pulled the trigger, watching Migdal's head snap back and his body collapse to the ground.

☆ ☆ ☆

Arik Allon never saw the ambush either.

One minute he was shivering quietly on the steps leading down into the Pool of Siloam, trying to stay warm. The next minute he was thrashing about wildly in the water. Two men were upon him. A hand was clamped tightly over his nose and mouth. A knife came slicing across his throat. He struggled desperately to get free. His lungs screamed for oxygen. He drove his nails into the flesh of those pinning him down. But it was all in vain. For a moment he could see the frigid waters around him rapidly turning red with his own blood. And then it all went black.

☆ ☆ ☆

Now they could see a large hole behind the plaster.

Bennett's arm muscles were burning. He could no longer feel his feet, they were so cold. But he could not stop. Adrenaline was taking over. He set his hammer down and grabbed his pick, as did Erin. All they needed was another few minutes, and the passageway they were uncovering would be wide enough to enter.

* * *

Mariano raced into the tunnel.

He and three of his men came charging from the direction of the Pool of Siloam. Four more entered the underground river from its source. Unencumbered by sledgehammers and backpacks, they moved quickly. By his calculations, the two teams should meet at the tunnel's midsection—trapping their quarry between them—in less than ten minutes.

* * *

Natasha tried the radio again.

"Roni, can you hear me?"

Nothing.

"Arik, you there?"

All she got was static.

"We've found a hole. We're almost in."

Again there was nothing.

"Hello? Hello? Are you guys okay?"

* * *

Mariano had Roni Migdal's radio clipped to his belt.

He had the earpiece stuck in his own ear. He could hear everything Natasha was saying, which meant he again had the element of surprise. Guns drawn, he and his men were ready to kill. The Bennetts had taken this hunt far enough. They had become a liability he could no longer afford. It was time to take them out, once and for all.

He stopped suddenly and held up his right hand, bringing those behind him to a complete stop as well. He whispered into his headset for the second team to stop and let the tunnel quiet down. A moment later, all was quiet, save the steady trickle of running water at their feet. Mariano closed his eyes and strained to pick up every sound. Finally he heard what he wanted. The picks were still chipping away.

"Go!" he barked into his headset. He and his men began to move again, faster now.

Their speed increased along with the headroom in the tunnel as they approached the center. Mariano was almost sprinting as he came around the last turn, his pistol ready to fire. But when the gunmen finally converged upon each other, they were stunned.

No one was there.

☆   ☆   ☆

It was as if Jon and Erin had entered a parallel universe.

On the other side of the wall was another tunnel, narrow but dry, running alongside Hezekiah's and back toward the Gihon Spring. It was level for about fifty meters but then began to decline sharply, down steps hewn from the limestone.

All three of them moved fast and sure.

At the last moment, they'd heard their killers coming. They'd had to assume Arik and Roni were dead. They'd slipped away from the main passageway just in time. But they still had no idea how many were behind them or what lay ahead. Their only goal now was to open up as much distance as possible between them and their pursuers until they could figure out what to do next.

They descended fifty or sixty steps, then once again hit level ground. The tunnel broke sharply to the left, moving perpendicular to Hezekiah's. It also began to narrow further, and zigzag wildly. Bennett quickly lost his sense of direction. He still had no idea where they were headed, except that it seemed they were now in some sort of subterranean complex of ancient cisterns and pipelines, winding their way underneath the City of David, under Mount Zion, and perhaps even under the Old City itself.

65

★ ★
★

Bennett stopped just in time.

As he rounded another corner, the tunnel came to a dead end inside a small cavern. At its center lay several dozen large rocks, arranged in a circle, with a hole in the center. With Natasha peering over his shoulder, Bennett shined his flashlight into the hole, revealing a shaft too deep for the light to penetrate beyond the first twenty or thirty meters. He picked up a stone and threw it down. No splash, no thud, no sound at all.

"What's down there?" asked Erin, watching their backs.

"I can't really tell," he said. "It's too dark."

"But we can't stay here," said Natasha. "If we do, we'll be trapped."

"We may be trapped either way," said Erin.

Bennett didn't hesitate. "Then we keep moving. Let's see where this thing takes us."

He ordered Erin and Natasha to go down first while he stood to hold off their pursuers. They quickly set down their backpacks; pulled out ropes, carabiners, and the rest of their gear; and prepared for the descent. Bennett donned a harness and gloves, then positioned himself on his stomach at the opening of the cavern, turned off his flashlight, and aimed his Uzi at the tunnel behind them.

He remembered the satellite phone. The last thing he needed was for it to start ringing in the darkness. Then again, this could be his last chance to get word to Costello. With one hand on the trigger, he used his other to reach down and pull the phone from his pocket. It glowed an eerie green in the shadows. But it was useless. No coverage.

He'd waited too long.

☆ ☆ ☆

Whoever was hunting them was coming on fast.

Natasha could hear footsteps and whispers echoing through the labyrinth. She quickly tied their ropes around several of the heavier boulders and cut her lights. Then she rappelled down first, lugging not only her backpack but Bennett's as well so he'd be able to move quickly if a gun battle erupted. When her feet hit the ground, it wasn't limestone beneath her. It was sand.

She pushed the packs aside, unclipped herself and tugged the rope several times to let Erin know she was free. Then she got down on her hands and knees in the darkness and felt around. *Sand?* Everywhere she touched, there was soft dry sand—loads of it. It certainly explained why they hadn't heard the stone Bennett had tossed into the shaft. But beyond that, it made no sense. *Who put it here and why?*

She continued feeling around with her hands, her Uzi strapped to her side. She crawled to her left but hit a stone wall. She crawled forward, but there, too, was a stone wall. There was one behind her as well. To her right, though, she finally found an opening.

That's when the shooting began.

☆ ☆ ☆

Bennett couldn't see a thing.

He could hear someone creeping forward in the darkness and decided not to wait. He pulled the trigger and the tunnel exploded. Fire and smoke poured out of the barrel as he emptied an entire magazine, following the tracer rounds onto his targets and watching at least two men drop to the ground.

Then the return fire started. Bennett rolled left, back into the relative safety of the cavern. He fully expected to be hit by ricocheting rounds, but when the shooting paused, at least for a few seconds, he was still alive. Someone was reloading. He did, too.

"Erin, go—you've got to go now!" he shouted as he fumbled in the dark to eject one magazine and pop in another.

But Erin had her own plans. Seizing the momentary lull, she jumped up and aimed down the tunnel. She, too, unleashed an entire magazine— firing directly over Bennett's head—before rappelling out of sight.

Bennett could barely breathe. A rush of adrenaline coursed through his body. He pivoted and pulled the trigger again, and again bloodcurdling shrieks erupted from the other end of the tunnel.

Four down, unknown to go.

☆   ☆   ☆

Four of Mariano's men were down.

Two were dead. Two more were seriously wounded and losing blood fast. He had only three men left, besides himself.

"Cover me," he said.

The tunnel again erupted in gunfire. Mariano fished a grenade out of his own backpack. He pulled the pin, rolled it forward, and scrambled for cover as his men—those who could move at least—followed close behind.

The cavern ahead of them erupted in a ball of fire. The ground shook. The roar was deafening, intensified by the sound waves echoing off rock walls in such tight quarters.

Mariano got up quickly and dusted himself off. Then, stepping over the charred bodies of men about whom he'd never given a second thought, he cautiously worked his way toward the opening of the cavern, sweeping his pistol from side to side. The air was thick with acrid fumes. He coughed. He waited a few moments for the smoke to clear, and then he and his men turned on their flashlights. But again, no one was there.

☆   ☆   ☆

Erin scrambled to Bennett's side.

She threw her arms around him and checked for a pulse. He was alive. He was breathing. But he was in pain from his fall. As quickly and quietly as she could, she checked her husband's body for broken bones. She couldn't believe he'd made it. He'd barely grabbed the ropes and begun descending into the shaft when she heard the grenade rolling across the granite floor above them. When it had gone off, he must have lost his grip and plummeted a good fifteen feet before slamming face-first onto the pile of sand. The force had clearly knocked the wind out of him, but he was going to be okay—as long as they started moving—*now*.

Bennett was covered with chunks of rock that had blown apart in the explosion. Erin brushed them off, took him by the arm, and whispered in his ear, "Jon, it's me. Are you okay?"

"I think so—are you?" he replied.

"Come on," said Erin. "Follow me."

They continued racing down one tunnel and into the next. When they stopped to get their bearings, they realized they were in another cistern of some kind, perhaps thirty or forty feet in diameter. It was clearly man-made, carved out of the limestone. Out from it fanned three tunnels like the spokes of a wheel.

"We've found the waterworks," Natasha whispered as they huddled together and charted their next move.

"What do you mean?" Bennett whispered, still trying to catch his breath.

"For years, scholars have believed there was an elaborate and complex system of tunnels and aqueducts running underneath Jerusalem, dating back to hundreds of years before Christ," Natasha explained, still keeping her voice low. "The tunnels supposedly channeled water from the Gihon Spring—and the winter rains—to large storage 'tanks,' if you will, and then on to various wells throughout the Old City. But until now, only a few remnants of the system had ever been found. The rest was just specu-lation."

"What are you saying?" asked Erin. "That no one's ever been down here before?"

"Not since the Romans sacked the city," said Natasha. "We've always assumed these tunnels were here, but no one ever found the way in. Don't forget, twenty centuries of construction, destruction, and more construc-tion—the entire Old City of Jerusalem–lies right above us."

Another buzz of excitement rippled through the trio, but they didn't have time to waste. They'd have company again soon.

"Jon, call Ken," said Erin. "We need backup fast."

"I tried," he said. "I can't get a signal."

"Check again," Erin insisted. "We can't hold them by ourselves."

Bennett pulled the phone from his pocket and powered it up. Still no signal. They had to split up, he decided. The best odds they had were by dividing their forces, luring their enemies into the tunnels, and taking them out one by one.

"Then we'd better hurry," Natasha urged.

They could already hear the men working their way down the shaft behind them.

Bennett took the lead. "Erin, you go left. Natasha, you go right. I'll take the middle tunnel. Move fast. Stay in the shadows. Conserve ammo. And pray."

66

★

Flashlight in hand, Natasha sprinted into her tunnel.

It was wider than the others, maybe four feet across. But there was no place to hide. The ground was solid limestone. If she'd had a week she couldn't have dug a foxhole deep enough. Nor was there a single boulder or outcropping behind which she could take cover. The only hope she had was to get low, stay low, keep quiet, and hope to God no one found her.

She turned off her flashlight and lay down, straining to hear any sound, any movement. She had never been in such utter darkness. It was unnerving. The limestone was cold to her legs and stomach. But it was dry. Somewhere, somehow, this system had once been sealed off from all the other waterworks running under it. *When? Why?*

She clenched her fists and noticed how wet with perspiration her hands were. They were trembling. She was scared—almost as scared of being alone as she was of dying.

With the death of her grandfather, Natasha was utterly alone in the world. Except for her cousin, Miriam, whom she practically never saw, nearly everyone she'd ever loved had died a brutal, senseless death. Were the Bennetts about to suffer that very same fate? She couldn't bear it. She had become close to them in the last few days. In some ways she felt like she'd known them all her life.

They weren't just newlyweds. They were so obviously in love. They were soul mates, as she'd once been with Binyamin.

And they had something else she envied. They really seemed to know God. Not *about* Him. They actually seemed to *know* Him—personally. Theirs weren't rote, liturgical prayers. They really seemed to be talking to someone who was listening and answering. How was that possible? She read the same Bible they did. But to her it was a treasure map, guiding her to the secrets of an ancient world. To them it was a letter from a God who loved them. And though Natasha dared not tell a soul, she was jealous.

She'd always considered herself a tough, smart, independent woman, and in many ways she'd become even more so since her husband's death. But the last few months—indeed, the last few days—had changed all that. She could feel the tectonic plates of history shifting under her feet. She wasn't sure if she bought into all of Uncle Eli's talk about the earth's "last days." But *something* strange was happening. That much was certain. And the death of her grandfather had rattled her, forcing all of her fears and insecurities to the surface.

She longed for Jon's and Erin's inexplicable sense of calm. It seemed to steady them, even when all hell was breaking loose. She coveted the sense of purpose and destiny that kept them moving forward when anyone else in their right mind would have given up and turned back. They were risking their lives every day, and for what? Even if they lived, what were they going to get out of all this? It was clear they loved Israel, and Uncle Eli, and it was clear they loved her. Humanly speaking it made no sense.

Being followers of Christ had certainly made a difference in their lives, she knew. Particularly Jon's. She knew just enough about him to know that being here cut against everything he'd been raised to believe, everything he'd begun to achieve on Wall Street and in Washington. There was something about becoming a follower of Christ that had radically reshaped the way he thought, the way he made choices. He had once been driven by wealth and power. But now he was willing to sacrifice everything for his God and for this woman he loved. It suddenly occurred to her how desperately she wanted to know this same God for herself, before it was too late.

The problem, frankly, was Jesus. He said He was the Messiah. She had read the New Testament. She knew He had said, "I am the way, and the truth, and the life; no one comes to the Father but through Me." She also knew He had said that the only way to know God personally was to be "born again." It's why His disciples loved Him. It's why His enemies hated Him. But was it true?

Logically, Natasha knew she had only two choices: either Jesus was the Messiah or He wasn't. If He wasn't, and He *knew* He wasn't, then He was a liar, not the good man or moral teacher she'd always described Him as. Then again, if Jesus wasn't the Messiah but *thought* He was, then He was crazy, a lunatic, a nutcase not worthy of a second thought.

But she'd read the New Testament in college, and the Christ whose life she'd read about didn't strike her as deceptive or delusional. To the contrary, she saw a man of love and compassion, someone who was kind to children and willing to take on the religious hypocrites of the day on behalf of the poor and the unloved and the widows. She saw someone humble and wise, someone with the ability to do miracles that astounded even His most bitter skeptics. The truth was, she liked Jesus, but where did that leave her?

If He wasn't lying or crazy, then He would have to be the Messiah. He would have to be Lord. Which would mean that when He said, "I am the way, the truth, and the life," He would have to be telling the truth. She wasn't sure if she could believe that. She wasn't sure if—

Natasha suddenly heard automatic gunfire coming from somewhere else in the tunnels. She feared the worst. *Was it Erin fighting for her life, or Jon?* She couldn't just lie here. She had to do something. She knew it could be a trap, luring her out into the open. Yet everything in her urged her forward.

She got to her feet.

The gunfire seemed louder. Was it coming her way? Natasha couldn't pinpoint its source, but it definitely seemed to be coming closer. Her fear grew.

A massive explosion shook the caverns. Then another. And a third. She gripped the Uzi in her hands and tried to imagine how this could possibly end well. She knew she should pray, but how? She didn't know how to begin or what to say.

The tunnel was suddenly filled with a blinding light. A split second later, she heard the explosion, felt the force of the blast, and knew exactly what was happening. It was a flash grenade. Their pursuers were systematically throwing one grenade after another into the tunnels to kill them or smoke them out, and now they'd found her.

And then she heard more automatic-weapons fire—very close—and felt the bullets tearing into her flesh.

67

★ ★
★

The flash grenade had exposed Natasha to her enemies.

But it had a second, if unintended, effect. It revealed—for a moment, at least—where their attackers were positioned, and both Jon and Erin seized the moment and opened fire. The tunnels filled again with fire and tracer rounds and a deafening roar as the Bennetts fought to save their friend.

A moment later, Erin shouted, "Jon, someone's coming your way."

It was still almost impossible to see people moving about. But Bennett took his wife's word by faith, if not by sight. He sprayed the entrance to the central tunnel with submachine-gun fire, back and forth until he heard someone cry out in pain and drop to the ground with a thud.

"*Got him,*" he shouted back.

"Great. I think I got one, too."

The gun battle raged on for another quarter of an hour. Every few seconds, Bennett rolled to one side of his tunnel, fired off a few rounds, then rolled to the center, fired again, and so forth, constantly changing his pattern, constantly trying to keep his hunters off balance. At one point, he pulled out his flashlight, turned it on, then moved to the other side of the tunnel as fast as he could. Predictably, the light drew fire, thus exposing the enemy's position. Bennett unleashed half a magazine before the man's screaming stopped and he made no other sounds.

And then, as quickly as it had begun, it seemed, all the shooting stopped.

Bennett lay still in the darkness, and time lost all meaning. Had it been ten minutes? twenty? a half hour? more? He strained for any possible sound, any shred of evidence that his pursuers were still alive, or that Erin and Natasha were. He could see nothing, not even the ground inches from his face. He could hear nothing but the pounding of his own heart. He prayed continuously for his wife, for her safety and comfort, and for Natasha. *Were they alive? Was it safe to go find them?*

Suddenly there was a tap on his shoulder.

Terrified, he instinctively turned and pointed the Uzi into the darkness. He was about to pull the trigger when Erin whispered, *"Jon, it's okay, it's okay—it's me."*

"Thank God," said Bennett. "How did you—I—I almost shot you. Where are you?"

Erin turned on her flashlight, covering most of the bulb with her left hand.

Trembling—but relieved—Bennett embraced her tightly as she turned off the flashlight, and they sat in the dark.

"How did you find me?" he asked.

"I heard you."

"What?"

"I heard you praying."

"You did?"

"I think you were also reciting the Twenty-third Psalm."

"Out loud?" asked Bennett in disbelief.

"Believe me," Erin whispered back, "it was a total answer to my prayers."

"What do you mean?"

"I mean when all the shooting stopped and everything got quiet, I was praying for wisdom—you know, when to move, when to find you. Then in the distance I heard a voice. It was faint, but for some reason I just started moving toward it. It was so soft, so quiet, I thought it might be Natasha."

"Have you found her?"

"No, not yet."

"You think we're clear?"

"I don't know," Erin said. "But, hey, I'm taking the fact that you weren't shot dead for praying out loud as a pretty good sign."

If he wasn't still so anxious, Bennett might have laughed out loud. "You think if someone was going to take a shot, he'd have done it by now?" he asked.

"That's my guess," said Erin. "It's been almost forty-five minutes since the last shots were fired."

Bennett couldn't believe it had been that long. He stood up and turned on his flashlight. Erin squeezed his hand, apparently more worried than she'd let on. He stood motionless for a moment, waiting, wondering what would happen next. But nothing did. It was quiet. So Erin followed suit, and there was still no gunfire.

Uzis at the ready, they shone their flashlights around the tunnel and found a man lying facedown at the entrance. Erin crouched and checked for a pulse while Bennett aimed at the man's chest. He was Caucasian, thirtyish, maybe thirty-five, with dark hair, olive skin, and a five o'clock shadow. But he was dead all right. Erin counted four bullet holes, though there may have been more. She picked up his weapon and checked for an ID of some kind. There was none.

They quickly spotted two more bodies, lying at the entrance to the tunnel Erin had been hiding in. Bennett rounded up their weapons and checked for IDs, but again there was nothing. Then they turned their flashlights farther down the tunnel to see if they could find any other bodies, and suddenly they couldn't breathe.

Twenty yards away was an opening in the tunnel wall. It had previously been hidden by large stones, but apparently the force of the grenade blasts had created an entrance. They grabbed their backpacks, raced forward, and began feverishly clearing the rubble. When they were done, they entered a world they could hardly have imagined.

Inside was an enormous room, ringed by iron torchstands, none of which seemed ever to have been used. Bennett found a box of matches in his pack and lit the torch closest to them, and the room filled with light.

Both he and Erin gasped, for before them stood three mountains of gold and silver and bronze coins, each towering at least twenty feet in the air. And that was just the beginning. As they cautiously inched their way forward, they continued lighting torches and finding more treasures. In one chamber they found ten gold lampstands, hundreds of solid gold sprinkling bowls, and piles of gold censers and dishes, all stacked on and below ten tables. In another chamber, at least as large, they found thousands of bricks made of pure gold. Yet another room was stacked floor to ceiling with bricks of pure silver, along with hundreds of gold items that looked like fruit of some kind—apples or perhaps pomegranates. The chamber beside that one held gold wick trimmers, gold tongs, gold nails and firepans and spoons, silver and bronze basins, pots, shovels, meat forks, and other articles related to the Temple sacrificial system.

Bennett's mind reeled. They had done it—almost by accident, it seemed, but they had done it.

As they probed still deeper, their minds could barely comprehend what their eyes were seeing. Before them now stood the golden altar of the Temple and a pair of sculptured cherubim overlaid with gold. Their eyes went wide and their mouths grew parched. They didn't know what to say and probably could not have gotten the words out anyway. Could these be the very ones that King Solomon had ordered built, Bennett wondered, the ones of which it was said in 2 Chronicles 3, "Then he made two sculptured cherubim in the room of the holy of holies and overlaid them with gold," with a "wingspan" of "twenty cubits"?

It didn't seem possible. And yet there it was. Illuminated by the flickering flames of the torches, the rooms glowed with the reflected glory of a lost world, now resurrected. The beauty and craftsmanship of the objects were beyond compare.

Jon and Erin wanted to touch everything, to feel the gold between their fingers, to reconnect in some small way with Levitical priests whose hands had last touched these precious artifacts two millennia before. But the truth was they were both scared, as well. Men had been hunting for these treasures throughout the ages, and now here they were, standing amid the greatest fortune man had ever amassed and willingly handed over to a God they could not see. And suddenly they felt unworthy even to be in its presence.

"I should find Natasha," Erin whispered.

"Good idea," Bennett whispered back. "I'll go with you."

"No," she said. "You should stay here. Start taking pictures. The Copper Scroll doesn't begin to do this justice."

68

TUESDAY, JANUARY 20 – 7:44 P.M. – THE JERUSALEM TUNNELS

Erin grabbed a torch and her Uzi.

She aimed them both down the tunnel. She was largely confident they were alone. But Langley training dies hard, and she took her time until she was sure.

★ ★ ★

Bennett, meanwhile, fished through the backpacks.

He pulled out a notebook and a digital camera and began taking pictures of everything. In one room his eyes locked on a small box—about the size of a jewelry box—made of gold and studded with diamonds but covered with centuries of dust and cobwebs. Not sure why he was drawn to it when far greater treasures lay all around him, he nevertheless carefully reached down to pick up the box and dust it off. He tried to open its lid but found it stuck—sealed, it appeared, with a strange combination of wax and tar.

He pulled out his pocketknife, scraped away the tar, and finally pried it open. Inside was a clay jar roughly the size of a soda can, with a clay lid also smothered in wax and tar. Again he used his knife to pry off the lid, which he then set down on a pile of golden bowls. With his left hand, he tilted the jar to the side.

Into his right hand there slid a scroll—rectangular, about six inches long, three inches wide, and a quarter of an inch thick. But it was not made of papyrus, or animal skins, or even copper. This scroll was made of gold.

Bennett's hands began to tremble. He set down the jar, wiped his left hand on his pants, and carefully cleaned off the surface of the scroll. Engraved on its face was lettering in what seemed to be a bizarre combination of Hebrew, Aramaic, and Greek letters, laced with yet another alphabet, none of which he could read. Like the Copper Scroll, it appeared to be a list of some kind, this one bearing seven entries. And then he turned it over.

He gasped, for on the back of the scroll was an etching of the Ark of the Covenant. Even in miniature, it was gorgeous, far more beautiful and detailed than anything he'd ever seen in books or the movies, and he couldn't take his eyes off it.

The Hebrew Ark. The most sought-after religious artifact in history. And the most dangerous. Could what he was holding in his hands possibly be a clue to where it now rested? He could only imagine the uproar that would be sparked around the globe simply by the unveiling of the Temple treasures. How much more tumult would the discovery of the Ark bring about?

Bennett's quivering hands slowly closed over the golden scroll. He needed Erin and Natasha.

★ ★ ★

Erin stared at the trail of blood.

And the broken flashlight, covered with bloody fingerprints.

"*Natasha,*" she yelled, but there was no answer.

Erin sprinted into the tunnel another hundred yards and finally found her new friend crumpled against a wall. She set down her Uzi and felt for Natasha's pulse. It was weak but still there. Natasha was breathing, but blood was everywhere. Erin shouted for Jon; then she leaned down and checked Natasha's pupils. They were dilated and unresponsive.

"Natasha," she said gently. "Natasha, it's me, Erin. Can you hear me? Move your fingers if you can hear me."

There was no movement. She called for Jon again. He didn't respond.

"Lord Jesus, please, *please* have mercy on this girl," Erin prayed. "I know how much you love her, and I pray that you would have mercy on her, Father. Let her live. Please, let her live. I can't take any more death. There's been too much dying, too much pain. Please, Father, spare her. Spare us, too. I pray in the name of Jesus. Amen."

Erin opened her eyes. Natasha's face was white as a sheet.

"Natasha, I want you to hold on, okay? Can you hear me? I want you to hold on. I'm going to get Jon. I'll be right back."

☆ ☆ ☆

Bennett heard Erin shouting.

He set down his camer, grabbed his Uzi, and raced to find her, nearly running into her as she reentered the main antechamber. He could see the panic in her eyes and instantly knew what had happened.

"Is she still alive?" he asked.

"Barely," said Erin. "Two shots. One to the stomach. One to the shoulder. We need to get her out of here now."

But her words had barely registered when they heard the pump action of a shotgun.

"That may not be possible," said a man's voice neither of them recognized.

Bennett looked over Erin's shoulder in disbelief. Beyond the mountain of gold coins beside them he could see someone in the shadows near the entrance. Someone who was holding a double-barreled shotgun aimed at their heads.

Bennett glanced back at Erin. He knew what she was thinking. But there was no way. He shook his head ever so slightly, just enough so she'd get the idea without drawing the gunman's fire.

"Set your weapons down slowly, both of you," said the man. "Then put your hands in the air and turn around."

"Who are you?" Bennett asked as he and Erin both lowered their Uzis to the floor.

"I am your executioner."

Bennett didn't wait for confirmation. He grabbed Erin, threw her to the left, then dove to the right, behind a mountain of gold coins.

The shotgun blast was deafening. Then came another. Both missed narrowly, but coins flew everywhere, forcing the gunman to duck. Erin scrambled for cover in one of the back rooms, then drew her Beretta.

Bennett, meanwhile, reversed direction, grabbed one of the Uzis off the floor, and dove into the next room behind Erin.

Another shotgun blast. Another near miss. The man was closer now. Bennett checked the magazine and found it half empty.

✷   ✷   ✷

Erin peeked around the corner.

That drew another blast. She waited a beat, then checked again. This time the gunman was coming in fast. She fired off three rounds. Two went wide but the third hit him in the shoulder, spinning him around and slamming him against a wall.

Erin caught Jon's eye and nodded. He took the cue, pivoted around the corner, and fired off two rapid bursts. The killer wasn't there, but his blood was splattered everywhere.

Erin took another quick glance. The tunnel was clear. She motioned to Jon to move on the count of three. She held up one finger, then another. On the third they both burst into the open, guns blazing, but the man was still nowhere to be found.

✷   ✷   ✷

Bennett was almost out of ammo.

There was more in his backpack, but just as he considered racing to the back chambers to get it, the gunman emerged from the shadows.

"*Look out,*" Erin yelled, but the man's gun went off.

Bennett ducked back just in time. Erin wasn't so lucky. Her scream almost paralyzed him with fear. He looked across the hall and saw the woman he loved holding her leg, blood all over her hands. Then he heard the sound of coins scattering in the main antechamber. The man was on the move, heading for the exit.

Bennett pivoted hard, found his target, and pulled the trigger, unleashing every last round he had. The man dropped to the floor, writhing in pain, screaming at the top of his lungs. Everything in Bennett wanted to attend to his wife, but he dared not let this monster loose. He raced across the room, dove on top of him, and lunged for the killer's throat.

69

TUESDAY, JANUARY 20 – 8:19 P.M. – THE JERUSALEM TUNNELS

Bennett's grip tightened around the man's neck.

"*Erin, I've got him,*" he shouted, but there was no response from the next room, and the man suddenly slammed his knee into Bennett's groin, sending him reeling.

The assassin scrambled out of the anteroom, heading back into the tunnels. Bennett was in excruciating pain, but with the pain came a torrent of fresh adrenaline. He dragged himself over to Erin as quickly as he could. The buckshot had ripped up her right leg, and she was bleeding profusely. He pulled out his handkerchief, made a tourniquet, and wrapped it tightly around the wound, trying to make her as comfortable as possible. She begged him to go after the injured gunman.

"I'm not leaving you," he said, wrapping his arms around her and holding her close to his chest.

"No, Jon, he's getting away. You've got to go after him—for Natasha," she insisted. "For Mordechai."

Erin's voice was weak, but she wasn't kidding. She handed him her Beretta.

"Just be careful," she added. "You've only got two shots left."

★　　★　　★

Viggo Mariano waited for Bennett in the shadows.

He had no weapon, no ropes, no way to climb out of these

underground cisterns. Escape wasn't an option. But murder was. He had the element of surprise, and that might just be enough.

* * *

Bennett couldn't bear the thought of leaving Erin.

What if he didn't make it back? Who would even know that she and Natasha were down here, in desperate need of help? But Erin was insistent. How could he let this guy escape after all the evil he'd done? Besides, she reminded him, he'd have to go at some point to get medical help.

He had no choice. He turned on his flashlight and headed out into the tunnels, trying to readjust to the overwhelming darkness. A moment later, as he turned a corner, he came across the body of one of the men they'd killed earlier. He would take no chances. He reached down to check the man's pulse.

Out of nowhere the assassin struck, smashing Bennett over the head with a rock.

Bennett collapsed to the ground, dropping the gun and the flashlight, both of which went skittering across the floor. His head was bleeding. He was conscious but woozy. It all happened so fast. He was on his hands and knees, frantically searching for Erin's gun, but the killer found it first. Before he knew what had happened, Bennett was staring down the barrel of Erin's Beretta.

"Almost, Mr. Bennett," the man said, short of breath and wiping away the blood trickling from his mouth. "You almost made history."

"Who are you?"

"Does it matter?"

"Are you Farouk?"

The man laughed. "I am Viggo Mariano. Farouk's dead. My team killed him in Jordan yesterday."

"A coup?"

"Hardly," Mariano sniffed. "Farouk was never the leader."

"And you were?"

"Let's just say I was the contractor."

"So who was the client?"

"You can ask the devil when you see him." Mariano raised the gun.

Bennett covered his face.

A burst of gunfire exploded through the tunnel.

But it was Mariano, not Bennett, who slumped to the floor.

☆   ☆   ☆

Bennett opened his eyes.

Mariano lay in a pool of blood. Twenty yards behind him was Dmitri Galishnikov and a squad of Israeli commandos. Bennett was too stunned to speak.

"You guys were taking so long," Galishnikov said. "I got worried. And when I took another pass over the city, I saw Arik's and Roni's bodies lying there, and I knew something had gone wrong. I called Katya. She said to turn you guys in, in exchange for special forces. So I did."

Bennett's head pounded. His hands were full of blood. But he was grateful to be alive, and he asked the commandos to go help Erin and Natasha. The medics moved swiftly while the others secured the tunnels and set up portable lights. Galishnikov, meanwhile, helped Bennett to his feet, and together they went to find Erin.

"God bless you, Dmitri."

"I think He has, my boy. I think He has."

"You're not going to believe what we found."

"You're kidding."

"I'm not."

But suddenly they heard a medic shouting.

"Mr. Bennett, she's not here."

Bennett raced inside to the chamber where Erin had been lying. "What are you talking about?" he yelled. "You've got to be kidding me. She was here just a minute ago."

But they were right. Erin was gone. There was blood where she had been lying but no trail leading anywhere else.

The lead medic grabbed his radio. "All units, be advised, there may be another hostile in the tunnels. I repeat, there may be another hostile in the tunnels." He turned to Bennett and Dmitri and ordered them to stay put until they could figure out what was going on. Then he drew his sidearm and cautiously moved back into the hallway with the others.

But there was no way Bennett was going to stay put. He didn't work for them. He didn't have to take their orders. He wanted his wife.

Just then he noticed a few drops of blood on the floor. He grabbed a torch and slowly began making his way to the back of the chamber, past the bowls and the censers and the acacia-wood tables piled up around him. What he hadn't realized the first time was how far the room went back. In his excitement, he'd snapped his pictures and moved on. But now he saw there was more. And there, in the back of the room, behind one of the tables stacked with treasures, was an archway, leading into another antechamber. It was there he found his wife.

Bennett set down his torch and rushed to Erin's side. He threw his arms around her, grateful beyond words to have her back. But she didn't move.

She was alive. She was breathing. But she refused to return his embrace. Instead she just stood there, motionless. And then he realized why. For there, not three feet away, stood the Ark of the Covenant.

Bennett froze, awestruck and trembling. He half expected to be incinerated, along with his wife, just for being in the room with the holy relic. In ancient times, only the high priest could approach the Ark as he atoned for his own sins and the sins of all Israel. Anyone else could die just for looking at the seat of God's glory or touching it improperly. So Bennett waited for death to come.

But it did not come. *Why? How was that possible?*

Bennett searched his mind as he had searched the Scriptures since this journey first began, and then it all became clear.

Mordechai had taught them, direct from the words of Jesus and Paul and Peter, that in the sight of God, all of their sins were now atoned for, washed away, gone forever—not because of their own good works but because of their faith in the blood that Christ had spilled from the cross. God no longer saw them as imperfect or impure. To the Judge of the earth, Bennett and Erin were now pardoned.

Now they didn't need a Temple or a high priest to approach the God of Abraham, Isaac, and Jacob.

What an honor, thought Bennett. *What an amazing privilege, to know Christ and to be able to enter His presence at any moment of any day.* Yet what an honor for him and Erin to be here, too. To be the first to see what men and women had longed to see for centuries. He began to weep, first for himself, for his weakness and his foolishness and his lack of faith, and then for so many souls who so desperately needed what Christ had bought them at Calvary. Beside him, Erin wept as well. They did not talk. They did not touch. They just cried, overcome by the presence of the God they loved and who loved them.

It could have been a few minutes or a few hours. Bennett had no idea. But when his tears had stopped and his heart had calmed, his curiosity began to grow and his eyes began to lift.

There it was, just as the Scriptures described, just as Barak and Natasha had described. It was a rectangular chest about five feet long and three feet high, covered in pure gold and resting on four gold feet. It was fitted with gold rings—two on the side facing him and, he assumed, two more on the other side—through which were resting long poles, again one on each side. On top of the chest was the mercy seat, where the blood was sprinkled by the high priest on Yom Kippur for the forgiveness of men's sins. And hovering over the mercy seat were two gold cherubim—angel-like creatures with large wings covering their faces, spread upward and almost touching.

Bennett wanted to touch it. He wanted to open it, to see if the rod of Aaron was inside, to see if the jar of manna was there too. But even as the thought crossed his mind, Bennett's body began to shake. Erin's did as well, he noticed, for she was looking too. It was as if they were on holy ground, and he again felt incredibly unworthy to be here. He felt like he *shouldn't* be here, that it was time to leave. He tapped Erin on the shoulder, and the two of them slowly backed out of the room, not looking at the Ark again.

When they were completely out, they closed the door to the antechamber where the Ark rested and sat down to catch their breath.

Bennett turned to Erin and tried to speak, but he couldn't. He looked around for Dmitri, or one of the soldiers, but for the moment they were alone. He wanted to explain what they had just witnessed. He wanted to shout it from the rooftops. The Temple *would* be built. The pressure to construct a house to hold the Ark would be an unstoppable force. He had no idea what their own futures held, but he knew for certain the world they had known was once again about to change forever.

70

★ ★
★

A light rain fell over Jerusalem.

Thunder rumbled in the distance. It was colder than it had been for weeks. Bennett stared out the window of Hadassah Hospital, sipping a hot cup of coffee and turning his BlackBerry on for the first time in days. He counted 114 e-mails and 43 phone messages.

"Anything urgent?" Erin asked.

"Salvador Lucente," Bennett replied. "Glad to hear we're okay, but he's still waiting for an answer."

"What, to work for him? He's lost his mind."

"Erin, he is about to become one of the most powerful men in the world."

"I'm not impressed," she said. "Besides, didn't we both promise each other to go through political detox and make a clean start of our lives?"

"That feels like a million years ago."

"It was only ten days," Erin reminded him.

Bennett sighed. "Don't get me wrong. It's not that I want that life again. Believe me, I don't."

"Then what?"

"I don't know," he admitted. "It's just that we keep getting pulled back into the game, and it makes me wonder if there's something specific God wants us to do with whatever time we have left."

The room grew quiet. Bennett could see in Erin's eyes how much she detested the idea of getting back into politics, especially with a man like Salvador Lucente. She had never trusted Lucente as much as he had, and maybe she was right. But that wasn't the real question. The real question was, how much time did they really have left before the Rapture, and how should they spend it?

Just then, the phone in the room started ringing. Bennett picked it up on the second ring.

"Hello?"

"Jon, sweetheart, are you okay?"

He was amazed by how quickly she'd tracked them down.

"Hey, Mom. I'm fine. I'm sorry I didn't call sooner."

"How could you do this to me? I was worried sick. What about Erin? Is she still in surgery? I saw on the news—"

"She's fine too, Mom," Bennett assured her. "We're both good. I'm actually with her right now. She's eating Jell-O and making faces at me."

"Someone said she was shot in the back. Is that really true?"

"No, no, in the leg," he explained, wondering how many other rumors were out there unchecked. "The doctors say they got everything. She'll be here for a few days, then on crutches or in a wheelchair for a while. But she'll be fine."

Ruth Bennett began to cry. "Thank you, Lord. Thank you, Jesus. I can't tell you how worried I was, Jon. I got a call from Helen—you know, the woman from my Bible study, the one I told you about? Anyway, she told me to turn on the news. And, of course, that's never a good call. But I did, and every network was covering it. They'd cut into all the regular programming. And when I saw the troops massed around the tunnels and people being airlifted out in helicopters, I just knew you and Erin were right in the middle of it."

"We were," he said. "But God's been very gracious to us."

"I'm just glad you're all right, Son," she said. "I remembered you telling me Hadassah Hospital was where they took Dr. Mordechai when he was shot. It took me a while to convince them that I was really your mother. But then I threatened to have President MacPherson call on my behalf."

Bennett had to smile. "And that shook things loose, huh?"

"They put me right through."

"You're tenacious, Mom."

"No, that was your father," she said. "Where do you think you got it from? Not from me. I'm just learning in my old age. Well, look, I know you've got a lot going on right now. I'm just glad I had a chance to hear your voice and make sure you're both okay."

"Thanks. I'll give you an update as soon as I can."

"Thanks, sweetheart, I'd like that," she said. "Oh, just one more question."

"Sure, what's that?"

"Is it true?" she asked. "What they're saying on TV? Did you really find *the* Ark of the Covenant?"

"Actually, it was Erin," he confessed. "But I saw it, Mom. I saw it with my own eyes. It was absolutely incredible. I can't wait to tell you all about it."

"I can't wait either," she said. "What are they going to do with it?"

"Good question. Everything's been moving so fast. I haven't heard."

"Is there anything you need? anything I can do for you before I go?"

"Actually, there is," he said, wondering why the idea hadn't occurred to him sooner. "Any chance you could drop everything and come over here?"

"What? To Israel?" she asked. "Right now?"

Bennett looked over at Erin, who smiled, nodding her approval, knowing how much it would mean to his mom to be needed at a moment like this.

"We're going to be here a little while," Bennett explained. "And there's also a friend of ours—she's actually still in surgery right now—but when she gets out, she could really use your help and your prayers."

"Is that Natasha?" she asked.

"Yeah, how did you know?"

"I told you, it's all over the news—the whole crazy thing."

He laughed and quickly filled her in on Natasha and Yossi Barak and how much they had both come to mean to them in the few short days since they'd met.

"For you, I'd do anything, sweetheart," his mother said. "I just want you to know, I love you very much, and I couldn't be prouder."

"Thanks, Mom, I love you, too," he said. "I'll have an e-ticket waiting for you at the Continental desk for the one o'clock Orlando flight to Tel

Aviv. It routes through Newark. And I'll have a car waiting to pick you up when you land."

*   *   *

Erin watched her husband hang up the room phone.

Only to have his BlackBerry begin ringing. It was Ken Costello in Washington, and Erin listened as Jon took the call.

"Hey, Ken, good to hear from you," Jon said, walking to the windows and staring out over the Old City. "No, no, we're fine. . . . Minor, but the doctors say she'll be up and around in no time. . . . Yeah, it *was* pretty close, but we got 'em, Ken, we got 'em. . . . No, Zadok hasn't stopped by yet. . . . His office just called—he's supposed to be by around five—Doron is going to call us around then as well."

Then Erin watched as her husband stopped cold.

"*What?* . . . What are you talking about? . . . Say that again."

"What is it?" Erin whispered, but Bennett wouldn't say.

"How long ago?" he asked. "But what about her husband? . . . Doesn't he . . . you've got to be kidding me. . . . I just . . . I don't know. . . . I can't believe that."

"*What?*" Erin pressed. "What's going on?"

"All right, Ken, call me back as soon as you know. Thanks."

"Jon, what in the world was that all about?" Erin asked.

"It's Indira," he said.

"What about her? Is she okay? Jon, tell me she's okay."

"They don't know. She's missing."

"What do you mean *missing*?"

"I mean gone, missing, disappeared. Nobody knows where she is."

"Have they talked to Peter? He's got to know where—"

"I'm just telling you what Ken told me. She's gone. And there's more."

"What?"

"Scott Harris at FBI just told the president he believes Indira was the mole."

"What?" Erin gasped. "Indira is the mole? You've got to be kidding! That's impossible."

"Maybe not," he said. "The FBI has found phone logs linking her to

Viggo Mariano. He's the guy who tried to kill us in the tunnels. Apparently he was leading the whole operation. They found a bank account she opened two months ago in the Cayman Islands. Harris believes she may have copied top-secret files and smuggled them out of the country. And Ken said she was supposed to take a lie-detector test over the weekend, along with a group of CIA and NSA officials who were suspected of being linked to Mordechai's murder."

"And?"

"And she never showed."

"What?"

"That's when she disappeared."

"Maybe she's hurt. Maybe she's . . ."

For a moment, Erin's voice trailed off; then she added, "It doesn't make any sense. I've known her for . . . I *recruited* her. . . . I . . ." Again her voice trailed off.

"Ken says the evidence is overwhelming, and it's mounting rapidly," said Bennett. "There was never a mole inside Doron's office, he said. It was Rajiv. She knew about Doron's Temple project. She knew about Mordechai's involvement, almost from the beginning. She knew about George Murray, Jaspers, the Baraks—all of them. She knew where we were in Israel, every step of the way."

"Of course she did," said Erin, still in denial. "Because I told her. I *told* her we were on Mount Ebal, and I told her we were heading for Hezekiah's Tunnel."

"Exactly," said Bennett, taking her hand to comfort her. "How could Mariano and his men have found us so quickly unless she was working with them?"

71

★ ★
★

A day passed, and then another.

There was still no sign of Rajiv, but Natasha was asking for them. She had been through three surgeries and was still in the ICU. But the doctors now felt confident she was going to make a full recovery and agreed to let her have ten minutes with the Bennetts.

"Hey there," said Erin as Jon guided her through the door in a wheel-chair.

Natasha smiled for the first time in days, though they could tell she was still in great pain.

"That bad, huh?" asked Bennett.

Natasha nodded. "I'm afraid so."

"Have you been watching all the coverage?"

"No," she said. "Maybe later."

"Don't worry," Bennett offered. "I asked the embassy to tape it all for you. You can watch it when you get out of here."

For some reason, the notion of watching all they had been through on TV made her laugh, which only triggered more pain. They both apologized but Natasha waved it off. They sat for a little while without saying a word. They only had a few more minutes together, but something about the lack of activity—and the silence that went with it—felt good to all three of them.

"I have a question," Natasha whispered at last.

Bennett didn't think she should speak. He didn't want her to be in any more pain.

"If it's about the Ark," he said, "the Sanhedrin and the chief rabbis still aren't sure how to move it. They asked Doron for a detachment of special forces to protect it and the Temple treasures, and he ordered an entire battalion to secure the tunnels and the surrounding area. Meanwhile, the rabbis and the museum are arguing over who is going to catalog everything down there. But they all seem to agree it will all be stored in the Temple, when it's done. Last night Doron and the cabinet approved plans to get started. They break ground on the Third Temple on May 14, Independence Day."

Natasha smiled, but there was clearly something else on her mind.

"You weren't indicted, if that's what you're wondering," said Erin. "Neither were we. But we're still not sure who this Viggo Mariano was working for. Farouk is dead. Al-Hassani's people are denying they had anything to do with it, which means this thing still may not be over. But—"

"No," Natasha said with great difficulty, "that's not it."

The head nurse popped her head in the door. "Five minutes," she said.

Bennett thanked her, then turned back to Natasha.

She looked at them both and finally just blurted it out. "I want to know God like you do."

Bennett was stunned. So was Erin.

"You heard me," said Natasha. "I want what you have. I just don't know how to get it. I wondered if you'd help me."

"What do you think we have?" Erin asked.

"Buried treasure," said Natasha, without emotion. "I want to know what Uncle Eli told you, Jon, at that restaurant on Gibraltar a few years ago. The night you became a believer."

Bennett wasn't trying to be coy, much less evasive. He was just totally surprised. "How did you know about that?"

"I told you," Natasha said. "He talked about you guys all the time. And when he got back from that trip, he told me how proud he was of me for following in my grandfather's footsteps, for becoming an archeologist. But then he took me aside and he warned me—gently, but firmly—that there was more to life than hunting for ancient artifacts like my grandfather or for oil like Dmitri and Miriam. He said he'd just had the same conversation with you, about finding real buried treasure, and that it had totally changed you. But he never said how."

Bennett sat down in a chair. He could suddenly picture himself back on Gibraltar, having dinner with Mordechai and Erin and Dmitri and the conversation they'd had burning in his ears and heart.

"Well," he said, "I remember Mordechai saying how moved he had been by reading the prophecies in the Hebrew Scriptures about who the Messiah would be. That Micah said He would be born in Bethlehem. That Isaiah said He would be born of a virgin and live in Galilee. I remember him saying how Daniel said after the Messiah was 'cut off,' Jerusalem and the Jewish Temple would be destroyed by an occupying power. And he talked about how David had written in the Psalms about how a band of 'evil men' would curse the Messiah, and mock Him, and gamble for His clothing, and then kill Him. And he said how moved he was reading Isaiah 53, that the Messiah would be 'pierced for our transgressions' and 'crushed for our iniquities' and that 'the punishment that brought us peace'—peace with God, our salvation—'was upon him, and by his wounds we are healed.' And I distinctly remember Mordechai saying, 'Look, I'm no rocket scientist. I just looked at the picture the prophets were painting and I said, who does that look like?'"

"Jesus," Natasha said.

"Exactly."

"And the part about buried treasure?"

Bennett sighed. He could feel the emotions of that night forcing their way back to the surface, and he had to discipline himself to hold them back, at least for now.

"Right, well, he said he was reading the New Testament one day— Matthew 12 or 13, I think—and he was reading a parable that Jesus told His disciples. Jesus said the kingdom of God is like a treasure hidden in a field. When a man found it, he hid it again and then in his joy went and sold everything he had and bought that field. Mordechai said it struck him that he was that man. He had finally discovered the truth that Jesus really is the Messiah. He had found buried treasure. The question, he said, was what was he going to do about it? Walk away? Forget about it? Act like it didn't matter? Or was he going to choose to follow Jesus Christ whatever the cost?"

Bennett got up, walked over to the window, and looked back out over the Old City, imagining the Temple where it would soon be standing.

"I remember going to bed that night thinking, that's me, too. I'd been brought up a skeptic, the son of two atheists, but now, somehow, I had no doubt that Jesus was who He said He was. And right in front of me, in Mordechai and Erin, I had two amazing examples of how God can totally transform the lives of people who choose to believe. They obviously had found buried treasure. They had a joy and a peace and a quiet confidence about the future that I didn't have. I wanted that. I knew Mordechai was right, and I knew it was time for me to choose."

"So what did you do?" Natasha asked.

"Mordechai made it pretty clear. Romans 10 says 'if you confess with your mouth Jesus as Lord, and believe in your heart that God raised Him from the dead, you will be saved.' So that night, I got down on my knees next to my bed and did it."

"That's it? That's all?"

"The Bible says salvation is a free gift," Bennett explained. "We don't deserve it. We can't earn it. We can't buy it. We just have to accept it. The hard part isn't what you say. The hard part is getting to the point where you're ready to say it."

"So what did you say, Jon?" asked Natasha.

"Well, it wasn't anything fancy," Jon conceded. "I think I just basically said, 'God, I really want what Erin and Eli have. I know I haven't lived a perfect life. I know I really need to clean up my act. But I'm ready to cut a deal, God.'"

"A *deal*?" asked Natasha. "You really said that?"

"Hey, it was new to me. I was doing the best I could."

Natasha laughed. "Is that all you said?"

"No, there was a little more."

"What was it?"

"You really want to know?"

"I really do."

"Then I'd be honored to tell you. I just said, 'God, I've got so much to learn. But I do believe that Jesus died on the cross to pay the penalty for my sins. I do believe that you raised Him from the dead. And I do believe that He is the only way to get to You. I'm ready to follow you with everything I have. I just want to know two things, God—first, that I'm going to be forgiven for every stupid thing I've ever said or done, and second, that I'm going to be in heaven with you if I never live to see another day. Amen.'"

"What happened?" asked Natasha.

"I wish I could say there were flashes of lightning or angels singing or some sort of supernatural sign that let me know I was really in, that I was really born again into God's family," Bennett confided. "But the truth is I knew that I had just done what the Bible told me to do. And that was that. In my heart, I knew the deal was done. I had my buried treasure. I was the luckiest guy on the planet. I just cried myself to sleep, thanking God for having mercy on someone as stupid and selfish as me."

Bennett looked over at Erin and took her hand. She had tears in her eyes, and when he looked back at Natasha, there were tears in her eyes, too.

"Is that something you're ready to do?" he asked softly.

Natasha nodded.

They all closed their eyes and bowed their heads, and when they were done, Natasha looked up and said softly, "Now I've got my buried treasure too."

EPILOGUE

✩ ✩ ✩

It had taken longer than expected.

Two weeks, in fact, what with all the news out of Israel. But Indira Rajiv was finally about to get the face-to-face meeting she had been demanding, in the safe house owned by the late Viggo Mariano on the outskirts of Rome. In less than two minutes, she'd be sitting alone with the man who had recruited her to betray her husband, her friends, and her country, and she could barely contain her excitement.

She was prepared to build and run the world-class intelligence operation he would need to see his vision through, and she was fully prepared to hand over files that would effectively cripple the national security of the United States.

But two million dollars a year was not going to be enough. Not for the services she could provide. Not with all the wealth her benefactor had at his fingertips. She could never go back, after all. She was being hunted not just by the CIA and FBI but by Interpol and the Mossad.

She didn't really need the money. Money was never what this was about. It was about respect. Money was just the tangible expression of the respect he was willing to afford her. And she wanted more.

Rajiv sat with her back to the door, staring out over the beautiful Italian capital. Her hands were perspiring. But she was determined to maintain a poker face at all costs. Any whiff of weakness and he could seize the upper hand.

Then the door opened and in walked Khalid Tariq, Al-Hassani's right-hand man. Rajiv stood and greeted him with the traditional Arab kiss on both cheeks. She would get to the issue of money in due time, she decided. First she needed to show she was in this for the long haul.

"So, what does His Excellency want next?" she asked.

The answer seemed to suck all the oxygen from the room.

"He wants you to kill MacPherson."

IS IT TRUE?

★ ★ ★

To learn more about the research used for this book—and to track the latest political, economic, military, and archeological developments in Israel, Jordan, Iraq, and other countries described in *The Copper Scroll*—please visit www.joelrosenberg.com.

You can also sign up to receive Joel C. Rosenberg's free e-mail newsletter,
>> FLASH TRAFFIC <<.

ACKNOWLEDGMENTS

✶   ✶   ✶

I have found few projects as fascinating as researching the Third Temple, the prospects of it being built in our lifetime, and the possibilities of finding the lost Temple treasures and perhaps even the Ark itself. For those interested in pursuing these and related subjects, I highly recommend the following nonfiction books and articles, each of which I found helpful in my own quest:

* *The Treasure of the Copper Scroll* by John Marco Allegro
* *The Copper Scroll: Overview, Text and Translation* by Al Wolters
* "The Mysterious Copper Scroll: Clues to Hidden Temple Treasure?" by P. Kyle McCarter Jr., in *Bible Review*, August 1992
* *The Complete Dead Sea Scrolls in English* by Geza Vermes
* *Understanding the Dead Sea Scrolls* by Hershel Shanks
* *Secrets of the Dead Sea Scrolls* by Randall Price
* *The Temple and Bible Prophecy* by Randall Price
* *Envisioning the Temple* by Adolfo Roitman, head of the Shrine of the Book and curator of the Dead Sea Scrolls (published by the Israel Museum, Jerusalem)

Thanks again to everyone mentioned in my previous acknowledgments for all your advice, encouragement, and prayers, and a deep, heartfelt note of thanks to Edward and Kailea Hunt, dear friends and kindred spirits, without whom this book would not have been possible; Dan and Susan Rebeiz, for their brilliant Web site, Power Point, and other graphic designs; Wendy and Colin Ligon, who went above and beyond the call of friendship to track down the original *New York Times* story on the Copper Scroll in libraries across Washington; our friends in Jordan, for their gracious hospitality and for taking Edward and me to see the actual Copper Scroll; Ron Beer, the best tour guide in Israel, for whetting my appetite with the drama of the Dead Sea Scrolls' discovery; and Leonard Buhler, Norm Schulz, and all of our new Canadian friends, with whom two weeks in Israel was not nearly enough.

A most-special word of thanks as well to Allen Roth, Steven Schneier, and their staffs for all the excellent advice and logistical assistance they have given me over the years in Israel; Joe Karlya, my long-lost friend from S.U., who first sent me to Russia two decades ago; Peter Robbio and his extraordinary colleagues at Creative Response Concepts, for helping turn this series into sales of one million plus; Beverly Rykerd, for all her first-rate PR efforts and counsel; Mark Taylor, Ron Beers, Becky Nesbitt, Jan Stob, Jeremy Taylor, Cheryl Kerwin, Andrea Martin, and the amazing family at Tyndale's headquarters and around the country, for their remarkable creativity, hard work, and passion for making these books reach farther than ever before; Scott Miller with Trident Media Group, still the best agent in the biz, for his continuing friendship, encouragement, and always-solid counsel; and, of course, the entire Rosenberg and Meyers families—especially my parents, Len and Mary, and Lynn's mom, June (a.k.a. "Bubbe")—who have worked so long, and so hard, and with so much love to make this dream come true.

Finally, to my dear wife, Lynn, let me say thank you again and again and again. Words cannot begin to express how much I love you, or how grateful I am for your love, your trust, and your undying friendship. I am yours for eternity.

JOEL C. ROSENBERG

Joel C. Rosenberg is the *New York Times* best-selling author of *The Last Jihad*, *The Last Days*, and *The Ezekiel Option*, with more than one million copies in print. As a communications strategist, he has worked with some of the world's most influential leaders in business, politics, and media, including Steve Forbes, Rush Limbaugh, and former Israeli prime minister Benjamin Netanyahu. As a novelist, he has been interviewed on hundreds of radio and TV programs, including ABC's *Nightline*, *CNN Headline News*, FOX News Channel, The History Channel, MSNBC, the *Rush Limbaugh Show*, and the *Sean Hannity Show*. He has been profiled by the *New York Times*, the *Washington Times*, and the *Jerusalem Post*, and was the subject of two cover stories in *World* magazine. He has addressed audiences all over the world, including Russia, Israel, Jordan, Egypt, Turkey, and Belgium, and has spoken at the White House.

The first page of his first novel—*The Last Jihad*—puts readers inside the cockpit of a hijacked jet, coming in on a kamikaze attack into an American city, which leads to a war with Saddam Hussein over weapons of mass destruction. Yet it was written before 9/11 and published before the actual war with Iraq. *The Last Jihad* spent eleven weeks on the *New York Times* hardcover fiction best-seller list, reaching as high as #7. It raced up the *USA Today* and *Publishers Weekly* best-seller lists, hit #4 on the *Wall Street Journal* list and hit #1 on Amazon.com.

His second thriller—*The Last Days*—opens with the death of Yasser Arafat and a U.S. diplomatic convoy ambushed in Gaza. Two weeks before *The Last Days* was published in hardcover, a U.S. diplomatic convoy was ambushed in Gaza. Thirteen months later, Yasser Arafat was dead. *The Last Days* spent four weeks on the *New York Times* hardcover fiction best-seller list, hit #5 on the

Denver Post list, and #8 on the *Dallas Morning News* list. Both books have been optioned by a Hollywood producer.

The Ezekiel Option centers on a dictator rising in Russia who forms a military alliance with the leaders of Iran, as they feverishly pursue nuclear weapons and threaten to wipe Israel off the face of the earth. On the very day it was published in June 2005, Iran elected a new leader who vowed to accelerate the country's nuclear program and later threatened to "wipe Israel off the map." Six months after it was published, Moscow signed a $1 billion arms deal with Tehran. *The Ezekiel Option* spent four weeks on the *New York Times* hardcover fiction best-seller list, and five months on the Christian Bookseller Association best-seller list, reaching as high as #4.

www.joelrosenberg.com

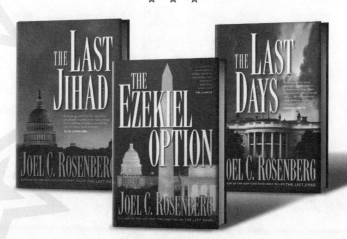

have you visited tyndalefiction.com lately?

Only there can you find:

→ books hot off the press

→ first chapter excerpts

→ inside scoops on your favorite authors

→ author interviews

→ contests

→ fun facts

→ and much more!

Sign up for your **free** newsletter!

Visit us today at: **tyndalefiction.com**